ZERO TO SIXTY

MARIE HARTE

Published by Sourcebooks Casablanca, an imprint of Sourcebooks, Inc.
P.O. Box 4410, Naperville, Illinois 60567-4410
(630) 961-3900
Fax: (630) 961-2168
www.sourcebooks.com

Printed and bound in Canada.
MBP 10 9 8 7 6 5 4 3 2 1

Chapter 1

ON A GOOD DAY, SAM WOULDN'T TOLERATE THIS kind of crap. But today? After spending all morning, afternoon, and early evening buried ass to elbows under the hoods of the most dicked-up cars in Seattle? It was like every transmission failure, radiator leak, and seized engine had landed at Webster's Garage—at *his* station.

Finally freed from having to listen to annoying talk about girlfriends and weddings—which didn't belong in a damn garage—he should have been heading to Ray's Bar to grab a beer. Instead, he'd just *had* to answer his cell. His own fault, really, that he now found himself crawling under the metal skeleton of an old Chevy on monster wheels—Willie's idea of backyard art.

"You see him yet?" the old woman yelled from three feet away. *Jesus*.

"I'm not deaf," he yelled back. "And no."

"*What?*"

He gritted his teeth and scooted again, scraping his forearms on the uneven gravel that no doubt hadn't been repaved since the early sixties, back when Willie had just been old. Not ancient as shit.

"Come on," he muttered at the shivering mess starting to growl. "It's okay, damn it. I'm not gonna hurt you." He continued to croon in a deep voice, reaching for the spitting furball crammed against a cracked rubber wheel. Willie's porch light gave him something to see by. A good thing, considering the late evening hour. Though spring had just arrived, the sun still set at a little past six. Over an hour ago.

He paused, close enough to grab the dirty cat, and held out his hand. It took a moment, but the growling quieted. A sandpapery tongue licked his finger. He sighed. "Come on, Tyrant. Willie wants you inside."

The old cat meowed as Sam gently dragged him out from under the truck. He cradled the feline and noticed the gash above the tomcat's left ear. "He's hurt."

"I know that, Sam Hamilton. Why the hell do you think I asked you to come get him?" The old lady shuffled closer, murmuring sweet nothings to the greasy feline while Sam got nothing but glares for daring to question Her Royal Bitchiness.

Granted, he liked the crabby quality that clung to Wilhemina Bower, glossing over the sickly sweet perfume and stale whiskey she wore under her hand-crocheted shawls. But he could only take so much of her demands.

He glanced down at the cat, now purring in his arms, while Willie scratched under its chin. She looked about as frail as a snowflake but had steel in those old bones. Her piercing features weren't beautiful, but they were memorable. A mishmash of striking meets cute, surprisingly enough. Willie looked exactly like the animals she helped—a mutt. Her tanned and leathered skin could have come from any number of ethnicities. She had one of those faces Hollywood called "ethnic," meaning she could have been an Italian playing a Mexican playing a light-skinned African American. Or dark Irish. Who the hell knew?

Sam only cared that she helped the animals, and she made life interesting. Anyone looking at her would see somebody's grandma, a woman who liked to bake cookies and pinch baby cheeks. Then she'd open her mouth and completely ruin the effect.

Willie frowned at Tyrant's ear.

He sighed. "Want me to call Doc Lee?"

"What the hell for? I still have some of that goop left from the last time we went in. It'll do. Bring him in." She turned and started toward the back entrance of the house, expecting him to follow. Her long, white hair fluttered in the breeze—the actual wind, sure as shit not from her snail's pace in those orthopedics.

Knowing it would be another ten minutes before she moved the four feet to her back door, he stomped past her into her musty, palatial home in the established Queen Anne neighborhood. He found the goop in the cabinet where she kept the rest of the medicinal supplies, and applied it and a makeshift bandage over the aptly named, hissing Tyrant.

"No one appreciates me. *Damn it*," he swore, having earned a huge scratch on the inside of his tatted forearm.

After he set the cat down and watched it tear away around the corner, deeper into the house time forgot, Sam walked into the living room and waited for Willie. She kept a neat if dusty pad. Everything had its place, from the collectible Hummels on doilies over the mantel to the tacky tchotchkes gathered with a rhyme and reason only Willie could understand.

She finally entered the house and sank into her favorite chair, a plush, hideous green-and-yellow-flowered La-Z-Boy that had probably been fashionable two decades ago. Like Willie, everything in the house had an expiration date that had long since passed.

The old cats and dogs with nowhere else to go didn't mind, though. According to Willie, they gave her a reason for living. And she gave them the love and affection they craved.

Probably why Sam couldn't make a clean break from the woman either. With his best friend "in love" and the woman who'd practically raised him borderline psychotic while planning her own wedding, he was at odds for companionship. Sure, he could have hung out with the other guys at the garage, but he didn't want to seem like a charity case. Just because Foley had hooked up with someone didn't mean Sam had nothing to do.

He didn't, but they didn't need to know that.

Willie leaned back and kicked up her feet with a sigh. Her elderly shepherd, Pygar, clambered by her side and sat on his haunches while she stroked his head. "Did you find Scruffy?"

Barbarella, a fluffy, white Persian that always looked dirty, and Mathmos, a long-haired Chihuahua, walked in together and sat on Willie's other side, in their shared dog bed.

They stared at him with flat gazes, as if he were nothing but giant prey.

He still thought it more than odd Willie had named her animals after characters in a sixties' science-fiction movie many considered soft porn, but whatever.

"Scruffy? He's safe."

"Where?"

"Some shop on Queen Anne took him in." At the remembrance of Scruffy's rescuer, his heart started thundering. "Some chick picked him up a few days ago. I would have stepped in, but it was dark and she threatened to call the cops."

Willie cackled. "Got a good look at you, eh?"

He scowled, knowing he looked like the ex-con he in fact was. But hey, better tats and muscles to scare away a threat than get his ass handed to him. He'd had enough of that growing up. And he didn't want to remember what prison had been like.

Tyrant appeared and twined his big, orange body around Sam's ankles. The purring sounded like a freight train, but the bandage remained around the cat's head.

"As a matter of fact, she didn't see me. I was in the shadows. But there have been a bunch of robberies on Queen Anne. I didn't want to get busted for something I didn't do just because I was in the wrong place at the wrong time."

"Good point." She nodded to the side table against the wall. "Grab me my sticks, would you?"

He stepped over the cat and grabbed her bag of yarn and knitting needles. After handing it to her, he watched her gnarled hands move like lightning. "What are you making this time?"

"A scarf."

"You know it's almost April, right?"

She gaped and feigned shock. "You're shittin' me. April? Here I was thinkin' I'd better get a turkey for Thanksgiving." She snorted. "It don't need to be cold for me to make a scarf. I make what my fingers want to make."

"Sure. Okay." He ran a hand through his hair, needing to leave but unsure of where to go. Ray's? Home?

Foley might be there. Then again, he spent most of his nights with Cyn anymore. Not that Sam could blame him. His best friend had somehow convinced the sexy redhead to date him.

Tyrant returned, doing figure eights around Sam's feet.

"Well? Shit or get off the pot, boy. You stayin' or going? What's up your craw?"

Woman had a real way with words. "You and the rescue gang. You get a home for Scruffy yet?" Casually, because he didn't want to seem too eager, he added, "Because I could check and see if that woman who took him plans on keeping him." He'd decided to do just that five days ago when he'd spied the pup in her arms.

But shell-shocked by the knockout blond and not wanting to deal with more estrogen when every woman around him lately was either getting married or landing a relationship, he'd kept his distance. He glanced at Willie. Suspicion overwhelmed good sense. "You're not shagging Old Rupert, are you?" Her horndog of a neighbor had a steady supply of funky, blue man pills. And yeah, Sam knew because Rupert liked to talk… too much.

She gave a sly grin. "What's it to you?"

"God." That was it. No more women for him. Except that blond, because she had Scruffy… He worried about the puppy.

Willie considered him. "Hmm. Probably wouldn't hurt to make sure the dog's in a good place. Lord knows we have plenty more to worry about. Be good to see one of 'em in a happy home." Willie and her small group of elderly friends had become unofficial fosters for animals needing permanence. They took in strays and cleaned up and cared for the animals while local vets and shelters put out calls for adoption.

All in all, the program helped more than it hurt. Animals no one wanted got a second chance, and Willie and her cranky friends found purpose in helping others.

Sam had stumbled onto the operation by accident, saving a pit bull from a dogfight going on outside an illegal underground boxing match he'd won a few months ago. The vet had sent him to Willie. Ever since, he and Willie had been working together to help strays in the city.

"Well?" Willie said.

"Well what?"

"Get your ass gone. And try not to scare this woman you're pretending doesn't matter. Plain as the nose on your handsome face you want some of that."

He flushed, still not used to such talk from an old lady, though he should have been.

She laughed. The shepherd gave a weird chuff that sounded like laughter. Willie laughed even harder. The Chihuahua yipped. The cat just stared.

"Hell," he muttered. "If I wanted this kind of abuse, I'd stay at work." *Or call Louise*. Something he'd been putting off. He shuddered at the thought.

"Give her hell, Sam Hamilton. And try to look less serial killer and more solid citizen. Smile, why don't you?"

He forced a smile at her.

Willie blinked. "Eh, maybe not. That facial hair makes you look scruffy—like the dog. Ha. And, well, keep your hands in your pockets and that prison ink covered up. Can't kill a woman with your hands tucked away."

"First of all, it's not prison ink. I paid money for this shit." His arms, chest, and neck were a canvas, according to J.T., his tattoo guy; thus, his body, a work of art. "Second, I don't hurt women," he growled. "Though if I did, I'd start with you." He glared at her and turned to leave, forgetting Tyrant under his feet.

The cat hissed. Sam tripped but managed to stay upright. Mathmos and Barbarella barked and growled respectively. Pygar howled. Willie slapped her knee, laughing so hard she snorted while trying to catch her breath.

Annoyed, Sam slammed out of her house, but not fast enough to avoid Willie's last bit of advice.

"Try not to fuck it up, boy. Prison ain't kind to a pretty face. And yours is prettier than most."

Like she had to tell him that.

Ivy Stephens waved good-bye to her last client of the day and hurried to close up her massage clinic. Technically, she now co-owned it with Shelby, the original owner. The thrill of finally owning a piece of the business stole over her once more, and the job was almost enough to negate her despair at losing Cookie again.

The adorable stray had come and gone twice in the past two weeks. But this time she'd thought she could hold on to him. She'd bought him a leash and collar. So small, he had to be no more than a few months old. He looked like some kind of ridgeback/shepherd mix, as best she could tell from having compared his features to many dog pictures online.

In any case, the puppy had big paws, the most

beautiful, soul-deep brown eyes, and too many ribs showing. He needed care, and he'd seemed happy enough when with her. Since the local shelter had no reports of a dog matching his description missing, she'd taken him home. Then she'd brought him to work. To her pleased surprise, he'd slept in the doggie bed she'd gotten him while she updated paperwork yesterday. No barking or bad manners. He'd simply waited for her to finish her quarterlies before showing he needed to go outside.

It was uncanny how well-trained he was for a puppy. But the moment she'd let him out the back, he'd managed to squeeze his way out of his collar and under the back fence of the courtyard to escape. She worried frantically that he'd be hit by a car, but he'd stayed away from Queen Anne Avenue. She'd spotted him once near the park behind the main drag before he'd disappeared into the neighborhood.

Ivy sighed. Time to go puppy hunting again. She double-checked to make sure she'd locked the front door, then used the restroom. She left through the back hall and had just opened the back door to leave when a large man appeared from out of nowhere.

She gasped and jumped back.

He just stood there, looming like a giant, his hands tucked into his jeans pockets. He had to stand well over six feet tall, and his frame looked massive. He wore a zipped-up, padded, black jacket that only enhanced his size. His short, dark-brown hair could have used a cut, and his eyes remained shadowed despite the overhead patio light. A beard and mustache framed his jaw and mouth, showing full lips. She thought she saw a hint of ink along his neck but couldn't tell because of the play of darkness over his features.

"Ah, hello," he said in a deep voice. A shivery voice.

When he didn't make any sudden movements, she started to relax. He backed up a step to give her more space, and she cleared her throat. "Hello. Can I help you with something?"

"Sorry. I knocked on the front door, but no one answered. So I came around back, like the sign said to."

A normal thing any client might do. But this man was no athlete or nine-to-fiver with tight rhomboids. This man screamed dangerous, in more ways than one. For some reason, when the light hit his mouth, she couldn't look away, thinking how pretty his lips were in a face chiseled from granite.

"We're closed. But if you'd like to schedule a massage, I can give you my card."

"Um, okay." He took another step back. "I can wait out here while you get it."

She fished in her purse and found it, then took a leap of faith and left the office, locking the door behind her. Leaving her with this stranger, alone, in the confines of the small back patio outside the office. The one fenced in for privacy.

Ivy got a grip on her runaway imagination, sensing no real danger from the man, just feeling overwhelmed by his presence. She held out her card. "Here you go."

He took it, careful not to brush her fingers. But jeez, he had big hands. "Ivy Stephens, LMT." Licensed Massage Therapist—since she'd put herself through school eight long years ago.

She nodded. "Bodyworks is closed now, but any of us here can help you. My number's on the card."

"Great. Thanks." He shuffled his feet. "I've been thinking about getting some work done."

"Yeah?" She walked cautiously around him and exited through the side gate. She continued along the side of the building, back to the lit and populated main sidewalk. Ivy blew out a breath, trying not to feel so relieved.

"Yeah," he said, walking next to her. "Name's Sam." He stopped to the side, out of the way of the foot traffic, and held out a hand.

She stopped and took it, to be courteous. The heat in his humongous palm startled her. As did the calluses. She glanced down, and his sleeve rose up his arm, revealing tattoos. A look at his neck showed she'd been right earlier. He had what looked like inked vines and barbed wire creeping up his neck from under that jacket. *Wow*.

He let go of her hand slowly, his gaze narrowed on her face.

He didn't say anything, and she felt awkward in the silence. "Um, so what do you do, Sam?"

He tucked his hands in the pockets of his jacket this time. "I'm a mechanic. I work at Webster's Garage over on Rainier."

"Oh, I've been by that place. Always seems so busy." She felt better getting his first name and a place of business. That information made him seem more real and less psycho stalker for some reason.

"Yeah." He drew his shoulder blades back into a stretch. Talk about a broad chest. "Sometimes my back feels tight and my hands could use some relief."

She nodded, thinking he'd be a challenge to work on. All that muscle had little give. When he continued to stare at her, she took charge of the conversation once more. "Well, I guess I should get home." Seven thirty on a Thursday night, and she had an eight o'clock appointment in the morning. *After* she looked for Cookie again.

"Sure. Right. Oh, one more thing." He paused. "You haven't by chance seen a small dog running around? A brown puppy, really cute, skittish? Darker around his muzzle and the tips of his ears?"

She stared, wide-eyed, both glad and sad he'd come to claim her stray. "You mean Cookie?"

He blinked. "What?"

"Cookie's what I call him." She flushed. "The first thing he did when I let him into the shop was steal a cookie. He's so cute. He looks kind of like a ridgeback mix. Is he yours?"

"Not exactly. I help some friends foster dogs and cats needing homes, and he's our latest rescue. But he keeps running away. I'm just glad he found a home."

"About that…" She bit her lip, not liking the intensity with which Sam watched her. He made her nervous. Such a big man. And so handsome, she realized, feeling an unwelcome sense of attraction. "Cookie ran away yesterday. I tied him up outside for no more than a few minutes, and he was gone. Wriggled right out of his collar. I looked yesterday but didn't find him." She studied Sam, then realized she could use some help if he offered. "I, um, I'd planned to look for him after work tonight."

"Right now?"

She nodded.

He took his phone out of his pocket, glanced at the time, then sighed as he pocketed it. "Let's go."

What the heck was that sigh about? "If you have something better to do, don't let me keep you. I can look for him by myself." She forced a smile. Ivy wasn't helpless, and she didn't exactly like the thought of him acting put out because he thought he had to help her find a puppy. "Call if you want some bodywork. You have my card."

She turned to leave when he stopped her, a hand on her shoulder.

"Wait." He let her go when she turned to face him again. "Sorry. I don't mean to act like a dick."

His blunt words took her aback. "Ah, okay."

"I'm tired. It's been a long day, and I've already had to deal with a bad-tempered cat for a friend of mine." He held out a thick forearm and pulled back his jacket. Cutting through a myriad of tattoos was a scratch several inches long that looked painful. Blood had crusted over it, but it appeared fresh.

"That has to hurt."

He shrugged and pulled his jacket back down. "Cat claws are a bitch, but it's better than dealing with Willie."

"Willie?"

"Tyrant's owner." He shivered. "Old woman is mean as hell. But she's good with the animals, so I cut her some slack. You ready to hunt down Scruffy? I mean Cookie?"

He seemed worried, and she thought he might be more attached than he'd let on. "Sure. But I mean it. You don't have to look for him. I can do it."

"No. It's dark out. Not exactly smart for a hot chick to be on her own in the city. It's safe, but it's not that safe."

Hot chick? That shouldn't mean anything, yet she felt warmer because of it. She stared at him, wondering if he realized he'd complimented her.

"I guess."

He nodded to the sidewalk in front of her. "How about we turn down Boston and look for him near the park? I've seen him over there playing with other dogs a few times."

"You have?"

They walked down the street and turned right. After a few more blocks, they passed the middle school, heading toward the park bordered by Blaine Street. Despite the late hour, a few parents and children still played on the swings.

Ivy felt a moment's envy that her own perfect family didn't exist and likely never would. She should be glad, really. Imagine if Max had gotten her pregnant the way he'd wanted to when they'd first started dating. All those years supporting him through undergraduate school had been difficult enough. But with a baby on board? Then his leaving her high and dry for law school and that perky blond would have hurt a lot more.

She should be glad to be strong and independent and single. Who the hell needed a man anyway?

Someone shouted from the other side of the street, and she started.

"You okay?" Sam put a hand on her shoulder to keep her from tripping over her own feet.

She felt safe next to his large presence. "Yeah, wasn't paying attention." Then, to prove she really *didn't* need a man to protect her or stop her from being clumsy, she stepped away and called out for Cookie. By herself.

They walked all around the park and deeper into the West Queen Anne neighborhood. Despite Sam still being a stranger, he seemed on the up and up. He called out for the dog. They walked near each other but not too close. She saw him watching her, but when she'd look at him, he appeared to make an effort to seem nonthreatening. Hands in pockets, keeping his distance.

She found his actions comforting—and charming, oddly enough—because he didn't seem to be trying to impress her. He'd sworn. Called her a hot chick, and he—

"*Sam*." She pointed to a small moving shadow near a house on the corner of Fourth and Blaine.

He nodded and raised his voice. "Scruffy. Come."

The shadow picked its head up and took a step in their direction.

"Cookie, come here," she added and made a few kissy sounds. "Come here, boy."

A tiny yip, and then the little guy was bounding toward them. Sam and she crouched low, so as not to threaten him with their size. But Cookie didn't seem to care. He went to Sam first, his tail wagging and his tongue licking everywhere he could reach.

Ivy watched Sam's stern demeanor melt into a smile that stole her breath. When he wasn't looking so serious or tough, he was…beautiful. His smile reached his eyes, and the joy on his face was infectious.

She laughed, and Cookie turned to her, half leaping on her with the enthusiasm of a dog three times his size. "Oof." She fell on her butt but couldn't stop smiling as she stroked the dirty little dog. "Cookie. Where have you been?"

"I think he likes Cookie better than Scruffy," Sam

said, sounding gruff. His smile had disappeared, but the happiness in his eyes remained, softening him the tiniest bit.

"Did you want to take him back to his foster family?"

He shook his head. "He's good with you, I think." Yet something in the way he petted the dog, the caring way he watched Cookie, told her Sam felt more than just a responsibility to see the puppy settled.

"I might have jumped ahead of myself," she admitted. "I felt bad for him so I took him in at work, because I didn't want him to be cold. Then somehow I bought him a collar and a leash. Some food. Nights at my house. Now he has a dog bed." She sighed. "But I haven't exactly explained him to my landlord yet."

Sam frowned. "Do you want him or not?"

"I do." She surprised herself with that truth. She hadn't wanted any relationship entanglements since Max. Including a pet. Yet Cookie was so cute, so desperate to be loved. And she finally felt ready to give that back. "But I have to okay it with my landlord." She felt silly for not having been better prepared. "And I'm not ready to take him full-time yet. I need to figure out when I can have him and how to care for him. I, well, I didn't exactly let my boss—I mean, my partner—know about him either."

Sam studied her. She didn't know what he saw, but a smirk curled his lips as he helped her to her feet while scooping up the wriggling puppy. "Suckered you into caring for him with those big, brown eyes, didn't he?"

She nodded, all the while being suckered into anything Sam said as she stared into *his* big, *gray* eyes. Gray-blue, she corrected herself, feeling a sudden connection to the giant man. She put her hand on the dog and somehow found her fingers curled around Sam's thick biceps as they walked past the park, back toward her car.

He cleared his throat. "Ah, just so we're clear, we don't give dogs away to just anyone who wants them, you know."

"Okay."

"I mean, puppies are popular. We'd have no problem getting him a good home. A friend of mine was asking about this little guy just the other week."

She frowned. "I have a good home."

"We'll see."

He didn't seem like he belonged to the typical animal rescue group that made a person sign an oath under God to take a dog. Just a do-gooder wanting to find homes for needy animals. With the amount of strays in need of homes, she'd have thought her word would be good enough.

She raised a brow. "Who makes that call?"

"I do." He seemed to growl the words.

"You're not going to charge me a fee or anything are you?" Was this some lame attempt to extort money out of her? But then, he hadn't known she'd actually had Cookie until he'd asked.

"Hell no." He scowled like a thundercloud. "This is about the dog, pure and simple. I'm not out to make a fuckin' buck."

Obviously, he hadn't decided on her as being suitable yet. Considering they'd just met, that only made sense. But it bothered her to be found lacking in some way.

She pulled her hand away.

He sighed. "I know, I'm being a dick again. Sorry."
After a slight pause, he added slowly, "If you want, I can
keep him while you figure things out. You think hard
about taking care of him, though. It's a commitment."
He frowned, and she saw a sadness that lingered. "He's
not a toy. You say you're keeping him, you keep him."

"I understand." She would have taken offense, but
Ivy knew how often people turned in pets because they
wanted a younger one. A different one.

A blonder, prettier one.

She studied Sam, seeing nothing soft about him.
Nothing forgiving. They had that in common, at least.
"I'd like that. Will you keep him for me?"

He nodded. "If you're serious about him."

"What? You want it written in blood? I said I am." He
was starting to annoy her. And it took a lot to annoy Ivy.

Sam didn't change his expression, but something in
the way he looked at her told her she'd amused him.
"Okay, relax. I'll keep the dog at my place. My roommate is never home as it is. And I have an in with my
landlady." He snorted. "She's too busy to notice a dog
anyway. Same with Foley."

"Foley?"

"The roommate." Sam sighed. "My best friend,
kind of."

"Oh." Some backstory there, but they'd reached her
car. "Well, um, you have my card, so you know how
to reach me. Do you want to give me your number so I
can let you know whether I can keep him or not?" *Why
does this feel like we're setting up a date?* She took her
phone out of her purse and punched in the numbers he
gave her. "Sam what?"

"Huh?"

"Your last name, for my contact list."

"Oh. Sam Hamilton."

"Okay. I just texted you. It's a 206 number, and you have my card."

Cookie chewed at Sam's finger, and Sam gently extricated his hand from the dog's mouth. "My phone's in my pocket. I'll text you back when I get in the car." He paused, staring at her with such intensity she felt uneasy.

"What?" She rubbed under her eye. Had her mascara run?

He cleared his throat. "So I'll call you." He rubbed the dog's head, and Cookie looked like he'd gone to heaven. "If you're not busy tomorrow night, we could grab a beer or something. Talk about plans for Cookie."

"Don't you mean Scruffy?" she teased, trying to play nice, her heart deciding to race like a rabbit chased by greyhounds. Or in Sam's case, a grizzly.

"Nah. Cookie sounds much more respectable." He stroked the dog just as she reached in to do so and accidentally ran over her hand in the process.

They both froze, then he slid his hand away.

She hadn't been out dating in over a year. Before that, she'd been with Max. But she'd never *ever* been with a guy this intense. Protective, dangerous, handsome. Sexy?

Since when did Ivy go for the bad-boy type?

Since I tried my best with the good-boy college guy and got burned badly. Even two years after their split, she held a grudge. It didn't help that the few guys after Max had been as needy and selfish as her ex-fiancé.

Sam seemed so different. *But I'm not looking for a*

man, she reminded herself, not wanting to go through that stupid hurt again. A beer and talk of a puppy didn't mean a date anyway. She needed to relax.

"So tomorrow night?" he asked again. "It's no biggie if you can't make it. We could always do it another time, or not. We can text and email details." He shrugged. "But I'm gonna need to know more about you before I hand over Cookie."

He seemed to be giving her an out. She could send him her answer. He wasn't pushing her into meeting up with him, so this definitely wasn't a date. She ignored the disappointment she felt. She didn't want or need a man. But she sure could use some puppy love. She rubbed Cookie's belly, and he licked her.

Her heart welled with need. For the first time in a long time, Ivy wanted to take care of a male again. But this one would give her love back. And he had fur.

"Actually, I think talk and a beer tomorrow night sounds great. I can use the break."

He looked up and weighed her expression. Then those lips that hadn't smiled but once all night curled into a breath-stealing grin. "It's a date."

Chapter 2

"I SHOULDN'T HAVE CALLED IT A DATE. PROBABLY scared her away," Sam said to the puppy chewing on a bone in the backseat of his pride and joy, a '74 Challenger. "But man, she was hot. Like, all gorgeous and curvy, kind of tall. Her smile…" He groaned. "Man, those eyes are just so green." Which had freaked him the hell out. Sam noticed tits and ass. Not pretty eyes and a beautiful smile.

Weird.

He glanced at the puppy in the rearview and felt awkward thinking sex thoughts with a baby in the car. Sure it was canine, but still.

"Never mind. Anyway, quit running away. You're gonna get hurt."

Sam had run away a lot when younger. By all accounts, Louise Hamilton had been—and still was—a shitty mother. But none of those early escapes had ended well. He'd only gone from bad to worse. Still, it was a toss-up as to which had been the real nightmare— living in alleyways with the drunks, stoners, and wackos or living with Louise. His mother had issues. *So many* issues.

Then he'd found Foley Sanders.

He remembered as if it had been yesterday. Just past his eleventh birthday and he'd already been to juvie twice. Social services knew his mother by name, and the principal had affectionately called Sam her "little brawler with a heart of gold." Still hadn't saved him from all those after-school detentions, though. Or from getting picked on when the teachers weren't around.

Foley had saved him from a major ass kicking after one such detention. Another bully who didn't like that Sam always wore the same clothes and smelled like stale cigarettes and funk had joined two other kids to pummel Sam into the ground. Then Foley arrived, already big for his age, and opened a huge can of whoop ass. A natural born fighter, his friend. Afterward, Foley had invited him over for dinner, and Sam, not being stupid and always hungry, had agreed.

They'd been screwing around and having a good time, reminiscing about how Foley had bitch-slapped that creep Joey Lindoney. Eileen had appeared out of nowhere. She'd tapped Foley in the back of the head, then did the same to Sam. "Language, boys," she'd said. Then she'd forced him to shower and put on some of Foley's clothes, because a person had to be clean to sit at Eileen's table. God bless her, she'd fed him.

Homemade waffles, maple syrup, and sausages. Nothing fancy. Foley joked that his mom always made breakfast for dinner when she was too tired to cook anything else. But Sam had lapped it up like cream. The only things better than Eileen's food had been Foley's friendship and having a warm, safe place to sleep when he'd needed it.

There was nothing he wouldn't do for the Sanderses.

He glanced back at Cookie. "Yeah, you got a good thing, boy. Ivy likes you. She's safe." He knew how to read the bad in people, and Ivy didn't have it. She might not be a saint, but she didn't have an abusive bone in her body. But just because Cookie seemed to like her didn't mean she wouldn't break the dog's heart in the long run.

The dog cocked his head, and Sam allowed himself a smile. He didn't often have crap to smile about, but this dog made him happy. Something about Cookie had gotten to him. "Don't fuc—screw it up. You don't want to get picked up by the dog police. Doggie jail is not a good place to be."

Cookie went back to his bone, and Sam drove home, for once hoping Foley wasn't in. They'd never had pets in the town house they shared. Eileen, doubling as mother and landlady, hadn't said no to a cat or dog, but Foley had never seemed too keen on things with four feet. Had actually made a point of insisting the house be pet free—*forever*.

Since working with Willie, Sam had taken to briefly hiding rescues in his room for those odd instances when they had to wait to farm them out to her friends or adoptive families.

He pulled into his parking spot at the town-home complex in North Beacon Hill and glanced around. He didn't see Foley's car. So far so good. Quickly leaving the car with the dog, bone, and a bag of supplies from the trunk, he locked up and hurried inside. He rushed upstairs to his room, prepared to hide Cookie all night, and froze when he saw Foley lying on his bed, looking at an old *Penthouse* magazine.

"*Shit*."

Foley quirked a brow. Nearly as big as Sam, the guy Sam thought of as brother was a carbon copy of Eileen. Same black hair and gray eyes. Except Foley had thick arms covered in tats, height, and the brawn of a pro wrestler. They used to do everything together. Up until Foley had grown up—three months ago—and got himself a real girlfriend, not just some one-night banger, but a smart chick with goals, her own house, and a job.

The kind of good girl who normally wouldn't glance twice at someone like them. But Cyn had good taste, and Sam liked her. Or at least, he liked her *now*, since he'd gotten used to her.

Foley sat up slowly. "What. Is. That?"

Cookie whined and shifted in Sam's arms, causing Sam to drop his pack and some kibble to spill out. The dog wriggled like an eel, so Sam set him down to eat the mess he'd made. "On my planet, we call this a dog. D-O-G."

Foley snorted. "Surprised you can spell such a big word."

"Suck it, Foley."

"I *knew* those cages were for something living." Foley nodded to the cages he must have obviously pulled out of Sam's closet.

"Seriously?" Rage built. "You're going through my closet now?"

"No, moron. You left those out."

Sam deflated. "Oh."

Foley's eyes narrowed. "Why? You have *more* cages in there?" He opened the closet door before Sam could stop him, and a mountain of stuff spilled out. "Christ, Sam, get help, would you? Hoarders has an eight-hundred number."

Sam flushed. "I am *not* a hoarder, I keep telling you. I just like to collect stuff."

Foley rolled his eyes. "Yeah, and you work at the garage because you love cars and the money means nothing. Give me a break."

They both studied the stacks of stuff Sam had piled in his room. Magazines over there. Clean clothes by the dresser on the floor. Dirty ones by the closet. Maybe *in* the closet, if he wasn't mistaken about that pair of crumpled socks. It had been a while since he'd opened that door.

Hmm. Seemed he also had some animal cages, tools he kept forgetting to take to the garage, a football and basketball, and maybe more clothes, though they had probably been hanging up at one time because he didn't see too many left on hangers. What *did* he have in his dresser?

"How can you live like this?" Foley sounded disgusted.

The neat freak. Sam bit back a grin. "What's wrong, your OCD flaring up?"

Foley shivered. "I have to get out of here. My skin is itching. I feel the need to clean."

"Such a pussy."

Foley shot him a finger and said over his shoulder as he walked out the door, "I have beer downstairs, where it's *clean*."

Sam considered the room, thought he might straighten it up later, then pointed a finger at Cookie. "Be good. I'll be right downstairs." He took two steps before realizing the dog might not be housebroken. He grabbed the puppy and another handful of dog food, and joined Foley in the kitchen.

The town house had been a gift of low rent from Eileen years ago, when Sam and Foley had made the permanent move back to Seattle. Though they'd grown up in the city, they'd left to explore the U.S. after that stint in prison. A fresh start. After several states and more automotive classes across the country, they'd managed to get enough education to be fully-fledged mechanics. Not that the shit was that hard to figure out anyway, but managers seemed to like book smarts. And when they got wind of Foley's and Sam's pasts, sometimes those classes had been all that stood in the way of unemployment.

Then they'd met Liam Webster and his daughter, Del, and hadn't looked back since.

Life was good in the garage. Or it had been, until everyone started making decisions with their dicks. Stick it here, get a girlfriend. Stick it there, move in together. Get stuck by one of those McCauley assholes, get married. He still wasn't sure about Del's guy, though his dog and kid were cool enough. Del had never seemed the happy-homemaker type. And the McCauleys were all about tradition, family, and the white picket fence. When Del had been dating the guy, her emotions had been all over the place. Especially when the dickhead had dumped her.

Sam would have bashed his face in for screwing with Del, but Foley had cautioned him to wait it out. Apparently, Del had been wrong about the rejection, because Mike McCauley had made it up to her with not only apologies, but also a freakin' *engagement ring*. Now the guy looked at her as if she could do no wrong. Sam didn't know what was worse—an annoyed Del or a cheerily happy Del.

He set the dog and the food on the floor. "Funny

finding you here." Sam sat at the table across from Foley. "What? No love time tonight with sexy Cyn?"

Foley smirked. "I wore her out. She's spending the weekend with friends in Port Townsend. A baby shower for a girlfriend, I think."

"You feel okay letting her out of your sight? I mean, what if she finds someone better than you? A guy not so into being a neat freak, who has a much better car?"

"No such thing." Foley slid Sam a beer and took a swig of his own. He stared at the puppy munching on kibble. "Now, about this dog…"

Sam held up a hand. "I'm just fostering. I swear. I'm holding Cookie until his new owner is ready to take him in. Besides, Eileen never said no to pets."

Cookie took a few tentative steps toward Foley, sniffing. But when Foley jerked his foot back, the dog ran into the living room.

"Quit scaring my dog," Sam warned.

"*Whose* dog?"

"He's mine until Ivy gets him back." Until he knew for sure she wouldn't turn her back on the poor thing needing her affection.

"Ivy?" Foley pounced with a shit-eating grin. "Who's Ivy? Do I know her?"

"No. She's not one of your bazillion ex-model girlfriends." *That I know of, because she's pretty enough to be one.*

Foley smiled through his teeth. "Oh, then I guess there's no reason to introduce her to Cyn, is there?" Foley still hadn't all the way forgiven him for the New Year's Eve fiasco.

Sam had been a little envious of all the attention Foley

had been focusing on Cyn, so he'd decided to test her—for Foley's benefit—by inviting a ton of Foley's exes to the party. Instead of being intimidated by a half dozen gorgeous women, though, Cyn had held her own.

Sam still felt bad about that. His insecurities had made him act like an ass. Foley would never dump him for some babe. Even if she *was* totally Foley's type—with long, dark-red hair, a pin-up body, smarts, and attitude. No way Foley would ditch him for all that, or so he kept telling himself.

"You know"—Sam toyed with the bottle—"instead of getting all pissy with me about that, you should be thanking me. Now you know for a fact she won't toss your sorry ass because you were a whore."

"I prefer the term 'player.'"

"Whatever. You had more sex than me and Johnny combined before Cyn. Not sure about Lou, though. He's a mystery." Johnny and Lou, their other garage buddies. Johnny was a charmer whose dad owned a strip club. Johnny knew how to seduce women like he'd been born to it. Lou was a dominant asshole who pretty much did whatever the hell he wanted and women loved him for it. He worked that dark Latin-lover angle and had a pretty good racket going for him.

"You got me there." Foley clinked the neck of his bottle against Sam's. "But admit it. You like Cyn. She's smart and funny. My woman is fine as shit."

"Yeah, yeah." Good. At least he'd gotten away from—

"But this Ivy. Who is she, exactly?"

Crap. "I told you. She's taking Cookie."

"How'd you meet her?"

How to explain without sounding like a stalker…

When Sam didn't answer right away, Foley sat up straighter in his chair. *Hell*.

Sam hadn't planned to tell Foley about Ivy yet, because the woman made him feel strange. He'd been with pretty women before. Nice, mean, thick, thin. Sam had done them all. He didn't know Ivy. But from the moment he'd seen her, she'd refused to leave his brain.

"Well?"

Despite the subject of conversation, it felt good to have his best friend back, talking, sharing a beer. They'd always spoken about women and work and whatever bullshit passed for a good story.

Cookie tentatively entered the kitchen once more. He made his way over to the food on the floor and began to eat again.

Sam drew in a deep breath, then let it out. "I've had a few strays wandering around First Ave, you know, near McClure Middle School and that playground, park area. I was looking for Cookie since I'd found Macho there last week and—"

Foley snorted. "Macho I get. But Cookie? That's what you named the dog?"

"She did it. I was calling him Scruffy. But whatever. Point is, I was there a few nights ago and found him at the back of her place, where Ivy works, I mean."

"Where's that?"

Sam studied his friend, but seeing nothing more than vague interest, he answered, "Bodyworks on Queen Anne. So it's—"

"She's a stripper?" Foley's eyes widened.

"On *Queen. Anne. Avenue.* Dumbass. She's a massage therapist."

"Oh." Foley looked relieved. As if he could throw stones.

"Anyway, it's dark, the dog is in the back of her place in a fenced-in courtyard, and I'm standing in the shadows hoping I don't get confused with the guys knocking places over."

Foley nodded. "Right. That string of robberies in Queen Anne. Yeah, that wouldn't look good, you being found there."

"So Ivy comes out to get the puppy, and I left. But Willie was worried, so I—"

"Who's Willie?"

"What? Are you writing a fucking book?"

Foley ignored his growl, so Sam grudgingly explained the rest. "Anyway, like I said, I'm holding Cookie for her. We're maybe going to grab a beer tomorrow; then I can tell you exactly when the dog will be gone. Okay with you, *boss*?" he asked drily. He pretended he couldn't care less about the date with Ivy. Date. Ha. It was just a meet up to see if she met his standards for the dog. Not anything personal. This was all about Cookie.

Yet his speeding pulse said otherwise.

Foley just watched him and drank his beer. "That's your story?"

"It's the truth."

"Uh-huh." Foley smirked.

"What now?"

"So this Ivy chick. What's her deal?"

"She's just some woman who wants a dog." Who had the prettiest smile. Big, green eyes that dominated a sweet yet sexy face. A husky voice that could talk all day and he'd never get tired of hearing it. Then there was that body that didn't stop, breasts and an ass that—

"That." Foley pointed at his face.

"Huh?"

"You only look like that when you're into a woman." Foley drained his beer. "What does she look like?"

Sam shrugged. "I didn't notice."

"Bullshit."

Foley was getting on his last damn nerve. "Fine. She's fuckin' hot, okay? Respectable."

"Yeah? Cyn was respectable."

"Until she fell for you," Sam muttered.

Foley ignored him. "I thought Cyn was too good for me once, but look at us now."

"But I'm not you, and Ivy isn't Cyn."

"How the hell would you know? You just met her." Foley stared at him. "You haven't looked this interested in a girl since Jennifer Roland."

"Yeah, and we both remember how that turned out."

"So we went to prison. We got out." Foley grinned. "You're older and wiser now. No way you'll break into Ivy's house to leave a love note, right?"

Sam rubbed his eyes. "I can't believe I was ever that stupid."

"I can. You're pretty stupid on a regular basis." Foley chuckled and ignored the hand gesture Sam shot him. "Look, you like this Ivy."

"Dude, I just met her. Give it up. This won't go anywhere. There's nothing between us." Though he might have wished for literally nothing to be between them while he took advantage of that smokin' body...

"She's pretty, and she's taking in a stray dog," Foley continued as if Sam hadn't interrupted him. "I'd say you guys already have that in common—you're both into animals. Why not see where it goes? It's not like you're asking her to marry you. Just enjoy a beer and some conversation together."

"I plan on having a beer, okay?" Did Foley not understand him? He'd already said that. Twice.

"Nothing to be nervous about," Foley just had to add.

"I'm *not* nervous." His palms were sweating at the thought of being near her again.

"I mean, it's not like she's someone you have to see after tomorrow night. It doesn't work out, you move on. The girls at Strutts are still asking about you. Johnny told me to tell you."

"Great." He'd served as security at Strutts, the strip club Johnny's dad owned. The girls were pretty and nice, and the sex had been good if not great. The last girl he'd been with had moved out of town, and he hadn't been back since. Not because he missed her, but because he'd lost his taste for easy sex that didn't mean anything.

And damn it, sex and Ivy didn't go together. Sam had no reason to see her other than to make sure Cookie would be getting a good home. Period.

If he wanted sex, he could go back to Strutts and take Bubbles up on her offer. What guy would turn down no-strings-attached sex from a woman who could kiss her own ass? Yet he forgot about Bubbles five seconds after leaving the club.

He hadn't stopped thinking about Ivy since that first time he'd seen her cradle Cookie to her chest.

Foley nodded, still watching him, so Sam grabbed them more beers.

"What's up with Eileen lately?" he wanted to know, since he hadn't heard from her in a week.

Foley groaned. "You had to ask, didn't you? Mom is losing it. She's all nervous about the wedding and calling me every other day, asking what I think about place settings."

Sam raised a brow. "You?"

"Exactly. Woman has lost her damn mind. I keep putting her through to Cyn. I mean, centerpieces and color schemes for a wedding? I say elope and put us all—and Jacob—out of our misery."

Jacob, Eileen's fiancé, would do anything for the woman he loved. "Poor guy. I like him."

"Me too. He has the patience to deal with Mom and her nuttiness, and he still hasn't called off the wedding. *And* he stayed with her even during her time in the cast. He really loves her."

The car accident Eileen had been in back in January had scared all of them. Worse, it had brought out the ugly patient in Eileen, a woman Sam would vote into sainthood without thinking twice. Yet Jacob had stood by her through it all.

Sam knew it had been difficult for Foley to accept his mother moving on without him. Granted, she was a grown woman living her own life while Foley lived his, but Eileen had never been devoted to anyone other than Foley since his father had passed. She'd taken Sam in, but that was different. She hadn't taken a husband or significant other.

Then she'd met Jacob last year and fell hard.

"You going to be okay with Mommy moving out?" Sam taunted. "I mean, no more tucking you in at night or wiping your ass once she's got a husband around."

"Dick." Foley sighed. "Yeah, I'm good. Cyn helps. Takes my mind off losing Mom." He sounded sad, but Sam caught the sparkle in his eyes. "When I tell her how depressed or confused I feel, Cyn *comforts* me. Takes my mind off my misery, you know?" He wiggled his brows.

"Nice." Sam raised his beer in a toast. "To finally growing a brain in that fat head."

Foley nodded and clinked his bottle. "To finally growing a set and asking a decent woman out. Even if you had to use a dog to do it."

"It's not a date," Sam growled.

A strange sound caught him off guard, and he glanced over to see Cookie vomiting up the kibble he'd just wolfed down.

Foley shook his head. "You're cleaning that up. With any luck, Ivy doesn't give you the same reaction tomorrow night."

Sam had a sudden image of her staring at him in horror, realizing who she'd accepted an invitation from. He wondered if he should just cancel the date that wasn't a date and save her the trouble. He could text her for details about her ability to care for a dog and—

"*Ow*." The balled napkin thrown at his eye startled him. He threw it back. "What the hell, Foley?"

"Stop thinking so hard. It's just a beer. Relax."

"I know that."

"So why are you so nervous?"

"I'm not."

"Bull."

"She's a nice woman," he admitted. "I don't have a great track record with nice. Not that it matters, since we're *not dating*."

"You spoke with her for how long and you know everything about her already? Maybe she's secretly bitchy and not nice at all."

She had put up an attitude when he'd questioned her about the dog. But when she'd looked at Cookie, when she'd petted him, he'd seen her heart in her eyes.

Sam scowled. "She's not bitchy. Don't ask me how I know. I just know."

"Fine. But check out the dog." Foley pointed to Cookie, staring at the mess he'd left. "He's as sweet and innocent as they come. Dumb animals seem to love you, and they can sense evil."

"Up yours."

"Hey, look at it this way. I doubt Ivy will throw up her food while you're out tomorrow."

They watched as Cookie stepped closer to his regurgitated chow and sniffed. Then he leaned nearer and…

Foley made a face. "Though if she eats her own puke, that might be a sign to dump her."

"You think?"

—⁓—

Foley watched Sam clean up the mess on the floor. He took the dog out for a walk. When he returned, he went to bed, the tired pooch snoozing in his big arms.

After cleaning the few dishes and wiping down their already-clean counters, Foley turned in early as well. It had been a long day, and he already missed Cyn, even though she'd only just left that day for the baby shower.

He readied for bed and slid under the sheets, feeling lonely without her by his side. Unlike Sam, Foley appreciated having a woman in his life. He loved Cynthia Nichols with his whole heart, forever and all that shit.

But he knew it wasn't that Sam didn't want a woman. Sam didn't think himself worthy enough to have one of his own. *A piece of shit like you doesn't deserve love and affection. A little snot who always demands too much needs to sit back and see himself the way others do. You can go or stay, whatever the hell you want, because I don't give a good goddamn. Because—*

Memories of that woman dogging Sam always left a bad taste in his mouth. Man, Foley hated Louise Hamilton.

Feeling unclean at thoughts of her, he dialed Cyn. "Hey, gorgeous," he said when she answered. "What are you wearing?"

"Foley." His lover chuckled, her husky voice turning him on without her trying. "I miss you."

"Me too." He sighed. "You coming back Sunday?"

"Yep. Try not to miss me too much. Absence makes the heart grow fonder."

"And my cock harder," he mumbled, staring down at himself.

"I know you did not just throw something sexual into my emotional confession."

"Big words, baby. Slow down, you're confusing me. Remember, I'm just a lowly mechanic."

"Lowly my ass." She snorted. "So what's going on with you?"

"Remember those cages in Sam's room?"

"Of course. So is he?"

"No." He blew out a relieved breath. "He's not

hoarding animals and hiding them in the house, thank God. He's rescuing them."

"Oh, that's so sweet. I told you so."

"You did not." He grimaced. She really had. Cyn saw the real Sam, the one he allowed Foley to see. That loving, kind soul under all the bluster, muscles, and badass. And the god-awful beard Foley had been on him to lose.

"Please. You've seen him with Johnny and Lara's dog. That puppy loves Sam. Heck, so does Jekyll." His boss Del's giant puppy. "Like you said, animals love him."

"Because beasts stick with their own kind," he drawled, and she laughed. "He brought home a puppy today. I finally caught him at it." He relayed their conversation, and she agreed with him.

"This Ivy. He's got a thing for her, hmm?"

"Yeah. I think so." Foley knew his bud, and the way Sam had talked about her, the way his eyes had glazed over in remembrance… "He hasn't been that way about a woman in a long time. Even Shaya, the chick he was seeing a few months ago, was just casual." He paused. "Ivy couldn't have come at a better time. I think he's been fighting again."

"Oh boy."

Sam had a lot of buried anger. He took that rage out by using his fists. Underground—*illegal*—matches where people made crazy bets gave him an outlet Foley wanted to condone. But if the guy got busted, he was screwed. Prison had been difficult for both of them, but Foley knew going back would break Sam. They'd both worked so hard to become better men. Without Foley to guide him, to help him stay on the right path, Sam might never recover. And despite their close bond, tighter than brothers, Foley wouldn't go back to prison again for dumb shit. To save his buddy's life, sure. But for illegal fighting? Hell no. Not even for Sam. Cyn would kick his ass, for one. And Eileen would finish the job.

"What do you think?" Cyn asked.

"I think the last time Sam got so wound up, Shaya was here to fuck the fight out of him. Er, ah, to take away the rage with some lovin'."

"Gee, thanks. I wasn't sure what you meant for a minute."

He chuckled. "But this Ivy… I don't know. He won't admit he likes her. Keeps saying it's not a date. But he looked nervous."

"He never looks anything but angry or stoic to me."

"I know him." Better than Sam knew himself, Foley liked to think. "He's into this chick. She seems okay on the surface. She wants to rescue a stray dog, and you know how Sam dotes on animals." Animals, kids—he protected the innocent. Though Sam would never see it that way, Foley knew his friend needed to do for others what had never been done for him. Not until Eileen had gotten her hands on him.

"That's good," Cyn said. "Sam needs softness in his life. Romance, love."

"Don't get ahead of yourself, woman. She likes dogs, yeah. But that's *all* we know. I want to feel her out."

A pause. "Oh?"

He chuckled at the frost in her voice. "But if I go check her out, he'll get mad. It'll get back to him one way or the other, and then he'll freeze me out. Then there's my girlfriend. She's not the sharing type, and she's nasty when she's mean. I'm a little scared of her."

Her throaty laugh turned him on even more. "Your girlfriend is a right bitch. And yeah. You do tend to stand out."

"But if *you* went in, Ivy the massage chick wouldn't think anything of some tall, gorgeous redhead with a kinked-up neck needing bodywork," he suggested.

"Hmm. How kinked up?"

"You get home and we'll try that position from that book you showed me. I can kink you up good, baby."

She laughed. "Okay. For you and for Sam, I'll sacrifice my body." Then she lowered her voice. "In fact, I'm in a mood to sacrifice it right now. I'm not wearing much, you know."

He jackknifed up in bed. "Keep talkin'..." Long-distance phone sex. Was it any wonder he loved her? "I owe you big-time when you get back."

"Yes, dear, you do." Then she made him groan.

Chapter 3

Ivy sat in the semicrowded bar and felt way out of her element. Sam had given her good directions to Ray's, even though the dimly lit sign outside read *Mazatlan*. The place smelled like a bar, with the odor of stale beer and greasy food wafting around the large, open room. Scarred wooden tables and chairs had been strategically placed for maximum seating, with a row of booths along the far wall.

By the back corner, a tiny dance floor, if one could call it that, sat in front of a jukebox playing a random assortment of alternative, classic rock, and grunge music. While she waited for Sam to return with their beer, she studied Ray's clientele. Most looked like blue-collar tough types. Lots of tattoos and piercings, scraggly beards, leather jackets—some with biker names on them, some without. More than a few scantily clad women hung around. The proverbial barfly was stuck to a seat at the bar.

In the twenty minutes they'd been there, the crowd had only grown, more people getting off work as the hour neared seven.

By far, though, the most interesting people in the bar seemed to be the staff. Most of them had tattoos everywhere—including the women—multicolored hair or *no* hair—again, including the women—and black shirts with their jobs stated plainly in white.

Ivy had no trouble making out the bouncers. The two men standing by the front door looked like they could eat a half-ton truck for breakfast, plus they wore shirts that said Bouncer.

She hid a smile and glanced away before a rather large, homely man swilling a beer caught her eye. He'd been looking at her for some time. Then again, so had many of the others in the place. Probably regulars not used to perky, blond massage therapists with no tats, piercings, or exposed cleavage darkening their door.

Sam totally fit in with this crowd. She noticed him talking with a few big, scary men at the bar. As if they'd sensed her study, all three of them glanced over at her. *Geesh, where do they grow these guys? On steroid farms?*

The one dark-haired man smiled at her and raised his beer in a toast. He was fierce, good-looking, and had sleeves of tattoos on both his muscular forearms. Sam slugged him in the arm and said something that caused him to laugh. The other man with them just watched her, his dark good looks a bit intimidating, as was the very direct stare that assessed her with a coldness she didn't like. He seemed almost out of place, not having any visible ink on his body—*almost* being the key word. He had a real, raw, powerful quality to him. When he smiled, she felt flustered under so much male regard.

A cute woman with bright, brown eyes, honey-colored, tight curls, and cocoa skin brought over a tray holding a pitcher of beer and a plate of…cookies? She wore jeans and a black T-shirt that said Waitress. "Hey, sweetie. You must be Ivy. I'm Rena." She set the cookies on the table. "Sam sent me."

Ivy smiled back. It would have been impossible not to respond to the sincere pleasure in the woman's eyes. "Hi. Is this for me?"

"Sam ordered the beer, but he's so busy jaw jacking that he's ignoring you. What a moron." Rena rolled her eyes. "The cookies are from Lara. She's in the back baking tonight. I know. Cookies and beer? Gross. But Lara's cookies are to die for, and Ray had a hankering. Ray's the owner."

Rena waited, so Ivy picked up a cookie and bit into it, despite needing to lose another five pounds that continued to linger like a cupcake hangover. "Oh. These are amazing." *So soft and gooey.*

"Yeah. Just make sure to eat them before the beer, or else the effect is way gross." Rena made a face and put two glasses and the pitcher on the table. "Enjoy." She winked. "And try to be gentle with Sam. He may not look it, but he's a pussycat."

"Thanks a lot, Rena," Sam growled as he took a seat in a huff.

"Anytime, handsome." She sauntered away and was lost in the masses waving for her attention.

"Getting crowded." Ivy poured them both a beer, to be nice, then finished another decadent masterpiece. God, that made three. She eyed the lonely cookie left, thinking she totally had room for that one too.

"Good, huh?" He nodded to the plate and snagged the last one.

A good thing or she might have eaten it.

"Lara's dating Johnny. He's not here tonight or he'd be flirting with you."

"Um, okay." She watched him finish the cookie, swallowed a sigh, then had a sip of beer. She must have made a face because he almost grinned. She could see the corner of his mouth wanting to turn up.

"Give it a minute and it won't be so bad." He drank half his glass. "Yeah. Better."

"Easy for you to say. If I drink that much, I won't be able to drive."

Before he could say anything, she felt someone looming behind her.

Sam's expression went from what she'd consider amused to annoyed, though his eyebrows barely moved. "Hell. We're talking. Go away." Sam sounded mean.

She hadn't heard him sound like that before, and it startled her. But the man—men—behind her only laughed. The two guys who'd been with him earlier by the bar sat with them.

"Hi. I'm Foley," said the tattooed one. He had gray eyes and a wide smile. Foley. Sam's best friend.

She smiled back. "I'm Ivy. Nice to meet you." She shook his hand, pleased he'd given her a gentle squeeze with that large paw.

The man across from him oozed sensuality. "I'm Lou. And the pleasure is all mine." He held out a hand and drew hers to his lips when she gave it to him.

"Cortez, hands off," Sam said, his voice cold.

"Easy, Sam. Just welcoming your lady to the fine establishment that is Ray's." She caught his Latin accent, as well as a healthy dose of sarcasm. "Classy joint you brought her to. I'm sure she's underwhelmed."

Foley coughed, to cover a laugh it seemed, because his eyes were shining with mirth. "It's not a bad place. The people here only seem rough."

As he said it, a scuffle broke out by the front door. But the bouncers tossed the assailants out in no time.

"Ah, just blowing off steam," Foley explained. "So how did you two meet?"

Sam shot him a look she couldn't read.

She might have been flustered if she didn't feel safer with so much muscle protecting her from the rest of the bar. "I found this adorable puppy, and it turned out Sam was looking for him too."

"How sweet. Love at first sight?" Lou asked. When she flushed, he added, all innocence, "For the puppy, I meant."

"Lou." Sam clenched his big fists on the table.

Lou, like Foley, ignored Sam's obvious mood.

"He—Cookie," she hastily clarified, not looking at Sam, "is adorable. I'm still waiting on an okay from my landlord that I can keep him. Pets are allowed per the lease, but you have to sign them on and get an okay before you bring them in." Then she turned to him. "Sam, how is Cookie doing? You haven't said."

"He's fine. Just missing you is all." Then he stood in a rush and hauled Foley out of his seat by the arm. "Go away." He turned and said to Lou, "You too. Ivy and me got things to talk about."

Lou smirked but stood all the same. "Easy, Sam. Don't blow a gasket. Didn't want to be rude and ignore your guest. See you at work on Monday. Nice meeting you, Ivy."

Before he could grab her hand for another kiss, Foley dragged him away, chuckling.

Sam sat with a grunt. "Assholes."

She watched the pair leave the table and head back to the bar. "Isn't Foley your best friend?"

"Yep."

"And Lou works with you." So Lou had said, because Sam hadn't exactly introduced them.

"Yep." Sam finished off his beer and poured another.

She continued to sip from her first glass, not even a third of the way finished. Sam just sat, watching her. The guy didn't talk much. That wouldn't have bothered her except that he watched her with such concentration. She felt as he if were looking through her, instead of at her.

"So about Cookie…" She'd called Sam earlier in the day, explaining that she still didn't have an answer about the dog from her landlord. But he'd still planned on going for a beer, so they could discuss her possible adoption. Intrigued despite herself, she'd agreed to meet him. Now she just hoped she'd survive the night.

"Yeah?"

"Foley was okay with him being there, at your house?"

Sam drank. "He was until Cookie puked up his dinner, then ate it."

Ivy was in the middle of taking a sip of beer. She put it back down, no longer wanting anything food or drink related. "Oh boy."

Sam gave a sly grin that caused her belly to do flips. Stern, he looked dangerous and sexy. But smiling? He was beautiful. Not just handsome, but bone-deep pretty in a manly kind of way. His blue-gray eyes seemed to light up, and his firm lips curled just enough to make a woman want to fan herself until the heat died down.

"Sorry if I ruined your appetite." He didn't sound sorry. "But it was funny as hell to watch Foley cringe. The guy is such a pus—ah, a pushover when it comes to dirt."

"And vomit, apparently."

"And that." He nodded. "But the puppy is hanging with Johnny tonight, so we're good."

"Johnny, who's dating Lara," she said, remembering the names he'd spoken of earlier. "Johnny works with you too."

"Yeah. Along with the assholes Lou and Foley. Foley and I have been friends forever. Worked together for the past ten years too. We met the others at Webster's Garage. Lou is a pain in the ass, but not a bad guy." That sounded like high praise coming from Sam. "He's also a hell of a painter. A real artist. But don't tell him I said that."

"I won't." As if she'd ever see any of these people again. Sam had been giving her a hot-and-cold attitude since she'd arrived. He'd been stoic and growly when escorting her inside. Then he'd introduced her to one of the bouncers. Earl, she thought, who'd acted nice enough. Sam had seemed glad to have her by his side. Until he'd dumped her at the table and gave her a command to stay while he found them refreshment. He'd said the stay part but nothing so sophisticated as "refreshment." No, he'd said, "I'll try to get us something that doesn't taste like stale piss."

Lovely, was all she could think.

"So what do you think of the place?" he asked, watching her.

"It's loud." She glanced around, saw that old man and

a younger, angrier one staring at her again, so she looked away in a hurry. "But the cookies are amazing."

He nodded, seeming pleased with her answer. "You got that right. Lara's an angel in the kitchen, and Ray knows it. He's gonna hate losing her when she gets her nursing degree and dumps this place."

"Oh."

"Johnny and she are living together. Probably get married once he gets the stones to ask her."

"I'm sure he will if she bakes for him."

Sam nodded, drank again. They hadn't spoken much about Cookie. And considering that's why they'd met up, she tried to get them back on track. Because tonight was *not* a date.

Ivy wasn't so much against relationships as she was about doing things right this second time around. She'd made major mistakes with Max, letting him walk all over her, being too nice, supporting him to the detriment of herself. So with a new man, she'd make all the rules and let him take care of *her* for a while. Not that she'd take advantage. No, she and her man would be equals, but she'd like to be pampered at least a little bit.

Going out with Sam was only about the dog. He'd said as much. And she kept ignoring her disappointment because of it.

When Sam's intense stare turned into a scowl, she followed the direction of his attention and looked to her left, to see him eyeballing the men who'd been staring at her earlier. "Who are those guys?"

He flicked an icy gaze back to hers. "Why? They say or do something while I was at the bar?" As if anyone would have dared.

"No. But they don't seem to like me much."

"Let's find out why."

"No, Sam, wait—" But he'd already risen and stalked to her unhappy fan club of two.

"What the hell's your problem?" he snarled at the younger man.

"Your bitch keeps making eyes at my old man." The younger one sneered. "Tell her to keep her snooty tits to herself. Unless she's willing to sit on my—"

Sam cold-cocked him before he could say another word. The younger man slumped to the ground, groaning and fingering his jaw. "Sac up, Goodie. I barely tapped you. Get your sorry ass gone before I rip your fucking head off. My friend and I are talking, and your attitude is on my last nerve." Then he shocked Ivy anew by grabbing the old man by the throat. "Drop the knife, Senior, or I'll gut you like a fucking fish."

She stared in surprise at the knife in the man's hand that clattered to the floor in the sudden silence broken only by the crackle of an old Bowie tune.

Senior grinned, showing missing teeth. "Sure thing, Hamilton. Don't turn your back next time, though. You won't see me coming."

"I won't, you old prick. Man, talk about some fucked-up genetics."

Before Sam could do any more damage, the bouncers ambled over and took charge, being a bit gentler, but not by much, before tossing the Goodie family out of the bar.

Sam returned to the table and sat, and the noise in the bar resumed. She just stared at the tight constraint in the man. Just moments before, he'd erupted into violence.

"You okay?" he asked quietly. "Sorry about that, but Goodie's a prick, and his old man is as bad—where he gets it from. They're mad because they lost money last week and they blame me."

"Why would they blame you for that?" she asked, her mouth dry. She drank more beer.

"Because they placed their bets on the wrong horse." He looked stone cold.

Suddenly, she needed to be anywhere but here. "I think I should go."

He blinked. "Go? We haven't talked about Cookie yet. Or you."

"Me?"

"Well, if you want Cookie, you have to prove you're the best one for the job."

She frowned. "Really? Because it seems to me that a man who starts trouble, punches people in the face, and is mean to his best friends shouldn't be the one having so much say-so on who gets a stray puppy."

He sat straighter in his chair, and for a moment, she wondered if he'd lean across the table and grab her by the throat, as he'd done the old man. When he set his elbows down and moved toward her, she jerked back.

He froze. "I'm not going to hurt you."

She flushed. "I know that."

"I don't think you do."

He sounded hurt, which confused her. He'd just beaten a man up. Knocked him down with one punch. "Well, maybe I don't. I don't know you that well, Sam. And I just watched you put a man down with a big fist. Then you held that old man in place with one hand. He was on tiptoe nearly *off the floor*. That's a lot of strength. Forgive me for being cautious."

He nodded, but the ice in his eyes refused to melt. "Makes sense."

"Look. It's been a long week, and I'd like to go home now." Before she did something silly and burst into frightened tears. Ivy was tougher than that. But she'd never been around such violence, and her distress that the night hadn't gone well added to her frustration and resentment. Just once she'd like to go out with a man, even for a simple beer, and not have it end in disaster.

"Yeah, fine." Sam stood when she did. "Put it on my tab, Rena," he called out and placed a hand on the small of Ivy's back.

She started but didn't pull away. Instead, she moved closer to him as they pushed through the rough crowd. The masses parted for Sam like magic. Before she knew it, he'd walked her outside.

"My car is over there." She pointed a few rows back. "Thanks for the beer and cookies."

"I'll walk you over."

She felt a sense of relief that she wouldn't have to walk through the dark and dangerous lot by herself. Whatever else she could say about Sam, he seemed the protective type.

At her car, he waited while she unlocked the door. He didn't cage her in, but stood back enough that she wouldn't feel smothered. Kind of like the first time she'd met him, when he'd given her a lot of space so she could get him her business card. She wondered if he did that a lot, because he gave the appearance of being so large and threatening.

She paused before getting in. Instead, she turned around to see him watching her. He seemed dejected, though she couldn't have said why she sensed that. As before, he wore a nearly emotionless expression.

"Well, it was interesting."

"My nights usually are," he deadpanned.

She smiled then and, unable to help it, laughed. "Sam, you sure know how to show a girl a good time."

He gave her a ghost of smile before shrugging. "What can I say? It's a gift." He shoved his hands in his pockets. He did that a lot too. "Sorry about the bar. I guess… Ah, hell. Well, I'll text you about the dog. Just let me know when you know something, okay?"

From her landlord. "I will. And thanks for standing up for me in there." At least, that's what she thought he'd done. For all she knew, she was a convenient excuse to pummel people.

He shrugged again, then turned to walk away. "Later."

It didn't seem right, this ending. She couldn't stop remembering that sweetness in his smile. The joy sparkling in his eyes as he'd cared for Cookie. She took a step and latched on to his arm, which stopped him in his tracks. He turned, slowly, to face her.

She tugged him toward her. When she could reach him, she kissed him tenderly on the cheek. Goodness, he smelled good. Like sandalwood and man—nothing off about Sam Hamilton. His beard had been surprisingly soft.

She pulled back and saw him frozen, his eyes wide.

"Thanks for keeping me safe in there. I'll talk to you soon." She patted his chest once, then stepped back and got into her car. She started up and left, checking her rearview. And saw him staring at her while she drove away.

———

Sam watched her go, not sure of anything as he let the feeling of her warmth fill all his cold places. Just… damn. Such soft, warm lips on his cheek. He touched the spot, still feeling her there. The despair that he'd ruined everything earlier faded, replaced by an unfamiliar sense of hope that hadn't been with him in years. Not since first realizing he and Foley had a home at Webster's.

He forced himself to drop his hand and turn, heading back to Ray's. Once inside, he moved through the throng of loud revelers and joined Foley at the bar. He didn't see Lou. A glance down at the puny guy sitting on the stool next to Foley had the dude leaving in a hurry. Apparently Sam didn't just scare women into leaving. He scared men too.

He rubbed his cheek, still feeling Ivy's soft lips there. Maybe he hadn't scared her too badly after all.

"I notice your friend isn't with you." Foley took a sip of his beer, staring at Sam.

"She had to go."

"I'll bet."

Sam sighed. "Probably shouldn't have asked her to meet me here on a Friday night."

"You think?" Foley snorted. "Dumbass. What the hell, Sam? You like this chick. I can see why. She is fine. Sweet. Much too nice for a place like this."

Sam frowned. "She's not all that nice to me." *Except for that kiss, or the way she looked at me that one time with Cookie. When she kept her hand on my arm the whole walk to her car.*

"Good. You'd eat up nice and spit it out."

"True."

Foley knew him so well. And he was right. Ivy was nice, despite the way she'd given him some attitude. What the hell did Sam think he was doing sniffing after her?

Foley frowned. "So what happened with Goodie?"

"He and his old man were dicking with Ivy. I didn't like it. So I made them leave."

"Oh. Good."

"Freaked her out, I think. She wanted to go home." He stared at his hands on the bar, seeing the calluses, the bruised knuckles, the roughness. "I walked her to her car." He looked at Foley. "She gave me a kiss on the cheek before she left."

Foley blinked, then gave him a wide smile. "Yeah? That's good, man. Means you're not totally up shit creek yet." He yelled for Lara, now working behind the bar. "Hey, honey, a beer for my buddy."

Sam glanced at the empty pitcher in front of Foley. "You know, I'm betting that's the pitcher I left behind. This next one's on you." While they waited for Lara to fill one up, Sam studied his friend. "You still pining for Cyn?"

"Always." Foley sighed, then ruined his sad effect by grinning. "It's kind of nice when she leaves, because when she comes back, I get rewarded for being the good boyfriend. I get her flowers; she gives me *looove*."

"I hate you when you're like this," Sam muttered. "Thanks, Lara."

Lara winked at him, her brown eyes deep, as dark as the straight hair pulled back in a ponytail. Hot and nice. Yet she'd chosen to take on Johnny. Like Cyn had glued herself to Foley. Maybe there was hope for him. If other decent chicks could see something beyond the ink and grease covering his hooligan friends, maybe Sam had a shot with someone as pure and sweet as Ivy.

His phone buzzed, and he drew it out, a small part of him hoping Ivy had changed her mind and wanted to get back with him tonight. Maybe a drink somewhere quieter? But when he checked the ID, he saw a number he dreaded.

But a reminder of the truth helped.

Ivy wouldn't want him. No woman did. When would he learn?

He drained his glass, still nowhere near to being even slightly drunk. "I'm done. Going home to turn in early."

Foley narrowed his eyes but said nothing more. "Cool. Want me to come?"

"Nah. Celebrate being alone for once. You know, not tied at the hip to the mean woman currently running your life."

Foley smirked. "Good point. Lou's driving, and I'm drinking. I just have to be careful he doesn't challenge me to darts, knowing I'm off my game."

Considering Foley was never on his game in darts, even when sober, Sam shook his head and left. On the drive to Johnny's, he called Louise.

And wished he hadn't.

—◦◦◦—

Monday morning at the garage, Sam felt as if he had the mother of all sober hangovers. And yeah, his mother had caused it. He hated the woman, as much as he reluctantly loved her. Just more proof he had nothing going for him, because what kid hated his mom? The woman who'd suffered to give birth to him?

Now he was out the two hundred dollars he'd been hoping to put toward a pneumatic impact wrench he'd had his eye on. His was about shot, and Foley kept giving him evil looks when Sam asked to borrow his. But Louise was short some cash, so he'd given her what he had.

She'd leave him alone for a few months, probably. That made him feel better about giving her the money. Not *loaning* her the dough, because the woman claimed he owed her a few bills here and there. And who was he to argue the fact?

He sighed and busied himself under the body of a Nissan Altima's broken catalytic converter up on lifts. The springs had 14mm nuts on them, but they were majorly corroded. He had a feeling he was going to have to torch the suckers. He did, melting them enough that he could remove them without breaking the studs. That's all he'd need, to have to drill those out too, making this repair even longer.

He'd checked what Del had scheduled for him today, and he didn't have time to waste on a stubborn assembly not wanting to come out. As it was, having to use the torch meant he'd need to wait for the components to cool off.

"So. Ray's? Really, Sam?" Johnny must have been feeling brave this morning, digging right into Sam's shit early on. Lou and Foley had focused on work, fortunately not much on conversation before nine.

Sam glanced at the clock on the wall, saw it had reached ten, and sighed. "What do you want? A fist in the gut, the face, or your nuts?"

He heard Lou laugh over the low drone of Alabama on the radio.

"Lara told me she met your friend. Funny you didn't say anything about it when you picked up your dog. So what happened?"

Sam sighed and stepped out from under the car. Johnny supposedly could charm a woman out of her panties in no time. At least, according to him. Though Sam had met enough of Johnny's ex-girlfriends to know the guy had skills. He also had looks. Prettier than Sam by far, though he lacked Sam's muscle. Johnny always had a grin and a smart comeback, and the guy could run like a deer. Most likely the reason he was still breathing was that he could outrace trouble.

Truth to tell, Sam liked the guys—and gal—he worked with. He considered them a loose kind of family even. Del and Liam, his bosses, treated him like he belonged, and he never took that for granted. Lou could be a dick sometimes, but the guy was a class act. Took care of a shitload of family—all women—and never did less than his best on any job. Sam liked that kind of work ethic. It was a lot like his and Foley's. Johnny worked hard too. He was a smart-ass, but Sam kind of liked his humor, mostly when it wasn't directed his way.

Getting back to Johnny's comment, he shrugged. "I came to get my dog, not to talk you to death."

Johnny gave him a sly grin. "Word has it, 'Cookie' isn't your dog. He belongs to some pretty blond and you're just holding on to him for her. That true?"

Sam noticed the sudden silence in the garage except for the radio. "Bunch of gossiping motherfu—"

"*Sam*," a female voice roared. "Watch that mouth!

I'm still collecting." Del Webster, soon to be Del McCauley in a few more weeks, rattled a glass jar half-filled with quarters. She could probably fund a honeymoon to Hawaii with all the money she'd been gathering from everyone who swore in her garage. Even her father wasn't immune.

Most likely the reason why Liam had been so scarce at the garage lately. That or he was continuing to cozy up to the current lady in his life. Sam liked her. Any woman who could put up with Liam had to be angling for a heavenly reward. The guy was sixty but looked forty, still worked out every day, and handled his kids with a firm hand. And a whip, mostly likely. Right now Del appeared a little wild around the eyes.

The eyes of a wolf—light gray and piercing. She wore her ash-blond hair in funky braids, had her own set of tattooed sleeves clearly visible on her muscular arms bared by a SpongeBob T-shirt. A nose stud and eyebrow ring complemented her striking looks.

But those eyes gave a guy pause more than anything. When she was in a mood, they fairly glowed. Yeah, she freaked him out a little, even after all this time. He'd never met a woman brave enough to face him head-on and not blink at witnessing him in a rage. Not too long ago, she'd stepped between him and Foley in a real doozy. Yet she'd still asked him to come back to work.

He lied, totally out of quarters and not wanting to get into trouble this early on a Monday. "I was just going to say mother *hens*."

"Well, okay then." Del huffed.

"Seriously?" Johnny gaped. "Motherfu and mother hen? Not seeing it."

Del arched a brow, and Johnny mumbled something and went back to his station to fix a beat-up Acura.

Pleased he could finish his work without all the emotional nonsense that lately seemed to clutter the garage, Sam moved back under the Nissan and—

"Ray's, Sam?" Del sighed. "Even for you, that's pathetic. A first date should be somewhere a little more romantic than sticky floors and Lara's cookies."

"Cookie. That's the name of Ivy's dog," Johnny added, *so* unhelpfully. "Ain't that cute?"

Sam swore under his breath. "Shut it, Devlin." Maybe if Sam ignored them all, they'd go away.

Del tapped her foot. "Waiting."

"Shit, Del. I'm working."

She just held out the jar.

He patted his pockets through his coveralls. "Foley, spot me. I'm empty."

"That's like ten bucks you owe me," Foley complained, but Sam soon heard the clink of change hitting glass. "What Sam's too embarrassed to say is that he screwed up by taking a sweet thing like Ivy to Ray's. So he's working on a way to get her to go out with him again without coming across as a—excuse the expression, Del—dumbass."

"No charge," she said. "It fits. Darn, Sam. You don't invite a nice girl to Ray's."

"*You* hang out there," Sam said.

"Yeah, but I ain't nice."

"She's not," an unwelcome voice added. Crap. McCauley was here.

"Yo, Mike," Lou called out.

"Hey, McCauley. You bring Colin?" Johnny asked.

Sam didn't have to ask if the big man had brought Jekyll, his goliath of a puppy, because the huge canine whined and danced by McCauley's big feet. Had to be on a leash, because otherwise Jekyll would have launched himself at Sam. The dog loved him, and Sam wasn't so hard-hearted he couldn't admit he looked forward to Jekyll's visits.

"Um, it's Monday, Johnny. Legally, I have to sit the kid in school."

"Oh, right. Forgive me for forgetting the laws and functions of the mortal world. Here in hell, with our demon mistress, reality fogs over."

"Johnny," Del growled.

"Nice one." Foley chuckled. "Truth hurts, Del. Ow, not the pitchfork."

Sam studied the underside of the Altima and snorted. Johnny truly was a pain in the ass, but a funny guy nonetheless.

"Del, leave 'em alone," McCauley said. Maybe he wasn't such a dick after all. "Just for a minute, though. Sounds like Sam needs help." Nah, the guy was a *huge* dick—both a jackass and a giant. He could have fit in at the shop, muscled and mean. But McCauley was also a family man. He worked construction and had a nice kid. And he loved the hell out of Del. For all that Sam got hives being near the Mr. Mom, he kind of liked that Del had found someone to treat her right. Because if the guy didn't, she'd kick his ass.

"*I* need help?" Sam had to say. "I'm not the one getting married in another—what is it, Foley? Four weeks?"

"Yep," Foley answered, way too smug. "Gosh, Mike.

That's only twenty-eight days away, not counting today. So soon. Are you ready, big guy?"

"Not getting cold feet, are you?" Lou asked, sounding amused.

"Shut up, guys." Del sounded nervous.

Uh-oh. In trying to worry him, they'd worried her.

Sam actually felt bad for Del. "You know, if he doesn't marry you, we can always hunt him down and beat him to death." The glare he shot McCauley told him Sam wasn't kidding.

But instead of doing the smart thing and looking scared, McCauley rolled his eyes. "It's not me you idiots have to worry about. It's her." Then he scooped up a hyperventilating Del and laughingly fireman's carried her toward her office. "Nope. Not letting you go, baby, so get used to being at my beck and call forever."

"The hell you say," she yelled, sounding much more like herself.

"I really like that guy." Johnny beamed, then called out, "Del, that's twenty-five cents for the swear jar." The Rattle of Oppression, as Johnny and the crew had taken to calling it.

They didn't hear her response because McCauley had slammed the door.

Nobody wanted to know what the pair got up to after it locked.

But they'd forgotten to take Jekyll with them, and he now stood quivering, his leash caught on a heavy floor jack.

"Sam, you're up." Lou nodded to the dog and started whistling in time with the Doobie Brothers.

Sam wiped his hands off on his coveralls and

gratefully left the shitty catalytic converter to pet Jekyll. The dog was in heaven while Sam rubbed his belly and ears, crooning what a good dog he was and trying not to laugh as he avoided the many licks and nibbles from the loving pup.

Sometime later, the office door opened, and a smug-looking McCauley and a rumpled-but-smiling Del walked out.

Sam stood and held the leash out to the guy. The dog clearly loved him, so McCauley couldn't be too bad, all said and done. "Seriously? That was, what? Like three minutes?"

"Best three minutes of my life." McCauley ruffled the dog's fur. "Come on, buddy. Let's get to work. Later, guys. Remember, you have to wear suits to the wedding." He gave Sam a thorough once-over. "You too, Hamilton." He ignored the jeers and fingers shot his way, kissed Del once more, then left with Jekyll.

Sam looked at her and shook his head. He stood in front of her to block the others and pointed to her shirt.

"Ah, thanks." She hastily rebuttoned the thing and blushed. "And it was closer to four minutes, really. Maybe even five," she said cheerily. "Now get back to work. He wasn't kidding about that suit, Sam. I can't wait to see you all sparkly and dressed up." She patted his arm. "I know you want me to be happy on my big day."

He groaned. "Emotional blackmail."

"You bet your ass. And yeah, I know, that's another quarter. But it was worth it." She turned and hummed on her way back into the office.

Sam sighed. *Great.* Now he was going to have to buy a suit. Renting one just didn't sit well. He'd lived too long wearing hand-me-downs. He had the money. Not like he spent what he earned on more than beer and car parts—or Louise. But still…he'd take tools over clothes any day.

He turned and went back to work, wondering when—*if*—Ivy would ever call him and half hoping she wouldn't, if only so he could stop his heart from racing every time his phone rang.

Chapter 4

IVY FINISHED UP WITH ONE OF HER FAVORITE regulars and waited for Mimi to leave. Shelby's mom refused to get work done from her daughter. Instead, she'd made it her life's mission to not only help Shelby increase her business, but to also guide clients to Ivy, because Ivy had "terrific energy." Mimi Vanzant was one of those woo-woo types who believed in destiny, used tarot cards and crystals to view the future, and had one of the most infectious spirits Ivy had ever met.

Big and bold, with short, dark-red hair, a brightly colored dress, and bangles that announced her coming far ahead of her actual arrival, Mimi never failed to make Ivy's day a better one. She also tipped well, and Ivy needed that extra income now more than ever.

Her car had been acting funny that morning. She had a bad feeling the clutch problems she'd suffered last week had returned.

"Well, dear, that was wonderful, as usual." Mimi smiled and gave Ivy air kisses on either cheek. "I'll see you in two weeks. I feel fabulous." Mimi sighed, then looked into Ivy's eyes. "I see good things coming your way. Ron and I have been concerned about you." Ron was Mimi's business partner and best friend. He too subscribed to otherworldly spirits for guidance, but she thought some of that had to do with his Native American roots. She didn't mind Ron. She just liked to look at him. An older man with incredible bone structure. Talk about eye candy.

"No need to be concerned about me, Mimi. I'm fine." Better than fine, actually. Her landlord had finally gotten back to her about the dog. For an extra deposit, she could have a pet. Since she always paid on time, gave her landlord little hassle, and gifted him treats at Christmas, he liked her. He hadn't given her any trouble about the dog at all. Not that she'd thought he would, but she hated to ever assume.

With the exception of the worrying noises her car had been making, Ivy felt great.

"Yes, you will be." Mimi smiled, then sighed. "I feel too good to work, but someone has to save my new house from Ian's terrible style choices."

Ivy grinned and took the money Mimi handed her. "Yes, well, I see good things in your future too. Like a happy husband smiling at the big screen TV you're surprising him with. He'll love it."

"I know." Mimi sounded smug. She laughed and left, and Ivy prayed the rest of her day went as smoothly.

As she cleaned up her massage room and put new sheets on the table, she wondered again how Cookie was doing. She tried to avoid that train of thought though, because inevitably that led her to thinking about Sam.

She'd dodged it for days, unable to do anything about the puppy until her landlord called back. But he had this morning. And now she'd have to face Sam again.

She dreamed about him. Embarrassing and stupid, because no way would a man who looked and acted like he did be so soft or gentle. Not unless she turned into a stray animal. Then she wouldn't mind being petted by him.

"Ack. Stop it!"

"Um, you okay, Ivy?" Denise, another of their therapists, stuck her head in the door.

"Sorry." Ivy blushed. "Talking to myself."

"Man problems, eh?"

Ivy laughed. "Puppy problems. But yeah, a man is attached. Kind of." She hadn't called or texted Sam in days. He probably thought she didn't want Cookie anymore. She should have texted to keep in touch, but she wanted distance to figure out her feelings.

Physically, she liked the look of him. She didn't mind his tattoos. Actually, they kind of made him more appealing. All that muscle and toughness. Heck, the ink went up his neck. His face could only be considered handsome. The scruff of beard and mustache only made him more intriguing. And those eyes. That bright blue gray just hit her, made it hard to breathe when she remembered him smiling at Cookie.

But then she'd recall the hardness there, that violent burst of power when he'd hit Goodie at the bar. How easy it had been to harm someone else.

Then he'd turned it off, escorted her to her car. Never touched her, never tried to kiss her.

Yet that kiss to his cheek had been impossible to forget.

Hell. The contradictions in the man gave her a headache.

Ivy chatted with Denise while they readied for their next clients. Then Ivy did her best to push all her concerns aside, her focus only to facilitate healing in her patients. Three hours later, she readied to leave early. But the worries she'd earlier pushed aside returned. Her clutch was still sliding, not quite catching, and she feared it breaking down if she drove it.

The car had a hundred thousand miles on it, and she'd bought it used, but it had been a terrific little thing for years. She couldn't afford for it to go bad now, not when she had a puppy to adopt and rent to pay. Her small savings would help if need be, she supposed. But the thought of those savings brought back all the bitterness and anger from Max's betrayal. She should have had a flush bank account. But she'd used her income, footing nearly all their expenses while he went through school. Supporting him so that, in turn, when he graduated, he could support her.

Instead, he'd saved up all the money from his meager job as a waiter to repay his student loans as well as his personal bills. He'd barely contributed to the food bill, but at the time, she'd been okay with what he could give. She'd wanted to help him. They'd had so many terrific plans for the life they'd build after he graduated. Then, when they should have been starting a new life, he'd left her behind for law school and some bimbo.

Untrustworthy men. She kicked the floor of her car. It had to be male; she just knew it.

After a moment more of letting herself wallow in self-pity, Ivy shrugged all that negativity away and focused on the good parts of her life. Surprisingly, Sam's bright eyes came to mind.

"I just can't shake you, can I?" She sighed. Then, because only an unintelligent person didn't know when to take advantage of a man with know-how about cars, she called him.

He picked up right away. "Yeah?"

She swallowed. "Um, Sam? This is Ivy Stephens."

No response.

"I'm the woman who found Cookie? We went to Ray's together Friday night?" How many women did he regularly see that he'd forgotten about her already? It had only been a few days.

"I remember you." That deep voice sent more shivers through her. Talk about dangerously sexy.

"Yes, well. My landlord finally called me back. He was out of town or would have responded sooner. He's actually a nice older man. I watched his grandkids once." *Stop babbling, Ivy.* "He had no problem with me having a dog."

"Uh-huh."

She frowned. "You do still have Cookie, don't you? You didn't give him away?"

"No. He's with Willie."

His friend who helped foster animals. She sagged with relief. "Oh, good. When can I get him?"

"I'm heading over to pick him up in another hour. She lives near Bodyworks, actually."

"Okay." And that brought her to another point. "I have one more thing to ask."

"Yeah?" He sounded hesitant.

"Well, I hate to bother you, but you're the expert when it comes to cars. My clutch isn't working right. I was hoping you could tell me if it's something serious or not. I'm afraid it's a big fix."

"Oh, sure." He sounded cheerful—for Sam. "I'm

wrapping up, but I can drop by and take a look at it for you."

"If it's no trouble. I don't want you to think I'm taking advantage or anything. But if you could just tell me—"

"See you in a few." He disconnected.

She stared at her phone and felt a slow smile work over her lips. Cookie and Sam. Now if her car would work all right again, she'd be happy as a clam in a cupcake.

Her stomach rumbled. Man, she had to stop thinking about sweets! She'd gained another pound this weekend making chocolate chip cookies that didn't measure up to Lara's.

Ivy went back inside and caught up on some client paperwork. She straightened up her office that was already straightened up. Then she manned the front desk for a while with nothing better to do.

Forty-five minutes after her call with Sam, he walked through the front door. He made the small studio look downright tiny.

"Nice place." He nodded, taking in the exercise balls stacked along one wall, the bands and small hand weights in another section. Sunlight filtering in through the big bay window highlighted the bright-white trim and made the bamboo floors and sesame-gold walls glow. When they had small yoga and exercise classes, they shut the front shade. But right now, the office shone with professionalism and healthy energy.

Maybe Mimi is rubbing off on me. I'm all about energy all of a sudden.

She smiled at him and stood, coming around the

small desk to greet him. She held out a hand. "Thanks for coming."

He slowly took her hand in his and squeezed. But the handshake felt anything but polite. A seductive warmth stole through her body, and the maintained eye contact made it difficult to breathe. To her surprise, her nipples beaded under her shirt. She hoped he hadn't noticed.

Sam seemed to keep his gaze on hers. He let her hand go and nodded. "Want to show me the car?"

All business. No problem. She could handle that. Putting a lid on her untimely libido, she shrugged on her jacket and gathered her purse, then walked him out back and past the patio.

"The clutch sticks."

"So you said." He held a hand out for the keys, and she handed them over.

He swore a bit when trying to get into the car. After pushing the seat back as far as it would go, he started the car and listened. "I'm going to take it for a little drive. Don't worry. I'll bring it back," he said drily.

"Don't be a jerk. I know that." *Not the thing to say to someone doing you a favor, Ivy.*

But Sam only gave her that amused expression she'd come to know. He drove away, and she saw it lurch once or twice. When he returned, she prayed he'd somehow fixed it. Through osmosis or something. Anything so she wouldn't have to pay through the nose.

He turned off the car and got out, then came to stand next to her, still staring at the car. He wore jeans, black boots, and a beat-up leather jacket over a heather-gray pullover. Nothing fancy, but on Sam, the impact was staggering. He looked impossibly large, intimidating, and downright kissable.

What the heck is wrong with me?

Ever since Max, she'd had a difficult time viewing men as desirable. Mostly she saw them as needy and clingy. Users and manipulators to be avoided. Unfortunately, the two men she'd briefly dated right after her breakup had been just like him.

But Sam didn't seem like anyone she'd ever met. She couldn't pigeonhole him. He confounded, intrigued, and alarmed her all in the same breath.

"Did you hear what I said?" He was frowning at her. "Ivy, you okay?"

"Yeah, fine. Say that again, please."

He talked slowly, probably figuring she was dimwitted, a stereotypical blond. "I can't be sure without looking into it, but you might need a clutch replacement. I'd take a look at the flywheel too."

She swallowed. "Will this be expensive?"

He shrugged. "Mostly in labor. I'd have to look at the car, specifically, but I'd bet parts won't run you more than two hundred, at most."

"Great." She clenched her fist around her purse strap. She'd have to dig into her savings. "So if you were to guess, how much would parts and labor cost all together?"

He scratched his head. "Ah, less than a thousand?"

"Not helping."

He patted her gently on her shoulder. "Sorry."

She forced a smile. "Not your problem. I appreciate you looking at it for me. I should be good to drive it home tonight, though, right? Maybe a few days more?"

"Nothing too far," he cautioned. "But, well, do you have a shop you take your car to? I wouldn't recommend waiting. You don't want to break down in the middle of I-5 or anything."

She sighed again. Crap. Two hundred she could handle, mostly. But a thousand? "I don't have a shop I go to regularly. I usually hit Jiffy Lube for my oil changes."

"Well, if you wanted, I could fix it for you. I won't rob you blind. I'll keep costs down as much as I can, just charge you for parts. That should help."

"I couldn't do that. You have to make a living too." But her mind was firing on all cylinders, even if her car wasn't. "Hey. We could barter for the labor. I can work on you, help fix all that tension I can see in your shoulders. But you have to let me know exactly how much I owe you. We'll do a bunch of sessions to even it all out. Would that work?"

—⁂—

Sam saw the hopeful look in her big, green eyes and nodded before her words registered. Anything to keep that smile there. "Sure." Wait. She'd put her hands on him? To help him get better? Right now, just the thought of those hands got him hard. No way he'd be able to hide an erection on her massage table with just her and him in a tiny, dark room.

The last adult flick he'd watched had been about a gal and a guy giving massage. Except in that case the dude's hands had been all oiled up and the chick naked on the table. He couldn't quite see Ivy agreeing to that, though God knew he was up for it. Right now, in fact.

He prayed she didn't look too hard at his crotch

while he tried to will the hard-on away. "Ready to go see Willie and grab Cookie?"

She nodded, still bubbly, and he let out a silent sigh. Man, staying away from her had been difficult. He'd had to forcibly stop himself from driving by Bodyworks yesterday. He wanted to be more concerned about her being a suitable dog owner, but the truth of the matter was that she'd hooked him with that kiss. A simple peck on the cheek, but she'd been so sweet about it. With him, a man not used to tenderness.

For all that Foley's mom had been there for him whenever he needed her, he'd always been aware she wasn't *his* mom. Didn't really belong to him, despite Eileen's protests to the contrary.

Ivy, however, wasn't a friend. Wasn't related. Didn't belong in his world. But she'd given him a measure of hope, of longing, he couldn't ignore.

She'd finally called. And not just about Cookie. Sure, he was the logical choice to ask about a car problem. But if the woman had wanted to avoid him, why ask him about her car? Why not just contain their association to the dog?

Feeling better about life, he suggested that he drive her to Willie's and back to save her from possibly having her car lock up on the way over.

"Okay. If you think that's best."

They got into his car, and he turned toward Willie's and said, "Actually, I think you should drop the car off at the garage tonight. I can run you home. I mean, if that's okay. Or you could have a friend do it. Your call." He was dying to know where she lived, but he didn't want to come across as stalkerish. "If it were my clutch sticking like that, I'd get it fixed right away. Unless you had another car you could use."

"Nope. One car, just me." She frowned. "Shelby lives in Green Lake, and Denise is in Fremont. They're not all that close to give me a ride. I guess I could use a car service."

He spoke with care, not wanting to spook her. Besides, he told himself, keeping in touch with her would let him see Cookie more, to know the little dog was doing okay. He'd taken a shine to the puppy, especially after it had grossed out Foley. "Well, you know where Webster's is, right? Are you close to that? I could always give you a ride until your car is fixed. Shouldn't take but a few days to see what's really wrong with it and get the parts in."

He waited, not daring to breathe, until she slowly nodded. They pulled into Willie's driveway and he tried to act casual.

"If you're sure you don't mind," she said again. "You'll really be doing me a favor."

He tried to downplay his victory. "Consider it my way to keep an eye on Cookie. I like the little guy."

She softened and smiled.

He had to work damn hard not to lean over and steal a kiss. But then, Sam didn't do things like that. He *never* made a move unless the woman told him he could. Yet with Ivy, he wanted to. And that alarmed him.

He hurried out of the car and locked up after she'd done the same. Then he cautioned her on her way to meet Willie. "She's a tough old broad. Says what's on her mind. No filter. Just…you've been warned."

Ivy chuckled. "Don't worry. If you didn't scare me, I doubt she can."

"Hey, just remember I tried to tell you." He shrugged.

They walked up the steps to Willie's front door. He rang the bell. Loud barking and swearing answered them.

Ivy blinked.

"Told you," he murmured.

Willie opened her door and stared at them through the screen door, her gaze lingering on Ivy. "Well? Come on in." She moved back inside.

Sam followed Ivy in and bumped into her when she stopped right in front of him.

"Oh my gosh. It's… It's…"

"Yep."

He knew the feeling. The first time he'd entered Willie's, he'd felt as if he'd stepped through a time warp. The woman had a thing for orange, green, and yellow. And clutter. Foley made fun of him for collecting shit, but at least he had a sense of order to it, no matter what Foley thought. But Willie…

"There's so much stuff." Ivy stepped over Tyrant, who meowed and wove through their feet. Sam had learned his lesson and glared at the cat before moving away. Pygar, Mathmos, and Cookie were playing tug-of-war with one of Willie's shawls, and she was swearing at the animals something fierce. Of Barbarella he saw no sign.

"Oh no." Ivy jumped in to get Cookie's teeth off the thing, while Sam did his best to break Pygar's hold and shield Ivy from a nipping Chihuahua.

Willie had gone from cursing to laughing. At Sam, no doubt.

"So," she drawled when she could catch a breath. "You the girl who wants my boy?"

Ivy finally got Cookie away and stood huffing. She handed Willie back her mangled shawl. "Hello. Yes, I'm Ivy Stephens. I'm here for Cookie."

Willie shot Sam an amused glance, and he realized she'd been referring to *him* as her boy, not the dog.

He flushed. *Interfering old bat*. "Willie, we're taking the dog."

"Not yet you ain't. Ivy, fetch me my sticks, would you?" She motioned to the bag on the side table.

"Her crocheting needles," Sam said.

"Knitting isn't crocheting, Sam Hamilton. You know better."

He rolled his eyes. "Yeah, yeah." Then he noticed she didn't have her usual evening tea. "You want some Earl Grey or what?"

"Yep. Ivy? Would you like a cup?"

Ivy blinked, dazzled no doubt by the glittery, naked collectibles in various poses in the corner hutch. "Um, yes. Sure. Okay."

Sam glared at Willie, mouthed *Be nice*, then went to the kitchen.

He didn't hear much, but when he returned, he saw Ivy staring with rapt attention at Willie's gnarled fingers moving like lightning with her yarn.

"Kind of mesmerizing, isn't it?" He brought over Willie's tea tray, on which a delicate teapot steeped tea next to two matching cups on saucers, and a set of sugar and creamer dispensers. The tea set meant something to the old woman, because of everything in the house, this seemed the most precious. No chips or scratches, no dust or stains. The pristine set had been meticulously cared for while being used daily.

The first time she'd offered Sam tea, he'd watched with rapt attention to the ritual of preparing it. Now he took it upon himself to make the stuff if she didn't have any made. But he didn't like Earl Grey. Not that he'd ever tell the guys, but Sam had a sensitive palate—according to Willie—and he now preferred a nice oolong or Lapsang souchong, which had a smoky flavor he enjoyed. Willie diluted hers with milk and sugar. He preferred his black.

"Wow. Do you do that every day?" Ivy asked, staring at Willie's fast moving fingers in awe.

"Yep, right as rain." Willie continued to knit like a woman possessed. Frankly he'd rather have his fingernails pulled out than have to perform such banal repetition, but it kept Willie busy and out of trouble. Speaking of which…

"You been having any problems with the burglaries in town?" he asked her. "I heard the thieves have gone from hitting businesses to neighboring houses. Somebody looking at this place from the outside might think there's something valuable in here. But, boy, would they be wrong once they got in," he added, half to himself.

"Asshole," Willie snapped at the same time Ivy admonished, "Sam."

"No manners at all. If you take him on, you're gonna have to fix him up nice. Not sure what he can do in the sack, but you'll know goin' in that he's something in the rough. Not sure I'd call him a diamond. More like a lump of coal that needs a lot of grindin'. You get me, girl?" Willie looked at Ivy's wide eyes and open mouth and laughed so hard she got the dogs going.

Even Cookie howled before starting marathon laps up and down the stairs, joining Pygar and Mathmos. Barbarella appeared and sat in the dog bed, vacillating between disdain and boredom for the humans in her space.

Ivy coughed and stood, her face aflame. "I'll get him." She darted away before Sam could.

"Damn it, woman. Be nice," he hissed at Willie. "Don't scare her away."

"Before you can, you mean?" She sighed. "Boy, you got to go easy with this one. She's pretty but soft. Not your usual type." Willie watched him. "I like her though. She took to Cookie, and Mathmos didn't bite her. That's a good sign."

Probably because the dog was going blind and couldn't see her; plus Sam had intercepted the Chihuahua's tiny jaw earlier. But hell. If Willie liked her, she'd be nicer. He hoped.

Ivy came back downstairs, her face beet red, holding Cookie. "Um, Sam, I think we should go. It's getting late."

"You okay?"

Willie wore a big grin. "Did he happen to go into my room? With all the straps and things?"

Ivy nodded, and he worried she might choke.

"You okay?" He glanced at the stairs. "I'll be right back."

"*No*." She gripped his arm. "I'm good. Just thought I saw a spider."

"Caught in a silky, black web, eh?" Willie hooted with laughter and slapped her thigh. "Don't worry about none of that, Ivy. That's for me and my friend Rupert to play with. But if you have any questions, let me know. I'm happy to help educate today's youth." That set Willie off again.

"Drink your tea before it gets cold," Sam scolded, curious as to what had made Ivy's face that red. He worried she might pass out, and her grip on the dog said it was time to go. "Thanks for watching him. I'll see you in a few days. Call if you need anything."

"Get out. I'm done with you." Willie waved at the doorway.

He tugged Ivy with him and shut them all in the car. After a moment, Cookie settled on her lap and took a snooze. "What the hell did you see up there?"

She shuddered. "You don't want to know."

They drove back to her car, listening to the radio. Then she followed him to the garage. He had her park her car close to the bay doors. He planned to go in early in the morning and work on it before the day began. That way Del couldn't bitch him out for doing a personal job during working hours. Not that she would, but he liked to cover all his bases just in case.

Besides, he had a real urge to help Ivy.

She rejoined him in his Challenger, with Cookie now sleeping in the backseat, and they drove toward her home. To his delight, she didn't live that far from him at all. Maybe fifteen minutes. Perfect for a midnight rendezvous.

If only.

She still looked to be in shock.

"Okay, I have to know."

She glanced at him. "Are you sure? It's in my brain permanently now, and I don't know that it'll ever scrub free."

"Tell me."

"I found Cookie caught up in a contraption hanging from the ceiling." She lowered her voice, which made him want to laugh. Like him, she tried to protect the baby canine's virgin ears. "It was a sex swing. And before you ask how I know what that is, she had pictures of herself using it, right there on her nightstand. Of her and her friend Rupert. Naked. *Wrinkly and naked*. And using the swing and, um, other stuff."

"No shit?" He let out a bark of laughter that woke the dog. "Sorry, buddy. Seriously though. Willie and Rupert swinging and getting nasty. Damn. Now I can't stop thinking about it."

"Welcome to my world." Ivy leaned her head back against the black vinyl seat.

He chanced a glance and quickly looked away. With her parted lips, her flushed face, and her eyes closed, she appeared as if asleep. Or flush from an orgasm that had left her breathless.

Man, not good thoughts with her right damn next to him in the car. He could smell her perfume, a floral type that seemed to go with the natural, intrinsic scent that was Ivy.

"You wearing perfume?"

"Oh, no. Sorry. That's probably leftover from the aromatherapy I used with my last client today. It tends to linger. I don't wear perfume much. Mostly because we don't wear it for work. A lot of people have issues with strong scents."

He hadn't known that. "How long have you been doing massage?"

"Seven years. Eight if you count my hours during

schooling. At first it was a way to make money while I decided what I wanted to major in. The certification only took a year, and it soon paid the bills. But then I found I really liked it. I love my job, but it's not easy. There are so many massage therapists in Seattle."

"Yeah? Well, there are a lot of mechanics in Seattle too. But if you're good, you're good."

"Like you?" she teased.

He liked her feeling comfortable enough to tease him. "Like me," he agreed. "And you too. You seem like you're busy a lot."

"I am. I also teach some workshop classes, which helps. And I might be getting a shot at teaching a class at a community college." She sounded pleased about that fact.

Sam hadn't gone past the twelfth grade and had no intention of going back to school. Sure, he took the occasional auto class to keep up-to-date on work. But that was different. He actually used what he learned. Not like the nimrods in college studying freakin' French literature and theoretical ass wiping.

But this wasn't about him. It was about Ivy. "That's cool."

"What about you? How long have you been working at Webster's Garage?" She pointed to a spot where he pulled the car in.

He parked and followed her out, locking up behind them once he saw Cookie in her arms. "About four years. Foley and I moved around a lot after high school. But Seattle's home, you know?"

She nodded. "I grew up in Portland, but once I came to this city, I just knew. I like it here." She shifted the dog, but he plucked the puppy from her arms so she could grab her keys. He wondered if she'd invite him in. If he should say yes if she did.

She unlocked the door and turned to him. He had to glance down to meet her gaze; she was smaller by more than a head. But as soon as he saw her eyes, he could look nowhere else. Until her mouth curled into a shy smile.

"Would you like to come in for a cup of tea? I hate to say it, but I'm not a fan of Earl Grey. I just accepted Willie's offer because I didn't want to be rude." Then she paused. "I have beer too, or iced tea." Then she flushed. "But you probably have a lot to do so—"

"Tea sounds great. Got any oolong?"

She blinked in surprise, then gave him a warm smile. "You know, I think I do."

Chapter 5

Ivy wondered if she'd made the wrong choice by asking Sam to come inside. She hoped he wouldn't take her invitation the wrong way, even if she had no idea in what way she'd actually meant it. She just knew she wanted to spend more time with him.

He set Cookie down, and the dog went exploring, disappearing into the short hallway leading to her bedroom and the bathroom. Not a whole lot of options for Cookie.

"This is nice." Sam glanced around.

"It's not much, but it's home." Trite but true. She'd moved into the apartment two years ago, changed the paint to a buttery yellow, added a dark blue to her bedroom walls, and hung a few pictures. Since it was just her, she didn't need much. The open floor plan made up for the small size of the place. At just under seven hundred square feet, it felt roomy enough to her—unless she had a big man like Sam standing in the middle of it.

He glanced at her small TV mounted on the wall above the tiny but functional gas fireplace, at the bookshelves on either side of it, and at the small table against the wall near the kitchen that served as her dining area. Both leaves in the table had been folded down to make the room appear more open, but she could always put them up when she had company.

Like now.

Ivy dropped her purse and keys onto their spots on

her funky, tiled hall table, took a quick glance at herself in the mirror above it, and knew she looked as good as she was going to get. Her hair seemed somewhat tame; her makeup remained tidy. Not that it should matter. It was just Sam over for a cup of tea, after all.

After kicking off her shoes and hanging her jacket, she joined Sam in the living room.

"Need to use your bathroom." Sam raised a brow in question.

"Oh, it's right there." She pointed to the hall. "If you find the bedroom, you went in the wrong door."

He grunted and walked away. The door closed shortly after.

She hurried to turn on some music, so she wouldn't hear him doing his business. The downside of a small space—she could hear everything in her apartment. Yet because she had an end unit in the fourplex, she hardly ever heard her neighbors. The landlord had informed her that a big plus of this unit, in addition to the price, was the upgraded soundproofing. She had to admit he'd been right. She rarely heard noise from the high school across the street or the musicians two doors down. Plus, she could walk right across the road to Seward Park, overlooking the water. What wasn't to love?

She set the kettle on the stove and dragged out two mugs and two tea bags. She liked a bit of sugar in her tea, so she put out a small bowl. Then she waited, humming to some funky jazz while she played a game of fetch with Cookie and his red rubber ball.

She smiled at him when he gave a small woof. So adorable. Her heart warmed. She'd been lonely and hadn't realized. She'd missed living with someone else.

Furry or not, Cookie was just what she'd been needing—someone who'd be loyal, affectionate, and love her no matter what. The perfect companion.

"So," Sam said as he returned. He held his jacket in one hand and glanced down at her feet. "Want me to take my shoes off?"

"If you wouldn't mind. It makes the carpet last longer." Beige carpet—a nightmare to keep clean. "You can toss your jacket on the couch if you want."

He did and set his shoes neatly beside it. It was odd to see Sam in socks. It should have made him more vulnerable. Yet he loomed as large without boots as he did with them. Nothing soft about the man. Until he crouched down by Cookie and sighed.

"You're gonna be one big-ass dog." He let the puppy paw him, accepting doggie kisses without complaint as he studied her home.

The living room consisted of her large, dark-blue sofa, a coffee table, standing lamp by the corner, and her bookcases. She didn't have much, but what she did have worked for her. No high-quality TV or sound system, but it let her watch the few television shows she liked. She played music through a Bluetooth speaker and her phone. And at the flick of a switch, she had a fire going. No chopping or buying wood for her.

"How long have you lived here?" Sam straightened and walked around. She didn't have many pictures—one of her family from years ago. Books littered the stacks, as well as a few knickknacks. An old eight-by-eight oil canvas, painted by her grandmother—an artist of some renown—took up her favorite spot on the mantel. A few pieces of pottery that had caught her eye joined some of her books. Nothing much of value to anyone but her.

"I moved in two years ago."

He nodded, picked up the picture of her and her family. "These your parents? Your brother?"

"Yes. Although my brother has since married and had a little boy." One she hadn't seen since he'd been born. The thought still haunted her. If Cheryl hadn't already been dead and gone, Ivy might have cursed the woman's name.

Sam glanced at her and looked like he wanted to ask another question, but he put the picture down and looked at her books instead. "You read all these?"

"Yes. I love books."

"Not me."

"So sad." She hadn't figured he was a reader. Not because he worked in a garage, but because he seemed like he had little patience to sit still. The kettle whistled, and she took it off the stove.

"Yeah." He turned and smirked at her. "Otherwise you and me could be having a terrific conversation about *What to Do with a Bad Boy*." He nodded at her romance collection. "Sounds educational."

She blushed. "Hey, I like to read about happy endings. Nothing wrong with that. God knows you don't get them enough in real life."

"You got me there." He wiped a finger across her bookcase and held it up to her, dust free. "Damn, Ivy. Not another clean freak. Bad enough I live with Foley... when he's there."

"Rest easy. I only cleaned this past weekend because I was overdue. I'm orderly but dusty."

"Huh. I'm told I'm disorderly on a regular basis."

She swallowed a smile. "My excuse is that I've been so busy with clients lately I've gotten behind on some chores." She poured the water and handed him the steeping tea bag and mug. "Careful, it's hot." Their fingers brushed before she pulled back.

Like before, the touch of him sent her pulse skyrocketing. Whoa. Talk about shocking chemistry between them. She didn't know what to make of it because Sam seemed so different from her usual type.

He just looked at her as they sat down at her too-small table. "Not going to blow on it for me?"

That the word *blow* made her immediately think of something dirty caused her face to heat. She could only hope her cheeks didn't show it. Ivy forced herself to stop thinking about sex and said, "I'll leave that for Willie. She seemed much more maternal."

He gave a rusty chuckle; she sensed he didn't laugh much. "First time she invited me in, I think I stood staring at her art collection for like half an hour. Woman has a skewed sense of collectibles. Half of 'em are ceramic naked people having sex in weird positions."

"I know." Ivy laughed and saw his answering smile. *That mouth is lethal. I wonder how he kisses.* Quickly moving on, lest she try him on for size, she said, "And her pets. All names from *Barbarella*, that old sci-fi flick."

He blinked. "You know it?"

"I'm kind of a sci-fi fan. I've seen a lot of old movies."

"Yeah?" He perked up. "Me too."

"Oh? Then you know about *The Beastmaster*."

"More fantasy than sci-fi, but okay. Plus it had Tanya Roberts."

"I see you're a fan of boobs and skimpy clothing."

"Um, yeah. I'm a guy."

She fought a grin. "I remember Marc Singer and those cute little ferrets of his."

"Marc Singer in a loincloth, you mean," he said wryly. "I'm not the only fan of skimpy clothing. How about a real classic like *They Live*?"

"With Rowdy Roddy Piper? The wrestler? Been there, done that. *Buckaroo Banzai*? Now that's a keeper."

"Seriously? Stupid." He snorted. "*Escape from New York*. Now that's a movie."

"Okay, I agree on that one." How much fun that Sam liked her kind of films. "Snake Plissken—the ultimate antihero—a prisoner who saves the president in a futuristic world where the criminals are forced to live in a fenced-in New York." She paused. "You know, I'm sensing a trend in your taste. You like violence."

"Surprised?"

"Ah, not exactly."

He withdrew his tea bag, wrapped the string around the bag to push out the excess water, then expertly set it on a napkin near him. "I'm sorry about that, you know."

"That you like violence?"

"That you had to see me hit Goodie. He's a jackass and had it coming." He sipped his tea, his gaze on her. "I'm used to guys thumping on each other. Sometimes I forget not everyone is." He sighed. "We should have met for coffee or something. Anywhere but at Ray's."

"It wasn't that bad."

He just looked at her.

"Okay, it was…" *Choose a word not so insulting.* "Crowded. And some of the people there seemed a little on the rough side, present company included."

"Gee, thanks." He glanced at Cookie pawing at his leg and sat the dog on his lap.

"But you were only trying to defend me." *I'm pretty sure*.

"Goodie and Senior aren't nice people."

"What did you mean about them losing money on you? I didn't understand that."

"A week or so ago, I was fighting some guy, just for sport, and people were taking bets. Apparently Senior doesn't like to lose."

She frowned. "Fighting some guy? As in boxing or mixed martial arts?"

"Yeah, except we're amateur. It helps me let off steam."

"Oh." She wondered what happened if he didn't get to "let off steam." "Is that legal?"

He smirked but said nothing.

She swallowed a retort and changed the subject. "So you're a mechanic. Do you like what you do?"

"Yeah. I got a knack for it." He sounded surprised by that fact. "What about you? Massage, huh?"

"Yes." She waited for some crack about touching people or naked bodies.

He looked thoughtful. "I bet you're good at it."

"Really? Why is that?" She took a sip of her tea, leaving the bag in and foregoing sugar for once. She didn't need a sugar rush on top of her hypervigilance around Sam.

He shrugged. "You just seem like the helpful type." He stroked Cookie, who looked like he'd entered doggie nirvana. "You're taking in this guy."

"Yes, but you rescued him. Seems to me you're the

helpful type too. And you've already been a lifesaver, taking him when I can't."

He drank his tea, saying nothing. They watched each other for a moment, as if trying to figure out what to say next. At least, that's what Ivy wondered. She truly had no idea how Sam's mind worked.

"So." She licked her lips, startled when he followed the movement with a raptor's attention. "You, ah, do you have a girlfriend?" *Oh my God. Why would you ask that, you moron? Now he's going to think you're angling for the position.* "I mean, you won't be in trouble for being with me tonight, will you? I wouldn't want to step on any toes, even though we're just having an innocent cup of tea." *Stop talking, Ivy!*

He frowned. "I was seeing this chick, but she left town a few months ago." He shrugged. "It was nothing serious. What about you? You seeing somebody?"

"No."

When she said nothing more, he prodded, "And?"

"Nosy, aren't you?" she muttered, nonplussed when he shot her a grin. *God, that smile.* She squirmed in her seat, not sure why she continued to physically respond to Sam. She wished her body would turn off. She didn't welcome the return of her sexuality. It was one thing to want companionship—in the form of a dog. Another thing entirely to desire a man again. And especially with a man who thought nothing of beating on another.

"Yeah, that's me. Nosy Sam Hamilton." He drank more tea. "Well? Why no man?"

She let out a breath. "Fine. You want to know why I'm single?"

"You're not a lesbian."

She'd opened her mouth to respond, then stopped at his words. "Huh?"

"You're not gay. I can tell."

"That makes no sense."

"I'm just sayin'. You don't give out gay vibes."

"What's wrong with gay people?" She readied to launch a diatribe against any homophobic slurs, but he took the sting out before she could get going.

"Not a thing. It's just you don't check out women the way you do men."

She frowned. "I check out men?"

"Not like you're interested or anything. But like, you put out signals you don't want to be bothered. You don't do that to women at all. It's a straight thing."

"Well, you're not gay either."

He raised a brow. "You sure?"

"Are you?"

"Why do you want to know?"

She let out a huff. "You're kind of annoying."

"That's what they say."

"Who?"

He didn't grin, but she heard the laughter in his voice. "Everyone."

"I can see why." Yet she felt amused by him. Not scared anymore. Entertained, attracted, and, blast it all, excited. "I never really answered your question. So I'll tell you." This would put him off. Men hated angry, bitter women. And she needed for him to not like her so much, if he even liked her at all. She had a feeling he was still checking her out for Cookie's sake, and likely because she was blond and female. Guys had a thing for blonds. Not because he had a thing for *her* in any way.

"Waiting."

"I met a guy when I was going through massage school. He was a little older than me, not by much. Nice, handsome. He had plans. Was going to be a psychologist, so he said." She felt the familiar anger return, could see Sam witnessing it as she spoke.

His eyes narrowed at her tone, but he said nothing.

"I loved him. So I put my own plans of college on hold. I finished school for massage therapy and got my certificate. I worked my butt off to pay the bills, rent, even any fun for the two of us, for the most part. Max worked hard, got good grades, and he waited tables to pay for a lot of his own expenses. So I helped, letting him do what he needed. He focused on school. It was all going to work out. I'd do the hard part first; then when he had a great job, he'd work so I could go back for classes."

She paused, trying to let the rage go. After all this time, she still wanted to belt the guy.

"What happened?" Sam asked, his voice low.

Ivy forced herself to calm down, to be glad she no longer had to deal with that scum-sucking, two-timing liar. "After graduation, he spent a year trying to get work, but he needed a graduate degree for the kind of job he wanted. I started losing patience with him. I was working my butt off while he took his time finding a job that would fit him. It never seemed to bother him that I'd come home exhausted every day." Would a part-time job at a pizza place have been so bad while he looked for his "ideal" job?

"What a prick."

She gave him a grim smile. "Then law school

happened. Max decided he wanted to become a lawyer and because getting a lower-paying job or going back for graduate school wasn't something I could afford, he found a richer, prettier blond and dumped me."

"Sounds like he was an asshole."

"You got that right." She blew out a breath, feeling better having shared her sob story. Normally, knowing she hadn't been good enough for Max was enough to turn her off to ever even liking a man again. But as she waited for Sam to say something else, she was struck by the color of his eyes.

"I've never gone through that kind of crap with a woman. Good thing. Because I don't like violence around women, kids, or pets, and I'd be tempted to beat her ass if she ever did me wrong like that douche did you."

Not a pretty boy or a scholar. A wild, fierce, predatory male sat across from her, sipping tea, agreeing with her wholeheartedly. The reassurance that she wasn't crazy for being angry felt good.

"I should let it go now, though, huh?" She sighed. "It's been two years since that jerk has been gone. I don't miss him at all. But I still get so darn mad."

"You know what your problem is?"

"Do tell."

"You need to let loose."

"What?" Was this where he tried to get her in bed?

"Stand up."

"Um, okay." She slowly stood. He stood as well and set Cookie gently down on the floor. The puppy didn't do much more than blink once, then close his eyes and go back to sleep.

Sam stepped around him and drew her with him away from the dog.

She was ready to send him packing. Loosen up? Heck, she'd feel looser slamming the door behind his lecherous—

"Hit me. And swear a little."

Not what she'd been expecting. "Excuse me?" She looked up, and up, at him. She stood five six in stocking feet. He had to be nearly a foot taller. Not six six, but close to it. "How tall are you?"

"Six four. Now focus." He held up a hand. "Punch me. Right here."

"I couldn't do that."

He ignored her. "When you do it, call me a motherfucker."

"*Sam*." She flushed. "Language."

He smirked. "I know. Come on. No one but me and you to hear it. Cookie's down. You can whisper it if you want. I won't tell."

She made a fist, and he shook his head. "No, not like that. You'll hurt your thumb. Wrap your thumb around your second and third knuckle. Then keep your wrist aligned. You bend it when you punch, you'll hurt it. Do it like this." He punched in front of him, slowly, showing her how to do it. "Again."

"Why am I doing this?"

"Trust me. I know all about keeping anger bottled up inside. When I fight, when I let it out physically, I feel better." He nodded. "All those pricks who stick it to you, who get away with shit, all the assholes out there, they get theirs when you hit back. Except you don't have to actually hurt anyone to feel better."

She thought about Goodie. "You do."

"Yeah, well, I'm fucked up. You're not. This will help. Trust me."

Why she should trust him, she had no idea. He put a hand around hers, helping her make a proper fist, and the assurance in his gaze was her undoing. She settled into the boxer stance he showed her, then gave a few air punches.

"Good, Ivy. Now hit my hand. You won't hurt me."

"You sure?" She felt strong, capable, and realized he might be onto something with that whole let-your-fist-fly-to-feel-good routine. "I don't want to do any damage."

He rolled his eyes. "I'm sure, Mike Tyson. Come on."

She concentrated, then hit his hand.

"That's it? That's all you got?" He snorted. "Willie hits harder than that."

"Hey." She straightened and put her hands on her hips. "Not nice."

He let out a loud breath. "That's the point. Use your anger, Ivy. Swear at me. Hit my hand. No, swear at Max. Hit him right in the mouth. Go on. You know you want to. Visualize, damn it."

She figured she might as well, if only to get Sam to stop with all the violence. As she settled into a boxing stance again, she did as he said. She remembered Max, his blond on the side, all the work she'd done for him, all the love squandered on someone who'd never cared the way she had.

Fury festered, and she launched her fist and swore. "Asshole."

"That's it. Again. You can do better. And a little louder than a whisper."

Another punch. This one stung her knuckles. "*Dickhead.*"

"He chose another woman over you. After all you did for him. All the work, the love, the—"

She didn't have to try hard this time. "*Motherfucker.*" Then she shook her fist. "That stung."

"No shit." He was clenching his fist and opening and closing it.

"Sam?" She hurried to take his hand in hers. His palm was red from where she'd hit him. "God, I'm so sorry. Are you okay?"

He didn't say anything, and she rubbed his hand, trying to bring more blood flow to the area. She smoothed out the sting, working on the palmar fascia, automatically going into therapist mode. Yet as she rubbed, she was too aware of the toughness of his skin.

She chanced a glance at his face, feeling horrible— because she felt terrific. Hitting him and imagining Max taking the blow had given her a primitive thrill. "I'm so sorry," she apologized again. "I hope you're okay."

He stared at her as if he'd never seen a woman before. "You hit me."

She blushed. "You told me to."

"I didn't think you'd really do it that hard. You gave it a whack." He looked a bit odd. He leaned closer, staring at her, checking for something, apparently.

"What? What's wrong? I didn't break it, did I?" She still held his hand, and this time she turned it over, more than aware of their disparity in size.

"Nah. I'm good. But you…" He paused. "You're not that nice or sweet, are you?"

"What did you say?" She stiffened and would have

dropped his huge hand, except he curled it around hers. "Sam, I—"

He lowered his head, standing so close she could feel his breath on her lips.

All thought left her.

"Not so sweet at all," he murmured.

The minuscule gap between them closed. Had he moved? Had she?

The feel of his mouth over hers stunned her. So much heat, so much electricity.

He froze and pulled back. "Shit, I'm sorry. I didn't mean—"

Ivy didn't give a damn. She yanked him back and plastered her mouth over his, needing more of that fire to burn through her, licking up the need and spreading it throughout her body.

For a split second, Sam didn't move. Then he groaned and wrapped his arms around her back. Before she knew it, he'd lifted her in his arms and seated them on her couch. Her knees straddled his lap while she continued to kiss him until she couldn't breathe.

Nothing made sense but getting more of Sam. She squirmed over him, hungry for something just out of reach. His taste, his scent, the sense of such strength underneath her. So much hunger for the man made it impossible to resist when, with a large hand, he squeezed her breast.

She moaned against his mouth, aware she was fast losing control. But her kiss had *nothing* on his. With a subtlety that impressed her, he slowly took charge of the embrace. The masterful way he kissed her, the varied pressure, the softness from such a large, ferocious man, stole her will to do anything but respond. Caged in his arms, lost to desire—hers or his, she couldn't tell—Ivy followed his lead. Between one moment and the next, his hand left her breast and pressed between her legs.

It had been so damn long, and she'd never been with someone like Sam before, someone so intense and desirable. She rocked into his touch, lost to everything but what her body needed.

He murmured something against her mouth, but she didn't care. She was so close, so amazingly right there, on the edge, then he—

"*Sam*," she cried and came, shuddering as he stroked her through her jeans, easing into a gentle petting that soothed the fiery rain of pleasure still pulsing through her. The cascade of release could have taken seconds or minutes. She had no concept of anything but letting herself float in his embrace.

After a while, those large arms holding her so close set her back from him, to give them space.

She blinked at him, aware he sat tense and still under her.

Pleasure gave way to mortification. She'd climaxed. On the lap of a near stranger after a tiny bit of heavy petting. Dear Lord, she'd been all over the poor man. Humping him through her clothes after he'd tried to pull back from that first kiss. Heck, he had been trying to *help* her, and she'd jumped him like a desperate, horny idiot.

She felt awful.

He must have seen her embarrassment because he hurried to move her off his lap. *As if jumping him wasn't bad enough, I all but smothered the poor guy!*

"I'm sorry," he whispered.

She took a peek at him and saw him rushing to put his shoes and jacket on. He said something else she couldn't understand and refused to look at her.

Probably as embarrassed for her as she was for herself. Women must throw themselves at him all the time. With a body and face like that, he had to be used to it. That thought didn't make it any easier to absolve herself of the guilt.

"Sam…" She didn't know what to say. What he must have thought of her. She glanced at her hands and clenched them into fists. Sam had helped, all right. All her memories of Max, her anger, had disappeared, replaced by a lust so extreme she'd attacked the man in her house.

She looked up, prepared to apologize, to grovel and hope he would keep this embarrassing incident just between them. She'd promise never to touch him again and—

"Sam?"

He was gone, the door closed softly behind him. As if he'd never been there.

Chapter 6

SAM COULD BARELY THINK, SO UPSET HE DIDN'T know what to do, where to go. He didn't know what had happened. One minute she'd been punching him, so cute with all that bottled-up anger easing up with every tiny punch.

As if she could hurt him.

Except she had—but not with her hands.

God. He drove faster, on automatic pilot as he followed a familiar route. Needing the release, he hurried toward the fights he'd been trying to quit.

Fuck. Tears burned, and he felt even more pathetic. She'd kissed him. Or he'd kissed her. Looking into her light-green eyes and inhaling that faint scent of flowers, he'd been unable to stop himself from touching her. Mouth to mouth. And then she'd been in his arms, they'd been on the couch, and he'd fucking lost himself to the hottest female he'd ever kissed.

Hearing her come had been a thing of beauty. He'd been so hard, so ready to take her, right there on her couch. But a glance at her fuzzy gaze, then seeing the horror on her face after…

He drove faster and pulled into a spot at the edge of the crowd. The owner of this particular empty warehouse took his cut of the proceeds. Illegal fights had become pretty popular with a lot of the major players, especially with MMA becoming such a huge legal draw.

Here, the owners and their bookies could make a killing with fights that had no rules. The refs would step in only if a guy verged on death.

Because corpses tended to involve the law.

Something he might have to deal with come the morning, he knew. How had a simple kiss turned so uncontrollable? Forcing the poor woman into an orgasm? Jesus. He felt sick.

Poor Ivy.

He turned off the car and sat, staring at nothing. She'd been so upset.

He hadn't meant to take advantage of her. The kiss had been good at first. He thought she'd been into it, into him. And then he'd gone from zero to sixty in a heartbeat. From a kiss to wanting to fuck her brains out. He could still taste her, could still feel her writhing over him while he made her come…

While she'd been trying to get away from him?

Had she been as lost in the kiss as he'd been? An amazing taste of Ivy had turned into a nightmare.

He knew more than most about rape. God, he'd been so young, known more than any kid should ever know about sex, period. Both parties didn't have to be willing for their bodies to experience a rush.

He closed his eyes, trying to put other older nightmares away, behind the closed doors where they belonged.

He could still see her, a pretty woman, young and vulnerable and barely old enough to be a mother. Half-drunk and laughing, then crying while someone bigger and meaner made her do things she didn't want to do. Or had she wanted it? He'd been confused. She'd laughed and cried, screaming at him to keep hiding while swearing at him for existing at all. And he'd done nothing but watch in shock and tears through the slats of that flimsy closet door, not sure if she'd wanted him to get help or if she'd beat him again for trying, like she had the few times before.

"Fuck." Sam slammed out of his car and stalked to the southern door, where a giant guard and sometime competitor stood. The guy smiled when he saw Sam, no doubt recognizing him as a top contender.

"Thought you were on break," Ritter said.

"Does it look like I'm fucking on break?"

Ritter studied him but didn't say another word. A good thing, because Sam actually liked the guy. In his current mood, he'd likely hurt someone and be sorry about it later.

But smart man that he was, Ritter simply stepped back and let Sam inside.

The dump of a warehouse had been somewhat transformed into a showcase for various arenas. The cement walls and support beams remained, as did the open wiring and cross supports in the two-story ceiling. The few upper windows had been blacked out by paint and lumber. Dim overhead lighting gave just enough illumination for the fights to go on.

Most of the small arenas were ringed by spectators dressed in a variety of clothing, from ripped jeans and denim jackets to thousand-dollar suits and fur coats. But every asshole in the place had the right contacts to be here, as well as the money to bet with the House, as the owners liked to call the place. It fit.

Sam hadn't been on the docket for the night, but word quickly spread to the right people.

Jerry O. hurried to Sam with a wide smile. The guy looked like a weasel and smelled of cheap cologne. He wore flashy, gold rings and had a thick, gold chain around his skinny neck. Dark-haired, light-skinned, and smart as hell, the guy did math in his head that would make a calculator jealous. Probably why the powers that be kept him around, in addition to Jerry's ability to manipulate people. He dealt with the fighting talent, keeping everyone scheduled and paid and content not to kill each other unless in a bout.

"Sam." It came out as *Tham*. "What a pleasant surprise." Jerry had a lisp. The last guy to make fun of it had been found floating in the sound. Cause of death undetermined.

"Yo, J. I need a fight."

"Oh?"

Sam could see the dude doing internal computations. "Jesus, I'm not in the mood. Do you have a spot or not?"

"I can fit you in," Jerry said in a hurry. "But your take will be five percent less. I'll have to move people around, and that's not that easy to—"

"Fine." Sam didn't care about the money. He needed the action any way he could get it. And since screwing a woman would only add to his misery, a fight would do. He could hit and be hit, taking his lumps like a man— one who might have assaulted a helpless woman who had wanted nothing but to share a cup of tea and the soft affection of a puppy.

The way she'd looked at him when he'd left, or rather, the way she *hadn't* looked at him, still crushed his heart into tiny pieces.

Thank God he'd at least kept it in his pants. He'd done

some heavy petting and kissing. But he hadn't hurt her. Well, no more than apparently fucking with her head.

He deserved to be kicked, beaten, burned.

Except his rage at himself made him *too* formidable.

They paired him with three different guys. He tore up all of them, every last one. •

The most he got for his trouble was a genuine workout and a shiner under his left eye. Because he'd needed something to hurt him, to remind him that what he'd done hadn't been all right.

People slapped him on the back. Jerry begged him to come back in two weeks, when he'd have a champ from Ecuador in residence, accompanied by some major players in the gun trade, according to rumor. Sam needed that trouble like he needed a hole in the head.

He preferred to stay away from outside competition. Because if the big guys didn't like losing, they had a tendency to take it out on the winner. Jerry was being persistent. Instead of an outright no, Sam told him he'd let him know.

He left in a rush, but on his way out, Ritter had the gall to grab him by the arm.

"You got a death wish?" Sam asked, glaring, ready for more action.

Ritter leaned closer, his expression one that had even Sam wary, and threatened, "Don't come back here unless you want trouble." Then he showed Sam the gun under his shirt. "You get me?"

Sam ripped his shoulder away and sneered. "Yeah? Well fuck you too." As if a gun were the worst that could happen to a guy. A bullet might kill him. But what he'd done to Ivy would haunt him forever.

On the way home, he couldn't stop thinking about her. She'd been so happy, smiling with him. Hearing her say *motherfucker* had almost made him laugh out loud. So sweet and pure and inherently good. Until he'd seen that lust in her eyes—at first, it'd been for violence. She'd sparked the attraction, because he'd stupidly thought he might deserve a taste of someone who wasn't so nice. That made her not quite out of his league.

The kiss had turned brutally arousing. Just thinking about it got him hard, and then the shame returned. Poor Ivy. He hadn't meant to force her into a yes. She'd been with him most of the way, he could have sworn. But she'd changed her mind, because there, at the end, she'd shut down.

And he'd finally done the one thing he'd never in his life thought he'd do.

He drove home, numbed to everything, and let himself inside. He hadn't expected Foley would be around, hanging instead with Cyn as usual at her swanky cottage in a better part of Beacon Hill.

But Foley was kicked back on the couch watching TV.

"Yo, Sam." He sat up and frowned. "What happened?"

Sam tried but couldn't contain his worry, or his despair, anymore. "I think I did something really bad."

"Talk to me."

Foley had been his best friend forever. But Foley didn't know everything about Sam's early life. And he planned to keep it that way.

But this…Sam had to own up to what he'd done. "I was with Ivy tonight."

"Yeah?"

He sat in the chair near the couch, not wanting to be too close to Foley when he admitted his wrongdoing. "We were hanging out. Having a good time." He explained everything, even up to the part where he'd left. "I don't know what happened. She was there with me, man. I swear I never meant to hurt her."

Foley studied him. "You sure she's upset?"

"She wouldn't look at me." Sam clasped his hands together, tired but still keyed up from the fights. "She looked scared, disgusted."

"Did she do that to you?" Foley nodded to his face.

"No." Sam knew Foley wouldn't like the fact he'd been fighting.

After a moment, Foley swore. "*Damn it*. We've talked about this. You have to stop. One of these days they're going to get raided, and you'll be fucked. Or worse, the next guy you trash might bring a gun to recoup his losses."

Sam immediately thought of Ritter. "I know." He ran a hand through his too-long hair, and the shiner started to throb. "I just… I couldn't handle it. I really like Ivy. I—" He swallowed hard, determined not to be a pussy in front of Foley. "I feel so bad about tonight. I swear I only went over there to help with the dog. I had to drive since her car is messed up." *Crap. Her car*.

"You know, you might be making a bigger deal about this than there is." Foley watched him, concerned. The big jerk was always looking out for Sam. Just like Eileen. They cared about him. But if they knew the real him, they wouldn't care. He could hear Louise's taunts, could see her sneers and disgust. He never wanted Foley or Eileen to look at him that way.

"How is this not a big deal?" came out harsher than he'd intended.

"Did you ever think she might be feeling shy or weird about being with you?"

"No. Should I?" Foley was reaching.

"Dumbass. You practically just met this chick. She doesn't know you all that well, except for watching you beat the shit out of Goodie with one hit. Nice job, by the way."

"Thanks." Sam's heart raced, wondering if he'd been wrong about Ivy's reaction, praying he'd made a mistake in his perception.

"So you just met her, you pounded Goodie, then you're at her place, and it sounds to me like she liked you a lot." Foley grinned.

Foley grinning meant things hadn't totally gone to shit.

"Then you get her off. Again, nice job. First Goodie, then Ivy. Two for two, man."

Sam flushed. "Get to the point."

"Well, your poor girl probably doesn't know up from down. She comes, you skate away without a good-bye—"

"I said good-bye." Had he? He'd been in such a hurry to leave he might not have.

"And she's embarrassed because she came like a rocket."

"You think that's it?" Relief made him light-headed. "That she's upset because she was so easy?"

Foley snorted. "Don't know that I'd call her easy to her face."

Sam's relief turned to upset again. "But if she's all nervous, she won't want to see me again."

"Now that could be a problem."

That was if Foley was right in the first place. Sam didn't know what to do. He'd checked his phone a lot tonight in between fights. She hadn't called or texted.

Then he realized he'd said he'd give her a ride to work in the morning.

"Her car bit it. I'm supposed to drive her to work tomorrow."

Foley nodded to the phone that had seemed to jump into Sam's hands. "Text her. Feel her out."

Sam shot her a text. Waited. Nothing.

Foley let out a loud yawn. "Let's deal with the drama tomorrow. I'm tired. Going to bed. We have work in the morning," Foley reminded him.

"No shit. So what's the deal with you?"

"What do you mean?"

Sam stood and clenched his phone in hand, hoping she'd text back. "Why aren't you locked around Cyn?"

Foley shrugged. "She had a project due tomorrow. Some business she's investing in. She says I distract her." Foley's grin eased Sam's worry. Seeing his friend happy made his own troubles easier to bear. "Woman can't take her hands off me. It's a curse." Foley shook his head.

"You're going to marry her, aren't you?" The familiar panic returned. That Foley would belong to someone else. Then what would Sam do, all alone? Lou was the only guy left at the garage without a girl. Hell, even his bosses, Del and Liam, had found happiness with significant others.

Sam's whole life was changing at rapid rate, one he feared would leave him far behind.

"I'm sure as hell going to marry her. Just as soon as she says yes."

"You asked her?"

"Well, she's kind of being backward about it. She's waiting to get knocked up before we say our 'I do's.' But she's only giving that six months. So in another three, if Foley Junior isn't already cooking, we'll set an actual date."

Sam blinked. "Foley Junior?"

"You'll be an uncle when that happens. Can you imagine?" Foley laughed, joy making his gray eyes bright.

Sam swallowed around a dry throat. "I can just see a baby with tats over his arms. I wonder how Cyn will feel about that."

"Very funny." Foley stood and stretched. "I'm thinking it will be a she. And yeah, Cyn will shit a brick when I get the kid ink to match mine." They both knew he was kidding. "Not up her neck though, like her Uncle Sam. Just her forearms, 'cause I want her to be all womanly."

"And neck tats aren't?" Sam said dryly, still coming to grips with the fact his best friend was moving on and growing up. A wife, kids. Would Foley ever have time for him anymore? And what kind of neurotic asshole thought about himself and his own problems instead of being glad for a guy he'd kill for?

"Before you start overdoing that weird panicked thing where you see everyone leaving you"—uncanny how the guy could read him—"you're *always* going to be in my life, dude. So suck it up and prepare for a lot of diaper changing and babysitting duty. Oh, and dinner at Cyn's place Friday night."

"Uh, okay." He paused. "Diapers? Seriously?"

"Hell yeah. If Cyn thinks I'm doing all that crap while she brings in the bucks, she's deluded." Foley shook his head. "Pretty and smart, but deluded. I'm roping the entire garage into the baby stuff." He paused, and a flash of nerves settled over his face. "You want to know something? Lately, she's been acting weird. She's either premenstrual or hormonal for another reason." The pleasure on Foley's face was impossible to miss. "I'm hoping for the kid."

Foley had only been dating Cyn for close to four months, but the guy had known she was it from the beginning. Foley was like that. He loved you or hated you, and there was no in-between. For all that he appeared like a murdering thug with that muscle and a glare he could turn on or off at will, Foley Sanders was the genuine article. A nice guy.

Cyn had lucked out when she'd met him, and she knew it. Now that Sam knew how much she loved his buddy, he could accept her. Especially because she seemed to want to include Sam on things. He couldn't be sure it wasn't Foley forcing her to invite him to stuff, but Sam wasn't too proud to accept a free meal or a movie with the pair.

"What's she making for dinner?"

"Does it matter?"

"Nah." The phone buzzed in his hands, and he tensed. After a moment, he looked down and read the text from Ivy. Dread once again settled in his stomach.

"What?"

He cleared his throat. "She's getting someone else to take her to work tomorrow, but she said thanks anyway."

"That's not bad."

"It's not good either." Sam shoved his phone into his back pocket. "I'm beat. Going to bed."

"Ice that eye. You know it'll look work worse if you don't. And know you're going to get a ration of shit from Del and Liam tomorrow because of it."

"Hell." With any luck, Liam wouldn't be in the next day, playing retired guy instead.

Sam had taken a few stairs toward his bedroom when Foley called out, "You know, if you want to try smoothing things over with Ivy, why not send her some flowers? That's always a nice touch."

Sam continued up the stairs and got ready for bed. He dumped his dirty clothes near the pile he thought were dirty. Then he sidestepped a few stacks of magazines and crap from the garage he'd brought home. A few sets of tools he should organize. When he had more time.

He slid into bed and pulled his phone and a pad of a paper close and made some notes. Flowers. *Not a bad idea, Foley*. Sam dragged a credit card out of his wallet and made it happen. He closed his eyes, feeling better about his chances.

Sometime later, he blinked his eyes open into a pitch-black room…and prayed Ivy wasn't allergic to pollen.

Wednesday afternoon, Ivy finished her third client and waved as he left her with a healthy tip. Her stomach distracted her with a rumble that let her know she'd missed lunch. After stripping the sheets and putting on fresh ones for her two o'clock appointment, she wandered to the tiny fridge and stared at her unappetizing salad.

Just as she prepared to reach for her drab lettuce and

bruised tomatoes with a side of low-cal, tasteless Italian dressing, the bell over the front door chimed.

She gladly left her lunch behind and moved to the front, aware Denise was currently working on someone in the second massage room.

A young woman carrying two vases of flowers set them down on the counter in front of her computer.

Ivy stared. "Can I help you?"

"Hi. I'm looking for Ivy Stephens."

"That's me."

"These are for you. Oh, and I'm not done. I'll be back."

Ivy blinked at a dozen yellow roses in a pretty glass vase and a colorful spring bouquet in a smaller, rounder glass container. The delivery woman returned with a bunch of purple irises mixed with lilies, what appeared to be daisies, and sprigs of baby breath in a purple vase; another bunch of daisies, these all white; and a potted lavender plant.

Ivy gaped, not sure what the heck was going on. "Who are these from?"

The lady shrugged. "There's a card with the roses. Oh, and another here." She pulled a larger envelope from beneath the lavender. "Have a great day!" She left before Ivy could tip her.

Stunned, Ivy couldn't look away from all the pretty flowers, wondering who on earth had sent them. Sam immediately came to mind, and she shoved the memory of his big hands and even bigger body behind her embarrassment.

A glance at the card in the roses told her nothing. "'I'm sorry'?"

Who had anything to be sorry about, especially in regards to her? It was too little too late to be from Max. Last she'd heard, he'd moved to the East Coast. She hadn't talked to him in two wonderfully long years.

She supposed the flowers could be from Sam, but what did he have to be sorry about? She'd jumped the poor man. Not only that, now she had to massage him— *nonsexually*, she reminded herself—in return for him fixing her car.

After all he'd done for her, Sam had once again been a nice guy and asked her last night if she needed a ride to work. She'd been way too embarrassed to take him up on his offer. So she'd taken the bus that morning. It had been a hassle but better than having Denise or Sue drive across town to get her. And with Shelby putting most of her efforts into her Green Lake office, Ivy had the management hat and said responsibilities for the Queen Anne Bodyworks.

As it was, she'd put aside some money to use Uber to get home tonight.

Staring at the back of the larger envelope she hadn't yet opened, she removed the note.

Handwritten in bold caps, it read:

> IVY, SORRY ABOUT LAST NIGHT. DIDN'T MEAN TO COME
> ON TO STRONG. HOPE YOUR NOT MAD AT ME. I REALLY
> AM SORRY. WILL FIX YOUR CAR NO CHARGE. HOPE YOUR
> OK. SORRY AGAIN. TELL COOKIE I SAID HI. —SAM

She read the note three times before understanding set in. The grammatical mistakes were oddly charming. But Sam was…sorry? What the heck had he done but give her an orgasm? She recalled exploding like a super-nova after about three seconds of his large palm grinding against her through her pants. Then she'd frozen, unable to look the poor man in the eye. That same poor man who had left her in a hurry, with a massive erection still in his jeans.

So, one, he'd given her a good time. Two, he hadn't gotten his. And, three, he'd left mistakenly thinking he'd offended her somehow. All that merited flowers, apologies, and free work on her car?

Conflicting emotions fought for supremacy. Mortification from coming like a shot. Pleasure that he cared what she thought. Dismay he obviously considered himself the reason she'd been unable to face him, and finally, and most importantly, a burning responsibility to make things right.

She glanced at the time and realized her conversation with Sam would have to wait. No way she'd do this through a text or phone call. They needed to meet face-to-face. Her next client would arrive in half an hour, and she had one more after that. She grabbed her phone and sent Sam a text.

He answered right away. He planned to work late tonight, so he'd be available anytime she wanted to talk.

As soon as she finished her massages, she planned to set the poor man straight.

Imagine being sorry for having given her more sexual pleasure than she'd had with a man in years? Max had been good in bed, but they hadn't shared the chemistry Ivy felt with Sam. Sure, she could chalk up her desire to it being a product of prolonged abstinence, but she knew it was more than that.

Sam had a powerful aura, one that screamed *sexy* and *dangerous* and *careful* all in the same breath. Anyone watching him with Cookie would be able to tell he cared, and deeply. Heck, he'd been a real softie with Willie, and that old lady had griped and ordered him around like she owned him.

Ivy ignored her salad, unable to stop thinking about Sam. She took care of her SOAP notes—patient forms that created a solid history for each client—then did some billing. Another reason Shelby had been more than willing to take Ivy on as a partner—Ivy could handle insurance. A real pain, but Ivy had patience and the smarts to handle it.

The bell over the door chimed, and she glanced up to see a tall, gorgeous redhead approaching the counter.

Ivy smiled. "Hello. Can I help you?"

The woman smiled back. "I'm Cynthia Nichols, and I'm here for my two o'clock appointment. But please, call me Cyn."

Ivy nodded. "That would be with me. I'm Ivy." She stood and circled the counter to hold out a hand.

Cyn shook it, a hearty handshake that told Ivy more about her next patient than looks would. Cyn walked with a steady posture and smooth gait. She had even shoulders, not internally rotated or uneven, despite the large bust size that led many such women to hunch their shoulders. Cyn was proud of her looks and confident. The steady eye contact and firm shake said as much.

"I received the online forms you filled out." A comprehensive history intake and release of liability. Ivy moved to a close-by drawer and fished out the clipboard holding Cyn's printed-out information. "Is this still good, or do you have info to add?" She handed it to Cyn.

After looking it over, Cyn gave it back. "Nope. It's good."

"Anything you'd like me to focus on today?" Ivy led Cyn to her room.

"Upper body and neck, but I'm hoping for an all-over massage. Work has been making me tense."

"No problem." She gave Cyn the spiel about using the bathroom prior to the massage and how to prepare for the session. Then she folded down the top sheet and blanket. "Get facedown, in between the sheets. I'm going to go wash my hands. I'll knock before I come back. Any questions?"

Cyn smiled. "Nope. Sounds good. I've been waiting all week for this."

"And it's only Wednesday."

Cyn laughed. "Can you tell I'm stressed?"

Ivy left her to her privacy, then returned shortly and entered after Cyn's okay. After adjusting the blanket and sheets, she began the massage to the accompaniment of soothing yet upbeat spa music. No reason a massage had to be given to pan flutes and tinkling pipes all the time.

Since Ivy liked to let her clients dictate the tone of the massage, she normally didn't speak unless spoken to. About a third of the way into the hour, Cyn murmured through the open portion of the face cradle, "Can I ask a question?"

Ivy dug into the middle of Cyn's back, working her rhomboids and upper traps. The woman sure had hypertonic tissue. "Ask away."

"What's with all the flowers out there?"

Ivy sighed. "They're mine, apparently."

"Yeah? Lucky girl."

"I'm not so sure."

"Oh?"

"Do you really want to hear this? It's your massage. You should relax." In fact, the woman seemed to be tensing up as they spoke.

"I'm always relaxed hearing about *other people's* problems."

Ivy knew better than to overshare with clients, especially new ones. So she kept it simple. "A friend and I had a misunderstanding. He thinks I'm mad at him. I thought he was mad at me. I'm going to fix it later."

Cyn eased back into the table. She hadn't been kidding about other people's problems. "Misunderstandings are the worst." She groaned as Ivy found a trigger point. "That feels *so* good. Maybe you should give your friend a massage. I bet he'd forgive anything if you did that to him."

Ivy chuckled and continued to soothe the knots in Cyn's back. The massage continued without issue, with Cyn sighing or groaning from the release of tension. After having her turn over under the blanket, Ivy proceeded to work on her neck, discovering more issues. "You have stuck scalenes," she murmured. "And your SCM is like a rubber band about to snap."

"Keep doing that." Cyn turned her head at Ivy's guidance. "Man. I wish I could teach my boyfriend to do all this."

"I hear that a lot from clients. Have him do this." Ivy demonstrated a particular spot on Cyn, then had

Cyn gently rotate her neck from side to side. "Just make sure he's not too firm. You don't want injury, just muscle release."

"I'll remember that." Cyn sighed.

Ivy left her neck and continued to work, eventually finishing up with the woman's elegant feet. The hour seemed over before she'd begun. She left Cyn to get changed and met her outside at the desk.

Cyn handed her a credit card without being asked. "Best money I've spent in months, and I buy a lot of shoes. I love shoes. I buy a nice pair at least once a month. That's telling you something."

Ivy grinned. "A true compliment. Thank you." She handed back Cyn's card, then heard a beep on her phone. "Excuse me for a minute." She handed over the credit slip to be signed, then read a text. "Shoot."

"Problem?" Cyn handed back the signed slip, which included a generous tip.

"Nothing serious." Her next client had something come up last minute, so they'd need to reschedule. Which Ivy would do with no problem. She loved Barbara Maycomb, and she totally understood.

Ivy reached for Sam's note and tucked into her purse, then grabbed her jacket while Cyn made small talk.

"Are you leaving too?" Cyn asked.

"Yep. Gotta hurry so I can catch the bus." Not to mention figure out which one would take her closest to the garage.

"Oh, hey, I can take you wherever you need to go. I'm heading back to work anyway."

"I couldn't ask you to do that."

"It's no problem. Really." Cyn rolled her neck on her

shoulders. "I feel *soooo* good right now. You could ask me for anything and I'd give it to you."

Ivy wasn't sure.

"Where are you heading?" Cyn prodded.

"I need to go to Webster's Garage."

Cyn beamed. "That's right on my way."

"Really?"

"Yep. I own NCB, the coffee shop, with my brother and his wife. It's just a few doors down from Webster's."

"Well, then." Ivy's day looked brighter. "Thanks. I'd love a ride."

What were the odds? All the signs pointed to Ivy having a talk with Sam. No sense in putting it off. She could only hope Sam would forgive her. She didn't think she had enough in her monthly budget to buy *him* a ton of flowers.

Chapter 7

Sam did his best to hide his face either under a car or under a hood. For the better part of the day, he'd been successful. Then Liam ordered his sorry ass to take a break, because he wasn't a "demon, whip-wielding, power-hungry manager without a care for his employees" like *some* people. Obviously it was aimed at Del, but she only grumbled and slammed back into her office while she did the monthly paperwork that always turned her bitchy. Well, bitchier than normal.

The woman had been on edge lately. The wedding that should have happened two months ago had been postponed due to issues with the venue where it was to be held. But nothing stood in the way of her becoming Del McCauley in another month. Nerves were making her brittle, and her father had way too much fun rubbing it in.

"That girl is stressed, no doubt." Liam's chuckle showed his lack of empathy. "Nothing like seeing my little girl freaking out because of her wedding to put a smile on my face. My soon-to-be little Delilah *McCauley*. I'm so proud."

Johnny, the dumbass, joined in on the teasing. But Foley and Sam knew to be quiet. With Lou painting at Heller's today, they didn't have his mouth to deal with. The paintwork had to happen where they had facilities to accommodate all the toxic fumes. Enter Heller's

Paint and Auto Body, formerly Heller's Paint Shop. The Websters and Heller had some kind of deal going on commissions, so they sent all their custom-art jobs there.

Sam didn't much care, so long as that daunting bastard kept his ass away from the shop. Sam had seen and done a lot in his life. But Heller made him uneasy. At six six and not an ounce of fat on him, he looked like the poster child for the Aryan race. Back when the guy had worn his head shaved, Sam had worried they'd been dealing with a skinhead. Since Lou was Latino, J.T. African American, and half their clientele something other than white, he'd wondered what the guy had on the Websters to make them deal with him. Turned out Heller had just had a bad haircut. Now he had longer hair. Still a scary motherfucker, but not so racist-scary anymore.

Thinking about Heller had done nothing but distract him, so that when Liam once again told him to get his head out from under that friggin' hood, Sam was less than careful about hiding his black eye.

"What the hell happened to you?" Liam planted his hands on his hips and stared.

Foley and Johnny joined him.

"Whoa. Nailed in the face, huh?" Johnny scratched his head. "It wasn't Foley?"

"Please. I'd never hurt poor Sam. He'd cry like a baby if I tried." Foley smirked at him.

Sam muttered, "As if you could."

"Believe it, Mary. I bet I could wipe the floor with you right now."

Sam gave him a mean smile. "Try it."

"Not in my garage." Liam glared, then noticed the

teasing smile Foley hadn't quite hidden. "You're a pain in my ass, you know that, boy?"

"Yes, sir." Foley saluted. "And that's my cue." He took off to the break room.

"So are you," Liam told Johnny.

The smart-ass took a bow. "Yeah, but I try at it. Foley's just naturally gifted." He paused. "Was it Goodie?"

Sam hadn't realized Johnny was talking to him until Liam stared at his black eye and repeated, "Goodie?"

"Yeah. I heard Sam pounded some sense into Goodie and Senior the other day at Ray's. Did Goodie hit you back?"

Liam raised a brow. It was where Del got the arrogant gesture, for sure. A hard man with muscles, good looks—according to himself at least—and amazing know-how when it came to cars and people, Liam was the man they all wanted to be.

Sam didn't like disappointing him, so he couched his answer. "Ah, no. Not Goodie. It's no big deal, really."

"Uh-huh." Liam stared at him, those dark-gray eyes piercing. "You aren't fighting again, are you, Sam?"

"Huh? Fighting?" Fucking Johnny and his big mouth. Sam scowled, but behind Liam, Johnny was shaking his head and mouthing, *Not me*. "Not sure what you mean." Playing stupid often worked for him with Del. But then, she usually went easier on him than she did the others.

"Please. I—" Liam turned to Johnny. "Get your scrawny ass out of here. Isn't Lara feeding you anymore? Go eat a sandwich."

"Yes, boss. Sure thing, boss. Thank you, boss."

Liam pinched the bridge of his nose. "Is he still here?"

Johnny danced away, laughing as he joined Foley in their crappy little break room.

"He's gone."

"Good." Liam grabbed Sam by the arm and dragged him outside, into the cold spring air, through the back door. Away from Del and the office. Only Liam would have the stones to put his hands on Sam. Foley had a few times before, but they were friends. And that one time a few months ago, they'd nearly ripped each other's heads off during one hell of an argument.

"Damn, Liam." Sam yanked his arm back but made no move to retaliate. He liked the old man. Not to mention he was smart enough to fear the wrath of Del and Sophie—Liam's squeeze—should he even think about messing with the guy.

"What the fuck, Sam? I thought you were done fighting."

"I, ah—"

"Like I don't know about the underground bullshit Jerry runs at the House. Please. Who the hell do you think works on all their cars? Owen's '62 Impala? Dixon's Mercury Cyclone? Or Jerry's fastback?" Oh yeah, that car gave Sam wet dreams. Jerry had a 1967 Ford Shelby GT350 fastback. A real thing of beauty. Figured he'd only trust Liam to work on it. "Jerry O. has been in the thick of shit for decades. Tried getting J.T. to fight a few years ago, but I set him straight."

"J.T.?" Sam snorted. "He'd get his ass handed to him. One pinky finger bent the wrong way and he'd cry like a pussy." He didn't care that he'd called Liam's son a wuss. They both knew it was true.

"I know." Liam sighed. "He's big and pretty. Like

tits on a bull when it comes to fighting. He's all about protecting his hands."

J.T. was one hell of an artist though. "Well, since he does my tats, I guess I can cut him some slack."

"But no slack for you." Liam slapped Sam in the back of the head, coming close to making Sam forget he should never strike his boss. "Get that look off your face," Liam hissed. "We both know you aren't going to hit me back. What *the hell* are you doing fighting again, Sam?"

Damn. No more pretending.

"You don't want to be there when the wrong people come to town. You know that. You sure as shit don't want to go jail. *Again*."

Sam bit back a sigh. "I know."

"So stop it. Because if Del gets a look at that face she'll—"

"What are you two doing out here? Sam?" Del gaped at Sam's eye. "What the fu—"

"Language, honey," Liam hurriedly interrupted. "Remember, the wedding is so close. Don't want to slip up in front of your future in-laws."

She clamped her mouth shut and shot daggers at her father. "Fine. What happened to the eye, Hamilton?"

Del didn't deal with criminals. You worked in her shop, you toed the line. Liam bowed to her wishes, since she'd pretty much taken over most of the work-load. He still came in to help, but he'd adapted to the idea of retirement better than any of them had thought he would.

"I, ah, well…"

"Apparently he got into a fight at Ray's, and a friend

of Goodie's sucker punched him afterward." Liam smacked him in the back of the head. For the second time. "Be more careful, boy. Never turn your back."

Sam bit back what he wanted to say, because Liam was giving him an excuse without having to personally lie to Del. "Good advice," he growled.

"Is that right?" Del didn't seem as if she believed him. "Fine. But be more careful. We won't get repeat clients if our employees look like they just broke out of San Quentin. You're bad enough without the bruises," she said to Sam, sounding gruff. But he knew she wanted only the best for him. "Ice that eye."

"Okay."

"Do you need to leave early or anything?"

He snorted. "It's a busted eye, not a broken hand." He'd had a sprained wrist before and worked through it. Sam was no stranger to pain.

"Good. Thought you were turning into a candy-ass, like my father." She ignored Liam's sputtering. "Take a break, then get back to work. And make sure Foley fixes the fridge like he said he would, okay? 'Cause we're not getting a new one until after I finish my taxes. The fridge needs to last a few more months, I'm thinking."

"You filing an extension?" Liam asked, following her back inside.

"Nah, just making sure I can cover it with this year's projections." She said something else, but Sam didn't hear. He thought long and hard about Liam knowing about his fights. Foley, Liam, Johnny. *Hell.* Lou probably knew too.

He couldn't keep going there, possibly getting

lumped with the other assholes and sent to prison when the cops busted them for gambling and whatever the hell else the House fronted for. Fighting was just the tip of the iceberg of what went down. He knew that. Hell, he knew *better*. With a sigh, he returned to the garage and sought Foley.

He looked in the refrigerator running on its last legs for the sandwich he'd slapped together. Johnny had already returned to a scrappy yellow Honda in the bay, but Foley remained planted at the table, stuffing his face.

"Liam knows," Foley said.

"You think?" Sam gave him a look. "Bastard slapped me upside the head. *Twice*."

"You deserve it."

Sam groaned. "I know. Look. I'll stop, okay? Next time I need to handle my aggression, I'll pound you." He wouldn't mention Ritter's gun. That would only freak Foley out more. And to be honest, it had alarmed Sam. Ritter had seemed like a decent guy. So what the hell did Sam really know about the people at the House?

"Or you could go to that gym McCauley uses. I overheard Del talking to him one day. He works out there religiously. Imagine pounding him instead of the guys at the House."

Sam considered it. "Yeah, but what if I really hurt him? Del wouldn't be happy about that."

"Hmm. Good point. We'll come up with something else." Foley paused. "Though if I remember right, you were pretty damn mellow when Shaya was around."

Good times. "Yeah, but then I was getting laid regularly." A nice girl. A hell of a stripper, and a woman with plans that included her sister out East. He hadn't minded, because he hadn't wanted anything more than some sex with a friend. He'd liked her. He also hadn't cared that she'd left, just wished her well.

"So do what you did with someone else." Foley talked in riddles sometimes.

"Huh? So I should fuck the shit out of someone else?"

Foley looked beyond Sam's shoulder and cleared his throat.

"What? You said it yourself that fucking or fighting relaxes me. So I should find some chick to bang? For how long? A few months on end?" He snorted. "That might leave her walking funny." As he said it, he could only imagine one particular chick to have sex with. And doing anything that might harm her didn't factor into his future. Nah, he only wanted to kiss Ivy. Touch her, pet her, bring her to a happy—

"Ahem."

Sam whirled around and stared at Del. She must have overheard him, because she gave him a look. His cheeks heated. "Ah, what's up, Del?"

"Someone here to see you. In my office." She paused. "What are you working on? The Tacoma in the back?"

"Yeah."

"I'll take a look at it. Hurry up so I can get back to work on my spreadsheets, will ya?"

He walked by her out into the garage, wondering if Ivy had come to see him, finally. Then he slowed down, rethinking all he'd rehearsed to say to her. If it was her, he couldn't screw up again. He needed to sound sincere, apologetic. He'd grovel if he had to.

Del must have followed him, because he felt her hard hands at his back, shoving him toward her office.

Freakin' pushy Websters. "Walk faster, Methuselah. We have a garage to run. But take your time with the convo." In a lower voice, she added, "Iron out your issues and quit moping around like a girl."

He blinked. "Like a what?"

"You heard me," she muttered. "Tell anyone I said that and you get extra oil changes tomorrow."

Shaking his head at Del, because he could always bully Johnny into doing his work for him, he entered the office and closed the door behind him. As he'd both hoped and dreaded, Ivy stood waiting for him. Seeing her looking so fresh and pretty caused him to lose all train of thought, and he stammered a greeting. "H-hey." He coughed to cover his nerves. "Uh, what can I do for you?"

She blinked. "What happened to your eye?"

He flushed, feeling like a huge bruiser compared to her and her gentle nature. "Ah, nothing really. Remember those fights I told you about? Needed to work off a little steam." She said nothing. "Would it help if I told you I won?"

"Oh, um, good." She swallowed audibly. "Does it hurt?"

"Nah. Seriously, I'm good. So what's up, Ivy?"

"I got your flowers," she said in a soft voice. *Well, shit.* She still looked upset.

"I meant to get more, but I didn't want to overdo it if you can't have them in the office." Alarm filled him. "You aren't allergic, are you?"

She gave a sad laugh. "Oh, Sam." Then she walked toward him and shocked him by grabbing his hand. She dragged him to sit next to her in one of the two chairs across from Del's desk. "You have nothing to be sorry about. *I'm* the one who has to apologize."

"Huh?" He was totally confused.

"Let's get a few things straight. One, you will not fix my car for free. If you don't want me massaging you, and I can't blame you for that"—her cheeks turned a bright pink—"then I'll pay you for your time. Two, you, ah..." She glanced around her before looking back at him and adding in a lower voice, "You were so sweet to me last night. I mean, you gave me a major orgasm."

"Yeah?" Fascinated at all she said and didn't say, he just waited. His heart hammered inside his chest, even more so when she continued to hold his big, ugly hand in hers and squeezed.

"I can't believe I attacked you like that." She sighed. "You were so cute." *Him, cute?* "Teaching me to hit, making me swear." Her slow grin turned her from beautiful to downright gorgeous. "I was having so much fun. Then, well, I'm not proud of it. I jumped you. I can't believe I did that. Although, I kind of can. You're so handsome. I mean, even the tickle of your beard turned me on. I bet you're used to women throwing themselves at you." She glanced down at their hands. "I shouldn't have done it, but it's like I couldn't help myself. Around you, I feel this superstrong attraction. I mean, *I* feel it. I don't know if you do."

He kept wondering when he was going to wake up. Or if someone had him on one of those prank TV shows. "Oh, I feel it. Trust me."

She bit her lower lip, and he stifled a groan. "The thing is, that kiss. It was so magical. Then I went too far.

I can't believe I...that I...climaxed from a little touching." She blew out a breath. "You have no idea how embarrassing this is for me. I'm usually not that quick to, ah, finish like that."

He chuckled, and her gaze shot to his. "Ivy, relax. I was worried I forced you into something you didn't want."

"*What?*"

Relieved, he relaxed in his chair and continued to hold her hand, not wanting to let go. "I was the one who kissed you first."

"You're not upset with me?"

"Hell no. What gave you that idea?"

"You left me so fast. I mean, one minute I was coming like some mutant, sex-starved fiend. The next you were racing out of the house."

"Ah, shit. I thought you were mad at me. The kiss got so hot, so fast. Before I knew it, I was touching you. Feeling you come drove me insane. I was two seconds from unzipping and shoving home." He flushed at her wide-eyed stare. "You probably won't believe me, but I don't do that. I never take what isn't offered. That's fucked up, and I'm not like that."

He *prayed* he wasn't. *Hoped* he'd never do what he thought he'd done. He was just so damn glad he'd been wrong about all of it.

"Sam, you were gentle with me." Her flush intensified. "Until you weren't, and it was *amazing*. I don't normally climax that easy or fast with a man. It's been over a year since my last date. I came across as desperate, I know, but I'm really not," she protested.

"Never said you were." Sitting next to her, so close while she held his hand, fixed all his doubts and fears.

Nothing existed for him at the moment but Ivy, and he could do nothing but gaze at her with rapt attention.

Seconds passed in silence.

She sighed. "Your eyes are so pretty."

"So are yours."

They both smiled and kept on staring.

The muted sound of Foley and Johnny swearing in the garage finally broke the moment.

"I, um, I wanted you to know you have nothing to be sorry about," Ivy said. "I do. And I promise not to jump you again."

He made a bold move, encouraged by her admission. He dragged his thumb over her hand, the lightest of caresses, the intimacy between them obvious. "You don't have to promise that, Ivy. In fact, I'd like it if you'd promise the opposite. Feel free to jump me anytime."

"Sam." She gave him a shy grin, and he wanted to hug and kiss her and never stop. "Cookie misses you."

"Yeah?" He cleared his throat. "I miss him too."

"I was thinking. Maybe…maybe you and I could share him for a while."

Best damn idea he'd heard in a long time. "You'd be okay with that?"

She nodded. "That way he gets a lot of attention. And you and I could become better friends."

With benefits, God willing. Or without. Hell, he just wanted to be around her however he could. He was totally turning into a pussy, but he didn't care. "Would you like to go out with me sometime? And not to Ray's. Like, on a real date?" How he found the courage to ask her out, he didn't know. But in her gracious mood, he could only pray she'd take him up on the offer.

She smiled. "A real date? That sounds nice. But no more flowers. I have enough." She leaned close and kissed him on the cheek. The one that she'd said tickled—he'd have to fix that.

He froze in place, not wanting to do anything to ruin the moment.

"I'd love to go out with you, Sam. Anywhere is good with me." She drew back and stood, and he immediately missed touching her. "I'm sorry if I took you away from work. I just asked if I could talk to you for a minute. I hope you're not in trouble or anything because I interrupted."

"Nah. Del's good with it or she never would have given up her precious office."

She chuckled. "Well, I'll let you go."

Which reminded him. "I worked on your car first thing this morning. Ordered the new clutch. Good news is the flywheel just needs to be resurfaced. I'll do that, and when the clutch comes in, you're good as new. Should be all fixed by Friday."

"Oh, thank you so much."

"How did you get here?"

"A client gave me a ride. She owns the coffee shop a few doors down."

He should have known. Nosy-ass Mr. and Mrs. Foley. "Great timing, huh?"

"Yes. I'd been wanting to call and apologize for my behavior, but my day was packed with clients. And, well, I was nervous. I didn't want to sound as pathetic as I still feel. Then I got the flowers, and I was so confused."

She still looked weirded out that she'd desired him, and her inability to control herself made him feel ten feet tall.

"When Cyn offered me a ride, with her working so close to the garage, I figured it was meant to be that I get down here."

"Meant to be," he agreed, deciding to have a talk with the curvy redhead. He appreciated the help, but he didn't want her or Foley meddling in his business. He could fuck up all on his own, thank you very much. "So about that date—what do you think about Friday night?" That would give Cyn and Foley time to do a little apologizing. "I have an invite to a friend's for dinner, but I'm always odd guy out because he has a girlfriend. They keep hounding me to bring someone. Would you like to come? She's a great cook."

"Are you sure they wouldn't mind?"

"Nah. They owe me." *And you an apology*. "Trust me, you coming is doing me a favor."

"Then that sounds great. What should I bring?"

He guided her toward the main office door leading into the belly of the garage. "Just yourself. So are you heading back to work or what?"

"Oh, yes. I have to grab my flowers." She gave him a tap on the arm that barely registered.

"How about I drive you to get them, then drop you off at home? Least I can do since you're without wheels."

"But you're working."

"He's on break," Del said as she approached them, wiping her hands with a rag. "Be back in an hour, okay, Sam?"

"Sure thing." He owed her a thanks when he got back. He walked Ivy to the break room, where Foley continued to eat on his long-ass break. There, Sam quickly removed his coveralls and hung them up in an open locker. He washed his hands and frowned at Foley. "Isn't that your fourth sandwich? How much did you bring to eat?" He recognized the uneven cut on the PB&J. "Hey. That's *mine*."

Foley shrugged and narrowed his eyes on Ivy. "I know you, don't I?" he asked around a mouthful of crunchy peanut butter and strawberry jelly.

She blinked. "Yes. I'm Ivy, Sam's friend. You're Foley, right?"

He swallowed. "Right. I remember you from Ray's. So what are you doing here? Slumming?"

"Funny guy." Sam gave him a warning glare. Ivy had just come back to him, so to speak. He didn't want anything to fuck up his chances. And that included an obnoxious best friend.

"Actually, Sam's fixing my car for me." She put a hand on Sam's arm, and he wanted to glue them together, so that they were always touching.

"Is that right?"

"Yeah, that's right," Sam growled, not liking the challenge in Foley's tone.

Ivy nodded. "He's doing the labor in exchange for some bodywork, I hope. I'm a massage therapist."

"Yeah? Heck, Ivy. I'll work on your car for you for that kind of trade. Just say the word."

She gave a tentative smile, and Sam forgave Foley for the slumming comment.

Sam casually mentioned he planned to drive Ivy home, since she had no car at the moment.

"Good idea." Foley nodded and took a last bite of Sam's sandwich, the bastard. "See you later."

Sam resolved to get back at Foley just as soon as

he returned. He took Ivy back to her office, packed her flowers in the car, then drove her home. She looked so pretty surrounded by colorful petals.

"You didn't have to do all this, Sam." Ivy held the plant in her lap, looking pleased.

"I know. But I felt bad I scared you."

"You didn't." She put a hand on his thigh, and he couldn't help tensing up. *All over.* "It was my fault."

"Do you think it might be your fault again?" he heard himself asking. "Because that kiss knocked me for a loop. You're damn right we share some chemistry."

"I'm glad it's not just me." She squeezed his leg, and he barely contained a groan.

"About that trade for massage. You bet your ass I want it. I get achy when I work long hours." Hell, he was achy now. If she moved her hand up a few inches, she'd see for herself.

"I'm very good at my job. You'll feel better in no time."

He could just imagine.

"But, um, you need to know that the massage won't be… It's strictly professional. Nothing like what happened at my house."

"So no happy endings?"

She lifted her hand from his thigh. "God no." She laughed. "Fastest way to lose your license—diddle the client."

"Gotcha." Ivy didn't do her clients. No one he'd have to rip apart, then.

"It's strictly therapeutic. Relaxing too. In fact, you might even fall asleep during a session. A lot of my clients do."

"Yeah? So when can I book an appointment?"

"I'll check my schedule at home, and we'll work it out. How many hours do I owe you?"

"How many can I get?"

She smiled. "Let's hope you like the first one; then we'll go from there. If you don't, you can be sure I'll pay you for your help with the car."

He'd like it even if she pinched him from head to toe. As if he'd balk at the chance to get her hands on him. "Sounds good. So do I get naked on the table or what?"

"You've never had a massage before?"

Not counting the happy ending kind. "Um, no."

"You're in for a treat." She patted his shoulder, then rubbed the dense muscle and frowned. "And you can use the work. You won't be easy, but I can manage you."

I sure as hell hope so. "Sounds like a plan. Now, about sharing Cookie, how about you tell me what you had in mind."

She did, and his life got even sweeter. A dog, a massage, and the prettiest girl in town. He was three for three and counting.

Chapter 8

FRIDAY EVENING, SITTING NEXT TO SAM IN HIS CAR with her newly fixed vehicle parked at home, Ivy couldn't stop looking at him. He'd shaved his beard and mustache, and the amazing face underneath blinded her. He'd been sexy as sin with that facial hair, but without it? It was all she could do not to reach out and stroke him...*all over*. She did her best to be still, though she found it difficult. And not just because of the new and improved clean-shaven Sam.

Ivy could hardly contain her excitement. Working things out with him had turned a corner in their relationship. She now counted Sam Hamilton as a friend. But from the looks he gave her when he didn't think she was looking, he wanted to be something more.

Not that she had a problem with that—shockingly enough. Memories of their intimate time together would hit her at the oddest moments. Like when he'd picked her up in his muscle car, a purring black beast that suited him to a T. It was rough yet gave a gentle ride, one that caused her to bubble with excitement.

With passion.

For so long, she'd been adamantly opposed to another relationship with a man. But somehow she found herself becoming attached to Sam, and without him trying very hard. Did that mean she'd healed from the pain of Max leaving? Or that she'd found someone worth trying for with Sam?

She shot him a side-glance, wondering if they'd get back to all that pleasurable touching. She never could have imagined Sam fretting about how he'd handled her. God, he'd made her come with barely a touch. Yet the big, handsome bruiser had been scared he'd been too demanding.

She forced herself to look out the window, afraid she'd sigh dreamily and spend the rest of the night staring at him. The more she looked at him, the more she *wanted* to look at him. His sexuality and brooding intensity attracted every ounce of her attention. The thought of a kiss against that smooth cheek played over and over in her mind's eye.

Even his scent intrigued her. He'd used a subtle cologne, but it couldn't hide the sensual manliness that belonged to him. It was hard to define, yet she knew it the instant she experienced it. And like the effect on the rest of her senses, desire rushed through her, turning her nipples rock-hard and the tingling between her legs to rev like his engine.

He glanced at her and curled his lips. "You look fine as hell, Ivy."

"Thanks." She warmed. His compliments never seemed prettied up. They were blunt, honest, and because of it, his words meant more. "So do you. I can't believe you shaved your beard and mustache. You look amazing."

"Didn't want you laughing if I tried to kiss you. You did say it tickled." He shrugged, as if shaving for her were no big deal. "But hey, my clothes are clean, at least. I'm not much more than a jeans and T-shirt kind of guy."

"I don't mind. This skirt is pretty much as fancy as I get. You should feel impressed I put it on for you." A light-blue floral skirt that reached her knees, along with a button-down blue silk top, a dark-blue sweater, and knee-high leather boots completed the outfit. Ivy's inner sex fiend, still raging for another go at Sam, had insisted she wear a pair of baby-blue lacy panties with the matching bra as a bonus. It closed in the front, so if Sam happened to unbutton her shirt, he could easily—"Are we there yet?" she asked with a bit of desperation.

So much sexual desire for a man she'd just come to know. Ivy didn't trust herself, and she didn't know why she felt so much when she'd been socially dormant for over a year. More like two years, in all honesty. Losing Max had damaged her to the core. Her trust in men had faltered, but so had her trust in herself.

She studied Sam, lingering on the tattoos creeping up his neck. Such a big man, so rough on the outside. She'd seen him take down a thug with one punch. A look at his fists showed them bruised, dense, his fingers long and thick yet curiously gentle when petting a stray dog—or a stray massage therapist.

Ivy shifted her gaze to the dash and stifled a sigh. She'd known she'd need to enter the dating scene again. She could only hope she would be smarter than to pin all her dreams on Sam. The poor guy had no idea his simple date had conjured fantasies of a deep relationship.

Ivy's problem—she wasn't a casual kind of girl. When she fell for a man, she fell hard. Her first boyfriend in high school had lasted three years before they'd mutually broken it off. Then Max and she had been together for four years. Four years living with the man, considering having children together, planning to purchase a home. Four years down the drain.

Maybe if her family had been more supportive, she wouldn't have thrown the whole of herself into Max. But he was all she had—until she had nothing. Now she had Cookie. And…Sam?

"You okay? You're awfully quiet. I promise they won't bite."

She smiled. "I'm good. Just telling myself to behave."

He arched a brow. "Not on my account." His deep voice sounded gravelly. Sexy.

She crossed her legs and tried not to think about all the tingling in her lower body. "On my account. I'm a mess, you know."

"Yeah?" He sounded intrigued instead of put off.

"Never mind. I'm trying to put on a good impression for you."

"Hey, I'm already impressed. I didn't scare you away after Ray's or from, well, before."

"Well, then I want to impress your best friend. How's that? I don't think he liked me much."

"Fuck—I mean, *screw* what Foley thinks. Besides, he liked you."

"Really? Because he had a mean look on his face even while he was acting nice. Trust me, I could tell." She had become an expert at reading body language. A bonus to her profession—reading postures, gaits, and looking for signs of pain or fatigue. Or in Foley's case, wary hostility.

Sam seemed startled. "Mean look? What are you talking about?"

She had a feeling Foley had just been acting protective about his friend. For all that Sam acted tough, he had feelings. Vulnerable ones she'd already witnessed—at her house, in Del's office, with Cookie. Only a sensitive man would feel sorry about something he hadn't even done.

"Maybe it's me. I still feel bad about before."

He pulled in front of a cute cottage in North Beacon Hill, one she'd love to be able to afford. Sage green, with white shutters and white Craftsman-style columns, the home had an abundance of pansies overflowing a tall, black pot by the front door. The house, the landscaping, the location—it all intimidated because it all looked perfect.

Sam turned off the car and faced her. He took one of her hands in his. "Ivy, let it go. We're good, yeah? Even if I hadn't been messed up about all that shit, I still would have sent you flowers."

She searched his face and saw only concern—for her. "Okay."

Then he gave her one of those rare smiles. "If you get jumpy again, know I'm ready for you at any time. Hell, say the word and we'll leave right now, so you can continue those feelings in the privacy of your living room. I'm partial to your couch."

Her cheeks felt hot, and she found it hard to breathe when he lifted her hand to his mouth and kissed it—all while staring at her.

His blue-gray eyes turned dark, and her entire body came alive.

"S-Sam?"

"Sure you're hungry for *dinner*?" The emphasis on dinner told her he felt it too.

Which made it worse. Because she really, really wanted another go at Sam. But they'd only just met a week ago. And Ivy didn't do casual. Sad she had to keep reminding herself of that fact.

She took a deep breath, then let it out. "I'm starved." Before he could ask what for, she withdrew her hand from his and darted out of the car. She thought she heard him sigh, but he joined her, wrapped an arm around her shoulders, and walked with her to the front door.

"Remember when I told you I had a surprise waiting for you?" The first thing he'd said after picking her up. "Well, here it is."

He rang the doorbell and waited.

The door opened, and Ivy stared in astonishment at a familiar face. "Cyn?"

Cyn Nichols blinked before a wry smile lit her face. "Busted. Come on in, guys." She stepped back.

Sam drew Ivy with him, almost protectively, and she couldn't help basking in his care. It had been so long since someone else had put her needs first. The years with Max had quickly progressed from his interest in her well-being to his interest in being taken care of—constantly.

"Yo, Sam, what's…" Foley tapered off as he saw Ivy with him. He glanced at Cyn, then back at Sam and Ivy. "Oh. You brought a guest. Ivy. Hi."

"Asshole," Sam snarled but kept a proprietary arm around Ivy. "What's with your super-stacked spy?"

Cyn chuckled. "Thank you?"

"Sam." Ivy tried not to be amused. "Just for the record, I told you Foley was acting weird."

Foley blinked. "What?"

Sam scowled, taking menacing to new heights, but Ivy felt nothing but protected in his embrace. "Why were you spying on Ivy?"

"Spying is a harsh word," Cyn interrupted. "Ivy, would you like a glass of wine?"

Seeing nothing but humor and goodwill in Cyn's smiling eyes, Ivy nodded. "A big one."

Cyn gave a husky laugh. "I wasn't trying to be devious," she said to Sam. "Or maybe I was. Rumor has it you were pretty upset not so long ago."

Ivy glanced up at Sam to see him uncomfortable. Knowing what he'd worried about, she wanted to comfort him. So she put her arm around his waist and held him close.

He glanced down at her and raised a brow. When she smiled up at him, his cheeks turned pink.

He cleared his throat. "I'm over it."

"Yeah, now." Foley sighed. "Look, you were acting all weird, and who the hell knew what Ivy would say or do? I mean, I know you aren't the type of guy to get all crazy. But some chicks are wacko, and for them, any hint of weakness in a guy can get him hammered."

Everyone looked at him.

"What? I had a life before Cyn." Foley shrugged. He wore jeans and a dark-green sweater. Like Sam, his forearms were covered in tattoos. Despite herself, Ivy acknowledged she was standing in a room with two very handsome men. Even if neither could seem to express himself clearly.

Cyn muttered under her breath, then said in a louder voice, "What my idiot boyfriend is trying to say is that, in his own way, he was trying to protect you, Sam."

"I know that. Or I'd have taken his head off when I found out he sent you to spy on her."

Ivy hugged him, then stepped away before she did something worse, like jump him again.

"For what it's worth, I truly went there for a massage," Cyn stated bluntly. She grabbed the bottle of wine on the dining table, which sat deeper into the large living space, and poured Ivy a glass. After handing it to her, she continued, "Ivy is amazing. I felt like a limp noodle after my massage. It was wonderful."

Ivy liked Cyn. Not just for the compliment, but also because she'd done something nice for Sam, even if he couldn't yet see it. "Thanks," Ivy said.

"Don't fall for her nice-chick attitude," Sam warned. "She's really a shark in heels."

Cyn beamed. "That's so sweet."

"Christ."

Foley smirked. "Ain't she fun?" He turned to Ivy. "I can't say I'm sorry for checking into you. Sam was acting like a dumbass, and he seemed to like you. Can't say if it's because you're a smokin' hot blond or because you like that furry mutt."

"Sam or Cookie?" Cyn asked, all innocence.

Sam shot her a look, and she seemed to choke on laughter.

"I'm pretty sure he meant Cookie." Ivy tried to placate her rigid date, trying not to laugh herself.

Then the air seemed to go out of him and he relaxed. He walked over to Foley and, quick as lightning, put him into a headlock.

Ivy watched as the two mock wrestled.

"You break it, you bought it," Cyn ordered in a stern voice.

They calmed some but not enough that Ivy wouldn't have worried if it had been her house.

Cyn sighed and turned to her. "Want to help me in the kitchen?"

Ivy took a sip of wine and saw the lack of tension in Sam's frame, except for his thick biceps around Foley's neck. She noted his pleasure in the microexpressions she'd come to recognize and knew Sam had already forgiven his interfering friends.

"Sure. What's for dinner? I hear you're a good cook." She followed Cyn into the kitchen, which was separated from the open dining/living space by a low wall. Knocked out by the gorgeous design, counter envy made it difficult for Ivy to focus on the good smells.

She'd *love* to have had a kitchen like this. Not that it was huge—far from it. But the stainless steel appliances, deep ceramic sink, and dark-mahogany cabinets were drool worthy. The white quartz countertops had her wondering what they would look like in her kitchen, where there was room for maybe one small area of food preparation. And Cyn had an island in the middle, where she had chopped veggies and what looked like ciabatta bread on a stoneware plate.

"We only use the good olive oil for company," Cyn teased and poured some into a small dish. She added some ground pepper, basil, garlic salt, and a dash of something else she refused to share, then broke off a bit of bread and dipped it in the oil before eating. "Ah, perfect. Help yourself."

Feeling as if she'd stepped into a restaurant and not someone's home, Ivy broke off some for herself and indulged. Paired with her wine, the simple appetizer tasted more like a feast. *Oh man. I think I just gained four pounds.*

"I'm going to apologize right here and now." Cyn shook her head. "When I heard how Sam was all gaga about some 'random chick'—Foley's words, not mine—I admit I was interested. Then Foley told me how you and Sam had had a misunderstanding, and he was really worried for the big guy. Sam's such a sweetheart, though you wouldn't know it to look at him. We wanted to see this woman who had our Sam in a knot."

Ivy arched a brow. *Our* Sam? She'd spoken with a firmness that told Ivy Cyn wouldn't be easy to convince of anything.

Cyn might be tall, gorgeous, and shapely in a way Ivy would never be, but Ivy had worked hard her entire life. She didn't need this woman's approval, and she wouldn't pretend to be something she wasn't in order to get it, had she wanted it in the first place. *What you see is what you get*—her personal mantra.

Then, what Cyn had said struck her. Sam was gaga over her?

Ivy swallowed a little cheer and tried to be as cool as Cyn. "And? What's the verdict?"

Cyn narrowed her eyes. "Too soon to tell. I know you're a goddess with those hands, though. And a genuinely nice person." Cyn's serious expression melted into a warm smile, and her dark-brown eyes shimmered with pleasure. "Plus, any woman who can handle a first date with Sam at Ray's and not run away screaming in terror has my vote."

That approval she hadn't wanted was all hers. Ivy chuckled, relieved to have at least gained Cyn's support. "Well, in his defense, it wasn't really a first date."

Cyn glanced over the low counter and, seeing the guys now engaged in a verbal battle instead of a physical one, leaned forward and said in a low voice, "Actually, it was. He's just that dense. Handsome as sin, dangerous, a natural brawler. But a bad first-dater."

Ivy laughed, a bit self-consciously, trying not to be so stuck on "gaga." "He said we were just meeting to talk about the dog."

Cyn raised a brow.

"Well, I didn't want to assume."

"He wanted to take you, a beautiful blond, out for a beer to discuss *a dog*? That's like asking me not to have chocolate during that time of the month. Totally ridiculous."

Ivy flushed. "He never acted like he was that into me. Not at first."

"Then again, in a place like Ray's, you were probably more worried about getting out alive." Cyn shuddered. "Don't get me wrong. I love Lara, Rena, and a few of the others behind the bar. But the locals? Not so much."

"Well, there was an incident with one or two of the guys there. Sam kind of hit one of them. Hard."

Cyn glanced over at an approaching Sam, Foley in tow. "I don't think Sam knows any other way to hit."

"I heard my name." He joined them in the kitchen. "Hey. You're eating already?" He gave Ivy a wounded look.

"She made me." Ivy pointed to Cyn.

Foley shook his head. "Bread for dinner? Way to impress our guest, babe."

"It's an appetizer, doofus. And I'm doing better than you are. *I'm* not the one that sent in an undercover agent to spy on Sam's friend. That was all you."

"Me? Please. You wanted to see who had Sam all confused more than I did. It was all your idea."

"My idea?"

As they continued to squabble, Sam leaned over Ivy's shoulder, ostensibly to grab a piece of bread to dip into the olive oil. He said in a low voice, right into her ear, "True love. Scary, huh?"

She wanted to agree, but that near him, she could do nothing more than nod. His warmth, his sheer presence, overwhelmed her. And she didn't think he was trying to make an impact. He just did.

He straightened and munched on the snack. Then he and Ivy moved closer and watched the entertainment as Cyn and Foley argued like an old married couple— her with a lot of hand gestures and rapid insults, him with a wounded growl thrown in every other defensive statement.

"This is kind of fun." Ivy sipped her wine. "Did you try some? It's really good with the bread."

"I'm not much of a wine guy. I'd be drinking a beer right now if my idiot friend had any manners."

"Seriously?" Foley swiveled to argue with Sam. "Me and my manners? Who regularly compliments women about their tits and ass?" Foley shoved a beer at him, then turned back to Cyn. "And I told you, woman, your ass is just perfect the way it is."

"Oh please, you…" She continued berating him without making much sense. It was like an argument for argument's sake, because half of her complaints had to do with Foley being too handsome, too muscular, and too fine for his own good.

Ivy chuckled. "I like this. It's much more entertaining than anything on TV."

"Yeah. You should see them when they really get going." Sam took a sip of beer, then leaned in again to whisper, "I hate to say it, but it's kind of verbal foreplay. When they start like this, it's a sign not to stay late after dinner unless you want another kind of show. And if you've seen Foley's ass once, you really don't want to see it again."

Ivy bit her lip to keep from laughing when Foley and Cyn turned to glare at Sam. "What did you just say?" Foley asked.

"Something about your fine ass, dear." Behind him, Cyn rolled her eyes, but her grin said she reveled in the argument.

Perhaps Sam had a point. There was a definite change in the energy in the kitchen. A lot…spicier than it had been.

Sam nodded. "One hour tops and we're outta here."

Ivy couldn't help it. She laughed.

Foley looked pained. "Oh, come on. My ass isn't that bad. I have dimples. Want to see?"

Before Ivy could protest, Cyn grabbed the hand poised at the fly of his jeans. "This is why we never have return company. It's like I'm dating a four-year-old."

Foley snickered and said to Ivy, "You should have

seen how fast Cyn's brother took off the first time I acted like I was going to drop trou in the kitchen."

"But you'll note Nina didn't blink during the performance." To Ivy, she explained, "Nina's my sister-in-law and best friend. Well, she was until she ogled my man." Cyn grinned, clearly not meaning it. "Not that there was anything to see, but she almost got dry eye from not blinking while he threatened to moon the room."

"Say no to crack, man," Sam deadpanned, then winked at her. "'Cause none of us but your poor, crazy woman wants to see that. Right, Ivy?"

Not willing to be caught up in their nonsense, she held up a piece of the ciabatta. "Man, this bread sure is good."

Cyn laughed with the others, then she tasked everyone with putting food on the table.

Ivy forced herself to splurge a little. She normally avoided bad carbs in favor of a highly nutritional diet, the occasional cookie notwithstanding. But life was for living, and great friends merited a great meal—pasta, salad, wine, bread, a cheesecake for dessert. She'd up her workouts this week.

A glance at her new friends told her it was more than worth it.

The evening passed too swiftly, and before Ivy knew it, the hour had reached nine. She and Sam had stayed for nearly three hours, and Cyn and Foley showed no signs of slowing down. The pair made her laugh, especially because they constantly harped on Sam, but in fun, loving ways. She'd learned more about him she liked.

He had a thing for classic cars. He loved rock music and alternative "crap," as Foley called it. Sam also seemed to be a momma's boy with Eileen, Foley's mom, whom he thought could do no wrong, even though he feared getting near her during her crazy marriage-planning phase. And he loved animals as much as they loved him. Foley had called him the "Pied Piper of Seattle," which had made Sam flustered. Compliments discomfited him. He apparently wasn't used to getting too many of them, and that was a shame.

After one particular nugget of information, she gaped at him.

"You're not really a hoarder, are you?" she asked, only to see him turn bright red.

Her favorite pastime of the evening—getting Sam to blush. Mr. Tough Guy could get shy about the simplest things.

"No." He gave Foley a finger he didn't even try to hide. "I just like to collect things."

"Okay, so hoarding is a slight exaggeration." Foley shook his head. "Note I said 'slight.'"

Cyn winced. "You are kind of messy, Sam."

"Yeah, but I know where everything is."

Ivy wanted to smile at his defense. "I do too, but my house is pretty picked up."

"Yeah? Well, that's because you're a chick. You too, Cyn."

"Thanks for noticing." Cyn chuckled. "What about Foley? He's superneat."

Sam snorted. "Because he's a huge pus—" He glanced

at Ivy and swallowed the insult. "I mean, he's a clean freak. You think I have issues? *He's* the one with crazy brain."

Sam dragged his hand over his hair, looking frazzled and mean and too sexy for his own good. His many tattoos captivated her. She'd been studying them without trying to appear obvious about it all night. He'd pushed up the sleeves of his long-sleeved T-shirt, so that the colorful artwork of a muscle car, barbed wire, vines, skulls, flames, and other manly things continued to peek at her.

He would have made a terrific massage therapist with forearms that thick. Talk about muscle.

"I'm getting the impression you don't believe me," he growled at her.

"Hey, you say you're not a hoarder, who am I to judge?" Yet from Foley's and Cyn's comments, she knew he probably wasn't the tidiest person.

"I'm not. Seriously. I'll prove it." He stood.

"It's okay, Sam. I was just teasing."

But now he seemed defensive. "No. It's not okay. Come on, Ivy. I've had enough." He shot a hurt look at Cyn, his face stoic as he looked at Foley. "I'll talk to *you* tomorrow."

Then he hustled Ivy to the front door, collected their jackets and her purse, and had them outside before she could blink.

"Sam, it's okay. Really…" A devious expression in those eyes told her she'd misread the situation. "You're not upset."

"Did you see Foley and Cyn looking all shamefaced? Oh yeah. The next time I see him, he's gonna feel so bad about making me look like a punk in front of you."

He guided her to the car. "It's getting late. I thought we should head out before they started undressing and making out in front of us."

"Sam." She chuckled. "Foley was kidding earlier about showing off his butt."

"Naive little thing. You have no idea." He got into the car with her and drove away. "Oh yeah. I can't wait to play this up. He'll be groveling like a bitch and I'll..." He paused. "I mean, he'll be all upset, and I'm gonna rub his face in it." He sounded positively cheerful.

Ivy put a hand on his arm, aware he seemed to tense anytime she touched him. She hoped that was a good thing, like the way she stilled whenever he neared. Then again, she couldn't help wondering if he was just being nice and not secretly thinking about how best to get her hands off him because she was one of those touchy-feely females. Guys might want to have sex with any available woman, but a man with deep feelings, like Sam, might also have regrets later.

"Sam, I had a great time tonight. But could you do me a favor?"

"Sure." He eyed her warily before returning his attention to the road.

"Would you stop censoring yourself? Just because I don't cuss doesn't mean you don't have to. I won't die from hearing the p-word or the f-word, you know."

He glanced at her and away, his lips curling into a hint of a smile. "You just can't bring yourself to say *pussy* or *fuck*, can you?"

She cringed. "No."

He gave an honest-to-goodness guffaw. "You crack me up. You're so pretty, so pure. But you're kind of not." His mirth was contagious, and she found herself smiling despite her embarrassment. "I remember you saying 'motherfucker' right before you pounded my hand. Nice hit, by the way."

"Thanks." She let go of his arm, then found her hand entwined in his. He'd reached for her, not looking at her, his attention on the road.

She didn't let go.

"So what now, Mr. Messy?" she teased.

He squeezed her fingers. "Watch it, or I'll start calling you Miss Happy Endings."

She cracked up. "Oh, please don't. It's never fun getting those kinds of clients."

"Yeah? How's that happen?"

"Every now and then, we get a weirdo who thinks a massage means he's free to be naked and get whatever he thinks he can pay for. I do not, and I repeat, I *do not* touch a guy's stuff."

"Stuff? What do you mean?"

She squeezed his hand tighter, knowing she'd cause him no pain. The giant man had giant hands. He seemed almost unbreakable. Unless he thought he might be hurting her. She warmed all over again. "You're teasing me."

"Yep. I want to hear you say a four letter word."

"Okay. O-K-A-Y. Four letters."

He grimaced. "I was trying to be clever. Please, no spelling. Let's not ruin tonight."

She laughed. "You're so much funnier than you seem."

"How do I seem?"

"Intimidating." She continued to hold his hand, feeling his strength in the tight, all-compassing grip. "Angry.

Quiet. Not always happy." She studied him, seeing those tattoos creeping up his neck, like the realization creeping over her that this man had many, many layers. "But that's all a front, isn't it?"

He shrugged. "Not sure what you mean."

"You're a big faker."

He frowned. "What?"

"You heard me." She was having fun. "You're a faker. You're tough on the outside. And God knows you look totally—"

"Hot? Sexy? Fuckin' raw?"

"Ah, I would have said menacing or threatening. And don't even try to pretend that bothers you. I can tell you're smiling."

"Am not."

She grinned. "Are too. You don't actually smile sometimes, but your eyes soften and your lip turns up the slightest bit. It's a Sam smile."

"You know me so well, huh?"

"Not yet." She paused, wondering if she should admit the truth. "But I'd like to."

He ran his thumb over her hand, and her body stirred, desire stoking to life the fires of the long-buried woman inside. "Well, then how about coming home with me for a quick tour? I'm not gonna do anything weird. I want a chance to prove I'm not a hoarder."

A chance to see Sam's home? More of the private man's life? "I'd like that."

She heard the smile in his voice. "Good. Then Foley, Cyn, and you, can kiss my lily-white ass."

"And there's the Sam I've come to know." And *like* a lot more than she should.

Chapter 9

SAM CALLED HIMSELF ALL KINDS OF FOOL AS HE took Ivy back to his place. He should have driven her home and dropped her off with the dog. Foley would have laughed his ass off if he'd known Sam had taken the woman to see the house. Because Foley was what a guy would call OCD neat, while Sam lived on the messy side of life.

He'd been in Ivy's place. The woman had orderly tendencies. But she didn't always dust, he recalled. That had to count for something.

They parked. After locking up his pride and joy, he walked her into the town house.

"Nice place, Sam." She glanced around with approval.

"I know, it's beige and boring. That's what Cyn's always bitching about. But hey, it's home." *Not "bitching" idiot. Saying. Complaining about. Hell.* He might not be that clean when it came to stuff, but he could tidy up his language.

She'd told him he could swear, but she still seemed uncomfortable with it. Poor Ivy. The girl couldn't even say *hell* without turning red.

And that made him want to smile. Why, he couldn't say. Sam's type typically ran toward stripper poles, sex for favors, and knowing the score, so surprises were few and far between. Women who knew *fuck* could be used in all kinds of ways. But a good girl like Ivy didn't use language like that.

"Beige is nice, neutral. You can put any color with it and it'll match." She defended him.

His heart tripped a beat.

Sam liked Ivy. A lot. She'd been so much fun at dinner. She didn't act stuck up, and she sure the heck could have. A woman with her looks and figure could have any guy for the asking. But she was a genuinely nice person. Cyn liked her. Foley did too. When Ivy had been in the kitchen helping Cyn clean up after dinner, Foley had taken him aside and given his blessing.

Sam appreciated knowing it wasn't just him, that his friend had also liked what he saw when he looked at Ivy. She had such a kind heart. Was such a giving person and so damn beautiful.

He had a difficult time forgetting how good it had been to kiss her, how responsive she'd been. *And what all had followed it, asswipe? You thought you'd scared her. Back off.*

Telling himself to behave, he gave her the quick tour. "This is the living room."

"I see that."

"Smart-ass," he murmured, pleased she felt at ease with him, even alone together. "So Foley got all the furniture, but we bought the stereo together. The TV is mine though, no matter what he says." Foley had a different recollection of who had bought the thing. But no way would Cyn let him move that "monstrosity" into her place. Sam didn't mind her taste at all—not if he got to keep what he wanted because of it. The damn TV was too huge for her prissy living room.

Watching a football game or boxing match on it was like being there. Poor Foley. Sucker.

"This is totally a guy's place." Ivy nodded, and her blond hair shimmied around her shoulders. So soft, so long and silky. He'd toyed with the ends a few times earlier, when he'd had his arm around her shoulders. She fit, as if she'd been made for him.

Trying to get his mind off another growing erection, he focused on the conversation.

He agreed with her. The oversized brown furniture fit him and Foley, but most women seemed to find it no more than functional. A few pictures of them with Eileen or with the gang at Webster's sat on the shelves of the lone bookcase holding the stereo. And with them sat a few framed pictures of classic cars he'd been dreaming about for years.

"Yeah, so, this is the kitchen." He led her into the attached kitchen, which had room for their table and chairs, tons of counter space, and cheap oak cabinets. Nothing homey, like Ivy's place, or fancy, like Cyn's. But the wooden table and chairs accommodated his and Foley's big asses, so he had no complaints.

"Wow. It's really clean in here."

"We don't cook much." More like they *couldn't* cook much. Sam could make a mean frozen pizza. Foley did him a few better by being able to fix mac and cheese or those tasty cinnamon rolls from the can. Or course, Sam could eat two of those cans by himself. Food didn't last long in the house.

Or at least, it hadn't when Foley had been living steadily in the place, doing most of the grocery shopping. A pang of longing for the way things used to be struck. Then he saw Ivy's shy smile and told himself to look to the future.

"What's down there?" Ivy asked, pointing to the short hallway.

"Foley's room and the bathroom." He showed her both, silently cursing Foley for being such a neat freak. The guy was going to make him look bad. Maybe he shouldn't have brought Ivy over until after he'd picked up a little.

"Your room is upstairs, I guess?"

"Yeah." He swallowed. "You, ah, want to see?"

She smirked at him. "You mean, to prove you're not a hoarder?"

"Freakin' Foley," he muttered and led the way, hiding a grin when he heard her soft laughter.

Being with Ivy filled him with joy. It made his cock hard too, but he could handle that. The joy part confused him. Because feeling good didn't come naturally. Anytime he had a reason to smile, something—*or someone*—would come along to ruin it. He grabbed his phone from his back pocket and muted it.

"Problem?" she asked.

"Nope." They'd reached the top of the stairs. "So, my room." He opened the door and wondered if she saw what he did—a guy who didn't have enough room for everything but was trying.

He saw the many stacks, the piles on the floor. Everything organized to his standard. It might appear a bit messy, but he knew where everything was. Foley could kiss his ass.

"What do you think?"

She blew out a breath. "You have a lot of stuff."

"Yeah, but it's organized, and you can walk through the room and all. In the hoarding show Foley makes me watch, people can't ever move around. They piss in bottles and have dead animals under their crap. I don't have any of that." He could clearly see his carpet…in spots.

She watched him moving around his organized stacks. "I see that."

He stopped and turned to face her. "You think it's a mess," he accused. "You're like all the rest."

She burst out laughing, which he hadn't expected. "You are so cute."

"Me? Cute?" He wondered if she'd hit her head and he hadn't noticed. No one called him cute. Not even when he'd been six and lost a front tooth. Never cute. Obnoxious. Annoying. Fucking retarded. Yeah, Louise had never been very PC about anything in her life.

"Adorable." She went to him and gave him a hug, her head coming to just under his chin. The warmth… He took every bit of stress and leftover anger he'd ever had and let it float away under her care.

He stood with her like that for what seemed like forever.

When she pulled back, he reluctantly let her. The happiness in her green eyes pulled at him. "Now let's go downstairs before I give in to my need to clean all this."

He groaned. "Not you too." He let her drag him back to the living room.

"I should probably go before Foley gets back. We all have work tomorrow."

"Yeah." He didn't want her to go. Ever. And Sam never thought in terms of forever. With a car maybe, but never with a woman. "I mean, no. Foley's not coming back. He's staying with Cyn tonight." And getting his rocks off, the lucky bastard.

Speaking of rocks…he'd been hard since they'd arrived, but his willpower and need to make Ivy feel safe had forced him to remain calm. With any luck, she hadn't felt the poker in his pants when they'd hugged. He'd tried to hold himself away when she'd pressed into him with those round, ripe tits—no, breasts. Ivy had mouthwatering, tight, little nipples.

And if he wanted her to leave before he came in his pants, he should stop thinking about sex.

"Sam?"

"Yeah?"

"My first client tomorrow isn't until eleven."

"Aren't you a lucky girl." A beautiful girl. Woman. Seductress. Her hair flowed over her shoulders, near the tops of her breasts. The yellow color looked like spun gold and brought out the green in her eyes. Like shiny gems, they sparkled as she looked at him. In that knee-length skirt, tall boots, and blouse, she looked fashionable. Too good for the likes of him. Hell, he'd worn a T-shirt and jeans to dinner. Only difference between his current outfit and his grungy work clothes, his jeans didn't have any stains or holes, and his T-shirt had long sleeves.

"So, I was wondering…"

His pulse sped up, and he told himself to relax. She probably wanted to talk about Cookie or the car. No way that look on her face meant what he thought—*hoped*—it did. "Yeah?" he sounded hoarse.

"Well, would you mind if I stayed for a bit? Not too

long, because Cookie's at home in his crate. But it's a little early to end such a great night."

"Sure." A no-brainer, that one. "We could watch TV or listen to music." *Lame, Hamilton*. But then, asking her to fuck like bunnies wasn't the way to go either. Ivy was a good girl. Nice, pretty, gentle, funny. Not someone who wanted to suck him down to see how fast he could come. Or bet on how many times he could in an hour.

Her slow smile made him sweat. *Crap*. This might not be the best idea he'd ever had.

But as he sat next to her on the couch, her warm, little body plastered next to his while a rerun of *Top Gear* aired, he didn't think he'd ever been smarter.

Ivy subtly wiped her sweaty palms on her skirt and snuggled with Sam. The guy put out heat better than an electric blanket. So hot, physically and metaphorically. With his jacket gone, his sleeves pushed up, and his frame eased into his big couch, he seemed so masculine. So different from her, and so fascinating.

Max had been an inch or two taller than her, and slender. In his arms, she'd felt cared for at first. But never so protected as she did with Sam. Granted, the guy could hold her down and do whatever he wanted to her with ease. All that muscle and power. But that wasn't Sam.

She hadn't known him long, but she knew the core of the man. He defended those who needed defending, and those flowers and his worry he'd upset her still made her feel so good. Sam cared about her—as more than a woman he wanted to screw.

He hadn't made a move all night. Even with her joined to his hip. Even after that hug that had shown her the excitement he felt—or at least, his body felt—in her presence.

She trusted him.

Imagine that.

She smiled up at him. He must have noticed, because he stilled. "You okay down there?"

She laughed. "Yep. I'm just loving this manly show. Vroom vroom. And there the car goes. Around another lap."

He frowned. "I can turn the channel if you want."

What she wanted was for him to kiss her and take charge again. To bring her to pleasure and not have her think too hard about why she shouldn't get involved with a man she'd just met.

But Ivy was also a realist, as well as a fair person. Sam had been the one to make her feel good last time. Shouldn't she return the favor? "Relax, Sam. I'm kidding. I'm fine watching cars drive around."

He gave a pained expression, then turned the channel to a show about tiny houses. "You like this, don't you?" He saw the grin she tried to hide and groaned. "I knew it. Chicks like you are into house shows."

"Chicks like me?" She casually wrapped an arm around his middle and felt him tense all over. A glance down his front showed his erection, loud and proud.

He swallowed audibly but kept his arm tight around her shoulders, his attention on the show. "Yeah, nesters. Women who are responsible, the kind who make good moms. You're good with Cookie, and you barely had dust in your totally organized house."

She wanted badly to see him lose control the way she had. She wondered if she could make him lose it like that. And why the prospect made her so excited. The idea of touching him, seeing him get off, had her wet and ready for him right now. Even for Max, she'd had to work to get in the mood. For Sam, it seemed like a natural part of being with him. Her body wanted what he had to offer.

Problem was, so did the rest of her.

Take it slow, Ivy. Don't rush him. A taste of pleasure is okay though. But back off the whole relationship train. Not yet.

Yet meant she was thinking about a future with Sam in it. She mulled over the idea while they watched two people on television try to cram eighteen-hundred-square-feet worth of possessions into a two-hundred-square-foot space. Idiots.

"Idiots." Sam snorted. "Why the fuck wouldn't they just get a storage shed? She wants to take all her shoes? What the hell is that about? Dude should say no, but he's all whipped and letting her lead the way. God."

Ivy bit back a grin, feeling the same. She and Sam had so much in common. It surprised her. She felt his hand in her hair, the way she'd sworn she'd felt him touch her earlier. That tender stroking, his soft sigh. Then he planted a kiss on top of her head.

She lost it. The sensual creature inside her threw caution to the wind. *He's mine tonight. Screw you, rational Ivy.*

Ivy scooted closer to Sam, loving how still he grew. He was totally aware of her and trying not to be. "Sam?"

"Yeah?" His voice could have cut gravel.

"Would it be okay if I kissed you?"

He seemed to stop breathing. He glanced down at her, and she did her best to appear innocent, batting her eyelashes.

"Uh, sure. Yeah. That would be okay." He coughed. "Just great."

She hid a smile. "I'm going to move so I can reach you."

"Yep. I'll sit right here." He put his arms out on either side of the couch. "Won't even touch you. All right?"

She nodded and gave him her version of a shy grin when really she wanted to mount the man. No, tonight would be all for him. Then they'd be even, starting over. Dating, she hoped, her fingers crossed. "You're okay with this? I know last time we had that misunderstanding. I don't want to make you uncomfortable or anything." She paused. "But I really want to kiss you."

He leaned his head back against the couch and groaned. "Ivy, baby." His voice was thick. "You can do any damn thing you want to me. I'm okay with it all. I don't want to freak you out or anything though. I'm a big guy." She'd more than noticed. "I don't want you to feel threatened if I kiss you back, so I'll just sit here and let you take charge, okay?"

"You mean you'll take it like a man?"

He looked down at her and narrowed his eyes. "You think this is funny, huh?" He looked amused as well. "Well, do your best, hotshot."

She hiked her skirt up so she could straddle his lap. She stood on her knees, now slightly taller than Sam. She took his face in her hands, holding him while she stared into his eyes. "You're so smooth." She stroked his clean-shaven cheeks. "So pretty."

He flushed. "That would be you, not me."

She shook her head. "No. It's you." She closed her eyes and leaned closer, fanning her breath across his lips. One thing Ivy knew she could do well—kiss. She heard Sam's breath hitch, felt him shudder as her lips lightly brushed his, and let herself go as she flowed into a kiss that showed him just how she felt about him.

Tender, affectionate, caring. She learned his mouth, what he liked and didn't like. And Sam, bless him, seemed to like it all. He was breathing hard, sitting rock still, letting her touch him with no more than her mouth.

Her breasts ached. She'd drenched her panties, and she wanted nothing more than to feel him deep inside her. He'd fit her so well, that huge erection doing her a world of good. But she wanted this to be for Sam, the unselfish lover, the giving friend, the caring protector of the innocent who could swear like a sailor and take a man out with one punch.

She leaned into him, trailing her lips to his cheek, then his neck.

He let out a moan. "Damn, girl."

Ivy smiled as she kissed his tattoos. "Your ink is amazing. I want to kiss every bit of it."

"Yeah, yeah, you do that," he said, hoarse and as tense as steel.

"You okay with this?"

"Ivy, shut up and kiss me again," he growled.

She gave a soft laugh and let herself lean into him. Moving her breasts into his chest while she kissed her way to his ear, she whispered, "Can I touch you too? Would that be okay?" She nipped his earlobe, and he jerked into her, bumping that thick cock, sadly encased in jeans, against her belly.

"Shit yeah. Anything you fuckin' want."

Ivy smiled and returned to kissing him, easing her tongue past his lips to duel with his. She stroked in and out, then teased the roof of his mouth, his teeth.

He pushed forward a time or two, then pulled back, barely breathing. She leaned back and stroked his chest, watching when his eyes opened. The brilliant blue in his blue-gray eyes had been smothered under a heady silver as he stared at her. And the heat in that look scorched her. She had to touch him, to see.

"Can you take off your shirt for me?"

His eyes widened, but he didn't speak. With hands that shook, he removed his shirt.

She gaped, amazed at such grace and beauty in the ink over such glorious muscle. "I have to touch."

"Fuck yeah," he whispered, leaned his head back once more, and closed his eyes.

Feeling such freedom, she ran her hands over his chest, in awe of the colorful flowers and skulls, the small phoenix rising from a fire. Vines and what looked like barbed wire twisted in patterns that framed small sections of Sam's pectorals. A hellhound with sweet eyes and a grin stared at her, right next to a grim reaper with vengeance blazing on his fiery scythe.

She traced every picture, first with her hands, then with her lips.

When she kissed that first skull, he flinched. "You okay?"

"Jesus." He said no more, but she felt a hand on her head, urging her to continue.

She moved her lips across his chest, amazed at her temerity, in awe of Sam's control. He didn't press her. He'd clenched his hand in her hair once, then quickly removed it. She saw it now clutching the couch cushion.

But the one thing Sam couldn't control—his jerking hips. He continued to thrust toward her as she kissed him, and she loved his reaction. Needing him on the edge, she moved her mouth to his nipple and lingered, licking the small bud.

"*Fuck me*. Damn." Sam continued to swear in whispers while she drew on his nipple, then did the same to the other. All the while she continued to touch him, enthralled with his tight abs.

She leaned back and saw his belly clenching, the rippled six-pack daring her to go lower.

"How far down do your tattoos go, Sam?" she asked softly.

He just moaned and raised his hips, showing off that massive cock molded by his jeans.

"You said I can touch you, right?"

"Yeah, don't stop. Just keep petting me, baby." He blinked at her once, then shut his eyes and groaned. "I'm gonna sit…right…here." He shook, then sat unmoving, breathing hard.

"God, you're gorgeous." She stroked him from his chest to his belly button, never having been so close to perfection before. Then, because she figured the poor man had suffered enough, and her underwear would never be salvaged if she kept stringing this out, she unsnapped his jeans.

He started, his eyes remaining closed.

"You still okay?"

He swallowed. "Yeah."

Barely a whisper, but he'd given consent. She smiled, pleased with herself. Ivy continued to unbutton his jeans, not an easy task considering the size of his erection. "I just want to relieve what has to be uncomfortable for you. Sorry."

He gave a harsh laugh and groaned again. "Don't ever be sorry for this. Oh, that's it."

She parted his fly and stared down at his underwear clinging to the thick, broad head and long shaft of his cock. A large wet spot stuck to his cockhead, and she had an urge to lean down and kiss him. But that might be a little too much for Ivy just yet.

So she eased her hand over him, underwear and all, and got his throaty plea for her to continue.

She stroked him a few more times, but she needed to feel him in her hand. To palpate that glorious muscle, her inner kinky massage therapist said. Ivy grinned, wondering if Sam would ever play the part of a client in bed; she was curious that, for all her talk of professionalism, she wanted to try that as soon as possible in private.

She eased her hand under his underwear and slid it over his wet shaft.

"*Shit*. Easy. I'm so close." He wouldn't look at her, keeping his eyes clenched tight, his hands gripping the couch like a lifeline.

"So pretty," she whispered and gripped him, amazed at his size. Then she pumped him, slowly, up and down, watching him take his pleasure. It was the most amazing thing.

"Fuck. I'm gonna come. So hard, all over your hand," he moaned.

"Do it. Let me see you, Sam. Come for me." She put her other hand between his legs to graze his balls and pumped him again, faster this time.

He jerked in her hold, his body so tense he felt as if he'd break. She teetered on that precarious ledge with him, so wet and needy, so consumed with his climax. "All for me," she whispered and squeezed.

Sam shouted and bucked up off the couch, his orgasm wild. He made a mess of his underwear, as well as her hand, his release not quick or short, but beautifully long and drawn out.

When he finally ceased, she started to release her hold on him, already missing the heartbeat pulsing beneath her fingers. But he trapped her hand around him and drew her closer.

"Kiss me," he rasped, "right now."

She leaned closer and moaned as he thanked her with a kiss. His mouth commanded, showing her how much he'd held back while he'd let her play. When she started to feel dizzy, he let her go and stared up at her.

"Best fucking orgasm I've ever had in my entire life." He flexed in her hand. "You… I just… Damn, Ivy. Just damn."

This time he let her release him, and she staggered to her feet, needing to clean herself up. She took her time walking down the hall to the bathroom, not wanting him to see her trembling, nervous and excited and scared at how much he'd impacted her.

She washed her hands and did her best to clean herself and her panties. The excitement remained, but now a sense of self-consciousness was there as well. He'd said she could touch him, but she'd done a lot more than that. Still, she refused to be ashamed of what she'd done. She'd owed him that bliss, and she now had a memory that would never fade. Sam coming—a true thing of beauty.

She returned to find him pacing in front of the couch, his clothing set to rights, his eyes a little wild.

"Ivy?"

She gave him a smile, forcing herself to pretend this was totally normal, that jacking him off hadn't changed something inside her forever. Like she did this all the time. She stopped herself from giving in to uncontrollable, nervous laughter.

"You okay?" she asked him.

He strode to her, lifted her chin, and kissed her. So light it almost wasn't there. "*Thank you.*" He gifted her with a true smile, delight in his eyes.

She relaxed completely. "You're welcome."

He continued to watch her, looking over her hair, her eyes, her face and mouth. "Thank you." He kissed her again. "Thank you." And again. Then he hugged her so tight she squeaked. "Thank you *so fucking much.*"

She started laughing once he'd stopped squeezing so tight. "I hope that felt as good for you as it did for me."

"No way possible. I saw heaven, baby. And it was all you."

She blushed and tried to make light of it. "Aw, I bet you say that to all the girls."

His humor faded, and he stroked her cheek. "No, Ivy. I don't. You are so damn beautiful. So giving." He sighed. "Sorry, gotta do it again." He kissed her, this time deeper than before. He pulled back with a groan. "We're sharing Cookie."

It took a moment to decipher that. "Ah, yes."

"So we'd better get used to spending a lot of time together. Like tomorrow night."

She blinked. "Are you asking me out on a date, Sam Hamilton?"

"I figure I have to."

"Oh?"

"Because if I don't, I'll just sit at home jacking off, remembering how you touched me. Held me. Fuck me sideways, Ivy. I'm still a little light-headed. You are so good with those hands." He leaned close and rested his forehead against hers. "Can I tell you something?"

She closed her eyes, wanting to say yes to anything he asked.

"I want to fuck you so bad it's killing me." He pulled back and stared down at her, all intensity and sexual fury. "I want to bury myself inside you. Take you until you scream and beg for more. I want to eat you out. Want that pussy gloving me while I ride you into multiple orgasms. And I want it so bad, it's all I can do to let you go home tonight. 'Cause I'm so freaked out I'm gonna scare you, and that can't happen. *Ever*."

She blinked at him, seeing the worry and the need and the confusion she felt too. "Sam, I'm not scared of you."

"Maybe you should be, Ivy. *I'm* scared of me. Scared that what I'm feeling isn't normal. I mean, I want you so bad I'm shaking." He lifted a hand, and to her astonishment, it wasn't steady.

Then seeing the worry on his face, she lifted her hand. "Yeah, well so am I." She showed him her trembling palm. "You were so open when you came. So gorgeous. Heck, all of you is a work of art." She let out a breath. "I just hope I can keep up. I feel like I'm out of your league."

He barked a laugh. "Are you fuckin' kidding me? I'm not good enough to lick your boots. The fact you came home with me tonight was more than I deserved."

They watched each other, each measuring expressions and words not said. Ivy couldn't contain her gladness with the situation. He didn't think he was good enough for her when she thought the exact same thing about him. They really were a lot alike.

"Um, not to nitpick," she said, trying not to sound as happy as she felt, "but that boot-licking comment. That's not a turn-on for you, is it? Because that might be a deal breaker."

His intense stare eased into an out-and-out laugh. He laughed so hard he cried, and she laughed right along with him. "Jesus, Ivy. No, I'm not into licking your boots. No foot fetishes here." He chuckled some more. "But I'm curious as to what else you like and don't like. I think we have a lot in common, besides you digging that shitty Buckaroo Banzai movie."

He'd remembered.

She grinned. "That's right. We both like loincloths."

"For you, I'd wear one. Anytime. But only if you let me return tonight's favor."

"Actually, that was me returning it to you. From before." She'd be only too happy to have him do her again. Preferably sooner than later, but she didn't want to come off as easy. Well, more than she already had. "Remember, Sam, last time you left my place before you were satisfied."

"Baby, if I was any more satisfied right now I'd be dead." He pulled her in close for another hug and kiss before leaning his head back to see her. "I like you a lot. Now that we're sharing the dog, I think we should keep seeing each other. For Cookie's sake," he teased, yet his gaze seemed deeper than his words.

"For Cookie's sake," she pledged and made a cross over her heart, then his. "So do you want to go out tomorrow night?"

"Hell yeah. How about we hang at your place, though? I've been told my room's a little messy."

"A little," she grumbled, then laughed when he squeezed her tighter as a warning. She cupped his cheeks again, and he closed his eyes in pleasure. Sam liked a caring touch. She planned on putting that info to good use, hopefully in the near future. "I take it you want me to cook for you?"

"Unless you want hot dogs or ramen. I'm good with those."

She grimaced. "Ah, no. How do steaks and baked potatoes sound?"

"Perfect." He beamed. "I'll bring the food. You cook it."

"That's okay. I can—"

"You cook; I pay. That's the deal." He tried to stare her down, using his intimidating presence.

To her surprise, Ivy didn't feel anything but affection for the big bruiser. "Yeah, yeah. Fine. But I'm getting the ingredients for the salad and the dessert."

He nodded. "Cool. But I'm not a fan of cucumbers."

"Oh. Okay."

"I mean, if you wanted to use them for something else, sure. But not to eat." The sparkle in his eyes should have warned her.

"Use for something else? What, like an eye mask?"

He bit his lip. "Ah, yeah. For that."

So he hadn't meant an eye mask. What else would she use a cucumber for? The wicked look on his face made her realize her stupidity seconds later. "Oh, you." She deliberately looked at the bulge in his jeans. "So you'd rather I used a cucumber?" Where naughty Ivy had been hiding, Ivy had no idea. But Sam seemed to love that side of her.

He gave her a smile. "You're not so sweet. Hot damn. I hit the mother lode." He gave her a kiss that heated her up a little too much. Then he pulled back and adjusted himself right in front of her. "Fuck. Sorry. You get to me, Ivy. It's like I can't help myself."

"Good. I feel the same way."

He nodded, grabbed her by the arm, then dragged her to the door. "Exactly. Now unless you want to be fucked up against the back of the door, condom or no condom, I think you'd better get your fine ass in the car."

She didn't argue, though she wanted to. Because the thought of having sex with Sam was a little too tempting just now.

They drove back to her home in silence. After Sam walked her inside, checked on Cookie, then kissed her senseless once more, he left without a word.

Moments later, he sent her a text.

Ivy smiled and got ready for bed. Six o'clock tomorrow night, she had a date with the most intriguing man she'd ever met. She dreamed about him and his smile. And woke up to Cookie whining at four in the morning, because she'd forgotten to walk him last night.

Nothing like waking to a dog mess to clear sensual cobwebs from the brain.

Chapter 10

SAM COULDN'T GET HIS HEAD OUT OF THE CLOUDS Saturday morning. Even Eileen dragging his ass with her on a shopping trip couldn't stem his utter pleasure with the world.

"Sam, what's gotten into you?" Eileen asked as she stared at him.

Foley's mother was hot. Like, MILF hot, not that Sam had ever seen her as anything but a mom figure. She had dark hair and gray eyes, like Foley. But her petite build and curvy figure, kept in shape by daily exercise and good nutrition, had her looking years younger than fifty-three.

Unlike Louise Hamilton, Eileen loved her own son. She always had time for him, supported him, and bragged about him to everyone who would listen. The same as she'd done for Sam for the past twenty years. She cared, and he'd move heaven and earth to see her happy and safe.

"I'm good," he said, trying to clear Ivy out of his mind.

"You're not on drugs, are you?" She yanked him down by the ear and stared into his eyes.

"Ow, damn it." But he kept immobile so she could look her fill. "Happy now?"

"You're not focused. You barely ate two pancakes this morning." With Foley out with Cyn, Sam had been left to Eileen's maternal devices. Woman was always trying to feed him. Normally he loved it because, as he'd told Ivy, he couldn't cook worth a damn. But today he had little appetite, filled with memories of a sexy blond.

"I wasn't hungry."

"Ha. Not hungry." Eileen let him go and wiped her hands together. "It's a girl, isn't it?"

He had no intention of sharing with Eileen, not when he was still trying to wrap his mind around his feelings. Being with Ivy had made him feel…something. Not just happy or sexually replete, though God knew she'd cleaned his clock. She made him feel like he could be more than just Sam Hamilton. Like he mattered.

She made him feel clean.

"Yep, it's a girl," Eileen said when he didn't answer. She glanced around her at the shoppers milling downtown. Then she spied the store he'd been dreading. "There we are." Sephora, his personal hell. Right across from Westlake Center, the bowels of the pit.

He groaned. "Shouldn't you be with Cyn or Jan for this trip?" Jan, her fiancé's pregnant daughter.

"Jan just had the baby, so no."

"No kidding?" He liked Jan and her husband, Noel. Hell, he liked Jacob too, though Foley was keeping an eye on the guy soon to be his stepdaddy. The thought still made Sam want to laugh.

"Yes. The baby's so cute, Sam. You should see her."

"Oh man, a girl. That's cool. Jan's okay?"

"Jan is just fine. Noel's a proud dad, and Jacob keeps taking pictures and showing them off." She smiled. "He's so proud of his family." She linked her arm through Sam's and tugged him with her toward the makeup store. "So when do you think Foley is going to marry Cyn and give me grandchildren to spoil?"

"Normally I'd tell you I can't snitch on my bro, but if it'll get you off my back, I'm game."

"I promise." Eileen's eyes glowed. "Well? What's the 411?"

"Have I told you I love when you sound all hip, like the kids these days?"

She smacked him, barely a tap. "Tell me, damn it."

He sighed. They'd entered the store. It was huge, and as they moved around, he saw maybe three guys. Two of them wore makeup themselves and seemed to be having the times of their lives. The other guy looked miserable as his girlfriend or wife dragged him around.

They made eye contact and gave each other commiserating nods of sympathy.

"Foley plans to ask Cyn to marry him pretty soon."

"I *knew* it." Eileen hunkered in front of a display, checking out various tubes of mascara. They all looked the same to him, but the two chicks who rushed over to help her didn't think so. He tried to pretend they weren't giving him the eye. In fact, a lot of women in the place had looked him over and apparently liked what they saw.

He'd love to tell them he was taken. What would Ivy think of him getting eye fucked in the store? Would she care? He had a feeling she might, and that amused the hell out of him. When was the last time a woman had cared about another woman wanting him? Try never.

All those lingering kisses Ivy had given him had been real. Not just sexual, but emotionally charged. He didn't feel like a pussy for thinking it either. Because to

Ivy, touch meant something special. She did it for work to help people. But those kisses she'd planted on his mouth, his chest, his nipples—they'd meant something else. Something intimate. Just for him.

"Oh my God, you're smiling. Are you okay?"

He coughed to cover a laugh. "Yeah, fine," he growled. "Can we go? I'm getting hives."

The saleswomen next to them tittered, and Eileen rolled her eyes. She ignored him in favor of asking the salespeople a few more questions about brands and prices.

On the other side of him, a dark-haired honey with large breasts leaned close. "Hey, handsome. You're blocking the Mac."

A glance showed a sign above a display saying Mac. Weird but okay.

"Sorry."

"No problem." She smiled, showing a cute gap between her teeth. "You busy tonight?" She nodded to Eileen. "That's not your date, is it?"

"Nah, my mom."

She softened. "Oh, that's so sweet. I'm gonna be downtown if you're interested in some company." Before he could say no, she wrote a number on the back of his hand with the sample stick she'd taken from the Mac display. "Call me. If tonight won't work, another time, maybe."

He watched her sashay to the counter to pay.

"Sam, really? What would your girlfriend think?" Eileen huffed.

"Hey, I didn't ask for her number. I'm trying to be fuckin' polite," he said through gritted teeth and accepted the wipe the girl next to Eileen handed him.

The saleswoman—her name tag read *Ashlee*—grinned. "Sorry about that. We don't get too many handsome men in the store. I think we scare them away."

Her friend laughed.

"Yeah, I get that."

Ashlee took the wipe from him. "I'll throw that away for you. If you come back to get your mom anything in the future, ask for me." She wrote something down on a business card and handed it to him.

"They don't get paid on commission, but they do get compensated," Eileen explained.

One of the women started talking about gratis, and he zoned out.

An interminable twenty minutes later, after they'd left the store and headed toward Westlake Center, he handed the card to Eileen. It wouldn't do for Ivy to find it and think he was cheating on her before they'd even gotten started.

She turned it over and chuckled. "Another one, Sam?"

"What?"

She showed him Ashlee's card. Scrawled on the back had been a cell number and, above it, a heart and "Call me."

He shrugged. "It's the tats. They all want a bad boy until they get one." He smiled, showing a lot of teeth.

Eileen gave a mock cringe. "Nicely scary. Now tell me about this girlfriend of yours, and I might—*might*—delay my shopping excursion and enjoy a latte instead."

He held her bags in one hand and directed her to a local coffee shop with the other.

Once settled down with caffeine and a bunch of pastries, he found himself under the gun.

"I'm waiting." She blew on her coffee and took a sip. "Is she pretty?"

Sam bit into his cinnamon roll and said, with his mouth filled to annoy Eileen, "No, she's a hag. But she has big breasts and a fat ass, so it's all good."

Next to them, an older man scowled while his teen-age companion grinned. "See, Grandpa? Thick is in, man. Told you."

The old man made them switch seats.

Eileen sighed. She tapped her long nails on the table, rolling them from pinkie to thumb. The woman was a real estate guru. She had the patience of Job between waiting on finicky clients and having raised Foley and Sam.

Sam swallowed his sugar and washed it down with black coffee. "Ah. Better."

"Try again."

He would have liked to give her the brush off, but he loved Eileen. She never judged, never threw him back to the mess that was his life unless he put himself there. Hell, she'd tried her best to get him to come live with them when he'd been younger, but his mother would never have gone for that—God forbid he find love and happiness away from Louise and her crap-hole of an existence. Yet he'd still spent as much time as he could at Eileen's or with Foley.

"Jeez, Eileen. What do you want me to say?"

"I want you to tell me that Ivy Stephens is exactly what she seems—a pretty blond massage therapist with eyes for my boy."

His eyes narrowed. "Foley has a big mouth."

Eileen gave a satisfied smile. "Yes, he does. And so does Cyn."

Sam groaned. "Fine. What do you want to know? Ivy's hot. She's smaller than me, but most women are. She's probably a little taller than you. Works out because of her job. She's sweet and nice. Makes me laugh. And she took in a stray puppy I was looking after." He told her all about seeing Ivy rescue Cookie, about her not freaking out at Ray's or at Willie's, but skipped over the sexual bits, ending with, "We have something between us. I think she likes me, and I know I like her."

"Of course she likes you." Eileen studied him over the brim of her cup. "Did you not just get hit on by at least two women in Sephora?"

"Yeah, but that's different. That's just for a quickie." Only with Eileen and Foley could he be blunt yet still feel okay talking about personal stuff.

"Sam, you're too handsome for your own good. And thickheaded too. You have more to offer than"—she lowered her voice—"just sex. Sure, those ladies liked the look of you, but it's what's inside that has them coming back. What's different about Ivy? You liked Shaya before she left. And Megan before that."

"Yeah, but they were like me. Kind of rough. We all wanted something simple. Ivy's different. She's kind."

"*You're* kind." Eileen looked angry. "What's wrong with you?"

"Easy, Mama Bear." He held up his hands. "I'm not saying there's anything wrong with me." *There's so damn much wrong it's not funny.* "I'm just saying she's not my usual type."

Eileen sat back and took a bite of a raspberry Danish. "You're saying she's not a stripper, hooker, or party girl?"

He flushed. "Um, yeah."

"*Finally*. Thank God. A good girl." Eileen leaned close and poked him in the chest. "Don't be fooled though, Sam. Good girls can be just as bitchy as worldly ones."

"She's not like that."

"So what is she like?"

"Don't you want to talk about your wedding instead?" She seemed a little too interested in Ivy for his peace of mind. Damn Foley and his flapping lips.

"I'd rather be shopping for centerpieces for my tables. Flowers and linens, maybe hitting some retailers. But since you look terrified at the prospect, I'd rather talk about Ivy."

"Fine. Sure. Whatever you say." A fate worse than death. He still didn't know why Jacob wasn't out escorting his future missus around town. But whatever. He took a huge sip of coffee. "You'd have to meet her to get what I'm saying."

"Oh, I intend to."

He blinked. "Ah, well, we've only been seeing each other recently." Like, last night, recently. "We just met, really."

"How lovely for you both." Eileen smiled. "Now cut the shit. What's her deal? What makes her so special that I can see you fogging over just thinking about her?"

"I can't explain it."

"Try."

"Such a hard-ass," he muttered, trying not to smile. "Ivy is…unique. She makes me feel good. I know she likes my looks." Both a blessing and a curse he'd been born with. "But she treats me right. Like a person who matters." He stroked his cheek, still feeling her hands cupping him. "She's nice to me, and I feel like I'm good when I'm with her." He shrugged. "I don't know. It sounds stupid. I just feel more with her."

Eileen reached across the table and clasped his hand. "Honey, I get you. I really do. And if this Ivy makes you feel good, then keep her for however long you feel good."

How to tell Eileen he wanted to keep Ivy forever? As impossible as the idea was, because sure as shit Ivy would grow tired of him or he'd do something to put her off, he wished he could have her by his side always. Feeling accepted, liked.

He wasn't holding out for love. Except for Eileen and Foley, he'd never had that. And he didn't think he ever would. But saying it was like asking to be pitied. Bad enough the Sanderses both thought him some lame ass who would break down without them around to pick up the pieces of his sorry life.

Probably true, but it hurt to think himself the weak link in the chain.

"Good advice, thanks."

"And when have you boys ever taken my advice?"

"We always listen to you." He frowned. "Why? What did Foley do? Want me to pound him for you?"

She laughed and patted his hand. "That's my boy. No, no. Foley is fine. But seeing Jacob's joy with Rowena, his granddaughter, makes me want some of my own. I know she'll call me 'Grandma,' but I want some little ones from my own boys." She raised a brow. "I know it's probably too soon, but what about you?"

He shook his head. "No way. Never having kids. I

told you that before. I still mean it." Not with his bad blood. No way in hell would he do that to a kid.

She sighed. "Sam, you are the best man I know, next to Foley and Jacob, of course. When you find the right girl, it'll work out. Just remember this for my big I-told-you-so moment later."

"Yeah?" He smirked, sensing the need to get out bigger guns. She was starting to make the backs of his eyes burn with all that best-man and lovey shit. "Well, how about this? Foley is trying to knock Cyn up. Thinks she might already be pregnant."

Eileen gaped. "Get out."

"Nope. Not that you heard that from me. He said she was being bitchier than usual."

"That's not nice." She frowned.

"Well, it was more like something about her being more hormonal than usual. But he's hoping she's pregnant, and according to him, she wants it too. They both want kids, and they plan on getting married soon. Like maybe in a couple months."

"I'm so happy right now." She dabbed the corners of her eyes. "I just need to get you down the aisle, and we're perfect."

"Don't you mean *you* down the aisle? Where the hell is Jacob in all this?" Sam tensed, worrying all over again that maybe Eileen hadn't told him the whole truth. "Tell me. Did he do something? Is that why you're so emotional all the time? And why we never see you guys together anymore? Want me to kick his ass?"

~~~

Eileen bit back a sigh. Sam's answer to everything

seemed to be an ass kicking. "No, no. He's fine. And handsome and charming. And apparently smart, because he's been leaving me to do this wedding any way I see fit."

"Yeah?"

She smiled at Sam's distrust. Though he and Foley both claimed to like Jacob, they were protective. Always had been. Foley had been the man of the house after his father passed when he was just four. Then, at eleven, he'd brought Sam home. A wounded, scrappy little brat who'd melted her heart with one look into his soulful eyes.

She'd done her best to keep him, but Sam's bitch of a mother had a stranglehold on her boy. Anytime Sam found happiness, Louise did her best to yank him back, tethering him to an emotionally abusive woman with her own mental issues. Eileen had her theories on why Louise was the way she was, but she'd been too worried about Sam to share them. And as he'd aged, that concern had never truly faded.

Foley confided in her that whenever Louise beckoned, Sam would go. And he'd come back a shell of himself for days, sometimes weeks, on end. Eileen hoped that Sam had become more confident and sure of himself after having been part of the Sanders family for so long. But she still caught remnants of the hurt, scared little boy inside the giant of a man.

All the ink and muscle and toughness couldn't hide the fact that Sam never quite thought of himself as loveable. If this Ivy woman could put stars in his eyes, she was all for it. Especially since both Cyn and Foley had confided they liked her.

Yet everyone worried that if things with Ivy, which were so new to begin with, went south, Sam might turn self-destructive. Those fights he used to get into as a boy had turned into something illegal he did as a man. Sam and Foley didn't think she knew about those. But Eileen had eyes, not to mention ears. She'd seen the bruises, and she'd heard from her friend Liam Webster that her boy Sam had better get his head out of his ass.

It appeared he might be doing that with Ivy. She could only hope.

"Sam, bring Ivy to dinner next week. Wednesday night."

"On the island?"

She nodded. She'd moved in with Jacob in his Bainbridge Island residence, and she'd never been happier. Well, once the wedding was over, she'd be tickled pink. But until then, she stressed over caterers and flowers and centerpieces.

"Uh, I guess."

"Don't guess," she snapped, stuck on how much she still had to do before her big day…in another two months! "I'm sorry, honey. I can't do this."

"Eileen?" He looked worried.

"I can't sit here and pretend I don't have shit to do. I don't care how much it hurts. We're going to Lela's and checking out her linens. I reserved them a while ago, but I need to make sure."

He groaned and stuffed half a sweet roll into his mouth.

"Good boy. Chew it all up. Get sugared and caffeinated, because it's going to be a long day. Oh, and don't forget, you have to wear a suit to the wedding. Foley too, so don't think I'm singling you out. But I heard you have to wear one to Del's wedding coming up. Just think. One suit for two weddings." She smiled. "Would you like us to shop for you when we're done with the tables?"

"Hell no. I'll do it on my own."

"Sure thing, honey. Now grab my bags and your coffee, and prepare to get crazy."

"With tablecloths and wedding shit? Right."

"Onward, soldier. Move that ass." Eileen grinned. Time to show her boy what a mother could really do when she had her mind set. "And don't forget that invitation for Ivy. I'm not kidding."

"Yeah, yeah." Like a good boy, he grabbed her bags, helped her to her feet, then followed her for the rest of the morning and into the afternoon, bitching all the way.

———⁓⁓⁓———

"You don't know, Ivy. It was like I was in hell," Sam whined as he stood next to her in her tiny kitchen, drinking a beer.

He saw her trying to hide a grin and continued to complain.

"I mean, there are a million freakin' shades of blue. Cobalt, aqua, navy, cyan. Oh, and then there's denim, azure, indigo. And don't get me started on the color wheel. Christ." He held the bottle to his forehead. "I'm getting a migraine just remembering the smell of stale fabric and cheap perfume—not Eileen, but that old biddy Lela, being all pushy about Eileen's choices."

Ivy pressed her lips together and nodded.

He sighed. "Go ahead. You know you want to laugh."

"I really do."

"Yeah? Well, I don't think you'll find it so funny when you're helping me find a suit for the weddings coming up. I've been ordered to dress up. Apparently a T-shirt that looks like a tux isn't considered fancy enough."

She laughed. "God no. I'm happy to go shopping with you. I don't mind getting clothes."

"And here I thought we had a lot in common." Watching her work, the graceful way her hands held a knife, pet a dog, or handed him a beer, was like seeing poetry in motion.

"We do," she agreed. "Neither of us tolerates BS."

"You mean bullshit?" he said for effect, getting hard at the sight of her pursed lips. "Isn't that what you mean, Miss Priss?"

"Yes, it is." She frowned at him. "Potty mouth."

He grinned. Around Ivy, he had a lot to smile about. "Oh, and we're invited to dinner Wednesday night on Bainbridge Island. Eileen insisted. Can you make it?"

She paused slicing potatoes. Instead of baking them whole, she was doing something sophisticated with slicing and spicing them up. His mouth watered. Nothing like a home-cooked meal prepared by his own hot chick to make a guy's day.

"Um, I guess so." She swallowed. "You want me to meet your mom already? Isn't that a little soon?" she teased, but he caught a hint of nerves he totally understood.

"First off, Eileen's not my biological mom. I mean, she's been like a mom, and I love her, but she's Foley's mom."

"What about yours?" she asked.

He didn't want to think about Louise. Not now, when

he was happy. "Ah, we don't get along much." She hated him, he loved her in spite of himself, and he knew nothing he ever did for her would be good enough. "Eileen," he said to dispel the ghosts of a past that continued to haunt him, "has looked after my sorry butt since the sixth grade. I never lived with her full-time or anything. But she helped with a lot of stuff I couldn't get at home."

Hopefully Ivy would let that be enough of an explanation. Because even thinking about the shit that was his early life took him down a very dark memory lane.

"And anyway, she loves cooking for me and Foley and our friends. Guy or girl, she's just happy we're not in jail and being social. Like, social without beating people up, social." Hmm. Maybe he'd overshared because Ivy just stared at him.

Then she slowly nodded. "You haven't beaten me up yet, so I guess you're making progress."

He flushed. "Shit. I would never... I mean, I don't hit girls. And I'd never *ever* hurt you. Anyone who even thinks of giving you a rough time has to go through me."

She gave a small smile. "Good to know. Eileen sounds wonderful. Dinner will be fine. My Thursday is lighter than I was expecting anyway, because I checked my schedule yesterday. I have a lot of clients on Friday though, so it all balances out." She finished with the potatoes, then put them in the oven. As she started on the salad, she asked, "What's she like?"

"Eileen? She's a trip. Beautiful woman, inside and out. Looks more like Foley's older sister than mother. Tell her that. She'll love you forever."

Ivy grinned.

"She's a sweetheart. Back before she met Jacob, she

went through a couple of bozos who tried to take advantage of her. Foley and me, we put a stop to that."

"I'll bet you did," Ivy said wryly.

"Hey, Foley never laid a hand on them."

"That's because you did, am I right?"

She read him so well. For all that they'd pretty much recently met, he knew her too. Weird and not a little troubling. He didn't mind her knowing surface details, but it would kill him if she ever learned the bad stuff, the Louise stuff.

"You're a little right." He shrugged. "Hey, when do I put the meat in?"

"*You* do nothing." She nudged him toward her dining table, now a full oval because she'd flipped the leaves up. "Your job is to drink beer and talk to me."

"I can do that."

"Good." She darted a look at him, then turned back to the lettuce. She wore jeans and a soft-looking sweatshirt that slid off her shoulder time and again. Her hair had been tied up in a loose ponytail, wisps of bangs and a few strays kissing her face and neck, the way he wanted to.

Barking took his attention for a second, and he stared down at Cookie, gripping a pig ear in his mouth. "You're welcome," he said to the dog, who wagged his tail so hard Sam feared the dog's butt would fall off. "I think he likes it."

"You're spoiling him." But she smiled. "You'll make a good dad someday, but you're going to have to watch it or your kids will be monsters."

She had the right of it in one. "Yeah." He cleared his throat. "So there's something I think I need to say."

She slowed down her lettuce ripping. "What's that, Sam?"

"I'm not a good guy for playing games."

She frowned. "I wasn't playing any."

"No, not you. Me. Hell. I'm not saying this right." He sounded like an idiot, and she looked confused. But he'd been practicing, needing to voice his concerns. "I just... after last night, I can't think about your hands without getting hard."

Her cheeks turned pink. "Oh."

"Yeah, oh. I've been happier than shit all damn day."

A softer "oh," this one with a smile.

"But I need you to know that I'm not just here for sex. I mean, I wouldn't say no, but you have to understand we'll only do something if you want to. I would never force you to do anything."

"I know that, Sam." She gave him a tender look. "I trust you."

His heart felt so damn full when she gave him that look. That trust. "Good." He coughed to clear his throat. "I wanted you to know that I like talking to you. Being with you. We don't have to do anything for me to be happy." So fucking weird he meant that.

"What if I want to?"

"Well, then. That's different."

"I mean," she continued, "I like just being with you too. I like talking to you. You have a dry sense of humor, and you make me laugh."

"I do?" He thought he was funny, and he could normally get a chuckle or two out of Eileen or Foley, but the guys at the garage tended to dismiss him as a sarcastic bastard. Which he was, but not all the time.

Other people ignored his sense of humor or shied away from him.

"Yes, you do." She nodded. "I also think you're amazingly good-looking. And I love your body."

"Huh." Just talking, she'd gotten him totally hard. She liked him. Damn it all, that felt good.

"But I don't want you to think I'm only after you because of your body. I want to spend time with you too. If that's okay." Now she seemed nervous. "I'm bad at relationships. I should probably warn you about that now. I can get too serious too fast. And I'm not all that sexual, I don't think."

He stared, amazed. "Seriously?"

"Well, it's been a long time for me. I might have been all sexy to you because I was in a dry spell."

"One you wanted, not because guys weren't into you."

She blushed. "That's true. But I was tired of dating and always having to take care of men."

"Good. I don't want to be taken care of." He got enough of that from Foley and Eileen. He liked it, but he also hated it. Hated being thought of as fragile. "I want to do for you."

Ivy relaxed. "You're so sweet." Again thinking him sweet and funny. She saw things in him he wanted to be. "But I don't need anything more than some laughter and conversation."

"Ivy, when's the last time a guy got you flowers before me?"

She shrugged. "I don't know. Max at the beginning of our relationship, maybe?"

"Or how about a guy taking you to dinner?"

"I did that a year ago."

"I mean, without expecting you to put out."

She sighed. "Again, Max. Maybe. Even then he wanted something from me."

"Well, here's the thing. You're sexy as hell. I want to fuck you, yeah. But I'm here, and we haven't screwed yet, and I'm not expecting you to." He loved that she smiled. "I'm here because I like you. No ulterior motive. No sex on the table or off, no gifts or rewards. Just being with you is good. Okay?"

"Okay." She used her shoulder to wipe some hair out of her eyes, and he crossed to help her, wanting his hands on her again. "You are the absolute best, you know that?"

He flushed, not comfortable with her praise. "Just being honest. Seriously, I still want you. But I… Us together is fun. Not complicated." Okay, that was a big fat lie. She confused the shit out of him, mostly because he'd never felt this way about a woman before. And especially not one he'd just met. "I need you to promise me something."

"Anything." Her green eyes seemed so wide, so deep.

Again, that trust. She killed him. "When you don't want something, you tell me *no*. No means no to me. Not some bullshit about really meaning yes. You get me?"

She nodded.

"I'm not into force. I mean, when—if—we get together, yeah, I like to be in charge. But that's only if you're good with what we're doing. I don't care if I'm two seconds from shooting my load. You say no, we stop." At least, he hoped he'd be able to stop. Anytime he got his hands on her, he felt lost to her taste, her touch. The woman drove him crazy, and she didn't seem to realize that. Or maybe she did now. He had come pretty hard for her last night.

"Thanks, Sam." She put down the veggies and gave him a hug. Then she drew his face down and kissed him.

Unlike the others, this kiss wasn't about passion. It was about faith, affection, care. To his surprise, the kiss hit him harder than anything they'd shared. When she let him go, he saw an odd look in her eyes.

"Ivy?"

She smiled and moved back to her lettuce. "Let me tell you about our puppy."

That "our" sounded way too appealing. Because with little effort, he imagined that *our* spreading to words like *house*, *family*, and *forever*.

And the shit just got real.

Chapter 11

SUNDAY AFTERNOON, IVY WALKED HAND IN HAND with Sam on a paved walkway along the beach. Cookie remained on a harness attached to a leash looped around her wrist, while she and Sam ate ice cream cones they'd grabbed before hitting the park. Seattle had a warm, sunny day on the books, and everyone seemed out and about, taking advantage of the weather.

He'd suggested Lincoln Park, and she loved the brisk wind, the tang of salt in the air, and the sun shining while Cookie investigated everything around him. He'd been doing better with a leash, though she noticed he had a tendency to want to jump when she held it. When Sam walked him, the puppy was completely docile.

"You know he's totally bossing you around," Sam said as he ate his cone of birthday cake ice cream.

"Probably because he's male, and men seem to want to boss me around lately." She arched her brow at him and licked her salted caramel before it could drip.

"You have no idea how much I wish I was an ice cream cone right now." He groaned. "I'm not looking at you until you finish that thing. Talk about cruel and unusual punishment."

"You want to talk punishment? Dealing with all your rules about food in your car, then listening to you complain about how I walk the dog. That's cruel and unusual, you big blockhead." She liked their bickering. It felt a little like Cyn and Foley's mock fighting.

Sam's eyes twinkled. "Is that right? You might want to hold him a little tighter," he said with a nod at Cookie.

"I've got this, thank you very—*Cookie!*" The puppy yanked her forward when he discovered a lab puppy coming closer. At twenty pounds and probably three to four months, he'd already become a handful. She could only imagine what he'd be like at sixty, then seventy pounds if she didn't get him under control now, when she still could. Her problem—she'd scold him, then look into his big, brown eyes and lose any sense of right and wrong to hugs and kisses.

Sam snorted. "Yeah, nice firm grip you have on our dog, there. Great discipline."

Our dog, he'd said. Every time he used *our* she felt like smiling. "I'll give you some discipline." She bit back a dopey grin as she reined in Cookie. "Come on, pup. Cookie, easy. Relax."

"I think the word you're looking for is *heel*," Mr. Helpful said as he continued munching on his ice cream.

"Would *you* like to take him for the walk?"

"No, no. You're doing a bang-up job."

She tried not to laugh, but Sam's condescension was too funny, mostly because he was so obvious about it. Max used to play passive-aggressive games, praising her out of one side of his mouth while insulting her out of the other. Sam didn't use subterfuge. If he thought her a bitch, he'd likely call her one. Fortunately, that hadn't happened yet. Not a fan of the b-word, she had no idea how she'd handle him if it came to that.

"You know, I want to strangle you and kiss you. Both at the same time."

He wiggled his brows. "Oh, kinky."

She chuckled and swung his hand in hers. "You wish."

"You're damn right I do."

Then why hadn't they done anything last night? The evening had been spent enjoying a meal together. The steaks and potato casserole had been cooked to perfection. The beer had been a great accompaniment, to her surprise. And the carrot cake had stayed moist, for once.

He'd devoured it all. They'd played a game of Jenga afterward, and she couldn't remember the last time she'd had so much fun. Cookie had been a doll, and they'd taken turns playing fetch with him until the poor little guy had run out of steam and conked out chewing on his pig ear. To cap off the evening, *Scanners* had been playing on TV, and they'd enjoyed telekinetics blowing heads up with possibly the worst special effects ever.

Totally a night to remember. Then Sam had turned his hot gaze on her. The moment had seemed frozen in time. A quick kiss and he'd been gone with a promise of a walk in the park the next day.

"Sam."

"Yeah?"

Another dog neared, and she took a firmer grip on Cookie this time.

"You're melting," he said with a nod at her cone.

"Crap. Cookie, heel." She used her ornery-patient therapist voice. To her pleased surprise, Cookie obeyed.

"Nice job." Sam nodded. He finished his ice cream.

"Here, give him to me while you eat that thing. It's so sad, the way you're dripping all over the place."

She handed Cookie's leash over. "How you can be so, and I quote, 'messy yet organized' at home, but a little bit of ice cream on my hands turns you into Mr. Clean?"

He sighed. "Here." He took her hand in his, then brought her finger to his mouth. She could only watch as he sucked her finger clean. The warmth of his mouth did funny things to her insides, turning her on in a big, big way.

"Oh." She swallowed.

"Yeah, *that's* why you need to keep that shit clean. Because if I put my mouth on you again, I might go down on you in public. In front of our poor dog. Then the little guy will be in therapy forever. You remember Mathmos and Pygar, don't you? Those dogs used to be normal before seeing Willie and Rupert swinging it up."

She cringed. "Don't remind me."

He grinned. "The cats were never normal though. Barbarella and Tyrant have always been evil."

A spear of sunlight landed on him just then, and he seemed to glow, a larger-than-life warrior.

And all mine.

"Hmm. What's that look?"

Her finger still tingling and her nipples now hard, she shivered. "Just thinking about last night. And what we could have been doing but didn't."

Instead of a frown or look of upset, Sam wore nothing but smug satisfaction.

"Something you wanted to say, Sam?"

"I told you. I'm trying to go slow. I want us to be friends."

"We are friends." She felt as if she were in an episode of the *Twilight Zone*, having *a man* put the brakes on their sexual relationship, not wanting to be viewed as a piece of meat. "But please, go on." Fascinating. Especially since he seemed…shy?

"I told you. I like you a lot. We can get together and have fun without it being about sex. I want you to know I respect you."

She looked around her.

"What?"

"I was just wondering if you were doing some kind of PSA about abstinence. Because trust me, it doesn't make the heart grow fonder." She snorted.

Sam blinked.

"Sam, you're a sweetheart. I believe you when you say you like and respect me. That still doesn't mean we can't get naked and sweaty." *Oh my gosh. Who* are *you speaking? Evil twin Ivy? Slutty Ivy?*

Honest Ivy, who was tired of being second best and not voicing her wants and needs. Screw that. It was a new era. There was no time limit on dating before having sex. And she could own her desire. She wanted him—and was proud of having a sex drive again. The dawn of Ivy Stephens, sexual princess. The She-Ra of nookie and her beastmaster's new queen.

Hmm. Maybe she should lay off the sci-fi for a while.

Sam stared at her as if she had three heads.

"What?"

"It's just…" He gaped. "I don't think I've ever been accused of playing hard to get. I'm trying to wrap my mind around it."

"Well, hurry up while you're doing that. Cookie is

circling that grass and getting ready to… *Ew*. He's definitely your dog now."

He huffed, muttered something about her being such a girl, then dragged a waste bag out of the small sack attached to the leash. After he cleaned Cookie's mess, he tossed the bag in a nearby receptacle.

She just stared at the hand he'd used to scoop poop. Granted, his hand had been protected by the bag the entire time he'd cleaned it up, but… She cringed when he tried to hold her hand again.

"Jesus. You're worse than Foley. Hold on." He dug into the small sack once more and pulled out a mini-bottle of hand sanitizer.

Only after he'd used the stuff did she accept the hand he held for her.

"You're such a wuss," he sneered.

"Thank you, Beastmaster." She grinned. "You've earned the title, you know. You mastered everything about Cookie. Even his poop."

"That's it. No more sci-fi for you."

"It fits. Your beast"—she pointed to Cookie, panting with his tongue out—"is quite the ferocious and cunning hunter."

They watched the puppy bark at a pinecone, then scoop it into his mouth.

"Yeah, he's a killer," Sam drawled. He yanked her forward and gave Cookie a gentle tug. "So since we're not having sex and being all friendly—"

"Who's fault is that?" She might have put a little too much snap in her answer, because he seemed far too amused.

"Easy there, Miss Frisky." He chuckled. "And don't

get all offended. I've been Mr. Horny since I met you."
That eased some of her concern that he thought her some
kind of nympho. "How about we talk? Tell me something about yourself I don't know."

"Like what?" Pleased Sam wanted to know more about
her, she debated what to tell him. Max had usually spent
his time talking about himself and what he wanted. As had
the few men after him. Sam seemed more interested in Ivy.
A nice but puzzling change. "Why do you want to know?"

"So distrustful." He sighed. "I told you already. I'm
trying to get to know you better."

"I like kissing." She watched for the telltale flush at
his cheeks, and seeing it, found pleasure in their conversation. *Ha. Take that, Mr. Horny.*

He cleared his throat. "How about some other details?
Like your family?"

She frowned. "What about them?" Was he trying to
ruin their good day?

"You haven't said much about them."

"You haven't said much about yours either."

"Good point. Look, I'll straight up tell you Louise
and I don't get along. Never have. I don't like to talk
about her. But I'll tell you anything you want to know
about Foley and Eileen." He studied her while they
walked. "If it hurts to talk about your family, just say so
and I won't pry. I hate that shit, people trying to make
you talk when you don't want to."

She raised a brow.

"And that's not what this is, you blond pain in my
ass," he muttered. "I'm not interrogating you. This is me
trying to show you I like more than your tits and ass."
His cheeks were *on fire*.

That was Sam—a man whose blunt honesty chipped away at her defenses. "Fine. It's not like it's a big secret." She dragged out her answer, testing to see if he really wanted to know or just wanted her to think he did. But he only waited while they continued their walk. "You asked for it."

"And…?"

She blew out a breath. "The sad truth is my parents always wanted a boy. When they had Ethan, life was perfect. But he got lonely, and they decided to give him a baby brother. Problem was, they got a baby sister instead. And in the Stephens household, women are tolerated because they make boys."

"Ouch."

She shrugged, trying to ignore the dull pain that never left. "It is what it is. Ethan was actually a pretty nice kid. I think he loved me when we were growing up." The only thing that had made life livable. Her parents had said and done all the right things in public, taking pride in their pretty little girl and her good grades and athletic prowess. But nothing Ivy did was ever enough to make them truly see her. And her mother had been the worst.

"Are you guys close now?"

She shook her head. "Growing up, Ethan felt sorry for the way my parents ignored me. Sometimes he'd pretend he wanted something that I wanted, just so I could have it." The memory still made her smile.

"Sounds like a good guy."

"He was. And then he met Cheryl." Ivy sighed. "Cheryl was pretty, smart. Head cheerleader and came from a good family. She and my brother fell in love. I was so happy for him. Until I realized Cheryl fit into my family better than I ever could. Like my parents, she focused everything on Ethan. I was the odd man out."

"That bites."

"Yeah." Depression settled in. Cookie trotted back to her side and kept trying to lick her hand. She bent down to stroke his furry head. "Ethan gave her whatever she wanted. And that happened to be a lot less of me. I kind of wandered away from home, and no one really missed me." She studied the water, seeing the waves come and go, that big, broad sound. Some things never changed. "They still don't. My parents got Cheryl and Ethan, the perfect family. Even better, I became an aunt to a baby boy three years ago. I wasn't invited to the birth or the christening."

"That's fucked up." He squeezed her hand.

"Yeah. I only know what goes on in their lives because my parents aren't tech savvy. I'm pretty sure they don't know how to unfriend me on Facebook or they would have." Sad but true. "You know what's worse? When Cheryl passed away from cancer soon after Greg was born, I was uninvited to the funeral."

He blinked at her. "That's for real? You can uninvite someone to a funeral?"

"I guess." She shrugged. "Not like I wanted to go. Cheryl was a real witch to me. But I felt bad for my brother and my nephew. Not that I've ever seen the baby outside of pictures online. My parents treat him like gold. That boy will never want for anything, which is a good thing. They're so keen on making sure Ethan recovers and Greg has a wonderful life that I might as well not exist."

"Man, what a bunch of pricks."

She nodded. "Total pricks. All of them."

Sam stopped her in her tracks, turned her to face him, and planted a smack on her lips. "That's for saying *prick* and meaning it. I knew you had it in you, babe." The goofy sense of pride on his face made her laugh.

Ivy suddenly felt better about her past. Her parents sucked. Her brother had turned into an ass, and she'd likely never see her nephew, who was being groomed to ignore her like the rest of her family. But with Sam by her side, her old life didn't seem to matter as much.

"You're a dork."

He let go of her hand to wrap his big arm around her shoulders. They continued along the walkway. "Louise, well, I don't talk about her. We'll just call her a prick too and leave it at that."

"Sounds good." Another thing she and Sam had in common—shitty parents. Or rather, parent. He'd never mentioned his dad. By the guarded way he now held himself, she figured the omission had been on purpose. "So what about Foley and Eileen?"

Sam subtly relaxed. "Now there's a pair. I told you they took me in when I was a kid. I was in sixth grade. I remember it to this day. I was mouthing off. Nothing unusual about that."

"Hard to imagine," she added.

"Hush. I'm telling my sob story now."

She chuckled.

"So these kids are all bigger than me. I didn't hit my growth spurt until high school. I'm this whiny little punk, insulting everyone. Especially the bullies. Hell, remembering my mouth, I would have picked on me back then too." She doubted that, but he continued, "So

I'm getting my tiny ass handed to me when Foley comes in. He was big for his age and had muscle when most guys were scrawny and covered in zits. Foley hates bullies. Always has." Sam didn't smile, but she saw his eyes light up, felt him ease even more beside her. "He decided to rescue me, invited me home to dinner even. Hell, I wasn't stupid. Free food?"

As he talked, she got the impression Sam hadn't been cared for by his mother at all. Because Sam's recollection of Eileen's warmth, of new clothes, food, and a heavenly shower told its own story. What sixth-grade boy loved being clean? One who didn't have the opportunity to bathe, most likely.

"Really? Pancakes is what it takes to get to you?"

"Well, pancakes and breasts." He wiggled his brows. "Not Eileen's, 'cause that's just gross. But yours, on the other hand…"

"My sympathy meter just took a nosedive." She watched Cookie continue to glance back at him, waiting for Sam to ease up on the leash. Like the puppy, Ivy felt caught in Sam's presence, wanting to please him, just to see him smile or hear him laugh. She tried to imagine him as a helpless little boy and stopped herself before she teared up. No one should ever treat innocence like that.

"So you're not feeling sorry for me at all?"

Nope. Not going there. This is a bright, sunny day. No more crappy parents with us on our walk. "Um, no. You had me with dirty little boy who swears a lot and lost me with breasts."

"Bummer." He snickered. "But, hey, it's a damn good story. Imagine anyone hitting me now."

"I have a hard time envisioning that." They walked

some more in silence, then she had to know. "So you're covered in all those tattoos. You seem pretty tough. How about filling in the parts between you leaving Eileen's house and her pancakes and getting here, to Lincoln Park, today?"

"That's a tall order."

"Yeah, well, we have nothing *better* to do," she said, goading him. "And before you offer something that'll scorch my ears, I actually agree with you."

"About?"

"This. Talking and getting to know each other. I like this." To her surprise, she really did. The sex would have been great, but it also would have put conditions and new emotions into the mix. And what if her first time with him had been a fluke? She'd feel the pressure to give him a good *O* face the next time around. Orgasms could be easy to fake, not so easy to achieve. She didn't want any falsity with Sam. This time she planned to do things the right way.

"So you want my life story."

"Hey, you're the one who wanted mine. I'll even tell you more about my disaster of a relationship with my ex."

He studied her before coming to a conclusion. "Fine. But you have to answer in detail. Anything I ask." He paused. "Even sex stuff."

"So do you."

"Yeah?" He perked up. "You want to know about my sex life?"

"I want to know about your time from high school to the here and now. I'll let you know if I want to hear the sexy parts."

He looked disappointed, and she did her best not to laugh.

"Well, go ahead."

"A little from me, then a little from you."

"Fine. But, Sam, no lies, okay? We're still new. Why not get all the ugly out from the beginning? That way there are no surprises later on. Heck, once you hear all I have to say, you can end things now and feel good about it," she teased.

He didn't look amused. "Yeah, fine. Okay." He handed her back Cookie's leash, and they waited while the puppy investigated a series of shrubbery. "My home life sucked, so I spent a lot of time with Foley. Hell, all my time, really. We'd hang on the streets or at his place. Eileen was always there, making sure we had enough to eat, washing our clothes, tucking us in if I stayed over. I mean, talk about a sucker. Foley could tell her anything and she'd believe it." He shrugged. "But that woman loves the shit out of him."

"And you?"

He nodded. "And me. God knows why."

Ivy liked the woman more and more.

"Foley and I managed to get through high school. We were a little girl crazy. But no way was I as big a player as he was. I'd say is, but Cyn's reformed him."

Ivy chuckled. "I can't see Cyn tolerating any fooling around."

"Woman has brass balls, so to speak. So no." They both grinned at that. Cookie finished sniffing everything, and they continued their walk. "I ran into trouble in high school. Lots of fights, suspensions, barely passing grades, but they were passing. Eileen didn't fool around when it came to graduating. Foley and me, we were doing good. Then came a girl…" He paused.

She waited.

Still he said nothing.

"And? Don't leave me hanging."

Sam shrugged. "Your turn."

"Come on, Sam."

"Nope. You first. So. Max. How'd that happen?"

She blew out a breath. "You're such a pain."

He smirked in response.

"Oh. Fine. I'd graduated high school with honors. Top of my class, and my parents couldn't care less. It was all about Ethan and his acceptance into medical school. I guess I finally realized nothing I did would ever be good enough for them." She still sometimes wondered what was so lacking in her that no one loved her. Not her parents, her brother, her exes. Certainly not Max. *Crap*. She felt the depression of her past creeping over her present once more.

"Hey, no doom and gloom," Sam growled, and Cookie froze, his tail low. "Not you, boy." He crouched and petted the dog as Cookie writhed in ecstasy. "You, Ivy. Remember, they're pricks. You're not. Tell me about Max."

"Yeah, yeah. I'm getting there." The big galoot wouldn't let her wallow. More, he'd recognized her unhappiness. Reason 302 to like the man. "Anyway, they gave me money for graduating with honors. Probably so I'd go away to school, anything to get me gone." *Those assholes*. Swearing inside made her feel better, especially because she knew Sam would approve. "Long story short, I had friends in Seattle, so

I moved out here. The money wasn't going to last, and I needed a career that would be easy to manage and quick to get going."

"So massage?"

She nodded. Cookie wandered over and gave her a lick. "Man, you are so cute." She turned her attention back to Sam. "I went to school for a year, got my one-year certificate and a license, and started massage. I planned on letting the massage pay for my schooling. I love sports and exercise, so I had planned to be an exercise science major. I would have become a trainer or sports therapist. I don't know. Something physical."

"Uh-huh." He gave her a lascivious once-over. "Physical, right."

"Stop." The man leered at her and she wanted to smile. She had issues. "Anyway, I told you all about how I met Max, how he was a psychology major."

Sam made a face. "I hate shrinks."

"Yeah, I do too. Now."

He nodded. "Good. So tell me why you fell for dickhead Max."

An apt description. "What can I say? I was young, he was handsome, smart, and he liked me. He treated me like I mattered. And I hadn't mattered to anyone in a long time."

Sam took her by the hand again. "I get that. That's the way Eileen and Foley made me feel. Important. Like if I died, someone would come to the wake."

She gave a sad laugh. "Exactly. I wish I could go back and tell my younger self to be more careful. But what's done is done." She shrugged, then narrowed her eyes on him. "Your turn."

"Oh, come on," he growled.

"Nope. See how you like it." She raised a brow, not at all bothered by his mean glare. "So what was this girl problem in school?"

He lost the glare and sighed. "I had a major crush on Jennifer Roland. She liked me right back. We made out after school and fooled around when she could sneak out of the house. She always told her parents she was with her girlfriends, I guess. I just figured it was because her parents were overprotective. I found out the hard way her dad was a fucking rich-ass dickhead."

"What happened?" She saw their walk coming to an end as they reached the parking lot where they'd left the car. So she pulled him with her to a nearby park bench and let Cookie have a lot of leash to play in the grassy area.

"Foley and I broke into her house, to leave a love note, if you can believe that. They'd gone on vacation, but I found out where she lived. It was like a mansion. Huge frickin' house with a maid and everything. I had no idea Jen came from money."

"She'd left her lipstick in my car, so I figured I'd return it. Fuck, Ivy, the house wasn't even locked up tight. If I had money like that, I'd have more than one tiny lock on the back door. That sucker jimmied free with a credit card."

"Breaking and entering. Nice."

He gave her a dark look, and her heart raced. She waited for him to finish.

"It was innocent. No one was home. I left a note in her bathroom, wrote in lipstick on her mirror. Something cute. Hell, I don't even remember it now. Foley kept bitching at me to hurry up. I started dicking around in her room, found a few notes she'd written me. She was into me. I was her first, and she was mine." He swallowed. "Not sex, but like, the first girl I fell for. Next thing I know, Foley is hauling my ass out of her room and out a window. Her dad came back early from their vacation to get something they'd forgotten, and he saw us leaving."

"Oh no."

His grim expression warned her that what came next wouldn't be pretty. "Oh yeah. The next day, the cops rounded us up. Eileen was all freaked out. But not angry, just worried. We were booked and, before we knew it, going to prison."

"How old were you?" she asked, pitying the younger, smitten Sam.

"Eighteen. I'd been in trouble before for some minor stuff like fighting and breaking shit that didn't belong to me. Our court-appointed lawyer tried to reason with the judge. Hell, we hadn't done anything. The love note I left was proof it was nothing dangerous. But the girl claimed I'd been bothering her."

"What? What about her notes to you?"

"The ones I had from her were no good. Because they said I must have written them. The girl's dad was loaded, and he hated the idea of his precious virginal princess out with a nobody like me." He shrugged. "Can't blame him for that. But I am still pissed he sent me and Foley to prison, not jail. Trust me, there's a difference. We spent eighteen months doing our best to get out in one piece." He gave her a look she couldn't read. "So there you have it. You're dating an ex-con."

They stared at each other. Ivy took in all he'd said and hadn't said. He looked the part of a convict, for sure. He'd done time—at eighteen, for breaking into a girl's house to write a note to his crush. How sad.

"So, um, have you been back to prison since?"

"Hell no. I might look stupid, but I'm not. And before you ask, even though I know you won't, it's a place where you *don't* bend over to get the soap. I didn't get to room with Foley until we'd been there nearly a year, but I got lucky. My roommate was an older dude who didn't play around that way. He was a jerk, but he never tried to get a good look at my ass."

"Sam."

He grinned, and she knew he hadn't lied. Thank goodness. Her life had been messed up, but he won the prize for awful adolescence.

"But, man, the guy could fight. I learned a lot, like how to dodge a fist. How to survive, who to protect, who'd protect you. It was harsh, and I never want to go back." Despite his lighthearted tone, his words were strong.

She stroked his fist lying on the bench between them, wanting to make him feel better but not sure what to say. Nothing he'd revealed turned her off to the man. Instead, she learned more, putting the pieces of him together. His fierce need to protect, the harsh face he showed the world. How little he thought he deserved from people who should have cared about him. She wanted to give Eileen and Foley Sanders a great big hug.

"Can I ask you something personal?" she said softly, reading his caution and knowing he had every right to tell her no. But she needed to ease his tension.

"Yeah?"

"Is it true every prisoner makes license plates? Did you wear black-and-white-striped uniforms? Have a ball chained to your ankle? Break up rocks with an Acme pickax?"

He blinked. "You watch way too much TV."

"And cartoons. My next question was if you'd ever shared a cell with Wile E. Coyote or Bugs Bunny. Because I'd swear they wore the black and white and looked good doing it."

The tension in his shoulders eased, and he shook his head. "Don't make me start with the blond jokes."

"Yeah? Watch it or I'll start with the ex-con jokes."

"Go ahead."

She bit her lip. "I don't exactly know any, but I'm sure they're out there."

He chuckled, and she knew they'd passed one major hurdle. "You really okay with me having done time?"

"For writing a note on a girl's mirror about how cute she is? Um, I think I can handle it. Oh, and I have a dead bolt on my door. No way a credit card can break that."

He smiled, and the joy in his expression floored her. "Good to know." He sobered. "I've seen some shitty things in my life, Ivy. I swear to God, you're always safe with me."

"You don't have to keep telling me that." That he felt he needed to broke her heart a little. Poor Sam. Big, brutish, mean-looking SOB, with a marshmallow for a heart. "I might look innocent and nice, but I'm not. If I thought for one second you might hurt me, I'd show you the door."

"Good." He nodded. "You do that."

"I will." She stood and glared down at him. Then she poked him in the chest for good measure. "Now, get off your butt and take me to lunch. I'm hungry."

He rose, stared down at her, and shook his head. "I don't know where you put it, but you eat a lot. Anyone ever tell you that?"

"Yep. Something else we have in common because I've seen you wolf down a steak or two."

His eyes lit up, and his lips quirked. "Well, come on then. Let's find a place that takes dogs and get you some food before you waste away." He looked her over. "You could gain a few pounds, you know."

"Oh, I think I love you for that, you wonderful man. Imagine me needing to gain some weight." She twirled and laughed. He gave her an odd look, but she grabbed him by the hand and hurried with dog and man to the car.

Chapter 12

MONDAY AFTERNOON, SAM COULDN'T KEEP HIMSELF from humming under his breath as he took a minute in the break room. It was either that or smile all damn day, and God knew the guys would razz him if they saw how happy he felt.

I think I could love you for that, she'd said. Sure, she'd been teasing. She hadn't meant it. But she hadn't dumped him after hearing about his murky past. Man, he'd wanted to break down and kiss her friggin' feet for that alone. She was giving him a chance. Ivy had taken his talk of prison time in stride, asked some silly questions, then shared hamburgers with him and Cookie.

He'd seen her slip the dog some of that Angus beef. He'd have to talk to her about that, because puppies didn't need to get too used to people food. Spoiling the mutt wouldn't help his training any. And speaking of Cookie…

He glanced at the puppy curled in his dog bed under the table. Good. One problem solved. Sam grabbed a cup of crappy coffee, shut the break room door, then hustled back to an engine repair. Buried under the hood, he hummed along to some CCR and finished in no time. After testing the car, he parked it out by the others awaiting pick up. Once back inside, he checked the list and saw a Dodge Ram waiting on him.

Silence in the garage alerted him something had

happened. He glanced up and saw Lou, Foley, and Johnny had circled him. *Shit.*

"What?" he snarled, waiting for it.

Foley answered, sounding way too low-key. "So I was telling the guys about how I'd made you look bad in front of your new girlfriend Friday night. How you'd probably lost the only shot you'll ever have at a decent chick."

"'Cause my sisters and cousins are totally off-limits," Lou reminded him. The guy had a bazillion female relations, all hot. Not easy to keep himself free from the Cortez connection, especially since one of Lou's sisters kept texting him. But now Sam had Ivy.

"I felt terrible all night, you asshole," Foley growled. "Cyn was on me for messing things up for you too. Even if you are a slob, she said I shouldn't call you on it in front of your girl."

His girl. Sam's heart raced. He could get laid, no problem. But a meaningful connection with a woman had eluded him. Until Ivy.

Foley's snarl turned into a grin, proving the guy could, indeed, act as well as Sam. "Except I know for a fact I didn't screw anything up. You spent all weekend with her when you weren't mooning over her with my mom."

"Don't even try denying it," Johnny added, gleeful and aggravating, as only Johnny could be. "I've never seen you this happy before. And humming to the radio? Wow. My man Sam must be in love. Can you believe it?"

Sam felt his cheeks heat. "Not in love, asshole. Ivy and I are dating is all."

Foley raised a brow. "Is all? That's everything for you, Sam. Rumor has it you have a date this week — at Mom's."

"Yeah?" Johnny positively salivated. "Taking her to meet the parents? Aw, Sam. That's so great." The gushing made Sam want to vomit.

"Why don't you and your girlfriends" — Sam nodded at the guys — "chat in the break room? Some of us have work to do."

"Well, see, there's a dog in the break room," Lou said, all apologies. "And I'm afraid of dogs." Bullshit. The guy played with his sister's pit bulls. "Where did he come from, anyway?"

Foley boomed, "I'll answer that one, Lou. You see, Cookie — that's the puppy in the break room — is *Ivy's* dog. Apparently, he's also *Sam's* dog, because they're *sharing* him."

"Joint custody." Lou nodded, thoughtful. "I see. So Sam and his girlfriend co-own a dog. Together. You bringing her to Del's wedding?"

Flustered, Sam hurried to checkmark the Dodge and get moving, away from the inquisition. "Look, dickheads, I have work to do, and I—"

"Why is there a dog in here?" Liam asked in a loud voice. Barking followed.

Sam closed his eyes, counted to five, then swore under his breath. "That's the dog I told you I was bringing today," he said through gritted teeth. "You fucking okayed him being here, remember, old man?"

"Fifty cents, Hamilton!" Del always arrived at the worst possible moment. "For the 'dickhead' and 'fucking' I just heard."

"Actually it's more like seventy-five," Johnny added to be helpful. "You missed an 'asshole' earlier."

Del nodded. "Thanks." *The suck up.* "So what's this about your date to the wedding, Sam? Do I know her? She work at your dad's?" she asked Johnny.

"She's not a stripper," Sam snapped as he took three quarters out of his pocket and handed them to Del. "Ivy's cool, okay? It's no big deal. We're dating. Maybe if you fu…"—he looked at Del and changed *fuckers* to—"fun-loving guys had your own lives, mine wouldn't be so interesting."

"No, no." Liam carried Cookie closer. The puppy licked his face, not a worried bone is his wriggly body. Like Del, Liam projected that safe-place aura. "You're fascinating lately, Sam. Del, look at this little cutie. Ain't he adorable?"

The guys left Sam to lavish affection on the dog. *Thank God.* Sam didn't like being the center of attention unless his activities involved fists, bone, and/or blood. Fights he could handle. Discussing his personal life? No way.

Del returned after petting the little guy. "You keeping him here permanently?"

"Nope. Just watching him this afternoon while Ivy gets him a crate for her office."

"She coming to the wedding?" Del asked again.

"I don't know." Why all this concern about the damn wedding? Didn't Del have more important things to do, like Eileen with her centerpieces?

"Ask her."

"Why?"

"Jesus, Sam. It's not a big deal. Why so suspicious?

It's not like we have designs on your woman. Except for maybe Lou. You'll need to watch that one, because he's hot even if he is obnoxious."

"Del, baby. Does McCauley know what a gem he has in you?" Lou crooned, his hand over his heart. "You use love words like *obnoxious* with him too?"

Del chuckled. "Haven't been using too many words lately, if you know what I mean. Been busy making Colin a baby brother."

"You're pregnant?" Liam asked, his eyes wide.

"Nah. Just practicing."

Liam groaned. "I'll put the dog back. Poor little guy shouldn't be hearing this kind of talk."

Sam cringed, not wanting to imagine Del or her fiancé naked. Del, maybe. McCauley? He felt ill. "No…kidding." He'd been about to say *no shit*, but Sam only had another quarter left. "Is this a garage or a nail salon?" He made sure to include Del in the insult, and she took it, by the dark blush on her cheeks. "Can we stop all the wedding and kissy talk? Let's work on cars. Or can't you get your nails dirty anymore, boss?" he asked Del.

She had the grace to look shamefaced. "I know." She closed her eyes and clenched handfuls of her hair. "Ever since I've been engaged to Mike, it's like I'm losing my mojo. In the garage," she added hastily with a glare at Johnny.

The smart-ass had his mouth open but wisely refrained from adding anything sarcastic.

Del released her hair, and even mussed, it looked stylish on her. A Goth-meets-punk look in her ash-blond braids and twists. "Okay, I swear. No more wedding, feelings, or baby talk." She grimaced. "And to prove I'm serious about us being a garage, you can swear for the rest of the day."

The guys gave a solid cheer.

Del handed his quarters back. "Take 'em. You'll probably need them tomorrow when we go back to the ROP." The Rattle of Oppression—great, even she was calling it that now.

"Fuck, yeah," he said, testing her.

She grimaced. "You have no idea how much I miss the f-word, but don't tell Mike."

He did his best not to laugh. "No problem. Mike and I won't be chatting at our next lunch date till...never."

"Shut up." She turned and strode back into her office, slamming the door behind her.

Everyone stood staring at each other, probably not sure how to handle this newfound freedom. Then Del opened the door back up and yelled, "And bring your damn girlfriend to the wedding, jackass," at Sam before slamming it again.

Liam sighed. "Ah, now there's my girl. Thanks for bringing her back, Sam. Oh, and make sure Ivy's at the wedding. I want to meet this paragon who can handle you."

"That's about right," Foley taunted. "'Cause sure as shit Sam has no idea how to handle *her*. Ivy is great."

Sam wanted to argue, but he couldn't. Foley had spoken the truth, all right. "Can you shut up and get some work done, princess? Or does Cyn have your balls all the time?"

Foley scowled, but Lou and Johnny high-fived.

"Oh, that was a good one." Johnny nodded.

Lou agreed. "And so spot-on."

Foley turned on Lou. "You want to throw down, Cortez? How about you tell us about the flower chick who won't give you the time of day? I hear she ran from the office the minute she laid eyes on your ugly face. What's wrong? Losing your touch?"

Everyone turned to Lou, who looked as if he planned on launching himself at Foley.

"Now, now, fellas." Liam stepped in, the ultimate peacemaker with those fists of steel. "We all know Lou can get any woman he wants." Lou calmed down. "Except for this woman with flowers," Liam added with a smirk. "What's the story, Casanova? She's got to be gay, right?"

Lou mumbled something and turned back to his vehicle.

"What's that?" Liam pestered. "She's too blind, deaf, and dumb to know a real man like you?"

Lou clenched his fists, considering Liam and his smirk. "Hell. Today sucks." He stomped to the Chrysler he swore was possessed, darted back under the hood, and let loose a stream of Spanish. A few words Sam recognized as not belonging in polite conversation.

Liam winked at him, then joined Del in the office.

"I thought he was retired," Lou muttered, swore some more, and started on the Spanish again.

Sam hated to laugh, because he felt the same way Lou did—not wanting to share his personal life with the guys, even though the bastards would eventually find out the truth. But Lou had made fun of him first.

As a peace offering, he said, "How about tonight at Ray's? Johnny, is Lara working?"

"Yep. I was planning to go. Darts match? I'll even spot you ten points, Lou."

"What about me?" Foley asked, wiping his hands.

"He could spot you fifty and you'd still lose by twenty," Lou snarked, down but not out. "Fine, Johnny. I'll take you up on that. Eight o'clock at Ray's. And, Sam, if you're smart, you won't bring Ivy this time."

Sam flipped him off. "Asshole. I might look stupid, but there's more under my hood than a pretty engine."

That got Foley laughing. Then Johnny said something about Foley's stupidity regarding Sue and a pitcher of beer over his head—an old relationship that had not gone well—and the insults started flying.

Finally. Things had gotten back to normal. Well, as normal as Sam having a girlfriend and Lou striking out with a chick.

Maybe hell finally has frozen over.

Sam gave up on the humming and started whistling. When the guys groaned and made fun of him again, he laughed and continued working, wondering if Ivy would like to do dinner Tuesday night—before he took his girl to meet the other most important woman in his life.

Yeah, life was sweet.

Later that night, Sam watched Lou and Johnny going neck-and-neck for points in their no-holds-barred darts match. Ray's still pulled in a decent crowd, but nowhere near the numbers on the weekends. The music remained low and the foot traffic slower, allowing for conversation and a decent darts battle.

Of Goodie or Senior he saw nothing. Lucky for them.

Lara kept coming over to flirt with Johnny, which screwed with Johnny's concentration. They all knew it. Lou, the smart guy, ordered everything from nachos to wings to *glasses*—not pitchers—of beer, so Lara had to keep returning, and gave generous tips each time.

"Kind of obvious, Lou." Sam shook his head.

"Hey, it's working. Shut up."

Foley laughed. "He's got a point. So you're really taking Ivy to meet Mom, eh?"

Sam took a few nachos and shrugged. Speaking through his food, he said, "Eileen made me."

"You are so disgusting. Chew and swallow, dickhead. Then talk." Foley frowned. "You know Mom's going to put her through the wringer. You sure you want to do that so early into the relationship?"

The dreaded r-word, and Sam had one. His heart full, he nodded. "Might as well." With Lou and Johnny goading each other, he leaned closer. "It's weird, man, but I feel like I've known Ivy forever. She's so cool about everything." He paused, then admitted, "I told her about prison. About Jennifer. And she didn't run away."

Foley gave him a wide grin. "I knew she was quality. Cyn likes her too. That's a good woman, Sam. You better do right by her, because it sounds like she's into you."

"I hope so." Sam downed his beer. "I really like her. A lot. It's—she's different than the others."

Foley watched him. "Cyn was different too. Don't believe all that bullshit about rules and dating and friggin' feelings. It's different for everyone. Sounds to me like you're seriously into her."

Sam glanced at Lou, now poking Johnny in the chest. "I am. It's like I don't even see other women now."

"Could be that this is new and exciting. First time you get a girl, she's hot. But it wears off over time." Foley shrugged. "Or maybe you're fucked up over her because a nice girl likes you."

Sam frowned. "It's more than that."

Foley clinked his glass against Sam's empty one. "Just make sure you like her for the right reasons, and not because you think you'll never get anyone else." Before Sam could protest, Foley shook his head and said, "I know you, brother. You always think you're not good enough, so you take little from women but some pussy. Not that there's anything wrong with that, but you're a good guy, Sam. And finally, a good woman is seeing that."

Sam grunted, not wanting to show Foley how much his respect meant. He cleared his throat. "Yeah, well, I'm trying to do more than just sex her up. We're, ah, holding off and talking and shit." He snorted, remembering her pique. "She was kind of pissed about it, like she wanted me and was wondering if I wanted her back. Wanted her back? She's fuckin' hot as shit. Who *wouldn't* want her?"

A glance at Lou and Johnny again had him fighting a laugh. Lou had Johnny in a headlock, accusing him of cheating, while Lara tried to talk him down.

"Should we help him?" Foley nodded at the idiots.

"Nah. Smart-mouth should learn when to keep his lips shut. Besides, now we get to see Lara in action."

They watched as Lara soothed the savage Lou, allowing Johnny to free himself from that elbow of death. All while Johnny got angrier and angrier at the guy flirting with his girl. As if Lara had eyes for anyone but Johnny.

And they all knew Lou would never poach a friend's girl. Lou was a dick, but an honest dick. Sam knew the guy respected love, because his sisters, his mother, her sisters, and his grandmother had beaten respect and affection into his sorry ass from day one.

"So what now?" Foley asked.

"I don't know. I'm going with what feels right. I just want Ivy to know I like her."

Foley watched him, a smile on his lips. "You mean before you do all the bad things to her you're dreaming about."

"Yeah, that."

Foley laughed, and Sam joined him.

Johnny, Lou, and Lara turned to stare at him.

"Did gargantuan laugh, Lara?" Johnny asked.

"I think I heard a mountain shake," Lou added. "Was that…? Could it be…? Sam?"

Sam flipped them off, then ordered another pitcher of beer, on him.

Lara winked and went to fill his order, calling over her shoulder, "Be nice, Johnny."

"For real? Honey, he's beating me up!" Johnny said a few choice words to Lou, who laughed them off.

"Suck it up," she called back, to which half the bar laughed.

"Fuck all of you," Johnny muttered, then proceeded to whip Lou's ass at darts.

An hour and a half later, Rena appeared, looking flustered but pretty as usual. Such a sweetheart, the girl worked her ass off. Sam knew she was close to opening her own hair salon. Hell, she did his and Foley's hair whenever they needed a cut. He ran a hand over his head, wondering if Ivy would like him better with shorter hair. She sure seemed to love him not having a beard.

He beckoned Rena closer and she rushed over. "Hey, Rena. How you been?"

Rena wore a shirt that said Waitress, so he figured he'd be seeing more of her tonight, especially since Lara had left early with Johnny.

"I'm good, sexy." She leaned down and gave him a kiss on the cheek. He didn't think Ivy would mind that. Everyone loved Rena.

She jolted back. "Oh."

Seeing the looming shadow over him, Sam turned and saw Heller, Lou's paint guy, at their table. The giant lurked, a dark and menacing presence. What set Sam off, though, was that Heller's attention fastened on Rena. Sam hurried to his feet, prepared for anything.

Heller didn't blink, staring at Rena like a wolf out for prey.

"Hey, Adolph, you got a problem?" Sam taunted.

Foley sighed. "I knew we couldn't go a whole week without someone punching you in the face."

Heller slowly turned his head and stared at Sam.

Jesus. It was like looking into nothing. The guy's blue eyes were dark, almost black, and lifeless.

"Easy, Sam." Lou stepped in and put a hand on Heller's shoulder. Brave fucker. "I invited him."

"It's not Adolph," Heller said, his tone as empty as his eyes. "Just Heller."

"Heller, you know Foley and Sam," Lou said by way of an introduction. "Johnny was here earlier, but he took off with Lara."

Heller nodded, but his gaze returned to Rena, who stood behind Sam, not moving. "Beer, *bitte*?"

Sam frowned. "Huh?"

"That means *please* in German, dumbass," Foley said and yanked him back down. "Sit. No fights. Easy does it, or I'll tell Ivy you were starting shit for no reason."

"No reason?" Sam thumbed at Heller. "Some psycho is staring at Rena like he wants to eat her."

At that, Lou started laughing. "Oh, I'm sure he'd like to *eat* her."

"Not funny, Lou Cortez." Rena slapped her hands on her hips. "Clean up your mind, you big jerk."

"Sorry, Rena," Lou apologized, sounding sincere, though a grin remained. "It's just…your expression."

To Sam's surprise, Heller seemed discomfited. "I am sorry…Rena." He paused, his German accent thick over her name. "I would just like a beer, please."

"At least *someone* has manners." She excluded Heller from her narrow-eyed stare. "Well, and Sam."

"Thanks."

"Hey." Foley made a sad face. "I agree Lou was rude. But I was laughing at some other joke, not at you. Gosh, I think Heller is just swell. Such a great guy." His obvious insincerity made Sam want to laugh. "The only thing we're eating here are wings. Like chicken parts, not lady parts."

"Oh, stuff it." She bit her lip to keep from smiling, Sam could tell. "Not buying it at all, Foley." She flounced away, muttering, "I'd better get one big-ass tip."

Heller watched until she disappeared behind the bar. Then he turned to the guys, frowning. "Don't fuck with her."

Sam blinked. "Us? Buddy, we've known Rena for years. You screw with her, we won't be the only ones handing you your ass. The whole bar will." Everyone loved Rena. So sweet and cute, but with a mouth and attitude that could cut you down right quick. "Look around."

Heller did. Earl, one of the bouncers, glared at their table. A few of the regulars around stared as well, their attention not on Sam and the guys, but on Heller, the newbie.

"Ah. I see." Heller nodded and sat. "I apologize."

Sam glanced at Lou.

Lou shrugged and sat as well. "So, Heller, you any good at darts?"

"*Ja.*"

Sam and Foley leaned closer. "How good?"

"I have not been beaten since coming to this country."

"When was that exactly?" Foley asked, sizing the guy up.

"Ah, let's see." Heller frowned, and had Sam not known the guy, he'd have gone for a gun. Heller was one mean-looking motherfucker. "I was born here, but then we went back to München."

"Munich," Lou translated. "Home of Oktoberfest."

"And beer. Nice." Foley nodded, approving.

"So fifteen years in München, then seventeen here." Heller nodded.

Rena returned with beer and a plate of cookies. She must have liked the guy, because she hadn't given *them* any of Lara's treats. "For you, because you've been nice."

Heller flushed. "*Danke.* Ah, thank you. And I'm sorry if I startled you. It's just…your hair is like…" He said something in German. The guy had balls, because he was straight-up flirting with Rena in front of all of them, three big dudes who'd threatened to castrate him if he messed with her.

Rena studied him. And she seemed different. Sam couldn't peg the strange look on her face. "What did you say?"

"Your hair is like sunbeams. Golden and ethereal." Heller smiled.

Sam wanted to run for the hills because that wolf had some damn big teeth.

Rena sighed. "Th-thanks. The beer and cookies are on the house." She smiled back. Then she slapped Foley in the back of the head. "You, be nice."

"Hey." Foley rubbed his head. "It's like everyone who's a Webster is hitting me lately."

Del had knocked him earlier before leaving for the day.

"Welcome to my world," Sam muttered.

Rena faced Heller. "Bye, um, what's your name?"

"Axel." He took a sip of beer, never blinking as he watched her. "Good stuff."

She smiled, flashing her dimples, and left with a bounce in her step.

Heller ignored them all and ate the cookies, without offering one, the bastard. "The beer tastes like piss, but these are amazing."

Lou nodded. "Lara, Johnny's girlfriend, made them."

"I thought he was her fiancé," Foley said.

Lou shrugged. "Did he ask her? Thought he didn't have the stones."

"He asked." Sam nodded. "She's making him work for a yes. Smart girl." Like Ivy. A nice woman who saw something in a man with a checkered past. If Johnny could land Lara, Sam had even more hope that he might be able to keep Ivy.

He poured himself another beer, determined to do whatever he had to in order to make that happen. Which meant showing Ivy what she'd be missing if she threw him to the curb.

Lou sneered. "He's smiling again. God, this shit needs to stop. He's freaking me out."

Foley laughed. "*He's* freaking you out? What about the mountain sitting next to you? 'Cause *he's* freaking *me* out. Yo, Axel."

"To you, it is Heller."

Sam hoped Foley knew not to push. He could tell Heller was not someone to mess with when riled. And in his good mood, Sam had no urge to mess up his own pretty face before Ivy saw him again.

"Heller," Foley corrected without missing a beat. "What's with all the staring at our girl Rena?"

Heller frowned. Not good. "Your girl?"

"Not mine, exactly. I mean, I have a woman. Sam and Johnny do too. Not Lou, though."

Heller turned to Lou so fast it startled him.

"No way, man. I value my life." Lou shook his head. "She's amazing, but you screw with Rena, you deal with the Websters. You know Del and Liam. J.T., though, he's not someone to fuck with."

Heller frowned. "Ah. Yes. J.T."

Sam and Foley exchanged a glance, and Sam asked, "J.T., a threat?"

Foley chuckled.

Sam was confused.

Lou nodded. "He works with Heller a lot. Pissing him

off wouldn't be pretty. You know, the temperamental artist type."

"Oh. For a minute there I thought you were scared he'd pound you or something," Foley scoffed.

Heller blinked, then gave a smile that wasn't scary at all. Hell, best not to let Ivy meet the guy until Sam had a lock on her. "J.T. Webster? Scary?" He started laughing. Of course, a guy his size wouldn't worry about a six-foot-four tattoo artist who had Liam for a dad and Del as a sister. Sam had wondered a time or two what J.T. would be like in a real fight. But then he'd remember J.T.'s easygoing nature and aversion to messing up his pretty face. Guy spent more time with a different piece of tail every other night than even Johnny used to get. Nah, J.T. would never fight when he could find a pretty lady instead.

Not that Sam thought that a bad thing, necessarily. But he'd much rather have Foley or Lou at his back, even Johnny, than J.T.

"He sure can draw though," Sam said.

They all joined in teasing the guy who wasn't there to defend himself. Sam would make sure to mention he'd stuck up for him before he got J.T. to do his next tattoo.

"J.T." Heller shook his head and drained his beer like it was water. "He's a lover, not a fighter. Besides, I need his hands not bruised. He's too valuable." Heller turned his gaze on Sam and Sam's hands. "Not like you. I hear you're the man to beat in a fight. Particularly when Jerry pays to play."

Around them, the guys stilled. Even Lou, so Sam knew the bastard was aware of what went down at the House. He glanced at Foley, saw his concern, and sighed.

"Nah. I'm retired. My woman wouldn't like me fighting." *My woman*. Just saying that gave him a secret thrill.

Heller considered him for a moment, then nodded. "*Ja*. This is a good thing. Especially since the *polizei* visited and closed the place down."

"Damn." Sam figured he'd dodged a major bullet there.

Foley gave him a look. "Told you."

Heller continued, "Love is a much better way to live." He left the table and headed to the bar or, more specifically, to Rena. He returned minutes later with a fresh plate of cookies and a large smile. "On the house."

The guy's accent must have ensnared Rena. He'd heard women went for foreign dudes. Sam grabbed his share while the guys grabbed theirs. As he enjoyed the treat, his thoughts once again shifted to Ivy. Would she make him cookies if he asked? Would she let him help? They could get covered in flour, maybe some cookie dough, then have to get clean. Together.

He drank more beer and willed away his erection, not wanting the guys to have more ammo to fire his way the next day. As he chilled, he made plans for his girl.

Time to step up his powers of seduction and see if sexy Ivy could handle him. Because Sam had skills she hadn't yet seen. And damn, but he was hungry…

Chapter 13

Ivy wished Cookie would get better at doing his business or, rather, faster. But no, the puppy had to sniff everything before peeing on it. How he could have so much in that tiny bladder still amazed her. She glanced around the park and noted the setting sun.

"Come on, sweetie. Time to go back and get ready for Sam."

Though their big date in Bainbridge wasn't until tomorrow, he'd asked to see her tonight. She hated to admit it, but she needed the confidence boost. She knew how important Eileen was to Sam, and Ivy liked everything she knew about the woman. What if Ivy didn't meet Eileen's approval? In the four years she'd been with Max, she'd never met his mother, because Max's family lived out East, and they hadn't had the money to fly both of them home for the holidays.

Her only access to parents had been her own, and they hadn't liked her much, let alone loved her. What if Eileen felt the same about Ivy? Despite Ivy's work ethic, smarts, and compassion, she apparently lacked something vital. Her exes and her parents had sensed the deficiency. Sam didn't yet, but she figured that was okay. But not if Eileen recognized it in her and put the kibosh on her new relationship.

Ivy had hoped she and Sam could enjoy each other before she scared him away. Maybe if she had more time to show him her value, he'd ignore her issues. She kept trying to take it slow, but her heart kept prodding her mind to wake up. Sam was much more than a friend. He had the potential to be someone special in her life. Yet reality told her he'd eventually go, like everyone else had. Still, she'd at least have shared in his warmth for a time. If anything, he'd woken her to the fact she still had a libido, as well as a desire for companionship.

She'd wanted to call him to go out Monday, but she knew they didn't need to spend every waking moment together. Thank goodness he'd asked to see her tonight, because she'd almost texted him first.

I am so pathetic.

She should have been more anxious about her fixation on the man, but excitement over seeing him overwhelmed caution. No sense in wallowing in the negative when she had a hot man on the way. Ivy smiled, played with Cookie some, then urged him away from the park back home.

She had Cookie tuckered out on the floor by the fire by the time Sam arrived. As usual, Seattle had decided to interrupt spring with a light snowfall, despite the prior day's record-breaking warmth. But the strange temperatures didn't bother Cookie. Ah, to be a happy-go-lucky dog.

She stroked him, loving his sighs of comfort. How right—and big—he looked in her home.

Every time she looked away, then back at him, the little guy seemed larger. He sure ate a lot. She wished she could go for the fancy, gluten-free, everything-bad-free food, but she could only afford basic puppy chow.

He didn't seem to mind though. In fact, he tended to eat anything not nailed down.

A knock at the door distracted her and woke the snoozing puppy. She stroked him between his ears, and he settled, blinking sleepy eyes. Then she hurried to the door. Peering through the peephole, she saw her favorite tough guy and those sexy tattoos. Remembering how she'd kissed each one last time, she did her best to calm her racing heart before opening the door.

Before he could say anything, she hauled him inside and locked up after him.

"Well, nice to see you too."

"Shh."

He stared her up and down but lowered his voice. "What's up?"

She nodded at Cookie, who wobbled over to Sam while yawning. "He's about to go back to sleep."

"Oh." Sam knelt to accept doggie kisses, then carried Cookie to his bed by the fire. "Hey, handsome." He caught one of Cookie's paws and shook his head. "You do realize he's going to be huge."

"Like someone else we know, eh?"

He stood, and she had to look up to meet his gaze.

He smirked. "What can I say? I'm a growing boy." He just watched her, no doubt waiting for her to jump on that phrase.

She refused. He could take his dirty thoughts—and hers—and sit on them. Because she feared if she said anything racy, she'd be tempted to act on her desire. He'd already set the pace, wanting them to be friendly without being too friendly. And the smart part of her agreed. It was nice to be wanted—as a person, not just someone to scratch an itch.

She cleared her throat. "To what do I owe the pleasure of your company, Sam Hamilton?"

He gave her a warm smile. "You know, you remind me of Willie. She always calls me by my full name. Weird, but that's Willie."

"Thanks a lot."

He chuckled. "Willie says hi, by the way. I'm supposed to bring you by when I can, so she can ask you a bunch of questions."

"About Cookie?"

"And me, I'm guessing. Woman considers herself a matchmaker." He looked pained. "She's hooked up all her single friends, and now a bunch of geriatrics are bumping and grinding in the neighborhood. I'm not even going there about her and Rupert and their swing."

She rubbed her eyes. "I think I'm blinded. I can't stop remembering pictures of Rupert and Willie in that contraption."

"I'm glad I didn't see it. Imagining it is bad enough."

Well, at least she no longer had an urge to jump Sam, even if he did look lickable. He wore his trademark jeans and biker boots. Tonight he wore an AC/DC T-shirt that must have been a size too small, because it clung to his upper body like it had been painted on him. *Oy.* A woman would have to be made of stone not to appreciate such fine art.

She cleared her throat and stepped toward the kitchen. "So this date tonight is about cookies—not the dog, but the actual chocolate chip kind. This wouldn't have anything to do with *Lara's* cookies, would it?" A niggle of jealousy lingered. Darn it.

He sighed. "I can't help it. The guys and I went to Ray's last night, and I got a hankering. Unfortunately, Lara's dating an asshole who refuses to let her make us any unless we're nice to him." He looked as if he'd swallowed a lemon. "I just can't do it."

She chuckled. "Yeah, that sounds terrible."

"It is. So, ah, can I kiss you hello?"

She nodded. "I—"

He took her in his arms and kissed the breath out of her, cutting off any semblance of thought. When he finally came up for air, he said, "Oh yeah. I've been dying to do that since Sunday."

"H-how nice." She took a few deep breaths to get back on an even keel. "Look, since we both know I can't compete with Lara's chocolate chip recipe, how about we make some killer peanut butter ones instead?"

The true test—how did Sam feel about peanut butter? A food so important she added it to each food group as a must-have?

"Oh man. Peanut butter is my favorite."

Of course it was.

Could Sam be any more perfect for her?

You just met the guy. Slow down, desperate Ivy! So sad how often she had to remind herself to ease back around this man.

"Ah, is that a problem?"

"No. It's my favorite too." She glared at him. "Do you do it on purpose? Pretend to like the same things I do?"

"You're cute when you're all cynical." He gave a

small smile. "Go on, swear at me while you're at it. Say *damn* or *shit*. How about a *hell*?"

"Shush." She tried to scowl and ended up smiling instead. Sam in a good mood was impossible to resist. Of course, Sam in a bad mood turned her on too, so she was in a lose-lose situation any way she looked at it. "Okay, buddy. I'll make you some killer peanut butter cookies, but you can't swear for the rest of the night. That's the deal."

"Damn. I mean, darn. Seriously?"

"Yes." She crossed her arms, hiding her erect nipples, playing hardball.

"I do it at work every day. I can do it here too." He shrugged. "Fine. But those cookies better be worth my time."

"You are such a pain."

"In the… Fill in the blank. I'm a pain in the…" He waited, but she didn't answer. "I can't curse, but you can."

"You have a lot of teeth when you smile, do you know that?"

He nodded. "Willie says I look serial-killer happy when I'm trying to show I'm nonthreatening happy. She's been working with me on that."

She laughed. "Um, yeah. Because she's your go-to when it comes to seducing women?"

"Not all women. Just you." He winked.

She wished she could believe him. But Sunday night she'd been all hot and bothered for nothing. *And I should be grateful he wanted to act the gentleman.* She swallowed a sigh and got out the ingredients for cookies. "It doesn't take much. Grab the peanut butter."

"Wait. What?"

"Good point. First, wash your hands."

"Hold on. Are we making these together?"

"No. I'm going to do all the work while you watch." He nodded.

"I'm kidding, Sam." She did sigh then. "Get that cute butt over here and help."

He raised a brow at her tone but obeyed, and she did her best to calm her raging girlie parts. Sam was so sexy, a bundle of sweetness trapped in a berserker's body. He washed his hands, then did what she told him to. Except when he rolled the balls for the cookies, he made them monster sized.

"No, no. That's too big."

"Huh?"

She nudged him aside and took the buttery dough into her hands, then rolled smaller balls onto the cookie sheet. "Oh, shoot. I forgot to preheat the oven."

Sam washed his hands. "I'll do it." But instead of heating the oven, he came up behind her, staring over her shoulder.

"You're blocking my light, Grape Ape."

"Really, Ivy? A giant purple gorilla? Another cartoon reference? That's the best you can do?" He leaned his head on her shoulder, and her pulse sped up.

"I can't help it. I'm distracted by peanut butter. I love peanut butter. Cookie does too."

"I'm sure he does," he said wryly. "You have to stop feeding him people food or he'll get fat."

"But he likes it."

"Well, I like this." He kissed her neck, and she froze. "But if I did it all the time, you'd never have your clothes on."

"Wh-what?"

"And this." He slowly wrapped his arms around her waist and pressed up against her, his rock-hard front against her back. "Is this okay?"

"Ah, Sam?" Embarrassing that she squeaked his name. "Y-yes. But I mean…" She held up her peanut-buttery hands.

He gently sucked at her throat, and a moan slipped out of her. She rested her head back against him, wanting him to take charge. Willing him to soothe that need inside her—for sex and for something deeper.

His hands came up to cup her breasts.

Oh, yes. That's what I need. She rolled her hips back against him, instinctively seeking his heat.

"That's it, Ivy. Give it to me." He continued to kiss his way up her neck until he found her cheek.

She turned her head and met him in a full-mouth kiss. One he took charge of before he backed off again.

"No," she moaned, "don't stop."

His breathy "Bedroom" relieved her.

She put shaky hands under the kitchen faucet, and Sam washed them for her. He took his time, pulling on her fingers, stroking her palms, the outside of her hands. Amazing how sensitive her hands were. She knew all about touch, but Sam's felt sexual. Hot. Blazing.

She let him control her, already aroused and wanting more.

He dried her hands with care, patting them in the towel. He looked into her eyes and must have liked what he saw, because his gaze darkened and he growled, "Bedroom. Now."

Too keyed up to speak, she led him toward her small

bedroom, entered, and stood in front of the bed, wondering what came next.

"You remember what I said," he uttered, his tone gravelly. "Anytime you're not sure, you just say no. And I'll stop."

He didn't touch her, waiting.

Always needing her permission. There had to be something behind that. But right now she couldn't bring herself to care. She nodded.

He eliminated the distance between them and kissed her. No preliminaries. Sam went straight for the power play. His mouth felt so firm, so hot. He caged her in strong arms, taking away her ability to move while he commanded her with tongue and teeth. His groan aroused her anew, because it vibrated through his body, and knowing he wanted her turned her on even more.

She clenched his forearms, needing to touch him all over, and felt him lowering her to the bed.

He stood over her, looking down. Breathing hard, sweeping her from head to toe with his gaze, Sam looked hungry.

And not for peanut butter cookies.

"Take off your clothes."

The moment of truth. But... Practicality had ruined many a magical moment for Ivy, yet she couldn't bring herself to turn off the cautious voice inside her.

"I, um, I don't have any condoms."

He watched her. "Uh-huh."

"So, ah, do you?"

"Nope. I left 'em at home tonight."

"Oh." Disappointing but okay.

"On purpose." He cleared his throat, finally meeting

her gaze once more. "Because if I'd brought them, we'd be fucking right now."

Her breath caught.

"I just want to play tonight. Okay? And, Ivy, you don't have to worry—"

"Sam, I know." She loved that he wanted her to feel safe, but he'd started to get redundant. "I trust you. Really."

He smiled, that look of pure joy that radiated from deep inside him. "Thanks, baby. But I was going to say you don't have to worry about me, because I always use protection. Biggest thing to worry about with me is not making babies, not about catching anything. I'm clean."

She felt her insides melt at thoughts of making said babies with Sam. "I've been on birth control since Max. I never went off it. But I haven't been with anyone in a long time. I'm clean too."

"Yeah?" He was still smiling.

She nodded.

"Then how about you stop stalling and take off your clothes?"

"You first." Nervous about him seeing all of her for the first time, she had to brace for his possible disappointment.

"Fine." He whipped his shirt off and onto the floor.

"Oh, wow." She gaped. That much masculinity made her entire bedroom feel dominated, intruded by so much power.

"You gonna kiss my tats again, Ivy? Maybe suck your way down my body?"

A glance at the bulge in his jeans showed he liked the idea. *A lot.*

"I don't know. We were supposed to be making

cookies…" She bit her lower lip even as she sat up and took off her shirt.

"Yeah, that's it. Now the bra." Sam didn't blink.

Nervous at being totally bare up top, she hesitated on the bed.

"Hey, I did it first."

"That's true." She swallowed and unfastened her bra, then took it off.

Sam stared. "You're so beautiful." Before she could respond, he lowered himself to the bed and pressed her back down again.

The feel of his chest against hers was incredibly erotic.

"Christ, that's so good." He rubbed his chest over hers. "I love your tits against me. I'm so damn hard right now."

The swearing got steadily worse as he continued to tell her how much he wanted her, until she'd made a mess of her panties thanks to him rubbing between her legs with a massive erection.

"I'm gonna take off my pants, okay? And yours are coming off too."

She could only nod, wanting to see the rest of him.

Sam left her to stand and remove all his clothes.

Just… She had no words. The sheer strength of the man was outlined in muscle. His arms, chest, legs. He had the *best* ass. She was tempted to ask him to turn back around, but he'd already knelt to take off her jeans. A bummer, because she'd wanted a better look at his cock.

It couldn't really be that big, could it? Long and thick and stiff as could be. She remembered feeling it before, but seeing it made an even bigger—literally—impression.

Sam shifted her on the bed so that she lay naked

in the middle of it. He sat on his knees, straddling her waist, and she got her much wanted close-up view of *all* of him.

"Sam." She stroked his thighs, what she could reach, feeling needy and so unlike herself. She shivered, craving his touch. "I want you."

"Not as much as I want you." He put his hands on her breasts and gave a gentle squeeze.

She gasped.

"You fit my hands. Just right." He flicked her nipples with his thumbs, playing with her breasts, until she wanted to scream. He looked in awe, so intent on her body that she didn't have the heart to tell him to hurry.

"I came over for cookies," he said in a soft voice.

"C-cookies. Right." Had they turned on the oven? She wanted to care about that, but she'd worry later.

"And I'm still hungry."

"Hungry." *Me too. But not for peanut butter.*

He moved down her body. She waited for him to lay on top of her, wondering how they would do this since neither had any condoms. Though he'd said he was safe, and she knew she was, she'd never had sex with someone without a condom so soon in a relationship. But part of Ivy didn't care, desperate to have him inside her.

Except Sam kept moving down her body. His kisses trailed down her belly to her hips, her upper thighs. He rested so close to her sex, his head just…

"*Sam.*"

He parted her folds with thick fingers, opening her while he looked his fill. The cool air felt like another touch over her most sensitive area. But the coolness didn't last.

"You're pretty everywhere." He kissed her, right between her legs, and she was lost.

Sam groaned and licked her. Sucked her. Kissed and teased her into a writhing mess as she climbed toward a killer orgasm. She pulled at his shoulders, but when he would only lick her harder, she bucked up into his touch. "It feels so good." Amazing yet lacking him inside her.

He ate her out as if he really had been starving. His big hands held her still, stimulating as well as oddly empowering. She could give in to her feelings and not worry about anything else. But she wanted him to feel it too, and how better than to offer the same?

"Turn around," she breathed.

He stilled and lifted his head, his arousal glowing in his eyes. "You sure? 'Cause one touch of your mouth on my cock and I'll lose it."

"Yes." She ran her hands through his hair, tugging him up.

Sam turned around and threw himself back into kissing and petting her, making her insane. But now she had something to occupy herself while he drove her to distraction. She reached for the thick shaft between them, and he moaned and shoved his tongue inside her, clutching her thighs.

She drew him down, pleasantly surprised they fit considering their height differential. But she had to lift up to make better contact. The moment her lips touched the head of his cock, he spread his knees wider and leaned into her, lowering his body.

Just what she needed. She grabbed the outside of his thighs and took him deeper, moving her mouth over him with greater speed. Her timing matched his rhythm, and they moaned and sighed and teased together, swaying into each other as their desire rose higher.

Sam's girth stretched her jaw, and his salty taste did nothing but make her desire him more. His scent, the feel of his need in the thickness of his cock. She cupped his balls, felt how hard they were. His thighs strained, and she grabbed his ass and tugged him down even more, taking him to the back of her throat before releasing him, stifling her urge to gag.

He shuddered and shoved a finger inside her, his lips like magic. She couldn't stop her body from reacting. And as she crested into release, she sucked him harder and her nails bit into his ass.

He groaned as he licked her and spilled inside her mouth. She swallowed him down, still caught in her own bliss, until she could barely breathe. He must have sensed her at her end because he immediately withdrew, his cock half-hard, hanging heavy over her.

Sam kissed his way from her sex, along her thighs as he turned, then up her belly to her breasts. He lingered over her nipples, sucking the peaks into taut buds. He met her lips, and she tasted herself. She wondered if he could taste himself on her.

When he pulled back and rested on his elbows, looking down at her, something between them clicked. She'd already felt close to him, obviously, but this... She couldn't feel so deeply for a man she'd met only recently, could she?

Staring into his eyes, more gray than blue right then, she saw only affection, lust, and that intensity that made words impossible.

He shook his head and kissed her again, this time

lingering before he pulled back. He felt heavy, leaning into her slighter frame from his belly down, but she didn't want him to leave. "You keep driving me crazy. Dam—Darn, Ivy." His soft smile and tender kiss earned a kiss back.

"Back at you, Sam Hamilton," she said on purpose, putting a mock frown on his face. She laughed. "Do I remind you of Willie, now?"

"Stop, Ivy. You're crushing my after-sex buzz."

She snickered, so happy and relaxed she wanted to never move again.

"You know this is just stage two, right?" he asked, running his fingers through her hair.

She closed her eyes and smiled. "What's stage three?"

"That's full-on sex. Me inside you, feeling you come around me," he said in a thick voice. "I can't wait for that."

"But we're taking it slow, right?" she teased. "So, what? We'll be hitting stage three tomorrow?"

"If you insist." He sounded happy.

She blinked her eyes open and saw him tracing her features with a tender gaze. She'd never seen him so at ease, so…well, soft before.

"Do you have any idea how tough it's going to be to not think about this all the time? I'll be getting hard-ons at work, at Ray's, hell, around town even." He grimaced. "At Eileen's. Damn."

She giggled and coughed to stop the giddy sound. Ivy didn't giggle. Ever. But around Sam, she felt girly and cared for and…well, loved. Too soon for that, but rationalizing her feelings didn't make them go away.

She hugged him, pulling him close for more kisses. They lay together, just kissing, resting, and kissing some more. Until the kissing turned deeper, more sexual than sensual.

"Wait, Ivy. Don't." Sam was thick and long against her belly, rubbing himself against her instinctively, she guessed. Because even as he told her to stop with the kissing, he continued to rock against her. "I want to fuck you so bad."

"It's been ten minutes at least," she teased. "That's enough time for stage three, isn't it?" Because she wanted him. Deep inside her, skin to skin. She ran her hands over his chest, intrigued at the lack of hair there. "Do you shave your chest? You're so smooth."

His cheeks turned pink. "Ah, no. I think we have some Native American in the family tree somewhere, maybe. I've just always been this way."

"But not here." She ran a hand between them to caress his balls.

He closed his eyes, his face agonized. Then he shifted, rubbing his cock against her clit. He settled between her legs, his tip resting between her folds. "You have no idea how much I want to come inside you."

"Sam." She kissed his neck and sucked.

He moaned and moved deeper. She felt him there, poised to take her.

"I want you in me."

"No condom?" he asked, his voice hoarse.

"Just you."

He started to push inside, and she gasped at how he filled her. He kept going until she didn't think she could take any more. And then he gave her the last of him. A light sheen of sweat covered his forehead while he remained very still.

"Don't move. Fuck. You're so hot and tight around me." He closed his eyes, gritting his teeth.

"Sam, more." She nipped his collarbone.

He withdrew until just the tip of him remained inside her. Then he thrust deep.

She didn't think it possible, but she started to seize around him, coming so hard she was lost to everything. Somewhere she thought she heard a bang and barking. Then Sam withdrew and left her all alone.

"Sam?" She felt drugged. Sam swearing and Cookie barking roused her in a hurry.

She rushed into the kitchen to see Sam picking up cookie dough off the floor and shoving Cookie's messy face out of it.

"Oh. We left the cookie sheet on the oven. He reached that?" She had a difficult time reasoning with a naked Sam in her sights and her body still coming down off that euphoric high.

He turned in his crouch and grinned at her. "You're sexier naked, for sure." He glanced at the dog. "No discipline. Oh, gross. Don't lick me. You're covered in peanut butter."

Peanut butter, a puppy, and chaos. And she'd never felt happier. She stared at Sam, seeing his erection flagging. "Ruined the mood, huh?"

"Maybe a little. But that's a good thing." He shook his head. "I have no control around you."

"So you didn't like where we were going?" She knew he had.

He stood, and she watched his cock bob, hard and pointing right at her once more. Sam didn't seem concerned about his nudity at all. "Damn it, Ivy. Of course

I did. But our first time is supposed to be long and slow. Candles and flowers and shi—stuff." He seemed embarrassed at what he was saying. "Like a date night."

She smiled at him, seeing the romantic he tried to bury under gruffness. "So cookies and sex don't mix? Not unless we're talking a sixty-nine or a blow job, is that it?" She laughed at his red face. "Why is it you can swear up and down, but mention of sex gets you all embarrassed?"

"I don't know. It's guy talk at the garage or the bar. But with you it's weird, okay?"

She walked to him and gave him a hug, which wrung a groan out of him as he ground against her belly. "You're so sweet. I owe you some peanut butter cookies. How about we get dressed and make some more? Then we can plan for our special first time together, hmm?"

He kissed the top of her head. "I know you're humoring me. I'm weird, but I—"

She pulled back to put a finger over his lips. "Stop. I love that you want it to be special. Because I do too." She rubbed his lips. "I can't wait for you to come inside me. I trust you, remember? And I think it would be amazing just you and me together." She didn't know if she should bring up her ex just then, but it needed to be said. "I don't just have sex with anyone, Sam. I was with my high school sweetheart for more than a year before he and I were intimate. And it was months before Max and I had sex. Even then, he wore a condom for the first two years, before I went on the pill. But with you, I'm protected." She paused. "You'd tell me if I should worry about you, right?"

He nodded and gave her another kiss. "Yeah. I'm

not gonna say I haven't been around, but a condom was always a must. With you, I don't want anything between us."

And he wanted a special night for it to happen. Such a sweetheart. What guy wanted to wait to make it memorable? Sam could have had her any way he wanted her tonight. But he wanted to make it right. Could she lo— like him anymore?

The other L-word unnerved the crap out of her, and she once again cautioned herself about getting in too deep too fast with him. But a part of her wondered if it was too late.

She gently extricated herself from his embrace and petted Cookie. "I'm going to get dressed. Then we're going to clean up this mess—"

"We?"

"And try again. I have enough peanut butter that it's not a problem."

"I'm always game for making cookies with you, Ivy." He winked at her.

Feeling extremely naked all of a sudden, she hurried away into the bathroom to do a quick cleanup. She dressed in pajamas and returned to the living room to see her guys sitting on the couch together, waiting for her. Sam, unfortunately, sat, dressed, stroking Cookie's head in his lap.

They both looked up when she cleared her throat.

My guys.

Feeling a ball of emotion lodge in her chest, she swallowed it down under the need to take it slow. To not scare either one of her guys away. "Well, since the cookies will take no time, how about seeing what's new and goofy in the world of sci-fi while I put a new pan in?"

Sam gave her a slow, panty-melting grin. "Great minds think alike."

So you're wondering if you're falling in love with me too? She gave him a smile, prayed he didn't see the panic in her eyes, and whipped up a fresh batch of cookies before sliding a tray in the oven. All while Sam watched and teased, commenting from where he played with Cookie.

Oh boy. Ivy had gone down this road before, and it never ended well for her. But watching her man with her dog, she wondered if she had the will to resist falling in love.

Chapter 14

SAM ENJOYED THE FERRY RIDE TO BAINBRIDGE Island with Ivy. She never sat still, always hungry for sensation. Her eyes danced as they sat huddled on the top deck, watching the sky darken from light blue to indigo. The setting sun made the clouds overhead appear orange, and the sky looked like an otherworldly painting.

"It's like the mother ship is up there, waiting to beam us into the hold before they suck our brains out." She wiggled her brows. "Am I right?"

He shook his head, trying not to grin. He'd been too damn happy lately. Everyone at the garage kept talking about it. Lou had given him an especially difficult time today, made worse because Sam had asked a favor. It was more like doing *Lou* a favor, letting his baby sister, Rosie, watch the dog, but trust the bastard to make things difficult.

"You want me to watch your joint-custody canine?" Lou had asked, a smug grin on his face.

"Look, your sister told me Rosie wants a dog. Think of this as a trial run."

"Which sister?" Lou's eyes had narrowed. "You flirting with Stella, asshole?"

"Don't be a dick. She texted me because she knows I rescue animals." But yeah, the sexy twenty-two-year-old had a crush on him, one he'd been trying to end without hurting her feelings. "How about you let

Rosie watch Cookie for a day or two to see if she can handle it?"

"A day or two, huh?"

"It's no biggie if you can't. I have a bunch of people who could watch him for me."

"Like Ivy, you mean?"

"She and I have a date." He'd felt an inordinate amount of pride admitting that.

"No shit? You get a good girl and get all soft and cuddly." Lou had chuckled, but his gaze had narrowed. "First a dog, then dates, you smiling—where's it gonna end, Sam?"

A good question.

Sam shot Ivy a look, saw her gazing at the water, and swallowed a sigh as he stood next to her, offering warmth and a buffer from the oncoming wind.

Sam had dated women before. Everyone acted like it was an act of God that he was seeing a "good" girl. Just because the women he'd happened to previously date had liked to take their clothes off for money didn't mean they weren't decent chicks. But those relationships had been superficial at best. He'd wanted sex and not much more than that.

His last squeeze, Shaya, had been friendly and sweet. And temporary—which they'd both known going into the relationship.

Hell, now that he thought about it, Sam hadn't seriously dated anyone since high school. And look at how that had turned out. Prison for him and his best friend. Maybe there was something to Eileen and her thoughts that the experience had scarred him, made him shy away from a meaningful relationship with a woman.

His phone buzzed, and he pulled it out to see the number that always caused dread to pool in his stomach. Yeah, and maybe he'd always be scarred from having a loving connection to a female. Because he'd been born that way.

"Who is it?" Ivy asked. Then she frowned. "Are you okay?"

Ignoring the summons to return the call, he muted the thing, pocketed it once more, then erased his frown. "Nothing that can't wait. I'm good." He hugged Ivy tighter. "I'm glad you came. It'll be fun. You'll see."

"Of course I had to come." She rubbed his belly under his jacket, and he tensed, aroused so easily around Ivy. "What would I do without my human heater at my side?"

"Funny girl."

She stuck her tongue out at him, and he smiled despite his unease. Lately, he'd had more calls from Louise than he normally received. She liked to remind him of his worthlessness as a human being every couple of months. Considering she'd brought him into the world, he knew he owed her—especially if he didn't want her screwing with the few people he did care about.

Nothing she did would be major. The occasional slashed tire, graffiti, trash cans set on fire. Making crass phone calls to his friends' places of business. But the personal intrusion, knowing he'd be the one responsible for her damage, that he couldn't handle.

Besides, Sam was a man who paid his debts. It should have been more difficult with Louise, considering how nasty she'd been for so long. But the thing was, Louise, though a real witch now, hadn't always been a shit to him.

Foley and Eileen hated her, he knew. But they hadn't been there for those times when she'd wiped his tears after he fell. Or made popcorn over the stove with him before they'd watched a movie together. She'd once collected pebbles with him, making memories, and showed him how to jump rope and ride a bike. Hell, she'd even baked him cookies a few times.

Some good stuff buried underneath years of abuse he wanted to but couldn't forget.

Ivy's arms felt snug around him, safe, and brought him back to the present. In Ivy, he saw someone his mother could have been if certain events hadn't transpired. If she'd eased off the drugs or sought counseling. If she'd seen her little boy as something to be thankful for, and not a curse she'd been doomed to bear.

He shook off his quiet despair, focusing instead on the important women in his life: Eileen, who treated him like a son, and Ivy, who treated him like a man worthy of affection. He saw her studying him when she didn't think he noticed. She looked the way he felt—uncertain, joyful, and feeling things that made no sense considering their short time together.

God, he *knew* her. So well. He couldn't wait to see what Eileen thought though. The woman cut through bullshit faster than Foley running through quarters at the garage. Nothing and no one could sway Eileen when it came to her kids. And she did consider Sam her son. Sometimes that warmth was the only thing keeping him from going off the deep end—knowing Eileen and Foley would genuinely grieve his loss. And then he'd met Ivy.

"There it is," she said as they neared the island. She

acted like a kid at Christmas, all energized and excited to hop on dry land.

"You have been here before, right?"

"Yes, but it's been a while. Heck, it's been years since I've been here. The last time, I breezed through Bainbridge to Port Townsend." Her excitement dimmed, and he had a feeling that last visit might have been with Max, her prick of an ex.

What kind of guy used a woman like Ivy? Hell, she was bolt of fucking sunshine. Anger on her behalf didn't surprise him. He'd been wanting to smash Max's face in ever since she'd told him about her sorry ex.

"Yeah? Maybe we could take a weekend trip some-time," he offered, wanting to put a smile on her face. "Just you, me, and Cookie."

A grin brightened her once more. "I'd like that." She stepped away from him, and he wanted to haul her back. An announcement came over the ferry speakers. Ivy tugged him by the hand. "Come on, we need to get to the car. We can't be late."

"Relax. We've got another ten to twenty minutes at least." Amused at her panic at the thought of being late, he tried not to smile. Ivy liked rules, and she had a bad habit of trying to make him and the puppy conform to them.

Sam, who'd been bucking the system straight out of the womb, shouldn't have had much in common with the worrywart. But to his surprise, he did.

Between silly movies, a love of dogs, caring for those who needed it, and liking each other a lot, they didn't seem to have much to argue about. He knew a fight would come sooner or later, and he wondered how they'd handle it. He didn't see Ivy as a rager. More a quiet withholder maybe? Would she ice him or lay into him? Throw shit at him or storm away and never see him again?

He didn't like that thought much. "Ivy."

"Yes?" She pulled him with her down the stairs.

"If, ah, *when* I piss you off, what are you going to do?"

They came to the bottom of the stairs before she answered him. "Do?"

"Yeah, like, will you bitch me out, do you think? Give me the silent treatment? What?"

"You know, we haven't had our first fight yet." She yanked him with her toward the car. "Although we might if you don't get the lead out."

He chuckled.

"I don't know. I guess it depends on why we're fighting. Did you lie to me? Try to cheat on me? Because we haven't exactly discussed it, but if we're seeing each other and fooling around, there's only you and me. No one else."

"Uh, yeah. I know that." That was a given. Sam didn't do infidelity. Eileen had influenced him while growing up, and he could only thank God he'd found her and Foley when he had.

He squeezed Ivy's hand. "I'm not talking something unforgiveable. I mean, like, if I say something stupid."

"You do that all the time."

He sighed. "I'm serious." She was humoring him, he could tell.

"Sam, why worry about a fight until it happens? For the record, unless you break my heart, I'll talk to you about any problems. I don't like to stew on things. When I'm hurt, I tend to get talky." She shrugged her pretty shoulders. God, everything about the woman seemed delicate overlying an inner strength. "I might get mad or cry."

"Christ, don't do that. I'd rather you were just quiet."

She smiled. "And that's why I like you, Sam. You act all tough, but you're really a big softie."

"Shut up, Ivy."

She snickered. "Yeah, one big old, gooey marshmallow covered in bitter chocolate."

He raised a brow as they got into the car. "Bitter? Baby, I'm nothing but sweet."

"And bad for me," she added. "You're the kind of guy who's all temptation and peer pressure. And before you know it, a girl's gained five pounds." She looked depressed at the thought.

"Um, I'm not sure how I'm causing you to gain weight by being myself."

"It's a metaphor." She sounded all highbrow, then ruined it by admitting, "I think. I'm not sure. Is that the right word?"

"You're asking me?" He started the car along with everyone else, and they listened to the radio for a few minutes, each lost in their own thoughts. "So, you're okay with tonight, right? I mean, you seemed kind of nervous before." He'd worried she might jet right after he'd picked her up. But then she'd relaxed once on the ferry. "I told you. Foley and me, we bring home friends all the time. It's not like I'm announcing to the world I'm doing you. Not yet." He winked.

"I'm good. It's just, I know Eileen is important to you. I want her to like me." She glanced out the window at the other cars. "Parents can be a tough sell."

"Nah. Not Eileen. Look, she put up with my crap for years. You're nothing but easy." He paused, thinking that didn't sound right.

"I'm easy?" Her lips quirked.

"I meant to say you aren't anything to worry about."

"So now I'm a nobody?"

He scowled and followed the guy in front of him off the boat. "No, damn it. Quit putting words in my mouth."

"See? We're having a mini-fight right now, and I'm not quiet or furious. I'm talking to you."

"This is a mini-fight?"

"Not really. I'm trying to ease your tiny mind."

"You're pretty funny all of a sudden." Yet he found himself grinning. "Smart-ass."

"Hey, I'm just trying to keep up with you, Sam Hamilton." She did that a lot, said his full name to mess with him, constantly reminding him of Willie. "And on that note, when are we going back to Willie's? I kind of liked her…minus her upstairs bedroom."

He chuckled. "She's an acquired taste, but I like her too. Never tell her that though."

She twisted an invisible key over her lips and tossed it over her shoulder. "Our little secret."

Every time she said *our* or *we*, he got a thrill. He constantly thought in terms of *them*, so to hear her doing the same eased his concern she'd tire of him too soon. If Louise would quit calling him, he'd probably stop worrying so much. But her presence was too much a reminder of what little he had to offer anyone, that Foley and Eileen pitied him, accepting him out of a sense of compassion. Loser that he was, he'd take it.

Ivy, well, she was so new, what she felt for him was barely more than like or desire.

Sam had no qualms about admitting to good looks and a strong frame. Women dug a man with muscle, and it protected him from getting his ass handed to him. But he had to wonder. If he were fat and ugly, would Ivy be interested in the guy buried inside all the tats?

He didn't want to know.

"You're too quiet. Now I'm nervous again." She blew out a breath. "Tell me about Eileen and… What's his name? I forget."

"Jacob Wynn, dentist to the stars."

"Huh?"

"That's what Foley calls him behind his back. Jacob's actually a good guy. We like him for Eileen. He's calm and good with people, though I think I freak him out. He always looks at me like he's waiting for me to punch him."

"Have you hit him?"

"Hell no." He scowled at her as he turned toward their destination. "Dude is in his fifties. I don't hit old men."

"Or kids, dogs, or women. I know. I was teasing you."

He blinked. "Oh. Right. Well, Jacob's a lot like Eileen, except he doesn't swear and he has a lot of money."

"He's rich?"

Sam heard her discomfort. "Yeah, I felt the same way when I first met him. I mean, his bathroom is almost bigger than my bedroom."

"It is?" Her green eyes widened.

He had to force himself to look back at the road. No sense in having an accident because he was too stupid to look away from his girl. "Well, maybe not. But it's big. He's got a friggin' chair in it. I mean, come on. The only throne you need in a bathroom is a toilet, right?"

Ivy chuckled. "Unless you're in a restroom in a fancy hotel or restaurant. I'm really curious to see this house."

"We were there for Christmas. He had the brunch catered. And yeah, I said brunch. It was all fancy and shit. Freaked Foley the hell out. That was funny."

"What happened?"

"Foley has been Eileen's focus for a long time. Then she meets and falls for Jacob. He's a nice dude. Has money, classy clothes, a cool place. And he thinks she walks on water. Trust me, Eileen is no saint. One of the best women I know though. She's real, and she's true. You could trust her with Cookie, your car, a million bucks. The woman is loyal to the bone." He nodded. "Anyhow, Jacob's no dummy. He fell for Eileen hard. Back at New Year's, they were in a car accident."

"How awful."

He swallowed, not wanting to remember how scared he'd been. Like being a lost little kid again with nowhere to go, no one to love him. Eileen anchored him in a way Louise never had. "Yeah, well, she broke her leg. Jacob felt responsible, but he wasn't. It was during the bad ice storm."

She nodded. "That was a terrible time to be on the road. We actually closed the shop for a few days because of all the ice."

"Right. Anyway, Eileen recovered, but man, she was so bitchy getting better. I've never seen her hurt like that, and you totally don't want to be around her when she's sick. She was a mean patient. But Jacob, he stuck to her like glue. Got her whatever she needed and never left her side. Look, I love the woman, but Foley and I both left her to Jacob. Eileen might be little, but she can be scary."

"You're not making me feel any better about our dinner."

"She's better now. All healed up." *Just psycho about her wedding*.

"Well, she's nice to you, so that's something."

"Eileen's nice to everyone. Too nice sometimes, that's why me and Foley step on the ones that get out of line."

"Will you step on me if I say the wrong thing?"

She sounded so serious that it took him a moment to realize she was teasing. "I might." He lowered his voice. "Then again, I might make you pay for it in bed."

"When we eventually get around to that." She sounded breathless. Good to know it wasn't just him.

"Oh, we'll get around to it."

"Really?" She smirked at him. "Because I've never had to work so hard to get a man to take me to bed before."

He felt shy and stupid and annoyed. "Hey, I'm trying to be a gentleman." It didn't help matters when she laughed. "I can be suave."

"I don't want suave or sophisticated. I want you."

They pulled into Jacob's driveway in the pricey Manzanita Bay area.

"Was that an insult or a compliment?"

"That didn't come out right," she teased, mimicking him from earlier. "My point is I like you just the way you are. Don't change, Sam. You're a gentleman at heart. And I appreciate your concern." She patted his thigh. "There's no place I feel safer than with you."

Now he was blushing for sure. "Yeah, yeah. You're laying it on a bit thick."

"Have I told you how much I love to see you turn red? You are so cute." She unbuckled her seat belt and leaned over to kiss him on the cheek. Then she caressed the other side of his face and froze him to his seat. "I sure do like kissing you. You always smell and taste so good."

Reminders of how she'd tasted him last night went straight to his cock.

"Damn it, Ivy," he growled. "I was ready to go in, and now I gotta wait out another hard-on. What are you doing to me?"

She blushed, looking edible. Man, he wanted to go down on her so bad right now.

"Sorry." She moved back. "But I do like kissing you. Deal with it." From the back of the car, she grabbed the peanut butter cookies she'd baked, then waited for him outside while he took a moment to collect himself.

He soon joined her by the front door. Jacob's house—and Eileen's too now, Sam thought—sat right on the water with a private deck and a boat parked out back. A large two-story with wooden shingles, it had a Craftsman design. And he'd never in a million years have enough money to buy something so expensive.

"I hope she likes me," Ivy said as she brushed the front of her skirt, the other hand gripping her plate of cookies.

"She'll love you. Trust me." He rang the doorbell.

Eileen answered in seconds. "I was waiting for you

two. Come in, come in." She closed the door behind them, then gave Sam a big hug. Sam thought she might have surprised Ivy, because the look on Ivy's face when Eileen gave her as warm a welcome made him smile.

"These are for you," Ivy said shyly, holding out the plate.

"Oh, peanut butter." Eileen smiled. "My favorite." She took the cookies. "It's so good to meet you, Ivy. So, this is the place." Eileen waved an arm at the interior.

Ivy stared, wide-eyed, not that Sam could blame her. He felt totally out of place in the designer home. It had built-ins made of quality wood, antique furnishings he worried would break under his weight, and fresh flowers. For no reason. Not like it was a holiday or anything. He felt like he'd been stuck in the middle of one of those millionaire house-hunting programs Eileen was addicted to.

"Let me take your coats." Eileen hung up their jackets in a big hall closet. Sam would have tossed them over the couch, like they did at Ivy's.

"Wow. This place is gorgeous." Ivy looked out the back windows at Manzanita Bay. Twinkling lights on the boats out at sea gave the outdoors a romantic vibe… if Sam were prone to feeling that kind of stuff.

A glance at the big, round dining table off the living area showed an aqua-blue tablecloth, floral centerpiece, and lit candles. Four place settings had already been laid out, with crystal glasses Sam feared breaking. Did the guy not own any plastic cups, for God's sake?

"…will be right out," Eileen was saying about Jacob, who apparently toiled over the stove in the closed-off kitchen. "Would you like the grand tour, Ivy?"

"Are you kidding? I feel like I'm on *House Hunters: Seattle*."

It was like he and Ivy shared the same brain sometimes.

Eileen laughed and took Ivy away. Sam would have followed, but Jacob ventured out from his gourmet kitchen. "Sam. Nice to see you." He strode forward with a big smile and held out a manicured hand. Dr. Jacob Wynn, DDS, had warm, blue eyes behind designer frames. He radiated sincerity and looked like the stereotype of what all older men should aspire to in his khaki pants and button-down, light-blue shirt.

Sam had dressed for the occasion—because it was Eileen after all—in clean black jeans and one of Foley's sweaters. The dark-gray one, because it was clean and hid stains, according to Foley.

"Where's this Ivy I'm hearing so much about?"

"She's getting the third degree from Eileen on a 'tour' of the house," he said, using air quotes.

Jacob grinned. Man, he had some nice, straight, white teeth. Then again, Sam wouldn't exactly trust a dentist with crooked, yellow fangs.

"Can I get you something to drink?"

"I'll take a beer." He followed Jacob into the kitchen and sat at one of the stools by the eat-in island, careful to make sure he sat apart from Jacob and didn't make any sudden moves. Normally he liked making others scared of him. But not people he cared about. And with Jacob soon to marry Eileen, the dude would soon be family. "Thanks." He accepted the bottle and, parched, chugged half of it. "Ah, that hit the spot."

Jacob grabbed a bottle and drank as well, no doubt to

make Sam feel at ease and not like a total slob for not using a glass.

"So, how have you been?" Jacob asked. "We haven't seen you in a few weeks."

Sam glanced around and leaned toward Jacob. "I've been keeping my distance. What is with Eileen and this wedding? She's like Bridezilla on crack."

Jacob smothered a grin. "An apt description." He sighed. "I don't know. I think she's nervous, so she's throwing all her energy into the wedding to ignore her cold feet."

Sam hadn't considered that. "Think she'll take off?"

"No. At least, I hope not."

Great, now Jacob looked anxious. *Nice job, idiot. Freak out the host, why don't you?*

Fortunately, Eileen and Ivy returned.

"Sam, have you seen this house? It's amazing." Ivy paused when she spotted Jacob. "Oh, hello. You must be Jacob. I'm Ivy." She held a hand out and shook Jacob's.

"A pleasure to meet you."

They stood smiling at each other. Sam knew what the other man saw—a gorgeous, sweet blond way too good for Sam. Ivy wore a long denim skirt and a pretty green sweater, her hair down, curled over her shoulders. She looked like a damn dream, and Sam worried he'd wake someday to find her gone.

He felt Eileen's stare. "What? Do I have something on my face?"

"You mean, in addition to that annoyed frown line right there?" Eileen tapped him between his eyes and laughed when he swept her into a hug, lifting her feet off the floor.

"My momma's getting married." Sam knew she loved when he called her that, and making her happy felt good. "I can't wait to see you walking down the aisle."

Ivy smiled at them.

And everything felt right. Eileen, his dream mom; her almost husband; and his girl—all together.

The dinner went better than he'd hoped. Eileen treated Ivy the way she treated Cyn—like a second daughter. He and Jacob lamented Eileen's wedding mania while Ivy defended her, saying the stress of hosting such an event would freak anyone out.

Eileen beamed.

Jacob kept the conversation flowing *away* from wedding talk, which Sam appreciated. When dinner ended, Jacob stood to clear the table. "You and I have dishes, Sam."

An odd command, since Jacob never let anyone lift a finger at his house. A guest was a guest. Period.

But a glance at Eileen and her nod toward the kitchen had Sam rethinking things.

"Ah, Ivy might want to—"

"Shoo." Eileen waved him away. "I want to talk to Ivy about wedding stuff I don't want Jacob to hear."

"Sounds good to me." Jacob made his escape into the kitchen.

"I won't tell him." Sam didn't want to leave Ivy alone. Eileen had a funny look in her eye.

"Yes, you will. You're male. You all share too much."

"What are you talking about?"

"Go." Eileen pointed in the direction of the kitchen, ordering him around like he was eleven all over again.

Ivy stared, wide-eyed, at the petite Eileen and her fiery authority. "I'll be fine, Sam. Better do what she says."

"See? Ivy's a smart girl. Boy, why are you still standing there?"

"Fine. I'm going." But before he headed in to join Jacob, he warned her, "I'll be right in the kitchen if anyone needs anything," in his meanest, most respectful voice.

Ivy could hold her own. Besides, Eileen seemed to really like her. It was all good.

And it was even better when he joined Jacob for a slice of devil's food cake and milk.

"Thanks."

Jacob nodded. "I'm glad you like it. I made it myself."

Of course he had. The guy probably shit rainbows too. Everything he touched seemed to turn to gold. Not that Sam minded, since the guy was marrying Eileen, but being near Jacob too much made Sam feel inadequate. He'd never be able to offer Ivy a place like this on the water. A sense of peace and sophistication.

Sam was engine oil and beer. Curse words, fighting at Ray's, and rescuing stray mutts from the street. Ivy was sweetness and light, neatness and a tender smile. Man, he was fucking doomed.

"I know that look, and it's not good." Jacob shoved the plate of cake at him. "Eat and forget your worries."

"Hey, this is good." Sam ate the whole piece in under a minute. Stress eating while he worried about Ivy? *Nah, it's just good cake.*

"More?"

"Hell yeah."

"Don't worry, Sam. Eileen likes her. I can tell." Jacob

dished him another piece. "Oh, and you don't have to worry about me and Eileen."

"What do you mean?"

"When I first met Eileen, I knew."

Sam forced himself to swallow before talking. It was one thing to gross Foley out, another when it came to Eileen's man. He had to make a good impression—until the guy was married and family. Then all bets were off. "You knew what?"

"That she was the one for me. I knew the moment I met her I wanted to marry her."

"That soon?" Sam felt a rush of nerves. Because he'd felt the same way about Ivy. But he didn't have Jacob's track record when it came to women. Jacob had been married once, had a beautiful daughter and grandkid to boot. He could do committed.

"That soon," Jacob agreed. "When you know, you know." Jacob smiled. "And like I said, don't worry about Ivy and Eileen. Your mother likes her, I can tell."

Yeah, but Eileen could be protective as hell. After that mess with Jennifer, the woman had said some things to the girl and her parents that had shocked even Sam. He groaned. "You don't think she's gonna grill Ivy or anything, do you? I don't want to scare her off."

"Who, Eileen? You know her better than I do. What do you think?" Then, because Jacob had a soft heart, he cut Sam another piece of cake. "More milk?"

Sam sighed. "A bigger glass would be great." He lost himself in chocolate, and not the bitter kind.

Chapter 15

EILEEN STUDIED THE FIRST GIRL SAM HAD BROUGHT to meet her in over ten years. Oh, Sam had brought friends of his home before. She'd fix them a meal or a snack and let the boys have their sleepovers. As they got older, she'd feed everyone before the boys and their friends hit the bars. Though Sam wasn't hers by blood, she'd cared for him when Louise hadn't. Which had pretty much been all the time.

Yet Sam had never brought home a woman he looked at the way he watched Ivy. Like the girl was something precious. Like he was scared she'd leave if Sam didn't remain close. That, and there was a curious fascination there, as if Sam couldn't *not* look at her.

He had good taste. Ivy was charming. Not only pretty on the outside, but on the inside as well. She'd been courteous and easy to talk to. Eileen liked her. But this was about Sam. She'd have to be thorough.

Ivy sat on the couch, watching the bobbing lights of passing boats on the water. The waxing moon lit up the night sky, turning it into a magical evening. Then again, everything felt magical to Eileen lately. She couldn't believe in just a few short months, she'd be marrying the man of her dreams. Oh, she knew Jacob worried she had her concerns about the wedding. But she'd worked those out. Now she simply stressed about making the day a success, which had to do with logistics, not emotions.

She wanted that same happiness for Foley, who seemed to have it with Cyn. But the man she worried about most sat in the kitchen with Jacob. Sam and his vulnerable heart—would they be safe in Ivy's hands?

"Yes?"

Eileen blinked.

"You're giving me that look," Ivy pointed out. "Did you want to ask me something?"

Eileen decided to go tits-out firm. If the girl couldn't handle some tough talk, she wasn't the one for Sam. And the boy could hem and haw about just meeting the girl, but hell. Eileen knew her boy, and he was hooked. "I have a few questions."

Eileen had intended to be pointed with the girl, but Ivy looked so nervous, so young, suddenly, she didn't have the heart to lay into her. "So you and Sam. Are you two serious?"

Ivy shrugged. "We kind of just started dating." The word *dating* sounded rusty on her tongue. "I like him a lot. He's sweet."

"Sam is sweet."

Ivy nodded. "He seems so tough, but he's a nice person at heart. I mean, he can hurt a guy. I saw him beat up a man at Ray's. But the man deserved it. Sam's been nothing but kind to me." Ivy blushed.

Eileen would bet that wasn't *all* Sam had been to Ivy. "He's a sweetheart of a giant, but because of his size and, let's face it, that stare, people can think the worst about him. Foley and I watch out for him." A warning.

Ivy nodded. "I think he's lucky he had you, and he knows it. It's what he hasn't said about Louise that made me realize that. You're a good woman, Eileen. Helping him like you did." Ivy smiled, and that soft look had no doubt pierced right through Sam's ironclad heart. That her boy had actually mentioned Louise to Ivy at all spoke volumes. "I don't know what he was like as a boy, but he's a good man. I like him a lot."

The girl had stared like a lovesick calf at Sam when he hadn't been looking. Eileen knew that look. Hell, she used it all the time with Jacob, but she kept that to herself. "I'm thinking you like him a lot more than as a casual friend."

"We're dating." Ivy nodded, then she smiled. "I like being with Sam. He makes me laugh."

"He's a little smart-ass." Eileen laughed. "Always has been." She paused. "Have you seen his house yet?" That was something Ivy should know. If the girl was afraid of dirt, Sam was not the man for her. "Because the man you're dating might have a soft spot for animals, but he's got a god-awful sense of organization."

"He showed me his room to prove Foley wrong about calling him a hoarder." Ivy and Eileen chuckled. "I've seen his stacks," Ivy admitted. "He's not the neatest man I've ever met, but hey, it's his room."

"His stacks. Lord. That boy and his collections." She shook her head.

"I don't mind." Ivy paused. "From the things he's said, I get the feeling he didn't have a lot growing up. That life with Louise wasn't…the best." Ivy shrugged. "So maybe he keeps what's important to him now because he can." She nodded. "We all have our stuff. What's best about Sam is that he's got a killer smile. And he's such a good person."

Eileen felt it. This girl—she saw the real Sam. "Ivy,

how are you not married with sixteen babies by now? How old are you?"

Ivy blinked. "Ah, twenty-six."

"Sam is thirty-two and never been married. You?"

"No. I was engaged once." Some drama there— Eileen could see it. "But it didn't work out. I've been single for a while. Men can be too clingy."

"Tell me about it."

Ivy snorted. "I was doing fine on my own. Then I found Cookie at the back door. And soon after, I found Sam there too." She sighed. "Now I have *two* boys in my life, and I couldn't be happier."

Eileen envisioned wedding bells for Sam, though she had no intention of telling him and scaring him away. "One thing you should know. Sam can be skittish. Go easy on him."

Ivy laughed. "Easy on *him*? He should go easy on me. He can be kind of intimidating."

"You can handle him. You have the stomach for it. I can tell."

They smiled at each other.

"So can I ask you a wedding question?" Ivy asked.

Eileen perked up. "Sure."

"What's your theme? Colors?"

The rest of the evening passed with the ladies talking wedding details until Sam and Jacob joined them and turned the conversation toward the water and boating, with a promise to take everyone out on the bay when the weather grew warmer.

Before Eileen knew it, Sam and Ivy had departed.

"Well?" Jacob asked as they got into bed. He pulled her into his arms, and she laid her head on his chest.

"I liked her. You?"

"She seemed sweet. Maybe too nice for Sam, though."

"Sam needs a little sweetness in his life. God knows he gets his share of vinegar from Louise." Eileen paused. "She sure was a pretty little thing."

"Little? She's bigger than you," Jacob pointed out.

"True. But next to Sam, she's small."

"Next to Sam, the Portland Trailblazers are small."

"Funny." She stroked his chest. "I love you, Jacob."

"Oh, Eileen. I love you too."

"I just want Sam to know the same kind of love I have for you. The way Foley feels for Cyn."

"He will someday. Remember, though, he and Ivy are new. There are bound to be tough times ahead."

"Especially when Louise calls him. The good news is he's not fighting anymore. Foley told me he's been a lot calmer at Ray's." And according to Liam as well, who'd heard it from someone else, Sam had laid off those illegal matches.

"I still haven't been to that bar. We really need to go there someday."

"We really don't." She cringed. "I've been there."

He laughed and hugged her to him. "Ah, Eileen. What would I do without you?"

She laughed with him, then they started kissing until she knew nothing but the wonder of Jacob, the second great love of her life.

—∞—

Thursday late afternoon, Ivy had no idea why she felt so nervous. She'd been giving professional therapeutic massage for eight years. She felt more than comfortable around Sam. And since her last client had rescheduled for Saturday morning, Ivy had nothing to do with the rest of her day. What better time than to fit Sam in for an appointment?

She hadn't forgotten how nice he'd been to fix her car, charging only for parts. She owed him big-time, and she didn't want him to feel taken advantage of.

As she waited for him, she wondered how Cookie was doing. Between all of Sam's friends and contacts through Willie, she seemed to have no end of dog-sitters, so her guilt at leaving Cookie alone so much didn't come into play.

Still, she missed the little guy. She and Sam would pick him up from Lou on Sunday. She'd been ready to get him today, but apparently Lou's little sister was in love and wanted more time with him.

Ivy had relented, because she'd remembered how badly she'd wanted a pet as a little girl. Something that would love her unconditionally. But Ethan had been allergic to cats, and her parents had no intention of letting a mongrel dog into their lives simply because Ivy wanted it. Bad enough they'd had a mongrel in *her*, she thought with bitter amusement.

Every now and again, she'd wonder about her family, about the nephew she'd never met and likely never would. Did they ever think about her? She'd pretty much resigned herself to having no familial connections, but she'd never understood why. What had she done but exist to make them all hate her?

Except hate was too strong a word. They'd have to feel something to hate her. Mostly they didn't care, and that hurt most of all.

The door chimed and Sam stepped through. He gave her a sheepish half smile. "I'm kind of cruddy, but I tried to clean up. Dirt won't come out of my nails no matter how hard I scrub. Friggin' low-viscosity oil, my ass."

"Don't worry about it. I'm just glad you're here." She felt better seeing Sam. He didn't play games, and he didn't do disinterest. He was too alive not to feel. "How was your day?"

"Exhausting." Yet he smiled. "The guys keep giving me shit about you."

"Me?"

"Yeah, I'm too happy for work. It's annoying the piss out of Lou though, and that makes my fucking day." He chuckled. "Sorry. I'd give you a quarter, but I'm out."

"What?"

"I told you about Del and her swear jar, right?" He quickly explained again, though she recalled him telling her before. "Woman should be able to go to the friggin' Bahamas for a month off what she's collecting from us in the garage."

Ivy stifled a laugh. "Must be tough to talk with manners."

He gave her a look. "Shut up."

She gave in to her smile. "Well now, time for that massage, right?"

She felt as if she'd just stripped down naked, because the raw expression of lust on his face shocked her into feeling it as well. And Ivy never did sensual stuff at work. No hanky-panky. No way. She considered that a breach of trust. A client getting undressed and vulnerable on the table needed a therapist who respected boundaries.

Even if she did want Sam in the worst way, she relegated her desire to off-the-clock time.

She cleared her throat. "Come on in and we'll get started." She led him into her office, which had never before felt too small for her. Then she did a quick intake interview with him, determining—as she'd already known—he could handle a massage without medical worry. Then she listened to him complain about tension in his shoulders.

"You're going to be a challenge." No lie. The man had muscles like rocks. "But I'm up for it."

"Yeah?" he said, his voice thick. "So am I."

She followed his glance to his crotch and blushed. "Sam, this isn't that kind of—"

"*I know*." He blew out a breath. "I'm not trying to do this. I can't help it."

She felt flattered, amused, and shy—which made little sense. So she shook it off. "Okay." She gave him the same talk she gave all her clients, determined to treat him like everyone else.

After she'd left him for a short time, she returned and closed the door behind her. Then she put on some relaxing music and turned to face him. Ivy dealt with bodies that came in all shapes and sizes. In her room, they were nothing but wounded people needing help. But she couldn't stop herself from seeing Sam as a beautiful man. Physically, he had the most amazing body. The perfect *V* from his wide shoulders to his trim hips. Such thick biceps, a strong neck, and wow, he was long. His feet dangled over the table.

She had to concentrate to focus on him as a patient and not a sexy man. After she made him more comfortable and tucked the blanket and sheets around him, only exposing the top of his shoulders, she grabbed a heat pack from the hydroculator. "This will soften your tissue so you're easier to work on. It will feel good."

He lifted his head from the face cradle to wink at her. "Work anything you like, baby."

She shoved his head back down with a laugh. "Stop. Now lie still. Oh boy. I might need to use the bigger pack. You're huge."

He said something she couldn't make out, then chuckled, so she thought it best not to ask him to repeat it. Grabbing a larger heat pack and a towel, she placed them both directly over his shoulders. The heat pack could get superhot, and she didn't want to burn him, thus the towel went on first. With the moist heat now over his upper traps, she could concentrate on his thick arms.

"While that heats up, I'm going to work on your arms and hands, okay?"

He mumbled a yes, and she got to work.

Twenty minutes later, after exhausting her hands on his steely forearms and hands, she worked his biceps and triceps and delts. She removed the heat pack, pleased to see his tissue had turned a nice pink.

"God, I feel good," he said, sounding sleepy.

She smiled and started on his back, working a healing cream into his muscle. He felt like a slab of slightly softened granite, and she was sweating by the time she'd finished his left side. Turning to the right, she saw him fidget.

"Are you okay?"

"Yeah."

"Face cradle bothering your sinuses?" Shaped like a

doughnut, it supported the head and sides of the face, leaving the nose and mouth open so the client could breathe.

"A little."

That much pressure for an extended period of time could be uncomfortable. "I'll turn you over after I work this side. Another ten minutes or so, okay?"

"Whatever. I feel so fuckin' good," he slurred.

Good old Sam and his potty mouth. Ivy continued to work the adhesions out of his tissue, using deep-tissue and trigger-point work together. But she'd never worked on a man of Sam's immense size before. Even the bodybuilders she'd massaged hadn't felt so dense.

The more she touched him, the closer she felt to him. Her intent to heal took her under once more, and she had to remind herself his face must be hurting from lying supine for so long.

"Okay, Sam. Now we're going to turn you over. I'll hold the sheet while you—"

"No. I'm good."

She frowned. "Are you sure? Because it would probably help if I worked your pecs and anterior deltoids to balance—"

"You turn me over, you're going to see how much I like this massage," he said in a rough voice, having turned his head to the side so he could clearly talk to her. "I tried not to feel turned on, but I can't help it. I'm fucking hard as hell, Ivy. And unless you want to finish me off in here, 'cause I'm more than happy to let you, I'd better get dressed." He paused. "But you know, you can always do me later tonight."

An offer she didn't want to refuse. "I—"

His phone buzzed, sitting on top of his jeans in a chair

in the corner of the room, and he propped himself on his elbows on the table. "Think about it. Now get out of here unless you want a real show."

"Well…" She smiled.

He raised a brow and started to get up.

"Stop. Wait. I'm leaving." She hurried out of the room. It might seem weird, considering she'd already seen him naked and touched and kissed certain parts of his body, but work was work. Such definite lines had been drawn for therapists, who'd been tagged with words like *masseuse* and were considered no more than prostitutes who kept their clothes on. Ivy was supercareful about always looking her professional best.

As much as she'd like to jump Sam's bones, doing it here felt wrong. What if Shelby or Denise or a client walked in the door and heard her moaning? Heck no.

She waited nervously by the front desk for him. Denise had already finished early today, and Sue had an evening yoga class.

Two young men, likely in their early twenties, entered the clinic. They wore grungy jeans and sweatshirts but looked like potential clients.

"Hey, what is this place?" one of them asked. He stood taller than his friend, closer to six feet. When he looked at her, she felt strange.

Ivy didn't get a good feel from him, but she didn't worry. It was still daylight outside, and none of the businesses on the strip had ever been robbed when they'd been open. She smiled. "This is a massage therapy clinic."

The men studied the place, the shorter of the two frowning at the hand weights and exercise balls along the wall. "What's this stuff?"

"That's for our trainer, Sue, who takes appointments for smaller groups. She has one later tonight, in fact. Did you guys want to book an appointment?" She noticed the smaller one seemed to favor his left shoulder. "I can tell you've got something going on with your shoulder."

His dark eyes widened in surprise. "Uh, yeah. I wrenched it yesterday moving furniture. That's what me and Derrick do. We haul stuff."

"Oh, are you guys part of that group, Junkin' and Funkin'? I've seen the trucks around town." For college students moving people for extra money.

Derrick nodded, studying her. "Yeah."

She turned to the injured guy. "Sounds like a good business." She nodded to his shoulder. "Where is it hurting exactly?"

He opened his mouth to reply, but Derrick shook his head and looked at his phone. "No time, Sean. Thanks, lady. But we need to go."

She grabbed two cards and approached them. Upon closer study, she thought them closer to her age. "Well, here you go. Take care of that shoulder. Rotator cuff injuries take a while to heal."

Sean grimaced. "Yeah, I'm getting that." He took the card and gave her a tentative smile. "Thanks."

"Anytime. We're here most days, but you can always call and schedule an appointment." She gave a card to Derrick as well. "And guys in your line of work can't be too careful."

Derrick took the car and nodded. "No kidding. If I have to lift one more sofa bed, I might lose it." He rotated his neck. "Might have to take you up on it. We came in because we thought you were some kind of spa place, and my girlfriend has been on my case to get her something nice for her birthday. But I don't see perfumes or lotions."

"Well, get her a massage. Those work too. I'm Ivy, by the way."

He grinned. "Not a bad idea." His smile left him' as he looked over her shoulder. "Thanks, Ivy. We need to head out."

He and Sean darted out the door. Ivy knew why. She turned to see Sam glowering after the guys who'd left. "Scaring future customers?"

He shook his head. "They looked shifty. I don't like you here by yourself."

"But I'm not." She crossed to him. "I'm with you."

His frown eased. "Yeah, you are." He rolled his neck and moved his shoulders. "Ivy, damn. You're amazing. I feel *so* friggin' relaxed right now."

Proud that she'd proved to Sam she was good at her job, she showed him a few stretches that might help ease his back and shoulders as well. "So do you want to come back for more sessions? I owe you a few more for the car."

Sam sighed. "Sorry, no can do."

"Oh." Hurt, because she'd thought he'd liked her work, she tried to figure out how to repay him. Maybe installments?

"Don't look like that." He pulled her in for a hug. "I feel like a million bucks. But, Ivy"—he lowered his voice—"I'm still in pain, and you can't fix that here."

She blushed. "Sam."

He grinned. "I'm afraid any visits to see you are going to end with me hard and you turning all red in the face. So instead of massaging me here, can we do it at my place or yours? And I'm not talking about sex. I felt a little weird being naked here. And I want to be totally relaxed with you. If I'm sporting wood on my back at home, you won't be all freaked out. Tempted, sure, but not worried I'll make you look like a ho."

She blinked. "Ah, thanks?"

He chuckled. "No problem. So what about tonight? Dinner? Or are you busy? 'Cause we can always do another day." He shoved his hands in his pockets.

Nerves.

But what did he have to be nervous about? "I'm done for the day and puppy-less. I have nothing but time."

He nodded. "Cool." Then he frowned. "Ah, I have to take care of something first."

"Your phone call?" The man never seemed to answer his cell.

He scowled. "No. Something else." He paused, as if in thought. "Can I swing by to get you at eight? And do you need to be in early tomorrow?"

"Not until noon. My Friday afternoon and evening are full, but my morning is free."

"Great." He withdrew his hands from his pockets and stepped toward her. "I guess I shouldn't kiss you here. Don't want to screw with your rep and all."

"No, that's okay. A kiss from my boyfriend is allowed." Boyfriend. That seemed too tame a word for what Sam meant to her.

But he seemed to like it. The kiss he gave her was chaste, sweet, and had her knees shaking. "I'll see you later tonight. Oh, and don't forget you promised to help me pick out a suit for Del's wedding. Saturday work for you?"

She should say no, should take some time away from Sam so she could breathe without obsessing over the man. "Sounds great. I'll see you tonight."

He left with a wave, and she wondered what he had planned for tonight, and why she suddenly couldn't think about anything else.

Chapter 16

HE'D PUT IT OFF LONG ENOUGH. WITH A SIGH, HE called Louise back.

"About fuckin' time," she said, her voice husky from years spent abusing cigarettes.

"What do you want?" No sense in being polite; she didn't care either way.

"I need some help with something."

Shit. He didn't want to see her. She always put him in a funk, and Foley told him he acted like an asshole for days after being with Louise. Not like Sam could help it. He needed time to decompress after being around his mother. But what if Ivy thought he was acting weird? Distance from Louise was the obvious answer, but the woman wouldn't stop bugging him if he ignored her.

She'd once threatened to come to Eileen's house when, as a kid, he'd refused to come home. Since he didn't want her ugliness around people he liked, he'd conceded to her demands. And as long as he kept doing what she wanted, she left him mostly alone.

Now she knew he worked at Webster's. He could just see her drugged-out ass busting up his job. He'd worked hard to fit in at the garage, and he liked it there. He didn't need her interfering, especially not now, with Ivy in the picture. He blanched, imagining his mother laying into her. God only knew what crap Louise would tell her.

"Well?" she snapped. "You coming or what?"

"I'll be there on Sunday."

"But I—"

"Sunday," he snapped back, "or you can fix your damn mess yourself." He'd never talked to her like that before. Despite all she'd done, he'd remained quiet, if not loving, then at least respectful. But he'd never had anything he feared losing like Ivy.

Foley and Eileen had met Louise. They knew she was bad news. Ivy didn't, and he wanted to keep it that way.

Louise remained quiet a moment. "Fine." Then she disconnected.

That out of the way, he could breathe a little easier. He started his car and drove downtown. Now to get to the next big project—making tonight unforgettable for Ivy. The big night. His palms felt sweaty, and he got the biggest hard-on thinking about what he wanted to do with her. Man, they were finally going to have sex. Make love. Whatever. Sliding inside her again, feeling that hot pussy gloving him while he stared into her eyes. Unlike his other sexual encounters, he connected with Ivy all over. He didn't want a faceless fuck. And with Ivy, it wouldn't be that way. He knew exactly who he was with in her arms. But this time he planned to finish inside her.

He groaned, the restriction of his jeans making his erection painful.

Her massage had nearly had him spilling on the table. Though she'd sure as shit relaxed him, she'd also aroused him just by being near. It was something about her, a lingering scent, her touch, feeling the caring in every stroke. He couldn't define it. But he hoped like hell other dudes on her table didn't feel the same.

He frowned as he drove to a certain hotel Foley had recommended. He'd spent a terrific night there with Cyn, so Sam figured Ivy would like it. If fussy Cyn hadn't complained, Ivy probably wouldn't. Much as Sam liked Cyn, she seemed too high-class for him. Fancy clothes, a fancy house, money out the ass. The woman totally made more than Foley, but Foley couldn't care less.

Sam cared. He didn't want to be so outclassed on every level. Sure, Ivy was better than him. But he had little in the way of expenses. He could handle some evenings out, dinners, getting her little gifts. It wouldn't be a lot, but he could take care of her. And judging by the size of her home and knowing her job, she couldn't be making all that much.

A night out in a romantic hotel would make her feel good. And then *he'd* make her feel good. He put a hand over his cock to calm himself and took deep breaths.

By the time he arrived at the small boutique hotel, he'd relaxed, eager to put his plan in motion. Hours later, he finished cleaning up his room at home. Well, he'd figured out which clothes were dirty and which were clean, and he'd done a load of laundry. Then he'd borrowed another of Foley's shirts, thinking he probably needed to get himself something nicer than a Bowie T-shirt if he planned on dating Ivy for any length of time.

He grinned at the thought. Imagine him and Ivy dating…like, for years. Imagine more…

He wanted that, so much that it hurt to think about. Because love and Sam didn't go hand in hand. "Shit."

He hated the emotional crap. Hated going down the path that led to memories he didn't want anymore. But he was helpless to stop them.

"Where's my little man? Come here, baby."

Sam peeked out from his room. When his mother used that voice, he knew it would be all right. No hitting, no cursing, and no men.

He thought about it, then grabbed his present for her. Now was the time to give her the macaroni necklace he'd made in school.

First graders did important stuff this year. His teacher had told him privately that his was the best she'd ever seen, and he'd been so proud. This would help him finally get Mommy to be nicer. He'd cleaned his room, not that he had that much to straighten up. She'd thrown away all his toys last week, when her last boyfriend had broken up with her.

Because of him.

Sam wanted today to mean something. It was special, maybe even her birthday. He wore his cleanest shirt, the one with only a tiny hole at the collar, and shorts because they were red—Mommy's favorite color. He ignored the cold in the house, determined not to mess up again. Not today.

He walked into the living room, where she sat with a coffee cup. Not a glass of stinky booze. He hated that stuff, and she always had bottles of it everywhere. A sneaky glance around showed the living room tidied up, no sign of pills or needles anywhere.

She seemed a little jittery, but she had showered and dressed nice in a short skirt and tank top. A cigarette burned in an ashtray, but she looked only at him, not at anything else.

He gave a tentative smile and held his present in hand. He'd wrapped it himself at school in red tissue paper. "Happy birthday."

She took the present with wide eyes. "For me?"

"I love you, Mommy."

Tears glazed her eyes, and she slowly unwrapped it.

"It's a necklace. For you to wear."

She stared at the stringy thing of colorful macaroni interspaced with beads.

"I made it with a lot of red because that's your favorite color. And you can wear it anytime you want."

She slowly put it around her neck. "It's not my birthday."

"But it will be." Or had been. He had no idea. "I wanted to make you something pretty because you're the prettiest lady in the whole world."

She held out her arms and he rushed in, getting the best hug he'd ever had. He knew it! She did love him. He never wanted to leave.

And then he made a mistake. "Someday, when I'm big, I'm going to marry you, Mommy. And we'll laugh and eat ice cream and live on the beach." Because his mother loved the water. "And you won't cry anymore." He stroked her hair, enamored with its softness. "And stinky Robbie will be all gone forever."

Her on-again, off-again boyfriend. A man who hit her, made her scream, and did sex stuff behind closed doors—stuff she'd educated Sam about after he'd seen them the last time, when she'd made him hide in her closet so Robbie wouldn't see him.

Robbie hated him. He brought the pills and the needles and made Mommy so different. Bad different, when she cried and screamed and laughed while Robbie did the awful things in her bedroom.

At mention of Robbie, she stiffened. Then she shoved him back, keeping a hold on his arms with a punishing grip. All traces of softness had vanished.

"What did you fuckin' say?"

"N-nothing. I love y—"

"You little shit." She ripped the necklace, the gift he'd spent a week making just right, from her neck. Pieces dropped to the floor and scattered. "You think this stupid crap makes everything all right?" She held what was left in her hand, shaking it in front of him. "You ruined everything!"

"No, Mommy. I'm sorry. I didn't—"

She slapped him across the face and shook him. "We were tight. He loved me. Then you opened your mouth and tattled. I know you did."

He hadn't meant to. But when the lady at school asked about the bruises on his arms and neck and the pain in his ribs, he'd accidentally mentioned Robbie. "N-no. I didn't."

"Liar." She shrieked and shoved him away so hard he fell into the table and hurt his back.

Now crying, he tried to scoot away, but she advanced, swearing at him, blaming him for everything, like she always did. Why had he thought today might be different?

"You're just like your father. That rapist piece of shit. Same eyes, same hair."

He'd always thought he had her color hair.

"He took everything from me." She started crying, and he felt ten times worse.

"No, Mommy. I love you. I'm sorry." He sobbed.

"You had to ruin it for me with Robbie. Jealous and controlling. Just like him! You made all the others leave too. It's always you, you little freak. Causing problems, needing so damn much. I hate you." She'd slapped him a few more times, then stumbled back, and he saw. Her eyes were too dark, the way they were when she took the pills—the ones that sometimes made her tell the bad truths she never remembered later.

"No one could ever love you," she whispered, staring through him. "Should have aborted you when I had the chance."

She walked away and didn't return for two days. But when she did, she'd cleaned him up, cooked him his favorite hot dogs, and sang to him while she drank her stinky booze. And then a new man had shown up…

Sam shook away the memory, the familiar litany of his being unlovable and ruining everything numbing, no longer painful. But it made him rethink tonight. Would Ivy consider tonight special? Did it need to be a big deal, or should they just fuck and enjoy it without all the worries of overdoing it?

He started overthinking it, he knew, and he cursed Louise and her fucked-up life for fucking up his. She'd made his childhood a living hell. She had issues, and God knew she'd earned them, but when they affected him now, after all this time, he truly hated her.

And then he hated himself, because a boy should never hate his own mother.

His resemblance to his masochist old man made it worse for her, he knew. So why did she continue to insist they spend any time together? Why not cut him out of her life forever?

He finished folding his clothes and grabbed a beer, feeling a headache coming on. Fuck. He didn't want this. Not tonight. Ivy shouldn't be tainted with bad memories. No. He refused to let Louise in. No more. He had to stop letting her influence his decisions, his life.

Tonight with Ivy meant something to him. And it might mean something to Ivy too. She liked him. He *knew* she did. Man. He sure wished he had someone to talk to about all this.

He took his cell phone out of his pocket and stared at it. Foley was hanging with Cyn and Johnny and Lara tonight. Some couples thing Sam wasn't a part of. Well, he'd been invited, but he'd wanted to be with Ivy more than being a fifth wheel at a cutesy party. Sometimes watching Cyn and Foley make love eyes at each other annoyed the shit out of him.

But…Cyn loved Foley. And Foley loved her. It wasn't a big deal to do something nice for a girl.

He nodded to himself. Screw Louise. This was for Ivy, and his mother didn't belong.

Tonight mattered. And he'd make it good for the woman he couldn't imagine being without.

—⁓—

Ivy had a bad case of nerves. Tonight, she and Sam would be together-together. What if she disappointed him? What if she froze up? What if he took a good long look at her and realized what a mistake he'd made?

She wished Cookie were there. She could pet him and love on him, and the puppy would lick her, make her laugh and forget her worries.

Telling herself to relax wasn't helping, so she checked her schedule for the next day, confirming her appointments. A full day's work would tire her out, but it would also pay the bills. So hurray.

A knock at her door caused her heart to race.

She glanced down at the knee-length, flared blue skirt and heels. She hadn't worn skirts so much in years, but she wanted Sam to see her as pretty, and yoga pants wouldn't cut it. So she'd worn thigh-high stockings, wanting some warmth and to feel sexy. Under her skirt, she wore her favorite white satin panties and a matching bra under a soft sweater. She felt girlie, sexy, and pretty.

A strong woman for a strong man.

Swallowing her nerves and reminding herself she'd aroused Sam without even trying earlier today, she opened the door.

He made her heart stop. So handsome, so big and rough, yet so gentle and vulnerable inside. She wanted to take care of him as much as she wanted to kiss and be with him.

"Man." He whistled. "You look amazing." He gave her a quick kiss, then stepped back.

"You too." He did. His dark jeans and sweater only emphasized his build. And those sexy tattoos creeping up his neck invited Ivy to explore.

She cleared her throat. "So where are we going?"

"It's a surprise."

"I love surprises."

He studied her, then broke out in a slow smile. "Good. I hope you'll like this one."

They drove for a while, and Ivy thought about the wonderful things Sam did for her without expecting much. How he cared for Willie and all those innocent animals he rescued.

She reached for his hand. "You're a sweetheart, you know that?"

He shrugged away her praise, as he always did, and held her hand. "Nah. But if you want to think that, go ahead."

"I will." She lifted his palm for a kiss. "I'm glad I'm with you, Sam."

"Me too." He blew out a breath, and she wondered if he felt any kind of nerves about tonight.

"Did you get everything done you needed to?" she asked.

"Yeah. Did some laundry."

"Wow."

He grunted. "Don't sound so surprised."

"But where did you put it when you were done? In the pile by the door or by your dresser?" she asked, all innocence.

"You know, you clean freaks are all the same. Picky about a little dust and all holier-than-thou. For your information, princess, I put my shit away. In drawers. Folded even."

She blinked. "Seriously?"

"Yeah. Figured I needed to organize a little. *A little*," he repeated. "Because you didn't seem to want to be in my room all that much, and if I wanted you over, I figured I should straighten up."

"You cleaned for me?" She gaped.

"So what?"

He seemed so defensive. This big man who could put a man down with one punch was uncomfortable when caught doing something nice.

"You are *so* getting lucky tonight." She grinned at the surprised look he shot her.

"Yeah? What do I get if I clear some more stuff out?"

"I'll have to take inventory and see."

"How about some more private massage? I gotta say, you made me feel so good." He paused. "But imagine how much better I could feel with some oil and a hand job?"

She knew she'd turned beet red because he started teasing her about it.

They spent the short journey in the car taunting each other about any- and everything. Until Sam pulled into the drive of a cute little cottage on the water.

"What's this?"

"This is your surprise. Wait here." He left the car, then opened the door for her. "After you."

She got out and took his arm as he walked them to the front door. "Are we visiting friends of yours?"

He shook his head, took out a key, and opened the door. "After you."

"You said that already."

"Gimme a break. I'm trying to act like a gentleman."

She entered the charming cottage and waited for him to join her. "I told you not to change on my account. I like you the way you are."

"So I'm not a gentleman?"

"Really? This is a surprise to you?"

He gave her a grin. "I really like you, Ivy."

Her heart fluttered. "I really like you too, Sam." *A whole lot. More than I should. More than you'd be comfortable knowing.*

"Good. Now, for the surprise." He showed her into the tiny living space, which had a love seat, fireplace, and a tray on the coffee table holding an ice bucket chilling wine and two glasses. Then he pointed out rose petals.

"What?" She stared, wide-eyed, and followed the trail into the bedroom. A king-size bed took up most of the space, along with an attached bathroom that had a Jacuzzi tub with more petals.

"Through there is a supersmall kitchen. This place centers around the bedroom." He took her into his arms. "Surprise."

"You did all this for me?" The cost of renting the place had to be astronomical.

A guarded look filled his eyes. "I wanted tonight to be special."

She felt the burn of tears. "Sam, every time with you is special."

He relaxed. "You like it?"

I love you. "Yes. It's amazing. Like you." She pulled him in and kissed him. "This is the nicest thing anyone's done for me in years."

"You deserve it, baby. You deserve nice all the time." He kissed her back. "How about some snooty wine?"

She laughed. "Snooty, hmm?"

"Well, it's not Boone's Farm. I was going for that, but I was told to do better."

"Oh? Who told you that?"

He sighed. "Cyn, if you have to know. Not that I

couldn't pick out something cool myself, but she's a wine snob."

"I'll have to thank her later."

He kissed her again. "Much later." He held her close, and she felt his erection, plain as day. "I've been hard since this afternoon. It goes away, then I think about you touching me, about your mouth over my cock, what you taste like, and I get so full." He put her hand over him. "Here."

She gave a squeeze, and he tensed. "I want you, Sam."

"Oh, baby. I want you too. I'm just afraid I won't last."

"I'm afraid I won't be good at this," she confessed. "I keep thinking us together before was a fluke. It was too good. I don't want to disappoint you."

He put his hands on her face and looked into her eyes. "Stop that shit right now. This, tonight, is for us. For you."

"No, for us. I like that better."

He stepped back and took off his sweater. "The wine can wait. I can't."

"Good. Me neither." She stared. "You are so handsome. I still can't understand why you're settling for me sometimes." She sighed. "I'm going to lick all those tattoos by the time we're done tonight."

"Done? I'm not gonna be done with you for a long time. Not tonight, tomorrow, or any day after that." He took off his shoes and socks, then stripped out of his jeans, leaving him naked.

"Commando, Sam?" She couldn't stop staring at that huge cock.

"I ache, Ivy. So much." He held himself, and her mouth watered.

"My turn?" she asked, holding the bottom of her sweater.

"Shit, yeah. But go slow." He moved to the bed and sat in the center, his back propped against the headboard. "I wish I had a camera."

"No way. Never take pictures of anything you're not comfortable sharing." She lifted her sweater over her head, praying she looked as good to him as he always did to her.

Sam stared, taking in her satiny, white bra and soft belly. "Fuck me. I'll be honest. The first time will be fast. But I swear I'll make the next few times better."

"Times? As in more than one?" she said, breathless, feeling aroused and needy under his stare. He made her feel good about herself in so many ways. But no doubt about it, knowing he wanted her triggered her desire faster than any physical touch could.

"Are you kidding? You see this, right?" He held his erection. "I'm wet, ready to come so hard. In you, right?"

"Yes." She blushed; she couldn't help it. Sam was so honest and frank. And so big. "I can't wait to feel you inside me again."

He groaned. "Okay, lose the skirt before I come from just looking at you."

She noticed he stopped touching himself. God, the power from his desire made her giddy. She slowly dropped the skirt, wanting to see his reaction to her heels and thigh highs.

He didn't disappoint. "Christ. You're keeping the stockings and shoes on. But everything else has to go. Right now."

Smiling, she shimmied out of her panties and bra.

He slid to his back on the bed. "Right now. Your pussy over my face. Hurry up."

She laughed. "So romantic."

"That's what the rose petals are for," he growled. "Now sit on my face so I can eat you out, then fuck you till you scream."

"Till *who* screams?"

He moaned. "Probably me. I'm so hard it hurts. Come on, Ivy. Stop teasing."

She joined him on the bed, walking up his body on her knees. But he wouldn't let her take her time. Sam pulled her over his face and sucked her clit into his mouth like a starving man. Already wet for him, it didn't take her long to come. Not with his hot hands gripping her hips, his tongue and teeth licking and nipping her into a powerful orgasm.

Before she knew it, he was moving her, positioning her over his cock. "Sit on me. God, yes." He groaned and positioned himself at her entrance. "Now, slide down, Ivy. *Fuck*."

She watched him, steadying herself on his shoulders while she eased her body over him. Even as wet as she was, he was a tight fit. Once he'd penetrated her fully, they both stilled, absorbing the pleasure, the rightness, of their connection.

"*Sam*."

"Yeah, baby. So good." He gripped her hips and started moving her, and each jolt of his presence inside her touched a deeper part that scuttled toward another, hardier climax. "I'm so close."

His abs clenched, and his pecs contracted as he moved her faster. And then she joined him, rocking over him and taking him deeper, needing him to feel the same bliss she'd just experienced. She stared at him, watching him watch her, so consumed with the man.

"Come in me, Sam. All in me."

"Yeah. Oh yeah." He felt so full, so thick inside her. "Fuck. Take it. *Oh, fuck.*"

He shouted and bucked up into her, then stopped as he came. She felt him shuddering beneath her, but he wasn't done.

He rubbed her clit as he continued to seize, and she jerked and came again, with such intensity she saw black for a moment.

He swore and continued pumping, but she could only moan, lost in ecstasy.

When he finally ceased, he pulled her down to his chest, still connected, inside her. "Can't move," he muttered, kissing the top of her head, her cheek, her mouth. "So good."

"Ung." She had nothing left to say, trying to catch her breath and get past the sparkles flashing before her eyes.

"Yeah, ung." He chuckled and spilled out of her. "Shit." Reaching beside them, he found a cloth and pushed it between her legs. "I left a lot in you, Ivy."

"You did." She remained on top of him, resting against his thick body and feeling his heart race while he cleaned her up. "Sam, I…" She wanted to tell him she loved him so badly. But she couldn't.

"Yeah, me too."

She doubted it. "So how about some wine while we wait for the next round?"

"I like your style." He grinned, his delight contagious. He wriggled out from under her, ignored her moan of complaint, and left, returning with wine and something else.

"Chocolate-covered strawberries?"

"I know. It's kind of cliché, but—"

"You know what *cliché* means?"

He smacked her ass, then scooted her over, sitting up next to her. "You like?"

"I love." She ran a hand over his thigh to his cock.

"Oh, I love too." He molded her hand around him. "You keep holding me, guaranteed we go again in a few minutes."

"Wow. That's some staying power."

"No, that's you in stockings and heels." He swallowed hard and poured them both wine. "Ivy, I'm just gonna say it. You're the best piece of ass I've ever had."

"Sam." She smiled, feeling amazing. "So are you, though I doubt I have as many partners to compare to yours."

"Maybe not, but you had guys you loved and all. I just had girls I slept with. Like, hot chicks. Strippers with big tits." He turned bright red and covered his eyes. "I can't believe I just said that."

She would have hit him if he hadn't been so pathetically amusing, because he seemed really embarrassed. "So bigger than mine?" She lifted her boobs.

"Damn. Uh, yeah. But none of those women ever made me lose it like that." He set the wine aside. "None of them made me want to be with them all the fucking time. None of them made me smile or laugh."

She sobered, feeling his truth. Knowing it. "Me too, Sam. This—us—it's different."

"Better than Max?"

She didn't have to think twice. "So much better. Because it's real."

He sighed and pulled her into his arms. "Real. I want this to be real forever."

Oh man. She did too. She nodded, unable to put into words what she felt, because she feared scaring him off the way she did everyone she deeply cared about.

"Ivy." He groaned and kissed her. "Can I feed you some strawberries and lick wine off your nipples?"

She laughed, coughed, then nodded. "Um, yes. But only if I can rub chocolate on your cock and nibble too."

"*Jesus.* Okay. You first."

"Thought you'd say that." She laughed. He hadn't been lying. It didn't take him long to get ready and willing again. But then, it didn't take her long either.

Chapter 17

SAM WOKE EARLY ENOUGH THAT IT WAS STILL dark outside. He had his arms full of a naked Ivy. He'd finally allowed her to remove her stockings and heels, but only because they'd needed to sleep.

He'd taken her three times, made her groan and sigh his name before he'd come. Even when she'd been blowing him, he'd refused to find pleasure first.

Man, this night... He'd never forget it. He'd never been around anything—*anyone*—so damn good for him. His mind and heart full of Ivy, he couldn't breathe in without taking some part of her close—her scent, her taste, her touch...

Her fuckin' taste. The woman had a golden pussy. Crude but true. He could eat her out for hours on end. And she loved it. She got so wet for him. She wasn't thinking about some other prick either. Ivy looked at him while they had sex. They stared into each other's eyes; they touched with care. He'd never been fucked the way she took him, riding him while smiling and looking like she...loved...him.

He tensed, because she hadn't said it or anything, but he felt cared for in a way he never had been. He hadn't been lying—he never wanted this with her to end.

Noting the gradual lightening of the dawn, he wanted to make another memory. This one a little kinkier and something he knew she'd go for. They hadn't just fucked last night. They'd laughed and talked too.

He knew she loved sweets, sci-fi movies, and manga, that she wanted to go back to school and learn more, that she still didn't understand why her family was so weird. He'd shared more with her than with anyone else except for Foley. Telling her about the guys at work, about his shameful fights at the House and why he used them to feel better about himself. About his same confusion in regards to family, though part of that had been a lie.

He knew why his mother hated him. But since he had tried everything in his power to make up for it and still struggled to make things right, he figured he could be forgiven the small untruth.

He'd told her how he loved going to Ray's because he felt like he belonged there.

And then his sweetheart had offered to go back with him because she'd liked it too. The little liar. But that she'd want to be with him where he felt good, that mattered.

A hell of a lot.

He also knew his woman had never been so well pleasured before. She touched him all over. Even in sleep, she reached for him.

Sam smiled. He'd make her scream for him this time.

He gave her his own massage, stroking lightly from her delicate feet, up her toned calves and thighs, then rubbing her sex, lingering over the sexy strip of hair over her pussy. She was still wet, moist from their last union and growing wetter as he touched her. He lingered over the small bud growing harder between her legs.

Unable to help himself, he kissed her there, teething

her clit the way she liked, and had her reaching for him, no longer asleep.

"Sam?" Her throaty question demanded an answer.

He kissed his way up her belly to her perfect breasts. Full but not overly large, they fit right into his hands. He kissed and sucked, rolling her nipples between his teeth.

She gripped his hair, hard, and he moaned, loving her roughness.

"Oh God. Yes."

He slid up her body, going higher, until he reached her mouth. She still tasted of wine and chocolate, and he sipped from her, drunk on desire.

She wrapped her legs around his waist, putting his dick right where it needed to be.

He pulled back. "Not yet, baby. Let's try something new." He'd feel even bigger inside her.

He flipped her over, onto her belly, then pulled her up, so she rested on her hands and knees.

"Sam. Please."

He angled himself so he slid between her legs, grazing her clit but not penetrating from behind.

Then he leaned over her and cupped her breasts, pinching her nipples, and continued to rock.

"Sam. More." She moaned as she bucked against him, her frailer frame no match for his powerful body.

"When you've earned it," he teased.

"*Sam.*"

"Tell me you want me to fuck you. Use those exact words." He loved hearing her talk dirty. His sweet girl with a mouth that could suck him to heaven.

"You're such a tease," she complained, still trying to get him to penetrate her.

"Uh-huh. Say it. Tell me you want my fat cock in your pussy, hammering until you come all over me." He was arousing himself, imagining taking her hard, emptying inside her once more.

He couldn't explain it, but coming inside her without a condom was as much a turn-on as her body was. It was like a claiming, leaving a piece of himself behind. The thought of her having his child both scared and thrilled him, even though he knew she was protected.

"Take me, Sam." She put her hand under herself to stroke his cock.

"Shit. Come on, say it." He closed his eyes, lost in her touch.

"I want you to fuck me. So hard. Until I come all over—"

He couldn't wait any longer. He angled himself at her entrance and thrust hard and deep. And then he was fucking her, owning her, stretching her tight pussy as she cried for more and pleaded with him to come.

"Touch yourself," he growled, unable to stop, nearing his own end.

But as he saw her reach between her legs, he eased up so as not to topple her over.

"Sam. *Sam*," she yelled as she clamped down on him, shaking, coming, and taking him with her.

Two more hard pumps and he jetted inside her, his tight grip on her hips enough to leave bruises. He would have been upset with himself if he hadn't known he'd brought her such pleasure.

She shivered under him as he pumped what was left of his seed inside her.

When he started to withdraw, she reached for him. "No. Don't leave me."

"Never," he agreed, meaning something completely different. But when he started to flag, he pulled out and flopped next to her.

"I'm a mess."

"I know."

She gave a weak chuckle. "You sound so proud."

"Baby, I am. I came so hard, all in you." Satisfaction mixed with love. "You're mine."

She turned, and he couldn't see her expression in the darkness, though the dawn continued to break. "This, us. It's more than sex, isn't it?"

She sounded hopeful, which overjoyed him. "It is for me."

"Oh good." She snuggled closer. "Because it is for me too." Then she reached beside her.

"What's wrong?"

"I'm leaking!"

He chuckled and handed her another washcloth. "Ivy, I want to do all this with you again. Like, in my place or yours. Just being with you makes me happy." So much easier to say without her looking at him. Because he knew he sounded like an emotional putz, but he couldn't help it. "I know this might seem too soon, but I want us to be together, like, just us."

"I thought we were just us."

"We are. It's just…" How to say what he didn't understand? "You called me your boyfriend."

"Yeah?"

"And I think of you as my girlfriend."

"Good."

He felt unsure. "But I think of you as more than that. Like, a maybe permanent girlfriend."

"What?"

"I want you to be mine. To go to the wedding with me. Hell, both of them. To share the dog. To, like, make dinner together and shit. Watch movies. Sleep together. Live together." *Hell.* That had just popped out.

The room lightened enough he could see her stunned expression and prayed he hadn't ruined things. "Live together?"

"Damn. Too soon. Sorry. It's just that I feel a lot for you. And I want to be with you more."

She sat up and stared at him.

"Please tell me I haven't scared you off."

"No." Her shy smile relieved him. "I've been worried I'll scare you off." She sighed. "Sam, I feel the same way about you. I want to be with you all the time. I have fun with you. I'm just not sure it's healthy to feel this way."

"Healthy?"

"What if I cling to you so much I freak you out? What if I start being too much, and you realize you don't want me anymore?"

"Are you high?"

She smacked him in the leg and gave a half laugh, half sob. "Oh, darn it." Tears poured in earnest.

"Shit, Ivy. Don't cry." Starting to freak out at her tears, he pulled her into his lap and rocked her until she stopped.

"S-see? I'm a mess." She sniffed.

He thought she was perfect. "What's all this about?"

"No one loves me." She moaned. "God, that sounds so lame. Even to me. But it's true. I think I'm unlovable."

He pulled back to stare at her. "Are you shitting me?"

"My parents have never liked me. My brother turned on me too. My first love dumped me, although to be fair I dumped him too. And Max, the man I loved and planned to have children with, he dumped me for someone else." She wiped her eyes. "There's something wrong with a person when their parents don't love them, don't you think?"

"Then there's something really wrong with me," he said bluntly. "My mother hates my guts."

"No. No, you're fine. I'm just—"

"Shut up. You're beautiful, smart, and kind. I fucking love you."

She gaped.

"I mean, I love being with you," he hurried to say but didn't think he'd successfully covered his slipup. "Your parents are fuckheads."

"Yeah? Then so's your mother. Any woman who can't appreciate your big heart, those gorgeous eyes, the way you help anyone who needs it, is a fuckhead too."

His heart totally belonged to her. No question. He had to clear his throat, full of emotion. "Yeah?"

"Yeah." She pulled him in for a rough kiss, her green eyes fierce. "Anyone can see you're a man worth keeping. So, what? We're two unlovable, dysfunctional morons who have amazing sex and want to be together, is that it? We can do whatever we want, right? No rules for us?"

He felt lighter than he ever had. "Hell yeah. No rules for us."

"Well, maybe one rule."

He would give her anything she wanted, do anything

she wanted, for this chance at a future together. "What's that?"

"You and that room. If we're going to be spending a lot of time together, the messiness has to stop."

"Shit woman. That's the way I organize—in stacks."

She glared, but he could see the happiness behind the tears she wiped away. "You have issues, buddy. And if our dog is going to be living in your place as much as mine, we need to fix your tendency to not put things away."

Damn. She was serious. He might actually have to fold his clothes and pick them up off the floor all the time. "Well, maybe."

She raised a brow and wiggled on his lap, no doubt feeling the return of his arousal.

He stroked her back. "So I'll make you a deal."

"I'll bet you will."

"I'll clean up if you'll help me. But only if you give me that massage you promised."

She blushed. "You're only with me for the kinky massage, aren't you?"

"I packed some oil in case you said yes." He winked.

"Tit for tat, then."

He laughed. "Tit it is. On your back, woman. You're first. And no more talking…"

Ivy existed in a state of delight and wonder for the next two days. Sam and she were a couple, and she couldn't get his words out of her head. He'd said he *loved* her. A slip of the tongue, but she treasured it, pretending he'd meant it.

Work went spectacularly well, probably because she

focused all her positive energy on her clients. To her relief, she didn't feel a single urge to give any of them an oiled-up sensual massage. Not even her handsome male clients toward the end of the day.

She flirted with Sam over the phone, laughing as he described how scared his coworkers were that he'd been smiling all day. His boss had even gone so far as to ask what he was on, because she had a policy against drugs in the garage.

She missed sleeping with him Friday, as if she always went to bed sleeping in the arms of a giant.

Saturday morning, after massaging two clients, she took Sam suit shopping.

Who knew fighting with the big galoot could be so much fun? He hated shopping the way she hated spiders—with all his being. After finding a suit that worked on him and made her want to do him right there in the store, she'd forced him to pay extra to get the tailoring done right. The idiot wanted to wear it straight off the rack, inches too long for his arms and legs but "doable."

"Doable my ass," she'd snapped. Then he'd laughed and put her in charge of it all.

And he wanted her to go with him to Del's and Eileen's weddings.

"So, about tomorrow," he said as he drove her home Saturday night. "I have to go out of town. Can you get Cookie? I'll give you Lou's address."

"Sure." She didn't like the way his fingers tightened on the steering wheel. "Where are you going?"

He pulled in front of her place and turned off the car.

"Sam?"

"Louise needs me."

Louise, his mother. She noticed he'd referred to her as his mother only briefly on Thursday night, but after that, he called her by name. Distancing himself, perhaps?

"What for, do you know? I thought she didn't like you."

"She hates me." He ran a hand through his hair. "But she needs my help. She's not right up here." He tapped his forehead. "Too many drugs and drink over the years."

Ivy didn't like it, but Sam had been dealing with his mother long before she'd met him. "Okay. Do you want me to go with you?"

He let out a breath. "Ivy, I totally don't deserve you. But, God, I am *so* glad you're mine."

She reached for his hand. "Come in with me and I'll make you some tea."

"Not that Lipton crap."

She rolled her eyes. "Come on."

Once inside, his precious oolong made, she sat him down with her on the couch. "What's really going on with Louise?"

"Hell if I know." He sighed. "She calls me when she wants something. I help her out, buy her beers or fix her shitty car. Sometimes I pay her rent if she's behind. Then she leaves me alone."

"But why?"

"I owe her."

"Why?"

He blinked. "Duh, I'm here, aren't I?"

"So because she chose to give birth to you, you owe her? No, you don't."

The bleak look in his eyes pained her. "I do."

"Sam, what about your dad? You never mention him."

He shut down.

"Is this something you don't want to talk about?" she said gently, knowing how parents could leave scars.

He nodded.

She took his fist in her hands and just held him. "Then we won't," she said simply.

He blinked. "Yeah?"

She smiled. "Yeah. You don't have to tell me everything, you know. I mean, I wish you would share, but I understand sometimes we need to hold on to things for ourselves. Sam, I..." *Love you?* Not now, when he needed compassion, not the burden of her feelings. "I know what it's like to have bad parents. Honestly? As much as I can't stand mine, if they'd apologize and take me back, I'd probably accept them." She sighed. "I'm a doormat, aren't I?"

He frowned. "Hell no. You're one of the strongest people I know. You got nothing from them. All alone and you never did anything bad. That's fucked up. Look, I was no angel. I stole. I beat people up. I went to prison."

"Seriously, Sam, unless you tell me you were a bully, everything you did was either in self-defense or a simple mistake. Right?"

He shifted on the couch. "Well, yeah, but I sound more badass if it's like I started it."

She huffed, and he gave her a small smile.

"Point is, you should have been protected and cared for your whole life. And you weren't. But I'm not as good as you. No," he said to forestall her denial. "You don't know all of it, and I don't want you to. I'm not so good, but I try. And so I get what Louise needs, and it's okay." He paused. "Foley and Eileen get mad at me for helping her. They don't like the way she treats me. Hell, I don't like it. But I understand it."

She nodded, stroking his fingers. "Okay."

"Okay? That's it?"

"Yes. I respect that you have your reasons. I know what it's like to have everyone expecting you to act a certain way or do something that you know isn't right for you. It's all right for you to keep some secrets." She stared into his eyes, loving him so much and wishing she could take all his pain away, dim the shadows lingering. "Not any secrets about other women on the side or kids I don't know about though."

"Uh-uh. I'm faithful, I swear." He didn't blink.

She believed him.

"And no kids. I'm not having any, ever."

"What?"

He sighed. "Shit. I hadn't wanted to talk about this now. It's too soon for us anyway, right?"

"Explain."

"I'm… I don't talk about my father for a reason. I can't have kids."

"Oh, Sam, I'm so sorry."

"I mean, I won't. I don't want to lie to you, but I'm never fathering children. Trust me, you don't want that anyway."

Talk about children was sudden, but it mattered. Because Ivy had been painting fantasies of her and Sam forever, and children had definitely been a part of that. It appeared her perfect man wasn't so perfect after all.

"You know what? You're right. This isn't the time to talk about kids. We just started dating, really." Yet she felt like she'd known him forever. "This is about you needing to help your mom, no matter what anyone thinks. I don't like the thought of anyone abusing you, but you're a grown man. If you need to help her, you need to help her. Just know I'm here for you."

"Oh, baby, I do." He sipped his tea and smiled. "And I'm here for you."

He stood and pulled her with him into the bedroom. Slowly stripping her, then himself, he joined her on the bed. "I think about you all the time," he confessed as he blanketed her. "I jack off to thoughts of you. I get hard when I remember going down on you." He kissed her, rubbing against her breasts with his broad chest. "I smile when I remember your laugh. When I smell lavender, I think about how gentle you are with me when we touch."

He was seducing her with words. Sam kissed her again, then spread her legs with his knee. He settled between them and slowly entered her.

"Your smile kills me, Ivy. It's so soft, so full." He moved inside her, taking her with words and deed and bringing her pleasure so effortlessly. "I love your body, your mind. The way you baby Cookie."

He moved faster, and she drew him down for a kiss, wanting more.

He broke the kiss, taking her hard. "You're so fine. So sexy," he rasped and palmed a breast. His thrusts shook the bed.

"And sometimes, when I forget to think about it," he

said in a whisper, "I imagine you with my baby. If there was anyone who could give me that peace, it's you." He shoved once more and she came around him, taking him with her as they crested fulfillment.

When she came down off her high, she stroked his hair and cheeks while he kissed her with slow, lingering caresses.

"Sam." *God, I love you.*

"Yeah, Ivy, I'm fucked up, but I feel it. I'm upside-down over you. You poor, poor girl."

She smiled. "A baby, huh?"

He grimaced. "I said I'm fucked up. That's one weird fantasy to have when you don't want kids, but I can't help it. You're sexy any way I imagine you."

She wouldn't argue with him now. Especially not in bed, and not when she wasn't ready for children anyway. But they'd have to come back to this at some point.

Sam left hours later, with a promise to call when he returned home. She hadn't asked where his mother lived, and he hadn't offered. It was enough he'd trusted her to tell her he was going.

So much about Sam made sense to her—their shared parental dysfunction, their need for connection, the way they both took care of people and pets who needed it.

The bed felt too big without him in it, and Ivy felt lonely in a way she hadn't in a while.

Sunday afternoon, she followed the directions to Lou's house, eager to get Cookie.

He lived in a mid-sized white house in Rainier Valley. She pulled up to find a dozen or more cars lining the street. Noise sounded from his house, like a party was underway.

She knocked but no one answered. So she tried again. The door eventually opened, and a striking, dark-haired woman stared at her.

"Hello. I'm here to see Lou."

The young woman, only a few years younger than Ivy, she'd bet, gave her a dismissive once-over. "Wait here." She yelled something in Spanish, to which several other women answered back with laughs, and walked away, leaving the door open. Festive music filled the house, an air of joy making it difficult not to smile.

Then Ivy heard barking. "Cookie?"

The puppy raced down the hallway when he spotted her, chased by a young girl. Cookie leaped at her, dancing at her feet and wagging his tail like crazy.

She laughed, so happy to see him again. She lifted the ball of energy in her arms and smiled through the licking.

"Hi, Ivy." Lou had joined the girl. "Thanks for letting us borrow him. Rosie's ready for a dog, she thinks."

"Thanks for watching him, Rosie."

The little girl looked forlorn. "Does he have to go?"

"I missed him. But maybe if it's okay with your..." *Brother? Father? Uncle?*

"Brother," Lou supplied with a half grin.

"Brother, then you can watch him again some other time."

Rosie perked up. "Okay. Thanks." She petted Cookie once more. "Bye, Cookie." Then she turned and skipped down the hallway back to the party.

"Well, thanks again." Ivy turned to leave.

"Wait. Want to come in? My family's here for the Sunday meal." He winced as something crashed and someone else chided in Spanish. "It's a little loud."

She smiled. "I have chores at home and a puppy to train, but thanks."

"And a man to get back to, eh?" Lou leaned against the doorframe.

He was sexy, enigmatic, and dangerous. Unlike Sam, who seemed open despite the few secrets he kept, Lou had a darkness to him, a depth that felt out of her league. "A man?" she asked. "Well, yes. But he's going out of town tonight. So technically, I'll be seeing him tomorrow." Or in a few days. He hadn't said when he'd be back.

Lou sighed. "Shit. He's gone to see Louise, eh?"

She blinked, not wanting to pry, but… "What do you know about her?"

"Only what I've heard. She's a bitch. Treats Sam like shit, but he still helps her out. He's a good guy, being there for his mother." With as many women that seemed to be in Lou's house, and no doubt in his life, she could imagine family loyalty meant something to him. "But he's always a basket case when he deals with her. He's usually quiet or gruff at work, but after dealing with Louise, he's scary quiet." Lou narrowed his gaze at her. "Then again, he's been smiling and laughing a lot lately. So maybe he'll be better when he gets back. Just watch out for his mood. She gets to him like nothing else does."

"Thanks."

"Nothing except for you." Lou smiled, and the expression lightened the impression of intensity, if only for a moment. "You're good for Sam, Ivy. He's really into you. I've known the guy for four years, and he's never been like this about anyone but you."

"Thanks."

"Yeah, don't mention it. I mean it. Don't mention it."

She laughed and left with a wave, feeling better in spite of her worry for Sam. She could only hope he'd survive Louise intact and that, when he returned home, he wouldn't shut her out.

Lou watched Sam's chick leave. *Man. What a hot piece, that one.* A genuine lady, sweet, and just what his buddy needed in his life. Softness.

He returned to the kitchen and to his million female relatives—could someone have a freakin' boy the next time one of his sisters or aunts got pregnant?—and tracked down Stella. She had a mutinous look on her face.

He sighed and motioned her over. She came, reluctantly, and he yanked her over his shoulder and walked her outside to the backyard, where his lone male cousin flipped spareribs over the grill. "Hey, J, get lost for a minute."

The kid nodded and left, calling for something to fill his growing body. One of his aunts would feed him.

He set Stella on her feet and knocked her hands away when she tried slapping him, swearing at him in Spanish.

He spoke in a language she'd understand—one from big brother to little sister. "Look, honey, I told you Sam's not for you. He's in love with that woman."

Stella sneered. "She's nothing. A ghost and a skank and a whore."

He raised a brow. "Really? A whore? Where did you get that?"

She shrugged. "That's the only way a bitch like her could keep a man like Sam."

Lou sighed and switched to English. "*Chica,* we talked about this. Sam let you down because he knows you're too young for him. And too good." And because Lou would rearrange Sam's body parts and bury him in concrete if the guy so much as touched his sisters. No one was good enough for the Cortez women in Lou's opinion. And watching over them was a full-time job. "Sam loves her."

Stella blinked. "He does not. See?" She pulled out her phone and showed Lou her texts.

That bastard hadn't said anything about Stella, but Lou had had a feeling. All he read were a bunch of messages from a guy who had trouble communicating to a young girl with a crush, and every message ended with Sam telling her in a roundabout way that he wasn't the guy for her.

Hell, now Lou couldn't in good conscience give the guy a broken nose. "Stella, he's not into you, baby. He loves Ivy."

"How do you know?"

"I've seen that man growl and snap at people, including his friends, for years. But now he has stars in his eyes. He's in love, and he's smiling all the time. It's freaky as hell, let me tell you. He's a good man, but he's taken. You need a man who has stars in his eyes when he thinks of *you*. And with Sam, that woman is Ivy."

Stella watched him, then sighed. "He really smiles?"

"Yep. And he and she have a dog together." Which for Sam, according to Foley, was major commitment right there. "He's happy, baby. If you really like the guy, you want him to be happy, yes?"

She nodded. "I really liked him. He was nice. He talked to me, and he didn't stare at my chest all the time either."

"Good, because then I'd have to kill him."

Stella rolled her eyes. "Really, Lou, ease up."

"Look, he's off-limits. Go find a guy *I* like, for once, huh?" He saw another of his sisters leaving the house. "Be the good girl Lucia isn't."

Lucia stopped in her tracks. "*What* did you say?"

Stella snickered. "Oh, *sí*. That's true. She is a slut."

Lou groaned. "I didn't say that."

"You bitch. You're just mad because Sam liked me first." Lucia advanced and started trash-talking her younger sister with a wink thrown Lou's way.

Lou nodded. They'd both known about Stella's crush, and they'd both known it would go nowhere. Although Lou hadn't realized Lucia had also made an impression on his friend, unless Lucia was talking shit.

Either way, he had an excuse to pull Sam aside and see what the hell was going down with the guy. Anything to keep Lou's mind on work and away from that aggravating woman at the flower shop.

He scowled as he entered the house and went straight for a beer. He glanced at the microwave, seeing his reflection, and swore.

What the hell kind of woman can walk away from all this?

Chapter 18

By Wednesday, Ivy had had enough. Sam had put her off with a few texts and even a phone call. But he hadn't stopped by to visit. She didn't want to hunt him down at the garage, but she needed to talk to him.

And one person who came to mind to help her happened to be dog-sitting Cookie while she worked.

The day came to a close, and Ivy drove to Willie's house. She parked her car, which now ran like a dream, and walked around the house to the back door, which Willie preferred.

Before she could knock, dogs barked, signaling her approach.

But after a few minutes, still no one answered. She knocked again. "Willie?"

She heard a shout and a long, male moan from an open window upstairs.

Oh, please, God, not today. I can't handle the swing again.

"Be right down," Willie shouted from somewhere in the house.

Ivy prayed the woman and her companion at least had their clothes on when they answered the door.

It finally opened, and a man, not Rupert, stared at her. "Hel-lo, gorgeous."

"Um, hi. I'm Ivy. I'm here to get Cookie?"

"That a question?" He laughed. "I'm Ross, Willie's

friend." The man looked to be in his midfifties, a redhead, not in bad shape, but definitely younger than Willie by a decade or so. He was slender, dressed in a sweat suit, and looked like he'd been exercising, if the sweat on his forehead was any indication. He sat on her ugly couch and waited.

Banging on the stairs told her Willie was coming down. And maybe…someone else?

Willie arrived, walking slowly, as usual, with her cane. She had on a housedress, but her hair looked frazzled. Behind her, Rupert came as well, dressed only in sweatpants.

"Ah, I came to get Cookie," Ivy announced as the pair stopped in their tracks upon seeing her.

"He's here…somewhere. Oh, wait. I think he's watching TV with Mathmos in the green room." Willie took a seat on the couch.

"Right." Ross stood. "I'll get him." He left.

Rupert took a seat next to Willie. "So this is Ivy? Sam's girl?"

"Mm-hmm." Willie studied her. "You been keeping him away."

"No. Well, we're dating, but I would have thought he'd have been by before now."

"Oh, he was." Willie nodded. "Yesterday. Found two more kittens to home. He's all fucked up."

Rupert nodded. "On account of his mother."

"Rupert."

"What? It's not a secret." He patted her knee, then tried to move his hand up her leg.

"Save it for later." Willie slapped his hand away. "Wait for Ross."

Ivy goggled the pair. No way. Willie and Rupert and…Ross? The old woman had a threesome going on?

Willie shot her a sly grin. "Something you needed, Ivy?"

Ivy coughed to clear her throat. "Yes. I mean, besides Cookie, I'm not sure what's wrong with Sam. He won't talk to me."

"He will. He's just scared of what he done. Not sure if he made the right call or not and it's eatin' him up inside."

"Oh." She didn't understand, but she needed to talk to Sam about this, not Willie. "I just want to help him."

Willie nodded. "You do, and you will. Just give him time. He'll come back." She leaned forward as Ross came down the stairs carrying a happy Cookie. "They all do. Especially if you work it just right." She made a thrusting motion with her hips from the couch that Ivy would have thought impossible.

Rupert started laughing. Ross saw and wiggled his brows. "Hey, Ivy. Got plans for tonight?"

She grabbed the puppy and left the three of them laughing so hard they cried. Not that she believed for one minute Ross had been involved romantically with the lovebirds. Yet…

Who knew with Willie?

The next day, Sam *still* hadn't called. But to Ivy's shock, on the news, reports of the duo who'd been robbing Queen Anne's shops made headlines. Apparently, Willie, Rupert, and Ross—an undercover policeman— had bungled the Junkin' and Funkin' Robbers. To Ivy's astonishment, the two men she'd met that day at work, whom Sam had scared away, had tried robbing Willie's place.

A big mistake and, from what she'd heard, a hilarious one. It seemed Tyrant had tripped up one of the men while Mathmos and Pygar had rounded up the others, with Rupert bludgeoning them with his cane while Willie placed them all under citizen's arrest. And somehow Ross had been directing the action, if the news report was to be believed. Already the YouTube video of the arrest had gone viral.

Ivy had to wonder. Had Ross really been sexing it up with Willie, or was that all a cover? What did Sam think of the arrest? She didn't know because he hadn't called.

More worried than angry, Ivy decided to drive to his house. She parked in a spot next to his car and knocked, having left Cookie at home. If things with Sam got ugly, she didn't want to have to deal with the puppy too.

Much as she wanted to respect his need for space, she worried about him. If he'd only talk to her, she'd go away and wait. But the distance made her itchy to at least see him, to know he was physically okay. She didn't like him pulling away from her.

She knocked. No one answered, so she knocked again. As she listened closer, she heard muffled voices.

She twisted the knob, and to her surprise, it opened. "Sam?" She walked inside and closed the door behind her. "It's Ivy," she called out.

To her astonishment, a gorgeous woman with long, dark-brown hair and hateful eyes glared at her. "So this is the bitch you're throwing me over for?"

Ivy stared, not sure she was hearing right. "Excuse me?"

"Fuck you," the woman snapped. Then she turned to Sam, who had followed her out of the kitchen to the living room. "And fuck you too. This ain't over, Sam. Not by a long shot." She pushed past Ivy, knocking her into the wall.

Stunned at the woman's violence, and at her own sick sense of betrayal, Ivy could only stare. She heard a car with a bad muffler screech out of the parking lot.

Sam sighed. "I'm sorry."

Ivy took a deep breath and let it out. "For what?"

"That you had to see that." Sam sat on the couch and held his head in his hands. "She won't go away."

Confused and not sure what the heck she'd just witnessed, Ivy cautiously approached. "Who was that?"

He lifted his head, his face blank. "Louise."

Ivy shook her head, incredulous. The woman had looked like she could have been his sister. But mother? "No way."

"Yeah. She won't leave me alone. I tried to get her to go to therapy this time. Told her I was done if she wouldn't clean herself up. Then I left." He looked desolated. "Ivy, she followed me home."

"I'm sorry." She sat next to him, shocked when he burrowed close and put his head on her chest. The poor guy. He seemed so miserable. "It's okay, Sam. It'll be okay." Not sure why he needed the comfort, she nevertheless gave it freely.

"No, it won't," he said, muffled against her shirt. "I'll never be free of her, Ivy." He pulled back and gave her the saddest look she'd ever seen.

"Sam."

"She's in the blood. Always here." He tapped his

heart. "Same as *him*." His eyes looked glassy, as if he might cry, and Ivy froze.

Good Lord. What had happened when he'd gone to visit his mother?

"How old was she when she got pregnant?" she asked quietly.

"Thirteen." He wiped his eyes and stood, so tense she feared he'd shatter if she touched him. "But she's always looked young for her age."

Ivy burned to know about Sam's father, but she knew now was not the time to ask.

"For a long time, I kept her out of my life," he said softly. "I did what she wanted, and she left me alone. But she won't leave now. I'm happy, and she hates that," he said bitterly and took a few steps away. He looked back at her, and her own tears burned, seeing him so hopeless. "I told her about you. My mistake. She seemed kind of normal, and I know better. I told her I couldn't bring her drugs. And no more booze, because it's killing her. I tried to do right by her. Said I had a future to think about, and so did she if she wanted it. But now…"

"Now?" She crossed to him, unable to stay away.

"Now she's going to haunt me." He clenched his hands. "You have to go before she ruins you too."

Ivy refused. "No. Come with me." She walked with him to his room, wanting privacy, and wasn't sure what to think when she saw it spotless, no dirt or stacks or mess left at all. What did that mean? Had he cleaned it for her or for some other reason?

"Ivy, you should go." He sounded so tired.

"Sam, look at me." She wouldn't budge until he did.

When he lifted his head to meet her gaze, she wanted to cry. "Sam, do you love me?"

A tear slid down his cheek, and her heart broke in two. "You don't understand." His voice cracked. "You don't know. She'll destroy you. Anything I care about, it's gone."

"You have Foley and Eileen."

"Yes, but they're different. They fought back and she's afraid of them. They…"

"I can fight back," she said when he didn't finish.

"It's different. Foley's a hard-ass, and he knows her. Eileen has Jacob now. But you have so much she could take away."

"Sam?"

"I think you should go."

Ivy hurt for him, for her, but mostly, she wanted to take that pain from Sam and turn it into something good. So she kissed him. Hard. Taking possession of the man who belonged to her.

At first he resisted, until she pulled out the big guns. She put his hand on her breast, and shoved her hand down his pants, stroking him into an erection in seconds.

"In me," she ordered and lay back on his bed, kicking off her shoes and shoving down her jeans and panties.

When he stood there, breathing hard, just watching her, she ran her hands between her legs. He opened the snap of his jeans. She started fingering herself, and he groaned.

He ripped open his fly and joined her on the bed. He reached between them to free himself, then she felt him pushing inside her.

He took her hard, and she gave as much back. They kissed and nipped, their passion rising as they each sought to overcome the other. A race to the finish line, and she came just as he did, in a swell of anger, release, and, on her part, hope.

He rested his head on the bed next to her, his body still joined to hers. She stroked his hair, loving him so much.

"You need to do what's right for you, Sam. Not for me or your mother. For you. I'm not sure why she scares you so much. But I know all about you, and I care. We connect—physically, like this." She swallowed, taking the plunge. "And so much more. Sam, I love you."

He tensed but didn't move, didn't so much as take a breath.

"She might be a terrible person. She might do terrible things. But if what we have is real, then you have to fight for it. I will." She kissed his cheek. "I don't have much that can't be replaced. I can get another job. Cookie could find happiness with another foster family. I'd miss him, but I'd be okay if he was in a good home. My car is crap, and my possessions mean less than nothing to me.

"But you… My heart would break without you. I'll fight for you, Sam. Now it's up to you. Will you fight for me?"

—‑∿‑—

Sam didn't know why he felt like Foley would be able to help him. The guy had the perfect life. A great mom. A woman who loved the hell out of him. Smarts and advancement in the job because, yeah, he was that good. People liked him, because he was charming and a good guy.

What was Sam but a burden?

Hours after he'd walked out on Ivy, sated, heartsick, and lonely, he sat next to Foley at Ray's of all places, because the guy was getting darts tutoring from Heller, that freak.

But seeing Sam, Foley took a break and sequestered them at a table by themselves.

"You look like shit," Foley stated, tactless as usual.

He glared. "Fuck you."

"What's up? You just said you wanted to ask me a question. I could have come to you, asswipe. We don't have to talk here." Foley and his giving, shitty, caring attitude.

"Here is fine." Sam's eyes felt gritty. Just thinking about how much it would hurt to lose Ivy killed something inside him. But they didn't know what Louise could do. How tough it could be if the woman took her wrath out on them. He'd protected Foley and Eileen for years. Now they might not be okay. Because of him.

"Well? You're worrying me, hoss. What's wrong?" Foley paused. "Or should I say, what did that bitch do now?"

Sam snorted. "Cut right to the heart of it. So my question is this: If you knew someone you loved was going to be hurt because you didn't protect them, what would you do?"

"Protect them, duh." Foley kicked back his bottle, finishing the beer. "But that's not an easy question, really. Because what am I protecting them from? And what's it going to cost me?"

"Who cares? Isn't protecting people more important than protecting yourself?"

Foley should know that. The guy was a natural when it came to looking out for the little guy.

"Let's cut the shit. What's really going on?"

Sam opened his mouth when Goodie and three of his friends walked up to the table.

"Not now," Foley growled at him. "Trust me. This is not a good time."

"Fuck off, Sanders. Hey, Sammie. Look at me, dick-head. You almost broke my jaw defending that whore. How about we make it right?"

Sam saw nothing but red. Trying to protect Ivy had become his world, and now another piece of trash thought he could hurt her? Words, actions, it was all the same.

He stood, needing to do something to solve his problems.

Foley hurried to his feet. "Sam, don't."

"Outside." Sam nodded to the back lot.

"After you, bitch." Goodie smiled.

Sam stalked off, ignoring Foley's nagging, Rena's look of concern, even Earl the bouncer's frown.

"Yo, Sam. Let me take care of this guy." Earl tried to stop him.

"I got this, Earl." Sam yanked his arm away from the bouncer and moved deeper into the shadowed lot, away from any potential interference. The lot was far enough back from the main road that the cops wouldn't inter-fere, not able to see much. And the clientele at Ray's had never been too law-abiding anyway.

"Well?" He waited for Goodie, in the mood to do some serious damage.

Out of the corner of his eye he saw Foley, Heller, and

a few others join the growing crowd now placing bets. That's when he saw Goodie's ace in the hole—a prick who'd been at the House once before being kicked out for cheating. And breaking a guy's neck.

"Stenson." He shook his head. "Really, Goodie? You can't fight me yourself, so you pussied out and hired this dipshit?"

Goodie flushed. "Shut up and fight. Or did your lady tell you not to? She leading you by the dick?"

Stenson, Goodie, and the two other douchebags with him laughed.

"You want to fight?" Big mouth Foley stepped in. "Fine. No more than two at a time."

Goodie glared. "Step off, Sanders. Before I—"

"He said—*no more than two at a time*," Heller repeated in a low voice, and the entire gathering grew quiet.

Goodie blinked. "Ah, hell. Fine. Won't matter none."

Sam was tired of waiting. He punched one of the unknowns, then the other. When the first one shook off the hit, Sam brought the guy's face down to his knee and broke his nose. He took a blow to the back, just above his kidneys, fortunately, and punched the other guy twice, taking him down.

Goodie didn't look so enthused anymore.

But Stenson practically salivated. "Finally." He rammed into Sam, taking him to the graveled ground. Then he kicked, his fucking steel-toed boot making contact with a few ribs before Sam could throw him off. Feeling a definite bruise in his side, Sam caught the next boot and jerked the dick off his feet, regaining his own.

The moment Stenson rose, Sam punched and dodged. And again. But Stenson was good, and fortunately, he gave Sam the fight he needed to relieve some stress. Breaking the guy wouldn't be easy, but in order to get to Goodie, Sam would have to take him down.

"Thanks," he growled at Goodie, showing a bloodied smile. His lip stung from a blow that had snapped his head back.

Goodie looked scared.

Sam smiled some more.

"Hell. That's his happy smile," Foley muttered.

"*Ja*. Nice." Heller approved.

Joy.

Sam took Stenson down in a wristlock, avoided getting bitten, then beat the shit out of him. Over and over. He was ready to finish the assbag when a hand grabbed his fist.

He tried to shake it off but found both Heller and Foley holding him back.

"*Fuck*."

"Sam, knock it off," Foley growled, "before Goodie gets away."

Goodie, that shit, had tried to run, but a few of the regulars held him steady.

"Your turn," Sam promised with relish.

Goodie paled. "I was just kidding. I'm sorry. Damn it. I—"

Foley and Heller stepped back, and Sam tapped Goodie harder than he needed to knock the little bastard down.

"One hit and he's out. Motherfucking pussy." He spat on the man. *Piece of crap*.

The crowd agreed, shaking their heads. Goodie wouldn't be welcomed back, that Sam knew.

He'd turned to leave when he saw Earl's wide eyes and heard Foley swear. He instinctively shifted to the side, aware of someone behind him. But he wasn't fast enough, because a sharp pain grazed him as he turned.

Senior stood holding a bloody knife.

And Sam's rage exploded. "That's *it*."

He hit the old bastard just once, knocking him back off his feet, and followed him down, intending to stop this shit permanently.

He only got two more hits in before a group knocked him off Senior and tackled him to the ground.

"No, no, Sam. No killing the old man," Foley kept saying while Sam fought to take the fucker right out.

Eventually he tired, and his side started to hurt like a bitch. Earl and the others took the trash to their vehicles, while Foley and Heller helped Sam to Foley's car, examining him on the way.

"Good fight, Sam." Heller slapped him on the back, and Sam groaned. "Ah, sorry. But you'll live. *Ja*. A good fight." He left with a nod at Foley.

Foley sighed. "Great. Now you *really* look like shit. And that stab wound. You're lucky he didn't hit anything more than he did."

"Just barely stuck me." Yet Sam was feeling lightheaded. "No hospital."

He heard Foley talking to Johnny on the phone, and the car roared out of the parking lot.

An hour later, while Lara stitched him up and complained about not being qualified to tackle split skin and possible infection, he tried not to look at Foley, who fussed like a mother hen.

"Shit. My mother, Cyn, Ivy—they're going to blame

me for letting you get like this." Foley paced. "And that conversation from before, we never finished."

"Not now, Foley." Sam groaned and drank more whiskey. "Thanks, Johnny."

Behind Lara, Johnny stood watch. "No problem. Want some more?"

"He's had enough," Lara snapped and turned her mean eyes on Sam. "Now, unless you want me dragging your ass to the hospital, no more alcohol. And *stop moving*." She glared at him.

He glared back but said nothing else.

Foley, *damn him*, talked for him. "So Louise fucked you over, again. Except this time, she's threatening people you care about."

"She always does that." God, he wanted to sleep for a week. Besides being tired, the needle Lara was dragging through his side freakin' *hurt*.

"So what's different?"

"I told her to shove it. That I was done."

"Good for you."

"Yeah?" Sam growled. "Well now you're going to pay."

Johnny looked from Sam to Foley.

"How's that?" Foley asked, not sounding as concerned as he should.

"She'll start badgering Del, trying to get you fired. Cars you're working on will show up with scratches in the paint, slashed tires. Your tools will go missing. Shit will stop working. And she'll fuck with Eileen. Yeah, that's right. The wedding, her real estate deals—Louise will screw with all of them. And Ivy." He swallowed hard, the sting of her loss too recent to bear. "She'll fuck with her business. Ruin her job at the massage place. That's Ivy's *job*, man. Louise is good at making accusations. Shit. She'll end up getting Ivy's license taken away." And then Ivy would hate Sam for ruining her life.

He never should have pursued her.

"All this because you said no to Louise for what?" Johnny asked quietly.

"For everything. No more trying to help her. Her threats about Foley and Eileen went away years ago. But I'm tired of her always telling me shit. Always talking down to me. I'm just done. I told her that. That I had someone who actually did love me." He sighed. *Ivy.* He looked at Foley. "She followed me to town, man. She's here, threatening to fuck with people. I know Eileen will be okay. She's got Jacob, and she's a tough broad."

Foley gave a forced smile. "Hell yeah."

"And she can't do too much to you now that you're all happy and shit with Cyn. I mean, if she even looked sideways at Cyn, Cyn would eat her alive," Sam continued.

This time Foley gave a real smile. "You got that right."

"But she can hurt Ivy. And she'll do it."

"Hurt her how? With a gun?" Lara asked, pausing in her stitching.

"No," Foley answered for him. "By screwing with her reputation, pulling stupid crap at the shop. Breaking a few windows, small stuff like that. Why didn't you ever tell us she was holding that over you? I thought you helped her because you felt guilty or something. Like you owed her."

"I do. I mean, I did." He'd been with Louise for so long because of what his father had done to her. And all the sacrifices she'd made to raise him. But for

Ivy, he'd wanted to cut Louise off, to finally be free of her negativity.

"So this is about Ivy?" Lara shook her head. "Man, you guys are always so dumb." She pulled particularly hard before tying off her thread.

"Lara," Johnny admonished. "The guy's hurting. Go easy."

She frowned at Sam. "Look, Sam, if it were me, and Johnny was having all these problems because of me, I'd want to know. Because if he were going to do something stupid"—she paused, and her eyes narrowed— "something like dump me to protect me, I'd nail him so hard in the balls he wouldn't walk right for weeks."

Johnny put a protective hand in front of his crotch. "Hey now, that's not necessary."

Foley chuckled. "Yeah, um. Could you two give us a minute?"

Lara stood, kissed Sam on the head, and muttered under her breath as Johnny and she left the kitchen.

"Is that what all this is about? You indenturing yourself to Louise for life so her hatred can't hurt us?"

Sam shrugged.

Foley punched him in the arm, hard enough to leave a bruise over the other bruises darkening there.

"Hey. What the hell?"

"*Idiot*. Seriously. What are you thinking? Cut the cord, dude. Mom and I will be just fine. But if you ditch Ivy, only the best thing to ever happen to you, all because of Louise?" Foley got down in his face. "Then you're a bigger pussy than Goodie."

Sam glared. "I'd hit you if I could without tearing my stitches."

"Great. Fight back." Pause. "Pussy."

"Damn it. You don't understand. She's toxic, man."

"Do you love Ivy?"

Sam stared up at the ceiling, not liking the emotional bent of the conversation.

"Do you, jackass?"

"Yeah. So what?"

"So act like you have a pair and fight back. I'll back you. Mom will."

"So will we," Lara yelled out.

"Shh. We're not supposed to be listening," Johnny said in a superloud whisper.

"Christ." Sam rubbed his aching head. "What am I supposed to do?" He wanted to fight for her, but his mother still had that ace in her hand—knowledge of where Sam had come from. His stupid birthright and a lifetime of making him miserable. Every time he hoped and reached for the mother who'd been nice to him, he got *this* Louise. The acidic, screeching witch.

His phone buzzed, and Foley grabbed it out of his hand before he could read it.

"Ah, you want my advice?" Foley's eyes widened at what he read. "Go home and be with Ivy before your mother gets there."

"*What?*" Sam stood, swore at the pain in his entire body, and wobbled on his feet. He would have fallen if Foley hadn't caught him.

"Come on. I'll drive."

Chapter 19

Ivy waited at Sam's, worried and feeling foolish. But she needed to talk to him. Sex had probably not been the best way to show him how they connected, but she hadn't been able to think past wanting him to feel better. And sex had definitely eased some stress from him.

But as the hours passed and she waited for him, staring at her phone for any word, she wondered if she'd done the right thing. He meant so much to her. He had to know she wanted him as more than a lover.

She texted him to let him know she would be waiting for him when he came home.

She sat on his couch, thumbing through the channels on his huge TV.

The door opened, and she stood, hoping he'd talk to her.

But Sam didn't stand there.

Louise did.

The angry woman let herself inside without closing the door. "So. You're still here."

"You're Louise Hamilton, Sam's mom."

"No shit." Louis sneered. "And you're the latest slut throwing herself at my son."

Ivy studied her. Louise wore jeans and a leather coat, neither cheap nor flashy-expensive. Her long, dark hair lay in waves around a face that could have graced magazines, she was that striking. She definitely had that heroin-chic look going for her. Yet despite her obvious good looks that even drugs couldn't tarnish, everything about the woman felt ugly.

"Why are you so angry?" Ivy asked, feeling surprisingly sorry for the vengeful woman.

"Why are you after my son?"

"I love him."

Louise snorted. "Right. You just love his cock and his money."

"He's not rich. And he's not the most charming man I've ever met," Ivy said calmly. "But he's the most decent, the sweetest man I've ever known. Why can't you see that?"

Louise fumed. "He wants nothing more to do with me because of you. Are you that desperate that you can't see he has other responsibilities? It's not all about you, bitch."

"My name is Ivy. And it's not all about you either, Louise."

The woman, incensed, came at Ivy, her fingernails poised as if to scratch Ivy's eyes out.

But Ivy refused to be intimidated. "Really? You're going that low? Scratching me? Heck, Louise. I'd rather you punched me instead. Don't lower yourself to stereotypes."

Louise paused. "What?"

Ivy sighed. "What's this really about?"

"I told you."

"No. Your son does everything you want when you want it. You blackmail him to be at your beck and call with threats to ruin his friendships. Who does that? Do you love him at all?"

"He's mine." Louise thumped her chest. "*My* son. I carried him. I gave birth to him. I raised him—"

"Sounds to me more like Eileen and Foley raised him," Ivy said, taking a shot in the dark. From what little Sam had told her, Louise hadn't done much good for him. "Eileen gave him food. Eileen gave him clothes. Foley looked out for him. What did you do? Drugs?"

Louise flipped her off. "Fuck you. What the hell do you know? I was thirteen years old when I got pregnant with him." Louise leaned forward. "You know how? Do you know what Sam's daddy did to me? He was a twenty-two-year-old convict who liked to rape teenage girls. And guess what? I got pregnant."

Ivy had wondered about Louise's young age. "I'm sorry, but—"

"But nothing, bitch. I was raped. I had a baby. At fourteen. It hurt, and I had nowhere to go. No one to help me." Louise dashed the tears in her eyes. "He was so cute, my baby boy. I loved him. But he started looking so much like that piece of shit. He has Cody's eyes, his size. God, he looks just like him." Louise seemed to be looking inward, not seeing Ivy at all. "I raised my boy by myself. No help from anyone. And when that fucker went to jail for raping and killing another girl, I was glad. He died in prison. Did you know that? Did precious Sam tell you that?" she spat. "Prisoners hate pedophiles more than anything. More than cops even."

"I'm so sorry, Louise." Ivy felt for the woman. "But that didn't mean you could punish your son for it. He was innocent."

"He's *a man*." Louise shook with fury. Or from drugs. Ivy couldn't tell. "They're all assholes." She cried in earnest. "But he's my son. The only thing I got. And *you can't take him from me*."

She darted at Ivy, but this time Ivy was ready. She made a fist the way Sam had taught her, and then she let it fly.

To her shock, she hit Louise in the cheek, and the woman stumbled and fell on the couch.

"Oh my God." Not sure what to do, she stared at Louise, who was groaning.

"Damn, girl. Nice shot." Foley entered half carrying Sam. He wore a big grin, so she had a bad feeling he'd heard and seen too much.

"Louise. Fuck." Sam shuffled to the couch, far away from his mother, and sank into it. "Go home."

"Sam, wait." Ivy helped Louise stand, not surprised when the woman ripped her arm away.

"I'll sue your ass. I'll make you wish you'd never met me or that piece of shit." She nodded at Sam. "And you, Foley. You dumbass. You're done. I'll find you, your whore, your mother, and I'll—"

"*Shut up*," Ivy yelled in her face, feeling a warped pity and fury that this woman continued to act so cruelly. "Look, bitch," she said to get her point across. She poked Louise in the chest as she talked, reinforcing who had the floor. "Enough. You're done. Whatever you think you have on Sam, you don't. I love him. He loves me. What happened to you was tragic. What you did to Sam to make up for it was worse. You're abusive, bitter, and just pathetic. He said he'd be there if you got help. Well? Get help! Stop threatening everyone. Stop blaming the world, and Sam especially, for your tragedy." Before the woman could speak, Ivy said in a loud voice, "Yes, you were raped. We all heard it. We all know. That's awful. I wouldn't wish that on anyone. But enough already. Sam's not to blame. You aren't either. And we sure aren't," she said of herself and Foley. "I'm going to tell you this one time. Leave him alone unless you're going to apologize."

"For what?" Louise snapped, sullen, sunken in on herself.

"For doing to him what was done to you," Ivy said.

"*What?*"

"His father raped you, took something from you. Just as you took Sam's childhood from him. He deserved better than a mother always blaming him for something out of his control." She poked Louise hard enough to bruise her own finger. "He didn't ask to be born. You made that call. Too late to take it back now. But the abuse, it stops here. He's not your bank. He's not your keeper. He doesn't owe you jack shit." She stopped poking the woman before she lost it and punched her again.

"You know what?" Louise steadied herself on her feet and glared at them all. "You want him so bad? You keep him. I'm done," she shrieked, and tears coursed down her cheeks. "No more." She hurried to the door, then turned and watched Sam.

Ivy saw him looking at his mother, so dejected it hurt her deep inside.

"You were such a cute little boy." Louise shook her head and whispered, "My precious baby. And now… You're nothing."

She left.

Sam leaned over, burying his head in his hands. He shook, and she thought he might be weeping.

Foley looked angry enough to punch through a wall. He walked to her slowly, and she didn't know what to expect. The huge kiss and hug threw her.

"God. If I wasn't in love with Cyn, I'd marry you tomorrow." He nudged her toward Sam, then moved to the door. "Need to talk to Louise myself."

He left.

Ivy cautiously approached Sam, then stopped when he lifted his head. "Oh my God. What happened to you?"

Sam felt so confused. He was elated that Ivy had stood up for him. Ashamed everyone knew he'd been conceived as a result of rape. Even worse that he looked just like the guy. And then, the ultimate rejection from the woman he'd tried so hard, for so long, to get to love him.

Shit. He didn't know why he was crying. But he couldn't stop. He hurt all over. And deep down inside, he worried the pain would never end. Only anger had ever worked before to stop the pain.

Anger…and Ivy.

But would she still love him now that she knew?

"Shh. It's okay, Sam. I'm here. And I'm not going anywhere." She sat next to him on the couch and cradled him to her.

The tears came harder, him crying like a damn pussy and unable to stop.

Foley returned, saw them, and left for his room. He shut the door and didn't come back out.

Ivy stayed with Sam until he had no more tears left.

"It's okay, baby. It's all okay. I love you." She stroked his hair until he fell asleep.

When he woke the next morning, he lay full out on the couch, a blanket over him, his pillow under his head. Someone was licking his face, and he hoped to hell the tongue was canine.

"Cookie?" he rasped, his voice hoarse.

He heard voices in the kitchen. It hurt to sit up, but Sam had lived with pain all his life. He slowly stood and forced himself to straighten, ignoring his many bruises, and joined Foley and Ivy in the kitchen with Cookie dancing behind him.

His best friend and Ivy stared at him in concern. "I can't look that bad."

"You look worse." Ivy didn't look too pleased with him.

Foley walked up to him and did the worst thing possible. He hugged Sam until Sam wheezed, his ribs throbbing, and murmured, "I love you, brother."

Shit. Sam's eyes burned again, and he had to blink back tears.

Then the bastard pulled back, glanced from him to Ivy, and slowly backed out of the kitchen. "Ah, I need to get to work. I told Del you're sick, so you've got the day. Good luck." Behind Ivy, he made a scared face.

Ivy didn't turn her head, watching Sam. "I can see you, Foley."

"Hell. She's just like Cyn." Foley hurried to his room, then reappeared with his bag and raced out the front door.

"So." Sam sat slowly, trying not to wince. Between Stenson's fists and Senior's knife, life would be full of aches for a while.

"*So?* That's all you have to say to me?"

"Ivy, I'm sorry, okay?" *For so much.*

"Be more specific," she snapped.

She was pissing him off.

"Hey, I tried to keep you out of it."

"How? By making me fall in love with a moron who picks fights with four men and a knife-wielding maniac?"

He blinked. "Ah, so that's why you're mad?"

She stared at the ceiling as if the answers were up there. Hell, Eileen had been looking for them up there for years and never found a one.

"Talk."

"I was upset, okay?" He'd tell her all of it. Most of it she knew anyway. "My visit with Louise was bad. I couldn't take her shit anymore. Her name-calling and orders were enough. But she wanted me to get her drugs, and I've never done that. Alcohol is one thing. Drugs? Boosting her a car? Hell no." He sighed. "Then she kept saying how awful I was, and I couldn't help it. I bragged about you."

"Me?"

"I told her someone loved me." He hoped she still did. "So I couldn't be that bad."

Ivy sat next to him and grabbed his hand.

Hope unfurled within him, edging out the despair. "I thought about you, about all you said, and I told Louise to get help. That I'd be there for her if she did. But she didn't want counseling. She wanted the boy who'd fucked up her life to get her some oxy."

"What a bitch." Ivy gripped his hand.

He bit back a grin, a good thing because his lip still hurt. "Yeah. She's got problems, as you know."

"Real problems." Ivy paused. "I'm sorry about your dad. But, Sam, you're not him."

"I know."

"You don't know." She looked at him, *through* him. "That's why you don't want kids. Because of him."

"And her. She's bad news too."

"You're an idiot."

He frowned.

"You're the best thing that's ever happened to me. And I've decided I'm awesome, even if I come from some messed-up people. But I'm not the one who ignored my daughter. I'm not the one who hurt a young girl. I'm not the one who abused her son for most of his life."

"Abused, huh? Good guess."

"Guess nothing. Foley and I talked."

"Oh." He felt weird, exposed. Foley had seen a lot of his bruises over his growing years. "So, ah, are we still good?"

She stared at him, shook her head, then laughed. She laughed a little too hard.

"What? It's a legitimate question."

"You are so fucked up."

Startled at her use of language, he didn't know what to say.

"*Yes*, we're still a couple. I love you, even if you need therapy and a few ice packs. And a solid spanking to keep you from fighting again without taking care of yourself."

"Ivy, honey, I—"

"*No*. It's my turn to talk." She poked him in the chest, and he felt for what Louise must have experienced last night. Ivy had bony fingers. "You and I are stuck together, buddy. First, we have a dog that needs us." Cookie pawed at her leg, and she lifted him into her lap, where he stared smugly back at Sam. "Secondly, I am *not* going back to Willie's alone unless you're with me. The last time I was there, I think I interrupted her in a threesome."

"What?" Okay, that he had to hear. That's once he got past being over-the-moon thrilled that Ivy wasn't throwing him away.

"Oh yeah. And somehow she and her threesome, and the pets, took down the Queen Anne robbers."

"Seriously?" He blinked.

She nodded. "But we're getting off track. Where was I?" She poked him again.

"*Ow.*"

"Third, we are going to date for a while. Then you're going to propose. I'm going to accept, and we're going to find a place to live that's big enough for Cookie."

"Ah, sure. Yes. Right."

She made like she was going to poke him again, and he flinched. "I'm not done. We're going to have kids." She sniffed.

"Hell. Don't cry."

She wiped her eyes. "You're going to be an amazing father, and I'm going to be an amazing mother. Because we are awesome people."

"Ivy—"

"No. It's one thing if you had a real concern about having children. Like, you had a genetic mutation that might make our baby suffer. Or you were a wife beater. Or a violent criminal."

"I'm violent, and I'm a criminal."

"You *were* a criminal. And you've never been violent

with me." She paused. "That's why you're always so careful with me, making sure I consent to everything—because of Louise and your father."

He shrugged. "Hey, it should apply to everyone."

"Yes, it should. And see? You're looking out for me. Protecting me." She leaned closer to kiss him on the cheek. Then a softer one on his lips. "I love you so much."

"Ivy." *Fuck.* Now he was going to cry.

"You put up with abuse your entire life, and you never hurt anyone who didn't deserve it. Foley and I had a long talk about you and your mother. Not your mom. Eileen is your mom. Louise just gave birth to you."

He looked into her eyes, praying this was no dream. "Louise wasn't always mean. She had moments where she cared. Not many, but they were there. I think the damage my father did and her having no one to help, that did her in."

"Yes. But that's not an excuse for her abuse."

"But—"

"No buts. Why is it okay for you to protect everyone else but not yourself? If my parents had done to me what she did to you, would you be so quick to forgive?"

"Hell no. I still think they're a bag of dicks."

She bit her lip, but a smile peeked out anyway. "A whole bag?"

"Yeah," he growled.

Cookie barked at him, then leaned forward, trying to lick Sam's face.

"So you think a kid of mine would be normal?" he asked, all casual, when inside, he felt like a bundle of nerves about to go off like a rocket.

"Never normal." She smiled. "Incredible, handsome, pretty, smart, big. All those."

"Definitely pretty," he agreed, thinking any daughter of his would have to look like her mother. Another image of Ivy pregnant stoked his lust. *Man, I am so pervy*.

Yet the thought of children didn't make him think about his father for once. Instead, he fantasized about a life with Ivy. A forever where she and he and their dogs, cats, and everything under the sink lived and laughed together. And maybe, if they were lucky, they'd have their own sex swing they still used long into their golden years.

"You really love me, huh?" he asked, needing to hear it again.

"I do." She smiled. "And someday you might tell me the same."

"God, woman. You know I love you. Why else would I let you badger me about kids when I'm clearly in pain? Besides that, I fucking cleaned for you. And I've had a few of those girlie magazines up there for years. Collectibles I tossed just for you."

"Ah, my own Mr. Messy loves me."

He frowned, wanting to come up with something as insulting. But all he could say was, "Yeah, yeah, and Miss Bony Finger loves me too." He paused. "You win."

"Nope. We both win." She lost her smile. "I come with baggage too, you know. No family, not much income, and a dog who doesn't obey very well."

"Please. You just met my mother, and my father's a dead rapist. I think I have you beat."

She blinked. "God, you really do."

He smiled, amazed not to feel awkward talking about his past. "Now, about all this pain I'm in."

She stroked his hair. "I've got some ibuprofen, and Foley brought over some pain meds Lara had. Do you—"

"I was thinking of some oil I have upstairs in my nightstand. I mean, Ivy, I'm really hurting, and you're the only one who can help me out." He took her hand and put it over his hard cock. "Besides, I did fix your car. And you do owe me more hours in trade."

"I am *not* 'loving you long time,'" she said, trying to keep a straight face, quoting one of his favorite sexual expressions.

"But you could give me some *medicinal* massage," he offered. "There's this site on the web you can use as a tutorial. I think it's called 'fun-time massage for those with a big dick,' or something like that. I looked it up after the first time I saw you."

She laughed, and he laughed with her. "Oh, Sam. What am I going to do with you?"

They stared at each other, then said as one, "Love me long time?"

And even Cookie added a howl or two.

Chapter 20

IT WAS THE WEDDING OF THE CENTURY. OR MAYBE the decade. Whatever. Lou was drinking and devising plans—some way to get that fine florist over to him without acting like he wanted her attention. He said hello and the woman turned in the opposite direction. What the hell?

Sam wandered over, a drink in hand. Weeks after his notorious fight at Ray's, most of his bruises had faded. Lou still lamented that he'd missed the big brawl with Goodie. According to Heller, a tough guy to impress, Sam had been a thing of beauty taking down Stenson. And even after being stuck with Senior's hunting knife, he'd raged like a demon trying to kill the old shithead. Battle-hungry Sam was a terrific guy to rage with. Focused, angry, mean. Going into a fight next to him guaranteed victory.

Unfortunately, this new Sam was pretty observant. And he liked to talk. "Shot you down again, huh?"

Lou groaned and tugged at his stupid tie. "I can't believe how you've changed. Now you never shut the hell up. And quit smiling."

Sam chuckled. "Yeah. I'm so pretty now, with my smiles, that all your sisters want a piece."

"Touch 'em and die."

"In fact, just yesterday I was hanging with Rosie, and she proposed. Mostly to get her hands on Cookie, but I can tell she's into me."

Lou smiled. "It's all about the dog, my man."

He saw the florist—not just Del's flower chick for the wedding, but also a guest—bobble her glass, then right it for a sip. Cyn said something to her, which made her chuckle. But this far away, he couldn't hear too much. Too many laughing, dancing people in the way.

"You are lame, Lou. Just… What happened to the guy who could get anybody?"

"I don't know." Lou groaned. "Leave me alone. Go flirt with Ivy, would you?"

"Sure thing." Sam slapped him on the back, and Lou had to work not to show the asshole packed a wallop. "But hey, if you need help scoring, let me or Foley know." Sam glanced to Foley, who lifted his glass at Lou and shook his head, mouthing, *Pussy.*

"I hate all of you."

"I'm so happy right now." Sam left, humming.

Del walked by, stunning in her dress. To her credit, she hadn't said one curse word through the ceremony and the celebration. She looked like a million bucks, her hair done in a classy twist, her makeup showing off the beauty they all knew was there. But now she shone with it, with love.

"Mrs. McCauley, you look radiant." Lou swung her in his arms, pleased to see her husband several feet away, frowning at him.

Del laughed. "Put me down, you maniac."

"I'm so happy for you, Del. You deserve it."

Near them, Colin McCauley twirled with a girl near his age. He looked like he'd rather be getting his fingernails pulled out one by one.

Del snickered. "See, we're all getting tortured a

little today. I can't swear. Colin's forced to dance with his second cousin twenty times removed or something, and Mike…"

"What did you do to McCauley?"

Her eyes twinkled. "I showed him what's under my dress, then told him we're staying for the whole party."

"Oh, evil. Why is it *we're* not married?"

"Because she's mine," Mike growled from over Lou's shoulder.

Lou chuckled. "Easy, Tarzan, just pulling your chain. Here. You can have her back. Come on, Del. Stop clinging. You're a married woman now," he added in a louder voice. "With Mike right here? I can't do that. It wouldn't be right."

Mike rolled his eyes while Del scowled. "Your ass is mine next week at work, Cortez. Oh, it's on."

"Easy, honey. You can beat him up later." Mike whirled her away on a laugh.

Lou moved back and bumped into J.T., Del's brother.

J.T. looked preoccupied. "Hey, man."

"What's up?"

J.T. frowned. "Is it just me, or do they only make pretty people in the McCauley family?" He nodded to one stacked, gorgeous blond talking to Mike's mother.

"Who's she?"

J.T. wrapped an arm around Lou's shoulder and turned him away, facing Lara and Johnny dancing so in step, they appeared as if made for each other. "She's one of the Donnigans, I think," J.T. said. "Mike's cousin or something. And not your problem. Look away, little man."

"Who you calling little?"

"I've got a few inches on you." J.T. grinned.

Considering they stood maybe an inch apart in height, Lou knew what he was *really* talking about. "Real mature, J.T."

"I try. But hey, let's talk flowers…and women… and you not getting the time of day." The bastard left Lou in the middle of Lou's insults about J.T's mother's mother's mother.

"Dick," Lou muttered and set his drink down on a silver serving tray. In its reflection, he saw himself looking fine as hell in a suit and tie, his dark good looks raging. He'd already been hit on half a dozen times by other guys' girlfriends, as well as by two cuties on the waitstaff. But the one submissive little bombshell he had his eye on kept avoiding him. Time to up his game.

Again, I ask, what the hell kind of woman can walk away from all this?

About the Author

Caffeine addict, boy referee, and romance aficionado, *New York Times* and *USA Today* bestselling author Marie Harte is a confessed bibliophile and devotee of action movies. Whether hiking in Central Oregon, biking around town, or hanging at the local tea shop, she's constantly plotting to give everyone a happily ever after. Visit marieharte.com and fall in love.

*Here's a taste of Lou's story, book four in the
Body Shop Bad Boys series*

*COLLISION
COURSE*

"Two dozen red roses and 'I'm sorry I screwed
your sister'?" Josephine Reeves stared over the counter
at the thirtysomething guy who badly needed a haircut,
thinking she must have misheard him.

"Yeah, that doesn't sound so good." He sighed,
combed back his trendy bangs with his fingers, and
frowned. "I was going to go with 'Sorry I fucked your
sister,' but that's a little crude. Probably just 'I slept with
your sister,' right? That's better."

She blinked, wondering at his level of stupidity. "Um,
well, how about ending at just 'I'm sorry'?"

He considered that and nodded. "Hey, yeah. That'll
work. Do I need to sign the card? Maybe you could
write that for me. My handwriting sucks."

*So does your ability to be in a committed relation-
ship.* Joey shrugged. "It's your call. But if it was me, I'd
prefer a note from the person who's sorry, not from the
woman selling him flowers."

Her customer brightened and chose a note card from

the stack on the counter. "Good call. Hey, add another dozen while you're at it. She loves roses."

Joey tallied up the order while he signed, then took the handwritten card. The guy really did have crappy handwriting. After he paid and left, she tucked the note into the folder of orders due to go out by two, in another two hours. For a Monday, the day had gone as expected and then some. Not chock-full of customers, but not empty either. Late spring in Seattle had most people out and about working on their gardens, not inside shopping for hothouse blooms.

Still, enough anniversaries, birthdays, and relationship disasters had brought a consistent swell of customers into S&J Floral to make Stef, her boss, more than happy.

Joey hummed as she organized the orders, thrilled that she'd gotten the hoped-for promotion to manager that morning. She'd worked her butt off for it, and that diligence had paid off. She wanted to sing and dance, proclaim her triumph to the masses.

Except it was just her, Tonya in the back putting together floral arrangements, and a half dozen shoppers perusing the store. It had been Joey's idea to add some upscale gifts to their merchandise selection. Teddy bears, pretty glass ornaments, and knickknacks went hand in hand with flowers. S&J had seen a boost in revenue since last December, when they'd implemented the big change.

Thank God it had worked. Joey appreciated Stef taking a risk by believing in her. And now...a promotion to manager and a $50K salary! With this money, she and Brandon could finally move out of her parents' place and start fresh, away from the history of mistakes her family never let her forget. She couldn't wait to tell her best friend, Becky, about it.

"Well, hello there."

She glanced up from the counter and froze.

"You work here?" A large grin creased a face she'd tried hard to forget.

The man who'd been haunting her sleep, who'd dogged her through a wedding and sizzled her already frazzled nerves, looked even better in the hard light of day.

"H-hello." She coughed, trying to hide the fact that she stuttered. When she could breathe without gasping, she said, "Sorry. What can I do for you today?"

The look he shot her had her ovaries doing somersaults and her brain shutting clean off.

The first time she'd seen him had been on a visit to her first wedding client, and she'd been *floored*. The guys who worked at Webster's Garage all looked larger than life, covered in tattoos, muscles, and that indefinable sense of danger they wore like a second skin. But it had been this guy, the tall Latin hunk with dark-brown eyes and lips made for kissing, who had snared her.

He had a way of raising one brow in question or command that turned her entire body into his personal cheering section.

"…for some flowers. I dunno. Something that looks like I put thought into it?"

Focus, Joey. Be professional. This isn't personal. Don't get all goofy on the man. "Ah, budget?"

He sighed. "For Stella, it has to be decent. Girl is like a human calculator when it comes to anything with value. If I skimp, she'll know," he said, still grinning. He took the binder she slid to him and leafed through the floral selections. "I'm Lou Cortez, by the way."

"I remember." He'd only introduced himself once, months ago, in the garage while she'd been going over flower choices with his boss. But Joey had never forgotten those broad shoulders, chiseled chin, or bright-white smile. Talk about too handsome for her own good.

She'd kept her distance, or at least tried to. She'd been invited to the wedding, having become friends with the bride. Of course, all the woman's employees had been invited as well. Joey had done her best to steer clear of the man women seemed to drool over. He was trouble she didn't need.

She realized he'd stopped looking through the binder and was staring straight at her. More like through her. *Wow. How did he do that?* Bring so much concentration and intensity, she felt as if his gaze reached out and wrapped around her, holding her still?

And why, when confronted with all that masculinity, did she want to stammer and obey any darn thing he said? She had to force herself to be strong, to speak. But she just stared, mute, at so much male prettiness.

His smile deepened. "And your name would be...?" God, a dimple appeared on his left cheek.

A dimple. Kill me now. Breathe, dummy. You can handle this. It's business. "Oh, right. I'm Joey."

"You don't look like a Joey," he murmured.

Her heart raced, and she forced herself to maintain eye contact. "Short for Josephine. So the flowers. Did you find anything you like?"

A loaded question, because his slow grin widened as

he looked her over. Then he turned back to the binder and shook his head. "Nah. I need something original. Do you design bouquets?"

"Yes." More comfortable on a professional level, she nodded. "We have some amazing florists and—"

"No. *You*. Do you put flowers together?"

"Yes."

"Good. I want you to do it." He shrugged. "Del, my boss at Webster's, you remember her?"

She nodded. How could she forget the woman with the cool gray eyes, tattoo sleeves, and funky ash-blonde hair braided in twists? The same woman she'd made friends with not long after meeting. Heck, she'd attended Del's wedding.

"She said you were amazing. My sister needs something amazing right now."

The flowers were for his sister. *Oh man. He's sexy as sin, has a body to die for, and now he's buying flowers for his sister?*

She softened toward him. "Do you know if she has a favorite flower or color? A scent maybe? Did you want sophisticated or simple? How old is she?"

"Ah, something cool. I don't know. She's gonna be twenty-three." He rattled off a few ideas, and she made quick notes.

"I can have this for you by…" She paused to check the computer. "Tomorrow. Would that work?"

"Hell. I really need them today. Her birthday isn't until Friday, but she got some shitty news, so I wanted to give them to her when I see her later. I'm willing to pay extra, no problem."

Adding *charming* and *thoughtful* to the Lou List, Joey

did her best not to moon over the man and keep a straight face. "Well, if you can wait until the end of the day, I'll try to fit them in. We close at seven. Is that okay?"

He broke out into a relieved smile. "*Gracias*, Joey. You're doing me a huge favor."

Ignoring his smile, she called on her inner manager. "Well, you're doing something nice for your sister. And I know all about crappy days."

"Yeah?" He leaned closer and she caught a whiff of motor oil and crisp cologne, an odd blend of manly and sexy that nearly knocked her on her ass. "Who tried to ruin your day, sweetheart? I can fix that."

She blew out a shaky breath and gave a nervous laugh. "Ah, I just meant I've had those kinds of days before. Not now. It's just a regular Monday for me." A great Monday, considering her promotion.

He didn't blink, and she felt positively hunted.

"Well, if anyone gives you any trouble, you let me know and I can talk to them for you. Nobody should mess with a woman as pretty and nice as you." He stroked her cheek with a rough finger before she could unglue her feet from the floor and move away.

Then he glanced at the clock behind her, straightened, and said something in Spanish.

"Sorry, Joey." Her name on his lips sounded like a caress. "Gotta go. I'll be back at seven to pick them up, okay? Thanks. I owe you."

"You don't owe me anything," she said. "But I'll probably have to charge you extra for the short notice. It's a rush order," she blurted, not wanting him to think she was giving him special favors.

"I'll pay, no problem." He slid a card toward her.

"My number in case something comes up with the flowers. Or a customer bothers you." He nodded to it. "You're a sweetheart. I'll see you soon."

He left, and she could breathe again. Still processing the overwhelming presence that had been Lou Cortez — mechanic, paint expert, and all-around heartthrob — Joey tried to calm her racing heart.

One of their regulars plunked a few items on the counter, her blue eyes twinkling, her white hair artfully arranged around her face. "Don't know how you let that one get away. If I was a few years younger, I'd have been all over him." She wiggled her brows. "Then again, he looked like he might be open to an octogenarian with skills. Think he'd mind if you gave me his number?"

They both laughed, even as Joey tucked the card into her pocket and rang up Mrs. Packard's items. The thing burned in her pocket, a link to a man she knew better than to step a foot near. She'd throw it away after he picked up his flowers. Joey had made mistakes with a charmer a long time ago, and she had no intention of ever going down that road again. Nope, not ever.

COMING SEPTEMBER 2017

*Now for a peek at book two in Marie Harte's
hot new Donnigans series*

Friday evening, Jameson's Gym

IT HAD BEEN ONE HELLUVA DAY ALREADY, AND IT
wasn't even six yet. Gavin had secretly called dibs
on the last remaining treadmill, needing to run out
some kinks.

Problem was, so had *she*—pink yoga pants.

He locked gazes with her before eying the distance to
the machine, then saw her doing the same. A gentleman
would let her go first, then stand back and watch her
work those magnificent glutes, those toned hamstrings
and calves.

But Gavin was no gentleman, at least not in the gym.
His domain. His jungle. His—

"Dude, you're blocking the Nautilus."

"Oh, sorry." He moved out of the no-neck's path,
now no longer able to see the treadmill. When he hurriedly stepped around another idiot standing in the way,
he saw her smirk at him as she stepped on the machine.

She kept his gaze as she slowly warmed up, making a huge production out of stretching her arms over her head, then smiling from ear to ear.

He frowned.

She grinned, gave him a mock salute—the sexy witch—then proceeded to ignore the holy hell out of him as she tuned out the rest of the world and ran. Not jogged, *ran*.

What he should be doing. Damn it.

That made half a dozen times she'd blown him off with that same smug expression, that same victorious, patronizing smile. Then she'd pretend he didn't exist. He'd like to throw her over his knee and spank the ever loving—

"Gavin. Today, bro. We have work to do before the class."

He groaned. Dealing with his older brother was no picnic, and especially not before getting some much-needed stress relief out of a run. "Landon, I need to work out first."

"Fine." The dick wrapped a thick arm around his neck and hauled him away in a headlock. "You want a workout? Let's see if you can get out of this. Then I'll throw you on the mat a few times and watch you flail as I beat your ass."

Gavin sputtered, trying to breathe as his behemoth brother dragged him down the hallway toward the self-defense classroom.

Not cool to headlock a gym trainer in front of his many clients. Gavin tried not to wheeze as he fought Landon's steel-hard muscles for breath. But the damage had been done. He heard snickers, laughter, encouragement for *Landon*.

Major Donnigan. What an asshole.

The former Marine choking him growled, "Now suck it up, princess, and let's see your moves. If you can't do it, you sure as shit can't teach it."

———∕∿∕———

Two hours later, Gavin heard familiar chatter. "Oh my God. Did you see the size of his arms? They're huge!"

"I swear, I would pay money for him to put *me* in a wristlock, headlock, bodylock…"

"Hey, he can carry me over his shoulder and take me away to do bad things anytime he wants. Bring on the stranger-danger, I say."

"I'd like to get some of that *strange*. Talk about a nice ass…"

Gavin cleared his throat from behind the group of early thirtysomethings still whispering things he knew they wouldn't want him to hear. Four guilty faces swiveled in his direction, their cheeks red, their eyes wide.

"Ladies? I just wanted to make sure none of you had any questions about tonight's instruction. We're getting a little rougher than just escaping wristlocks." And preventing douchebags from turning women into victims. Landon's self-defense class had been hugely successful.

The boldest of the four managed a shaky smile. "Uh, um, no, Gavin. No questions." She swallowed loudly, glanced at his eyes once, then lowered her gaze to his chest. "I found it really helpful."

The others nodded like bobbleheads. "Awesome class."

"I feel safer already."

"I'm so glad you're the ones teaching us."

"Will you have a third session?"

The first had gone so well two months ago that Mac, his boss, had asked Gavin and Landon to do a second set. "I'm not sure yet. You'd have to talk to Mac. I'm glad the class is helping, though. Make sure you practice at home, and see you next Friday, unless I run into you in the gym first."

They scrambled to leave, but he overheard mention of his smoky gray eyes and to-die-for abs between a few breathy sighs. He resisted the urge to power flex as he straightened up the large room, setting the mats to rights.

Another successful self-defense class at Jameson's Gym, courtesy of the Donnigan brothers.

Of course, it helped when *both* brothers did the labor instead of the lamer one panting over a hot chick.

Gavin sighed, wishing he could be more annoyed with his older brother, now laughing at something Ava—his fiancée—said. Trust Landon to find happiness and laziness all at the same time. The same guy who would throw a shit-fit if Gavin forgot to put the toilet seat down or wipe up a water mark on the kitchen counter now saw nothing wrong with mats askew and a few plastic water bottles laying around.

He gave his brother a look, but Landon pretended to ignore him. "Dick," he muttered loud enough for Landon to hear him, despite there still being a few stragglers still gathering their things before leaving.

The jackass continued to dismiss him in favor of Ava's sexy grin. Though the finger he stuck up behind his back hinted he might not be as focused as he pretended. Good to know Major OCD still understood when he was getting insulted. Gavin straightened after tossing another bottle into a bin and nearly tripped over the finest ass to grace the gym since he'd started working at the place.

Well, well. The treadmill thief hadn't darted out of class the moment it ended. There was a God after all. He gave her a thorough once-over. Mostly because she was hot as hell, and yeah, it bugged the crap out of her. But something had to get her to notice him as more than a rival to the gym equipment.

"Well, hel-lo, pink yoga pants. Hope you enjoyed the class as much as you enjoyed your run earlier."

She straightened, gave him a baleful stare, then sighed. "It's wonderboy, in the flesh. Or should I call you Smoky?"

He frowned, then smiled at the earlier reference to his eyes. "Did you hear the part about my rockin' biceps and bitable abs too? And don't forget these glutes." He turned around, presenting for her, and looked down at said ass. "Rumor has it, there's no sight finer in all of Seattle." He squeezed his cheeks together—looking impressive, if he did say so himself.

"This has been *such* a long day."

He'd swear the corner of her lips curled in the hint of a smile before she glanced down and fiddled with her shirt. He turned back around to fully face her. "Hey, if you'd rather, I can put you in a headlock so you can be up and close with the Guns of Steel." He flexed his biceps. "I call this one *sexy* and this one *as hell*."

She sighed even louder. "A long, never-ending day."

But so worth it, if only because he got to see *her* again—Zoe York. The woman was as obsessive about her workouts as he was. Tall, athletic, gorgeous. Now if only she'd stop saying no to a date with the magnetic Donnigan everyone wanted but couldn't have. Well, not counting Michelle. Amy. Megan. Maybe Brenda, now that he thought about it…

Gavin poured on the charm. "You looked great tonight. Terrific form." He tried not to laugh at her scowl. "How about going out for a drin—"

She hefted her bag over her shoulder, and he had to step back so he wouldn't get smacked in the face. "Have a great weekend, Romeo. I have more important things to do tonight than date your guns of tinfoil."

"Like?"

"Like wash my hair, clean lint from my dryer. Oh, and breathe. I have to do that too."

And like that, she was gone.

Behind him, he heard a whistle, then his brother's loud clapping. "Strike three. He's out, ladies and gentlemen."

Well, crap. "Gentlemen?" Gavin snorted, trying to ignore the fact that he'd failed. Again. "Please. It's just us, Landon."

"He's got a point," Ava agreed. "You're no gentleman."

Gavin turned to see her smirking at his brother.

"Shut it, Doc." Landon frowned, then winked at her. "I'm only trying to encourage my poor, battered baby brother to—"

"First of all, I'm only younger than you by two years, ass-wipe." He hated it when Landon lorded those two frickin' years over him. "Second, Theo's the baby. Not me. And third, I was just kidding around with her." Joking until the stubborn woman said yes.

Landon, the bastard, knew it. "Yeah right. Talk about a crash and burn."

Ava perused Gavin.

"Hey." Landon growled. "Eyes over here." Landon pointed to his own behemoth frame. He and Gavin shared the same height, but Landon had a linebacker's build whereas Gavin was more quarterback, all lean lines and sinewy strength. "Remember, Doc. You belong to me."

"*To* you? You mean *with* you, don't you?" Oh boy. She was using *the tone*.

Landon blinked. "Ah, right. With me, of course. Come on, I was just kidding."

Gavin got a kick out of seeing Ava take his domineering brother down a notch. "Oh?" She raised a brow at the Neanderthal.

The twinkle in his brother's eyes skeeved him out.

He'd seen this play out at home. Their version of kinked-up psychological foreplay, in Gavin's opinion. Ava pretended to shrink his brother. Landon got riled up, faked being pissed off, then swept her into his bedroom for a few frenzied hours.

Gavin started for the door, leaving the rest of the room for Landon to clean. "I'm out of here before you start doing it on the mats."

"Gavin." Ava sounded scandalized, but a glance at her cheery grin and blush said otherwise.

"Gavin," Landon mocked. "I would never…"

"At least lock the door," he mumbled and left on their laughter.

A happy couple. Two people in love who deserved to find that special someone. About time Landon got his head out of his ass and chose a woman who could handle him, a real woman who had opinions and wasn't afraid to share them.

As if thinking of opinionated women had conjured her, he saw Zoe by the water fountain near the exit.

She was staring at two women chatting and laughing on treadmills, and her face lost all expression. That sadness he'd seen in her eyes on previous occasions showed itself, making her bright-blue gaze muddy with emotion. But Zoe didn't linger. She saw him watching her, scowled, then turned and left.

What would make a vibrant woman like Zoe so sad? Had she lost someone, like he'd lost so many? At the thought, it was as if she'd passed him the baton, letting him take the grief she'd worn so briefly.

The gym started to fade as memory overtook him. The slam of weights like car parts raining down after an explosion. The garble of low voices like insurgents around a rickety table, plotting, while he stared through his scope and—

No. He didn't need that. Not here. Not in his safe zone.

He refused to let the anger and pain get a toehold. Instead, calling on the exercises Lee, his new therapist, had shown him, he concentrated his energy elsewhere, on what he was good at. Gavin sought one of the unoccupied treadmills in the corner, the one facing the wall-mounted TV showing a stupid sitcom. He hopped onto the thing and ran. Faster and faster, until his lungs burned and his legs strained. The pain cleansed, allowing him to wheeze in laughter at the televised antics of some brainy scientist types trying to hit on girls. Much better than raging at all he'd lost.

Balance, he kept telling himself. *It's all about balance.*

With that in mind, he once again donned a mantle of false cheer and willed himself to believe life was good.

Visualize, and it will come, Lee liked to tell him. Gavin needed to have a discussion with the shrink, because he'd been visualizing Zoe York in nothing more than a smile, but that sure as hell hadn't happened. Thoughts of her turned his fake cheer into a real grin. He slowed down and let himself enjoy the TV show. But once it ended, he needed something more.

With the help of a spotter, he used a nearby weight bench and lifted until muscle exhaustion. Finally ready to go home and hit the rack. Where he could dream of a stubborn, sexy woman with long, wavy black hair... and sad blue eyes.

Zoe drove home, annoyed with herself for getting overemotional. Treadmill girl's pink laces on her silly, adorable-if-useless fashion sneakers had been all too familiar. Just the kind of impractical crap Aubrey used to wear.

She sniffled, then blinked rapidly to still the tears that continued to come from out of nowhere. Pink laces? Really? But that pink led her to recall something else. *"Hel-lo, pink yoga pants."*

Without meaning to, she felt her mood lift, and she chuckled. Had Gavin Donnigan actually flexed his ass at her?

Yes, he had.

For months she'd been coming to this gym. For months he'd said silly things to her to get her to smile and finally go out with him. No way, no how. He was *so* not her type. Ripped with muscle. Sexy. Doable, sure. He'd already proven that by hooking up with a half dozen—that she knew about—women at the gym. Dark hair, *smoky* gray eyes, a firm yet sensual mouth. And yeah, okay, he had an amazing ass, really amazing thighs, and topped off with an amazing torso.

So annoying that he was charming too. Few people had been able to make her even want to smile since the accident. But Gavin had been obnoxious, obvious, and somehow charming all at the same time. He made her smile despite herself. Just what the doctor ordered.

COMING JULY 2017

RECKLESS
HEARTS

Collin

"DAMN IT, MAX. HOW MANY TIMES DO I HAVE TO TELL
you not to mix the reds with whites when you're washing clothes in hot water?"

I tossed the laundry basket holding my newly ruined
rugby jersey on top of the dining room table. It landed
with a thud, knocking down one of the musical toys my
nine-month-old daughter, Chloe, loved.

Raising a baby daughter with a couple of guys is a
lot like being a marine. It's an intense experience that
requires constantly being all-in just to save someone
else's back while he manages to save yours. It smells
like shit ninety percent of the time, and every time you
move, another body is up in your space. But you do it
because you love it. There isn't any other option but to
live and breathe it. In my life, my daughter—and the
guys who helped me through—were all I needed.

That, and maybe a cleaning lady.

I spun around on my untied cleats, the sound of "Mary Had a Little Lamb" playing in the background as I rushed toward the breakfast bar to grab Chloe's diaper bag.

In the hallway to my right, my roommate—and certified laundry screwup—Max stood grinning, holding my girl in his arms. Dressed and ready to go, thank Christ, she sported a tiny green Carinthia Irish Rugby jersey her aunt Lia had made for her when Max, Gavin, and I joined the intramural club a few weeks back.

"You yelling at me, Colly?" Max kissed the top of Chloe's head, probably holding her on purpose 'cause he knew I wouldn't lay into him with Beaner in his arms.

With a thumb in her mouth, she snuggled closer to her pseudo-uncle's chest, still half-asleep from her nap. My throat grew tight as I took in her gorgeous face. Lucky for Max, the anger I'd been harboring disappeared with that one look at Chloe.

My daughter was my world—my peace, my rock. And even though the past eight months hadn't been picture perfect for us as a family or as far as life went, we were good as a unit—me, her, and Max, along with Gavin, who lived in the attached duplex.

Except that none of us could do laundry to save our asses.

"What were you thinking?" Glancing at the clock on the wall, I dropped the diaper bag on the floor next to my rugby bag and grunted. "Now the thing's pink and green, which means the guys are gonna rag on my ass all day." On the table sat a stack of five diapers. I grabbed a couple and shoved them into the bottom of the diaper bag, along with a couple of baby toys.

"Where's your spare?"

"Dirty."

Max set Chloe inside the playpen by the TV, then handed her the bottle I'd made up a few minutes back that'd been sitting on the coffee table. "Dude, pink is kick-ass."

I shot him a look. "Watch your mouth."

Ignoring me, he walked over to the basket, thumbing through it for a pair of socks, taking his time, chatting like a little kid, and acting like we weren't fifteen minutes behind schedule.

"You've got the pink-for-breast-cancer thing going on, like the *Save the Ta-Tas* T-shirts." Max picked his jersey—the one that had managed to stay green and white—out of the pile, then shoved it inside his rugby bag on the floor next to mine. "Then there's pink bubble gum that never loses its flavor…" He waggled his dark eyebrows and jogged over to the breakfast nook that separated the dining room from the kitchen. He tossed two Gatorade bottles my way. I caught both, tucking them in my own bag, along with my *pink*-and-green jersey.

"*Finally*, there's my favorite reason that pink is cool. Wanna hear it?"

Not really. But I shouldered my duffel, along with Chloe's diaper bag, and waited for him to finish anyway. When he didn't say squat, I sighed and finally said, "Jesus, don't leave me hanging. I won't be able to sleep at night without knowing why it's *cool* to have a *pink*-and-green jersey."

With a smirk, I turned to face him again, just as he tossed me the baby wipe container. I caught it one-handed and shoved it into the side of Chloe's bag.

"Mock me now, but I'm serious. Pink lip gloss looks hot as hell when it's on a woman's lips. Especially when those lips are wrapped around the head of my—"

"Shut it." I pointed a finger at him, glancing back at Chloe. Wide baby blues stared back and forth between us, watching, waiting, almost like she knew exactly what we were talking about.

Max shot his hands up in defense while I sat on a chair to tie my cleats.

"Just saying. Pink is a good color." He winked at Chloe. "Adds character. Right, Beaner?"

Eyes damn near sparkling, she babbled something or another from around her bottle, her blond hair sprouting all over the place. Before I could bitch about Max using my daughter against me, Gavin came busting through the front door, sandy hair hanging over his eyes. Any longer and he'd have the old Justin Bieber hairstyle beat.

But then I saw what he was holding and froze, while trying to ignore the snorts coming out of Max's nose.

"New car seat's ready." Gav kicked the door shut behind him with the bottom of his foot, meeting my stare.

Max laughed harder, reaching down to grab Gav's jersey this time. He tossed it at him, a perfect shot that landed on his shoulder. Like Max's, Gavin's was also still green and white.

"What?" Gav looked back and forth between the two of us, his lip curling as he set the *hot-pink* car seat down on the floor. "Quit looking at me like that."

Teeth gritted, I stood and attempted to tie the string on my rugby shorts.

"Nice choice of seat colors, don't you think?" Max

smirked, pointing toward the car seat, before he took off out the front door, car keys spinning around his finger.

I rolled my eyes and shoved my bags at Gav. He took them, trying to defend himself as he said, "You told me to get a new car seat, so I got one. Chloe's a girl, and girls like pink. What's the big deal?"

"Colly's just struggling with his masculinity today. Nothing new," Max hollered from outside on the porch.

Ignoring my asshat of a best friend, I pulled Chloe out of her playpen and smiled as I tossed her in the air. The sanity that came with being a dad definitely outweighed the occasional insanity of my two best friends.

I buckled her into her new seat. Gav had already messed with the straps, adjusting the things to the perfect size. He was a genius like that, a certified master of all things safety and organization. He'd been that way from the second I met him in basic training six years ago.

"You going to fill me in?" He grabbed his cleats by the front door and tied them to the strap of his bag.

"You don't wanna know," I said, setting the handle of the car seat, now filled with my girl, over my forearm.

Gavin grunted something under his breath, then nodded before heading toward the door. I followed, not ready to face my teammates in my fucked-up jersey but more than ready to play.

"What's this?"

I rammed into his back on the threshold, Chloe's car seat digging into his ass. She let out a happy squeal and grinned up at me, bare feet kicking the air.

"What's what?" I glanced over his shoulder.

His hand was in my bag, humor lacing his words as

he said, "Think you need to borrow my other jersey." He yanked the collar of mine out, a rare grin on his face.

I shut my eyes and yelled out the front door, "It's *pink*, Max."

"Real men wear it," he yelled at me from the street before getting into his car.

Scratch my earlier thoughts. I needed my daughter, a cleaning lady, *and* a new roommate.

NOW AVAILABLE!

BEAUTIFUL CRAZY

First in the Rock 'n' Ink series from author Kasey Lane

Kevan Landry has one shot to sign the metal band Manix Curse and get her fledging PR firm off the ground. If she doesn't succeed, she'll lose more than her company—her brother will be forced out of rehab early.

Mason Dillon heads the most successful music PR firm in Portland and has been commissioned with signing Manix Curse. But after going head-to-head with Kevan over the band, work is the last thing on his mind.

Forced on tour with Manix to prove their marketing skills, the pair wages a battle for the band. If they can set aside their differences, they may find together they're the right mix of sexy savvy to conquer the bedroom and the boardroom.

"Kasey Lane gives readers a rockin' romance that sings!"

—Marie Harte, *New York Times* and *USA Today* bestselling author

For more Kasey Lane, visit:
www.sourcebooks.com